SPRING TIDES AT THE STARFISH CAFÉ

THE STARFISH CAFÉ SERIES BOOK 2

JESSICA REDLAND

Boldwood

First published in Great Britain in 2022 by Boldwood Books Ltd.

Copyright © Jessica Redland, 2022

Cover Design by Debbie Clement Design

Cover Photography: Shutterstock

A CIP catalogue record for this book is available from the British Library.

Paperback ISBN 978-1-80162-424-4

Large Print ISBN 978-1-80162-425-1

Hardback ISBN 978-1-80162-423-7

Ebook ISBN 978-1-80162-427-5

Kindle ISBN 978-1-80162-426-8

Audio CD ISBN 978-1-80162-418-3

MP3 CD ISBN 978-1-80162-419-0

Digital audio download ISBN 978-1-80162-420-6

Boldwood Books Ltd
23 Bowerdean Street
London SW6 3TN
www.boldwoodbooks.com

To Sharon Booth: talented author, amazing friend and fellow lover of cake, with love, hugs and eternal gratitude xx

'With courage, nothing is impossible.'

— SIR WILLIAM HILLARY, 1823

— FOUNDER OF THE ROYAL NATIONAL
LIFEBOAT INSTITUTION (RNLI), EST. 1824
(ORIGINALLY KNOWN AS THE NATIONAL
INSTITUTION FOR THE PRESERVATION OF LIFE
FROM SHIPWRECK)

Recurring Characters from Snowflakes Over The Starfish Café

Hollie Brooks
Owner and full-time manager of The Starfish Café
Owner of wood craft business Hollie's Wood
Trainee volunteer with RNLI
Lives with Jake

Jake 'Mouse' MacLeod
Charge nurse on A&E at Whitsborough Bay General Hospital
RNLI crew member (helm)
Lives with Hollie

Pickle aka Mr Pickles
Hollie and Jake's shih tzu (found abandoned)

Heather Brooks
Hollie's mum, who set up The Starfish Café
Died of cancer over six years ago

Joe 'Sparky' Brooks
Hollie's dad, RNLI crew member, killed in tragic rescue seven
years ago

Isaac 'Silver' Brooks
Hollie's brother, RNLI crew member, killed in tragic rescue seven
years ago

Angie Swinton
Assistant Manager of The Starfish Café

Had been best friends with Heather for fifty years
Estranged from husband Martin

Martin Swinton
Funeral director
Estranged from wife Angie

Kyle 'Jaffa' Bradbury
RNLI Mechanic (full-time paid crew member)
Was Isaac's best friend since childhood
Married to Bex

Rebecca (Bex) Bradbury
Was Isaac's girlfriend
Married to Kyle

Mia Bradbury
Kyle and Bex's young daughter, aged four

Isaac Bradbury
Kyle and Bex's young daughter, nearly three

Violet MacLeod
Jake's nanna, who raised him
Died following a stroke nearly six years ago

Robert (Bobby) Reynolds
Jake's dad
Drowned trying to save Jake on Jake's ninth birthday

Michelle Reynolds
Jake's mum

Died from complications following Jake's birth

Larissa Kent
Jake's older estranged sister
Blames Jake for their parents' deaths

Andrew Kent
Larissa's husband

Irene Trent
Former neighbour of Jake's and a family friend
Lives in Bay View Care Home

Adrian Daniels (Uncle Adrian)
Retired police sergeant and Bobby's best friend
Recently reconnected with Jake

Maggs Daniels (Auntie Maggs)
Had been friends with Michelle and Bobby
Recently reconnected with Jake

Katie Vickers
Recruitment consultant
Hollie's best friend
Lives with Trey

Trey O'Sullivan
Recruitment consultant
Lives with Katie

Betty and Tommy
Long-standing customers at The Starfish Café

Sylvia Braithwaite aka Mrs Sultana
Regular customer at The Starfish Café
Recently befriended Hollie

Avril
Works in The Starfish Café

Artie 'Chief' Briars
RNLI Coxswain (full-time paid crew member)

Finley 'Bart' Scott
RNLI crew member (obsessed with *The Simpsons*)

'Spaniel'
RNLI trainee crew member (excitable like a spaniel)

1

HOLLIE

I placed the final batch of cheese scones in the oven at The Starfish Café and glanced at the clock: 7.55 a.m. Two hours until opening time and I was way ahead of schedule.

'We came in far too early again, didn't we?' I said as I wandered through to the customer side of the café.

Pickle – my gorgeous brown shih tzu – looked up from his bed below the staircase and yawned as though in agreement. I crouched down beside him and stroked his soft ears.

'I'm sorry for dragging you out so early this morning. Can you forgive me?'

I'd arrived shortly before five – completely unnecessary but I struggled to sleep when Jake was on a night shift at the hospital. The house felt empty and the bed cold without him. There was no point lying there fighting a losing battle with sleep when there was so much I could be getting on with.

Leaving Pickle to settle back down, I made a coffee and took it out onto the large terrace at back of the café. With my hands wrapped round the mug, I rested my arms on the railings and breathed in the cool morning air. The sun had risen an hour earlier and the cloudless sky was powder blue with bands of lemon and pale peach, promising a gorgeous day on the North Yorkshire Coast.

The Starfish Café was set on a clifftop two miles south of the popular seaside town of Whitsborough Bay. The beach below – Starfish Point – was home to a colony of two hundred grey and common seals. This morning, the sea was calm and I could see several seals resting on the curved rocky outcrop of Starfish Arc. What an honour to have a thriving colony on the land my family had owned since the 1950s.

I was glad I'd come in early after all because the beautiful morning, the tranquillity, and the views were such a gift. No wonder the terrace was so popular with customers.

My mum had opened The Starfish Café nearly thirty years before on the site where her mum had run a smaller café, Norma's Nook, for twenty years. When Mum lost her battle with cancer a little over six seven years ago, I became the third-generation owner, ensuring it remained a warm and friendly place where everyone was welcome and made to feel like part of the family.

I smiled contentedly as I sipped my coffee, watching the seals and listening to the gentle lapping of the waves on the beach. Despite the tragedy of losing my dad, my brother Isaac, and Mum in the space of a year, I was blessed in so many ways. I had amazing friends, an incredible boyfriend in Jake, and the most adorable, loving dog. And I had this place. The Starfish Café, our customers, my staff and those gorgeous seals were part of me and I couldn't imagine ever wanting anything different.

* * *

Angie, my assistant manager and Mum's lifelong best friend, pulled into the car park shortly before half eight while I was replenishing some hanging Easter-themed Hollie's Wood products – wooden chicks, bunnies, and lambs – on the display hooks by the till.

Hollie's Wood was a crafting business I ran alongside The Starfish Café to raise money for three charities close to my heart: Macmillan Cancer Support, the RNLI, and local animal charity Paws Rehomed. Every time a Hollie's Wood product was bought, it gave me a warm and fuzzy feeling, knowing there was a little more money in the pot to distribute among them.

My passion for crafting wood had passed down the generations on Mum's side of the family, although I was the only one who'd turned it into a business. Hollie's Wood specialised in products made from driftwood such as candle holders, picture frames, coat hooks, street and harbour scenes, and Christmas tree decorations. I also made pictures using pebbles, shells and sea glass. Foraging on local beaches had given me a much-needed distraction after the tragic RNLI rescue in which my dad and Isaac had both lost their lives just after Christmas, seven years ago.

'What a gorgeous morning!' Angie declared. 'Should be busy today.'

'I really hope so, because I might have gone overboard on the baking.'

She raised her eyebrows. 'You were in early again? Should I be worried about you?'

I gave her a reassuring smile. 'No. I just miss Jake when he's working nights.'

She returned my smile. 'You two are the sweetest. Warms my heart.'

* * *

My favourite customers – octogenarians Betty and Tommy – arrived shortly after we opened. They'd been coming to the café for tea and scones every day except Sunday for as long as I could remember, and it had been an honour to host a sixty-fifth wedding anniversary party for them at the end of February.

Tommy, ever the gentleman, tipped his trilby at me. 'Good morning, darling girl. What a beautiful day!'

'It's gorgeous, isn't it?' I said, coming round from the counter. 'How are you two today?'

'Wonderful,' Betty said as they slipped into their favourite window booth. 'Sylvia's joining us shortly, so we'll wait until she arrives before we order.'

'That's good. I haven't seen her for a couple of weeks.'

'Neither have we,' Betty said. 'She says she has exciting news.'

'Ooh, sounds intriguing. I'll leave you to enjoy the view in the meantime. The scone of the day is raspberry and white chocolate.'

Betty's eyes lighting up made me laugh. She had a penchant for chocolate scones.

I returned to the counter while they waited for Sylvia to arrive. Also in her eighties, Sylvia was another of my favourites. She'd started coming to the café six years ago after losing her husband but had never engaged in conversation. We'd affectionately christened her Mrs Sultana because she always ordered a fruit scone but picked out all the fruit. On what would have been her husband's ninetieth birthday, she finally opened up to me and it broke my heart discovering how lonely she was. I'd introduced her to Betty and Tommy and finding new friends seemed to give her a new lease of life.

I was curious as to what her news was. Could it be a new romance? She'd been absolutely devoted to Albert, but the love they'd shared wouldn't lessen if she felt ready to let love and companionship into her life again.

I didn't have to wait long, as the next customer to arrive was

Sylvia. A petite woman with a sleek white bob, she looked radiant in a dusky pink tunic and cream silk scarf over black trousers.

'Hollie, dearest,' she said, smiling warmly, 'can I borrow you?'

She greeted Betty and Tommy and slid into the booth next to Betty, indicating I should sit beside Tommy. We all looked at her expectantly. Her eyes shone and it seemed she'd burst if she didn't share her news.

'I'm going on a cruise round the South Pacific!' she announced, clapping her hands together. 'Can you believe it? I've never been abroad before but I'm going on a cruise.'

We all spoke at once, firing questions at her about when she was going, the stops on the cruise, and whether she was going alone.

'I'm going with my neighbour, Dorothy,' she said, laughing at our enthusiasm. 'Albert was never interested in travelling when there were so many beautiful places to visit in the UK and Dorothy's husband was the same. She lost him two years before I lost Albert. A couple of weeks ago, she was telling me about all these wonderful places she'd visited since he died and said I'd be very welcome to join her if ever I fancied getting myself a passport, so I decided what the heck.'

'Good for you,' I said, full of admiration for her taking her first overseas adventure.

'Thank you. We're going in mid-May, flying to Honolulu and staying there for a few days before a cruise round the South Pacific. We'll be away for three weeks.'

'If somebody had told me a year ago that Mrs Sultana was capable of going through this transformation, I'd never have believed them,' I said to Angie when I returned to the counter.

'And it's all thanks to you,' she responded, her voice full of warmth. 'All it took was one kind person to show some genuine interest and compassion. You got a lonely woman to open up and doing so helped her face up to things. You changed her life for the better and I'm so proud of you. Fulfilling your mum's legacy every day.'

As Angie took the order she'd been preparing to her customers, I glanced over at the driftwood framed photo on the wall showing the evolution of the café from Granny's version – Norma's Nook – to The Starfish Café. My eyes rested on the image of Mum in the cab of the bulldozer when Norma's Nook was demolished. Yes, I was fulfilling her legacy and I'd do that forever because kindness cost nothing but time. I'd always have time for my customers.

2

HOLLIE

'That's my computer boxed up,' Jake said the following morning. 'How are you getting on with...?'

He broke off laughing as he turned and saw how far I'd got with removing his photographs from the whiteboard in his studio. Or rather, how far I hadn't got.

'Sorry. But I haven't seen these ones printed off and they're amazing. Why can't you see how talented you are?'

'They're okay.' Even the word 'okay' was full of doubt.

'They're a million times better than okay.' I shook my head and sighed. 'That sister of yours has so much to answer for.'

'She'd claim it's the other way round.'

Jake's dad had loved photography. When Jake was eight, they'd spent a happy summer taking photos together. However, his older sister Larissa vandalised them all and left a vindictive note telling him how useless he was and how he'd wasted their dad's time and money. The effect on Jake had been so profound that he hadn't picked up a camera again for nineteen years.

Larissa had always hated Jake, blaming him for the loss of their mother, who'd died following complications during Jake's birth.

She made his childhood hell and, when their dad drowned in rough seas in North Bay on Jake's ninth birthday, her hate campaign escalated. It broke my heart every time Jake shared something she'd said or done to him and his nanna, culminating in a final showdown after his nanna's will reading.

'Larissa's a troubled woman.' I lightly ran my forefinger across the scars on his left cheekbone from where she'd attacked him with a gardening fork after their nanna disinherited Larissa, leaving her home – Lighthouse View in Whitsborough Bay's Old Town – and her life savings to Jake. 'She's out of your life now.'

Running my fingers into his dark wavy hair, I drew him into a kiss, my heart racing as he responded passionately.

'This isn't going to get the packing finished,' I said, reluctantly pulling away.

'And neither is studying all my photographs,' he quipped. 'Do your work!'

I stuck my tongue out at him. 'You're a hard taskmaster, Jake MacLeod, but I'll speed up if you promise me we don't have to unpack at the other end and we can pick up where we left off with that kiss.'

His blue eyes twinkled mischievously. 'You're on.'

We laughed as we raced to remove the photos, sending the colourful magnets scattering across the floorboards in our haste. Pickle scampered after them, barking excitedly.

And then Jake's pager beeped.

Perspiration prickled my brow and a shudder ran through me from head to toe as my pulse raced and my stomach churned.

Jake glanced down at it then up at me, his eyes full of concern. I tried to smile but my hand automatically fluttered to the gold chain round my neck and grasped Granny's and Mum's wedding rings.

'Hollie, I...'

I swallowed down my nerves and tried my hardest to keep my

voice light and breezy. 'I'm fine. Go! Save lives! We'll see you later.' I scooped Pickle up and waved his paw at Jake.

'I love you,' he said, giving me a quick peck on the lips before racing down the stairs.

'I love you too. Stay safe.'

I carried Pickle over to the front window and watched as, moments later, Jake rushed along the garden path and through the gate. He turned and blew a kiss in our direction then sprinted down the hill towards the seafront, disappearing from view.

Over the tops of the houses, I could see Whitsborough Bay Lighthouse in the distance, but the lifeboat station where Jake was heading was obliterated from view. It was another beautiful day, just like yesterday, with a clear pale blue sky and gentle warmth from the sun – a far cry from the stormy seas Dad and Isaac had experienced that fateful day – but that didn't stop my legs feeling shaky or fear gripping me.

I sat in the armchair near the window, stroking Pickle's brown fur and teasing out a sticky bud that he must have picked up on our walk this morning.

'It'll be fine,' I said to him, trying to reassure myself. 'The sea's calm. It's probably a fishing boat conked out and needing a tow.'

Most of the time, I didn't know Jake was on a shout because we'd made a pact that he wouldn't let me know. There was no point distracting me from my customers and having me worry unnecessarily while I waited for news of his safe return from a rescue. Better to live in ignorance. On the few occasions he'd been paged while we were together, my immediate reaction had been fear and panic, but ever so slowly it was getting easier.

I suspected the nerves would always be there to some extent, but I knew I needed to stay strong. Fate couldn't be cruel enough to tear Jake and me apart too after we'd both already faced more tragedy than anyone should ever have to endure in a lifetime.

Jake had passed out as RNLI crew towards the end of last year after working hard for several years to overcome an extreme fear of water following his dad's drowning. As soon as I discovered he was crew, I'd pulled away, unable to see a future for fear that I'd lose him in the same way I'd lost my family, but I loved him too deeply to cut him out my life. Inspired by the amazing way he'd tackled his fears head-on, I contacted the coxswain at the lifeboat station, Artie 'Chief' Briars, and asked whether there was any chance I could start training with the crew on Monday evenings to attempt to overcome my own fears. Artie had been with Dad and Isaac on their final rescue and, even though there was nothing he could have done to change the tragic outcome, I knew he bore the burden of guilt and was eager to do whatever he could to help me move forward.

Pickle stretched and adjusted his position on my knee.

'You're tired, aren't you?' I said, stroking his ears.

After an extra early start yesterday, we'd risen early again today like we did most Sundays to catch the sunrise on the beach and forage for driftwood.

'How about you have a snooze and I finish the packing?' I gently lifted him up, draped a fleecy blanket across the chair, and settled him back on it. He tucked his paws in, closed his eyes, and soon drifted off.

I returned to the whiteboard and removed the last few photos, added them to the box, and retrieved the scattered magnets. Desk drawers next.

Jake and I had decided to make a proper go of our relationship on my thirty-fifth birthday on Christmas Eve. Two months later, I'd asked him if he'd move into Sandy Croft – my family home on Sea Cliff overlooking the southern end of South Bay. I'd anticipated some comments from friends and customers about it being too soon, but everyone had been really positive, and their support was so very appreciated.

Over the past month, we'd gradually moved Jake's belongings from Lighthouse View to Sandy Croft and the relocation of his photography 'studio' was the final task for now. I wanted him to feel like Sandy Croft was his home too and not like he was having to work round me, so we'd prepared his new studio in what had been my parents' bedroom as the double-aspect windows provided the best light.

We'd removed the furniture, painted the walls white, taken down the curtains, put up new blinds, and replaced the lighting. It wasn't as big as his studio at Lighthouse View – which took up the entire top floor – but it was ample. More than six years after losing Mum, repurposing the room as Jake's studio felt timely and right.

It only took me half an hour to clear Jake's desk, pack away his photography books, and bubble wrap his Hollie's Wood lifeboat station. Pickle was sound asleep and I didn't like to disturb him, so I crept down the two flights of stairs to the kitchen, made a coffee, and wandered into the lounge with it.

Jake had told me that he'd existed rather than lived after his nanna died and, looking round the lounge, I felt that strongly. While the top floor and his bedroom were very much his domain, the rest of the house clearly still had his nanna's stamp on it. I knew from personal experience how hard it was to clear out and move on but it had to be done and I made a mental note that our next project needed to be refurbishing Sandy Croft's lounge so it was to our joint taste.

I'd been certain that Jake would want to live with me, but unsure how he'd feel about making Sandy Croft his home. He'd told me that, although Lighthouse View would always be special to him because of his nanna – the amazing woman who'd opened her home to an angry, confused, scared nine-year-old boy – it held memories of many sad and difficult years as he struggled with his grief, so he felt ready for a fresh start.

Sandy Croft was closer to The Starfish Café, had a double garage I used as my workshop, and was bigger for the family I hoped we'd have, although we hadn't yet had that conversation. Things had moved so quickly for us that I didn't want to spook him by throwing children into the mix so soon, although, if he didn't want a family, I'd still choose him. He hadn't been the only one existing instead of living.

I returned to the kitchen to study the large collection of recipe books on the shelves above the wooden table. I recognised several of the older ones as duplicates of those I'd inherited from Mum, passed down from Granny. My heart leapt as I spotted a copy of a family cookbook that had never recovered from an incident with a jar of tomato passata. Smiling at the prospect of a replacement, I removed it from the shelf and opened it up, immediately tearing up as I read the dedication inside:

To the best mum and mother-in-law in the world on your 58th birthday. Some more family recipes for you to perfect before our family grows with your second grandchild due in November.
　　All our love forever, Bobby & Michelle xx

I sat down heavily on one of the wooden chairs and ran my fingers across the beautiful, sloped handwriting. Jake's nanna's birthday had been the end of May so Michelle would have been about three months pregnant with Jake at the time. She'd have been so excited and hopeful for the future; a future snatched away from the whole family five months later.

A key turning in the lock made me jump and I looked expectantly down the hall, wiping at a rogue tear that had slipped down my cheek.

'That was quick,' I called to Jake.

'A fisherman reported a suspected body in the water, but it turned out to be a boat buoy snagged in some rope and driftwood.'

'That's a relief.'

He narrowed his eyes at me. 'Have you been crying?'

'No! Well, maybe a couple of tears. I found this.' I slid the book across the table and pointed to the dedication.

'That's Mum's writing. That was probably the last gift they gave to Nanna.'

'It made me sad thinking about how excited she must have been and then...'

He drew me into his arms, and I took a deep calming breath.

'None of us know what the future holds,' he said gently. 'All we can do is live our best life each day. How's the packing going?'

'I've finished your studio, there are some cushions I'd like to liberate from the lounge, and I'd love some of your nanna's recipe books, including this one, if you don't mind.'

'You can have them all. There's a book of Nanna's own recipes buried on the shelves somewhere which I kept meaning to dig out for you. We'll box them up and take them home to sort through. In the meantime, they're holding the "body in the water" at the station for me. Do you want to come down while I take some photos? We can grab some lunch on the seafront afterwards.'

'I'd love to.'

Jake collected his camera bag and we decided to leave Pickle sleeping as we wouldn't be out for long.

'Have you had any further thoughts on what to do with Lighthouse View?' I asked as we headed down Ashby Street towards the seafront.

'I keep changing my mind. I know the sensible thing would be to sell it, but I'm not sure I'm ready to fully let go.' He squeezed my hand. 'I'm not sure I'm ready to have a stranger renting it, either. Maybe another week or two to think about it.'

'Take as long as you like. You won't get any pressure from me.'

I completely understood his reluctance. Even though he'd downplayed it, it was a huge thing him moving out in the first place, so I certainly wasn't going to push him to do anything else when he wasn't quite ready. Although it was a shame for such a beautiful house to remain empty.

3

TORI

I stared at my reflection in the full-length mirror on the wardrobe door, twisted and turned to get a better look at the maxi dress, then shook my head. They wouldn't like it. There'd be some comment – masquerading as a compliment – about it being too long, too baggy, too bright.

I ran a brush through my long dark auburn hair and fastened it back into a clip. Long hair at the dining table was 'uncouth' apparently, even for a thirty-eight-year-old.

'Tori! We need to go!' Leyton yelled up the stairs, his frustration evident, as it always seemed to be these days.

The desire to feign illness was strong but I wasn't one for deception. I knew how hurtful it was being on the receiving end. I pushed back my shoulders and forced a smile.

'Coming!'

I glanced at my reflection once more and slammed the wardrobe door closed. It was too late to change outfit now, not that anything in my wardrobe would please Leyton's parents. They were all about designer labels and the only labels I had in my clothes were supermarket ones on the basic T-shirts I wore under the dresses and dungarees I designed and made myself.

'Sorry,' I said to Leyton as I settled into the front passenger seat of his Mercedes. 'Wardrobe dilemma. Not sure I made the right decision.'

I wasn't fishing for a compliment, but it would have been the perfect cue for him to say something nice. He didn't take it.

'I can't believe it's already the last Sunday of the month,' I said, trying to keep my voice light. 'I swear it comes round every week.'

He flashed his eyes at me before pulling off the drive and my stomach sank. I'd actually meant it as an observation of how quickly time passed, but I could see how it might sound like a criticism of his parents. I'd learned early on in our relationship that Leyton could rant and rave about them but it was never an invitation for me to join in, even though I usually wholeheartedly agreed with everything he said.

'It's only three hours once a month,' he mumbled, his voice low and edgy. 'It's not a lot to ask.'

I opened my mouth to explain what I'd meant but thought better of it. Explaining would sound defensive and he'd find a way to twist it. He'd been so touchy lately and I couldn't seem to do right for doing wrong.

He paused by the junction to pull out of our estate and surprised me by turning and winking. 'I'll be ready for a stiff drink afterwards.'

I smiled back at him but remained quiet in case I said the wrong thing again. I wasn't sure I'd be able to make it through Sunday lunch at his parents' without a couple of relaxing drinks so I've no idea how Leyton managed it. I'd previously offered to drive so he could drink but I wasn't allowed to drive his Mercedes after an altercation with a bollard. It had only been a small scratch, but the trust in me driving his car was never repaired.

Taking Carrie, the campervan, wasn't a viable alternative. Apparently she was an 'eyesore'. Bit rude. I love my VW camper. I couldn't believe it when my Uncle Hugh rang me to say that they'd found her in a barn on the land they'd bought from the neighbouring farm and would I be interested in a restoration project? Would I ever? I'd since lovingly restored her to her former pale teal and cream glory and how Leyton's parents could refer to her as an eyesore was beyond me. Although most of what they said and did was beyond me.

Only three hours, as he said. Best get it over with.

* * *

Fifteen minutes later, we pulled onto the sweeping gravel driveway at Fenby Heights. A stunning early twentieth-century red-brick mansion with seven bedrooms, six bathrooms, an orangery, a pool and six acres of land, it occupied an elevated position at the end of the Fenby Grange, a village north-west of Whitsborough Bay, exclusively for those with money. Lots of it.

Like everything about Eveline and Ernest 'don't call me Ernie' Clairmont, Fenby Heights was a statement about their wealth and status in the community. Leyton was their only child, he was forty, and he'd left home years before they moved here. Nobody ever stayed overnight, so why the seven bedrooms?

Leyton reached for my hand and gave it a gentle squeeze before exiting the car. The rare show of affection gave me comfort and strength. I pushed my shoulders back and forced a smile as the heavy oak front door opened and Eveline stepped out, arms wide. Looking effortlessly glamorous in a white blouse, tailored grey trousers and burgundy stilettos, she reminded me of Helen Mirren with her stylish white-blonde bob and statement jewellery.

'Darling!' she cried, air-kissing Leyton on either side. 'Wonderful to see you.'

Her over-the-top enthusiasm suggested she hadn't seen him for weeks when I knew she'd stopped by the Whitsborough Bay office of Clairmont Properties on Friday morning – something she did with alarming regularity despite her and Ernest retiring five years back and passing the running of their estate agency and property development empire to Leyton. It was frightening how much power they still wielded by retaining the controlling share in the company. They might as well not have retired.

Eveline turned to me. 'Victoria!' she said with less conviction as she air-kissed me too. I hated being called by my full name and she knew it.

'Come inside. Your father's in the kitchen, checking on the pheasant.'

Pheasant? I caught Leyton's eye and he gave a shrug. A good old roast chicken was never on the menu at the Clairmonts'. Always had to be something a little more impressive.

In the grand marble-floored chandelier-lit entrance hall, Leyton took my coat, and Eveline looked me up and down.

'Is this another of your creations, my dear?'

'Yes. I finished it last week.'

'Well done you. It's very floral. Reminds me of a pair of curtains my mother had.'

Smile of a beauty queen, sting of a scorpion.

'Thank you, Eveline.' I childishly pronounced her name as Evil-Lynne instead of her preferred Ever-line. I had to take small wins where I could get them. 'Glad you like it.'

'You're welcome, Victoria.' She emphasised the 'Vic'. Touché.

Her Louboutins click-clacked as we followed her into the enormous lounge, which looked like a showpiece from a country living magazine. Fresh flowers burst from a dozen or so ceramic and crystal vases. I'd brought flowers the first time we'd been invited for Sunday lunch, but my selection looked so inadequate compared to her high-end florist's arrangements. I'd also taken a packet of Jaffa Cakes – a triple pack, no less – but from the withering look she'd given me, you'd think I'd presented her with arsenic. Lesson learned. No more gifts for Eveline.

'Good afternoon, all,' Ernest announced, stepping into the room with a silver tray in his hands. 'Sherry is served.'

I always felt like I was at meeting of a board of directors when Ernest spoke. Dressed in a charcoal grey three-piece suit with a paisley silk tie and matching pocket handkerchief, I wondered if the man even knew how to relax.

'Thank you, Ernest.' I smiled politely as I took my glass, the smell turning my stomach. I'd told them on several occasions that I didn't care for sherry. Leyton had told them too. And yet the sherry kept coming – tradition, apparently – so I'd learned to sit beside one of the ceramic vases so nobody would notice the discolouration of the water as I steadily tipped in the rancid liquid when they weren't looking. They employed a cleaner and, if she'd ever commented to Eveline on the strange smell and aroma when changing the water, it had never come back to me. Or maybe it had and that was why they kept plying me with the stuff.

We were invited to sit and I pretended to take a sip from my drink as I anxiously watched Ernest settling into the large high-backed chair. Leyton referred to it as 'the throne' and Ernest only ever sat there when he meant business. I think the straight back and extra height made him feel even more superior than usual.

He straightened his trousers and adjusted the sleeves on his suit to avoid rumpling, then fixed his steely gaze on his son. I bet the entire workforce at Clairmont Properties had breathed a collective sigh of relief when Ernest retired and handed over the reins to Leyton. Ernest had a reputation for paying well, but his staff pretty much sold their soul to the devil. Standards were high, expectations were higher.

'Your mother tells me the Whitsborough Bay branch is an absolute shambles. Explain yourself.'

Wow! No preamble at all. Straight in for the kill!

Leyton's jawline tightened and I knew he'd be grinding his teeth. His dentist had instructed him to wear a mouth guard in bed because it had become that bad over the past few years.

'It's not a shambles,' he declared, his voice strong and confident. 'There are a few issues to resolve and they're all in hand.'

'A few issues? You've had the worst performing March in over twenty years, you've lost a key client, and you're facing an employment tribunal. That's not a few issues, Leyton. That's an unmitigated disaster.'

I glanced from Ernest to Leyton and back again. There was no mistaking they were father and son – the same intense deep blue eyes, chiselled cheekbones and strong jaw. Ernest's hair and immaculately coiffed beard were a distinguished silver, but I'd seen photos of him when he was younger and he'd had the same light brown colouring Leyton had.

It wasn't just looks they shared. I'd known from first meeting him that Leyton demonstrated many of his father's traits – ambition, drive, determination – and I'd admired that about him. They were qualities I possessed myself, which had been essential for making a success of my business, Tennyson Designs. But lately, I'd seen more of the qualities surfacing that I resented in his father – ruthlessness, intolerance and an element of cynicism – and I didn't appreciate how they'd crept into our personal life. I kept telling myself it was because he was under immense stress and it would get better, but I'd been telling myself that for quite some time now.

'It's all in hand,' Leyton insisted, drawing my attention back to him. Ernest's use of 'unmitigated disaster' was a bit harsh, but I knew that all was not well at Clairmont Properties and the resolution would neither be quick nor easy.

'How? Please share your brilliant plans. We're all waiting with bated breath.'

'March was only low because Easter is in April this year and we're expecting several sale completions then. And we had one of the best Februarys ever, so I'm not unduly concerned.'

'Not unduly concerned? You should *always* be concerned when it comes to business. Have I not taught you anything? And what about losing the Durling account? That's got nothing to do with when Easter falls. What genius plans do you have in place to rectify that?'

Ernest continued to interrogate Leyton, and Eveline watched, wearing a ghost of a smile as though this was a great piece of dramatic television unfolding. I glanced down at my sherry and at the vase next to me. The only way I was going to get through three hours of this was alcohol. I necked back the drink in one.

4

HOLLIE

'What do you reckon, Pickle?' I asked as I released him from his seatbelt harness. 'Is this going to be the best sunrise so far?'

I held out my hand for a high-five and he placed his paw against my palm before jumping down from the back seat into the car park.

'Good boy!'

'I'm feeling confident it'll be a good one,' Jake said as he hoisted his backpack containing his camera and kit onto his back and lifted his tripod out of the boot. 'Although every sunrise I spend with you is the best one.'

'Aw, you old romantic,' I said, giving him a soft peck on the lips. 'Here's to thousands more sunrises and sunsets together.'

It was 5.30 a.m. on the first Monday in April. It was dark and cold, so we'd wrapped up warm in several layers topped with waterproof jackets and hats.

We pulled on our head torches over our hats and I held Pickle's lead as we descended the steps to the right of The Starfish Café. I smiled as we passed it, a familiar feeling of pride sweeping through me.

By the time we made it down to the beach, the sky had turned from inky black into a deep shade of petrol blue and we could just make out dark clouds. Any sunrise was beautiful, but clouds added more drama and interest to Jake's photographs. We dimmed our head torches, not wanting to startle any of the seals while they were sleeping.

The sun would rise behind the red and white striped lighthouse beyond Starfish Arc so Jake set up his tripod opposite the lighthouse, ready to move it when it was clear exactly where the sun would peep over the horizon.

I chose a flat boulder nearby, removed a waterproof seat pad from my backpack and placed it on the top. Pickle clambered onto my knee and I stroked his head and back as the sky gradually lightened. With each passing minute, bands of colour streaked across the sky, changing hue from pale to deep to vibrant. Lemon gave way to yellow then gold. Lilac become purple then violet. It was as though an artist was sweeping their brushes across a blank canvas, increasing the depth and beauty with each stroke.

'Isn't it stunning?' I whispered to Pickle.

I poured a cup of coffee from my flask and breathed in the aroma of the cocoa beans mingled with salt, seals and seaweed. A gentle breeze tousled my hair beneath my pink bobble hat and I pulled it down a little further over my ears.

'Nice hunk of driftwood for you,' Jake said, placing a gnarly log beside me.

'You spoil me.' I blew him a kiss as he returned to his tripod.

My family had all loved the sea – particularly Dad and Isaac – so being on the beach had helped me feel closer to them after their deaths. Looking back now, I could see what a lonely existence I'd created for myself in my grief. Watching a sunrise with Jake and Pickle was so much more meaningful than on my own. Although my whole life was so much more meaningful since they'd burst their way into it on Bonfire Night last year after Jake found Pickle abandoned on this very beach.

Pickle adjusted his position and I stroked his warm belly. 'We're so grateful to you, aren't we? Changed our lives.'

Since they'd moved in, the house felt alive with laughter and chatter, just like it used to. I sighed contentedly as I watched Jake reposition his tripod.

A grunting sound beside me pulled me back from my reflections and I smiled at one of the most recognisable grey seals on the beach as he rolled onto his back and shuffled back and forth.

'Morning, Tank,' I said quietly. 'Good to see you too.'

I owned the beach but welcomed visitors, providing they followed a few rules to take their litter home, keep dogs on leads, and remain a safe distance from the seals, especially when there were pups around.

I watched Tank getting himself comfortable on the sand, then turned my attention back to the sunrise. An arc of flaming light nudged over the horizon, inching higher, spreading a warm glow across the sky.

As the sun rose and the light strengthened, bringing depth and colour to the lighthouse, beach, rocks and seals, I felt alive and happy. I'd never stop thinking about and missing my parents and brother, but there was hope for a future without them. Thanks to Jake and Pickle, I looked forward more than I looked back and, when I did look back, it was with happy memories instead of an overwhelming feeling of sadness.

* * *

'They're amazing, Jake.' I peered over his shoulders at the sunrise photos as he scrolled through them on his computer back at Sandy Croft later that afternoon. 'Please tell me you see what I see. You have a gift. Seriously, you do. And I'm not saying that because I'm biased.'

'I'm pretty pleased with them,' he conceded.

'And so you should be! But can we have a bit more enthusiasm, please?'

I wrapped my arms round his shoulders and nuzzled his neck. 'When I look at your photos, it's like I'm there. I can feel the sun, hear the sea, smell the salt. You, Jake MacLeod, are an extremely talented photographer. What else can I do to convince you?'

He spun his seat round and I laughed as I landed on his knee.

'A kiss might help.'

I melted into a tender kiss.

'Which one's your favourite?' he asked.

'I love them all, but that one's something else.' I pointed to a silhouetted image of a seal sitting on a rock as the sky behind it exploded with colour. 'It's perfect.'

'Then I'll print it off for the whiteboard.'

I looked round the room. We'd only moved his things over a week ago, but it now felt like Jake's studio instead of Mum and Dad's bedroom – another significant step forward.

'I'll take Pickle round the block while you do that,' I said. 'Come on, Pickle. Walk time.'

Pickle jumped down from the cushion where he'd been napping and followed me down the stairs. Jake and I would be heading down to the lifeboat station shortly for Monday evening training, followed by optional drinks in The Lobster Pot, opposite the harbour.

We walked along the esplanade where the trees that lined the cliffs gave tantalising glimpses of the sea. Where the trees ended was one of my favourite parts of Sea Cliff. The path curved either side round a grassy area in which a brightly painted wooden rowing boat nestled, surrounded by winter pansies, behind which was the most spectacular unbroken view across South Bay.

While Pickle sniffed round the boat, I looked down towards Whitsborough Bay lifeboat station. I'd been so proud of Dad and Isaac for volunteering as lifeboat crew. I remembered many dog walks with Mum on Monday evenings where we'd watched the Shannon-class ALB (the large all-weather lifeboat) and the D-class ILB (small inshore inflatable lifeboat) launch and speculated as to what skills they might be focusing on that evening.

For a long time after the accident, I couldn't walk to this end of the esplanade. I avoided South Bay. I even avoided the beach for a while. I never dreamed there'd come a day when I started to train with the crew myself.

My first few training sessions in January had been terrifying and I'd even been sick after the first one, although Jake was the only one who knew that. First steps are always the hardest and, as each week passed, it became a little easier.

I'd been worried I might be treated differently because of what had happened. I didn't want to be the person they all felt sorry for and acted awkwardly around, but every single crew member had been amazing. Those who'd known Dad and Isaac – or Sparky and Silver as they'd been known to the crew – didn't need to express their sorrow or tell me how proud my family would have been that I was continuing their legacy. I felt it in their hugs, handshakes and smiles as they warmly welcomed me. I wasn't the only one who'd suffered a loss; they'd all felt it too.

Artie – I was still trying to get used to calling him 'Chief' – was convinced that the sea was in my blood and in my soul and there was no way I'd be able to walk away at the end of my training.

'I guarantee you'll be the second fourth-generation member of the Brooks family to become RNLI crew and the very first female,' he often told me. I laughed and reminded him that wasn't my intention. I was going to train for between six to twelve months, depending on how long it took to lay my demons to rest, and then I'd back away and continue to support the charity through sales proceeds from Hollie's Wood.

'Keep telling yourself that, Starfish,' he said, using the nickname they'd assigned to me early on. 'But, deep down, you know I'm right.'

And with each passing week, my protests were a little weaker.

5

TORI

As I drove Carrie the campervan towards South Bay on Monday evening, a week after Sunday lunch with Leyton's parents, I stole a sideways glance at Leyton. He was hunched over, reading through emails on his phone, his frown deepening. I could feel the tension emanating from him and suspected I was about to add to it.

'Tough day?' I asked gently, hoping a little empathy might cushion my news.

'Every day is a tough day at the moment,' he responded with a sigh.

'You'll soon forget about it when you're gliding across the sea.'

He snapped his head up and stared at me. 'You're kidding! Have you any idea what's going on at work?'

'Not really because you don't tell me. But if you want to talk about it...'

'What good would talking about it do? Can you make the tribunal go away? Can you win back the Durling account?'

'No, but—'

'Well, then.'

I bit back a frustrated sigh. I hated it when he uttered those two words which translated as *so shut up and butt out*. Another unappealing habit he'd picked up from his father.

'I'm really looking forward to getting out on the board,' I said, my voice a little too bright and excitable. 'First paddleboard outing of the year.'

'The weather's going to turn,' he said for what I swear was the twentieth time since he'd arrived home from work.

I ignored him. 'Tell you who else is looking forward to getting out on the water. Matt and Charlee. Charlee hasn't been on a board since she fell pregnant with Teddy. She can't wait.'

'How thrilling for them. Get them to send us a postcard.'

I wasn't allowed to say anything against his parents, but he seemed to think it was okay to make snide comments about my cousin and his wife. So he really wasn't going to like what I had to say next.

'They won't need to. They're joining us tonight.'

'They're what?' The volume and high pitch of Leyton's voice conveyed his displeasure.

'It'll be fun,' I said.

'Your definition and my definition of fun are clearly poles apart.'

Poles apart? Yes, like pretty much every aspect of our lives at the moment.

I pulled into a parking space outside The Bay Pavilion and gazed out at the sea.

'We won't be going out anyway,' he said. 'Because like I've already said, the weather's going to turn.'

I winced at the smug, patronising sing-song voice and checked my weather app again. 'It isn't forecast to turn until midnight.'

'But it's going to turn sooner.'

'Why are you so convinced? Look!' I held out my phone. 'And look!' I swept my arm along the sea. 'It's perfect.' It was a beautiful evening with the gentlest of breezes rippling the sea and, from what I could tell, near enough perfect conditions.

'A hurricane wasn't forecast in 1987 but the Great Storm still hit.'

'Seriously? The best you've got is 1987? When we were both kids?'

His eyes flashed angrily at me and I knew I'd pushed it too far. He hated being challenged on anything – just like his father – and he'd been touchier than ever all week following the worst Sunday lunch in the history of horrendous lunches with his parents. When we'd returned home, he'd been in a foul mood, stomping round the house, slamming doors, swearing under his breath. Fair enough. I was livid for him because the way his father had laid into him had been embarrassing and condescending. I have no idea how he'd stopped himself from storming out that afternoon, instead managing to calmly responded to the barrage of criticism hurled at him. I'd therefore completely understood the need to let off steam last Sunday. I also understood that it wasn't something he was going to get over by the morning. What I didn't understand was why he was still so snappy with me a full week later.

'Come on, Leyton,' I said in a gentle voice. 'It's our first outing of the year. You know you've been dying to get the boards out.'

He drew in a deep breath then shook his head. 'I've had a crap day and what I'm dying for is a pint. You can do what you like. You usually do.'

I didn't appreciate the dig, especially when he was the one who tended to do his own thing.

'You liked the idea a few days ago.' It had been the only thing I could think of that might cheer him up. I'd been a surfer when we met, but he'd dismissed it as a stressful sport and had introduced me to paddleboarding and kayaking.

'And now I'd rather have a pint.'

I glanced across at Leyton and fought back a sigh. He was an exceptionally good-looking man with those mesmerising blue eyes, sun-kissed hair and a muscular six foot four build. He looked even sexier after developing a stubble beard as a fresh look for his fortieth birthday and deciding to keep it thanks to all the compliments it drew. When he laughed and his eyes sparkled, I saw the gorgeous man I'd fallen for when we met nearly eight years ago. But when he sulked, I couldn't see anything of that man. He looked ugly, petulant, rude. I'd seen too much of that side of him recently and it was wearing me down.

'So you're not coming?'

'No.'

'But you won't be annoyed with me if I go?'

'I'll be the one who's safe on land alerting the coastguard when you're swept out to sea.'

I could have done without the sarcasm. He was being overly dramatic – his default position when he didn't get his own way – but he'd get even more dramatic if I called him out on it.

'Are you sure it's not because you don't want to spend time with Matt?'

'For God's sake, Tori, will you *ever* let that go?'

I raised my eyebrows at him. 'Will you?'

He pushed open the passenger door and jumped down. 'I'll be in The Anchor when you're done.'

Slam went the door.

I scrambled across into his vacated seat and wound the window down.

'I thought you didn't like it in there,' I called to his back.

'Closest pub to the lifeboat station, so I can watch for them towing you back in,' he yelled without even turning round.

'Stupid arse,' I muttered as I wound the window back up. Why did he have to be so stubborn? The answer that came back terrified me: *Because he's morphing into his father.*

I shuddered at that thought and turned my attention to the sea, unable to see what his issue was with the weather tonight. No matter what Leyton claimed, he was still at odds with my cousin because of some stupid fight they'd got into over a girl back in their college days. Neither of them would give me the full story and I wasn't particularly interested in something that had happened half a lifetime ago anyway, but Leyton couldn't seem to let it go and there was always tension – and usually words – when they got together. He claimed it was Matt who started it, but I'd seen them together and it was *always* Leyton who made the first dig. Pathetic, really.

I probably should have double-checked with him before I invited them, but it wasn't like it was a complete surprise. They'd regularly joined us before Charlee got pregnant with their son, Teddy, now two and a half, and then Aria who'd soon be celebrating her first birthday – and they'd both said on several occasions in Leyton's presence that they were dying to get back on the water the first chance we got this year. This was the first chance.

The beeping of a horn snapped me out of my thoughts and I looked up to see Charlee had parked beside Carrie and was waving at me. Smiling, I waved back and clambered out for hugs.

'I'm so excited about this!' Charlee cried as she squeezed me. 'A child-free hour on the open water. Bliss. I've missed it.'

Matt peeked into Carrie. 'Did I imagine it or did we drive past Leyton just now?'

I sighed and rolled my eyes at him. 'Nope. Didn't imagine it. Leyton Clairmont, weather forecaster extraordinaire, has declared that the weather is about to turn and it's not safe to go out.'

We all turned to face the sea and the gentle ripples.

'Looks good to me,' Matt said, shrugging. 'His loss. So what's the plan?'

* * *

Ten minutes later, we were all standing upright, heading south along the coast in the direction of Starfish Point. There was a light breeze pushing against us, which would aid us on the return trip when our muscles would be aching. For Matt and me, it was the first session since October, but it had been about three years for Charlee.

'I love this!' Charlee called. 'It's so peaceful.'

I had to agree. I still loved the adrenaline buzz from surfing, but there was something special about paddleboarding that had captivated me from my very first go. I loved being able to switch off from work or anything else that might be preying on my mind – like Leyton's perpetual grump – and just focus on keeping my balance as I cut through the water.

We were about halfway to Starfish Point when the wind suddenly whipped up and I fought to keep my balance as the gentle ripples became more of a swell. There was a squeal and a splash as Charlee fell in.

'Are you okay?' I called.

'Yeah.' She groaned as she hauled herself back onto her board, but she was still smiling.

Next moment, the increased swell knocked us both off balance and I gasped as I tumbled into the cold sea.

'You both all right?' Matt called.

'I'm fine,' Charlee said. 'Not got my sea legs yet. I'll soon be in double figures.'

'Tori?' Matt asked.

I rubbed my stinging eyes before clambering back onto my board. 'All good. That first plunge is always the worst. You'll be...'

I didn't get to finish my sentence as Matt toppled into the sea, followed by Charlee for a third time. Matt had only just stood up again when I found myself back in the water, spluttering on a mouthful of salty sea.

A feeling of unease clawed at me. Even when I was first learning, I'd never fallen twice in such quick succession and Matt's balance was superb. Charlee and I usually joked that he superglued his feet to the paddleboard.

Clinging onto my board, I took a moment to look round. What had started as gentle ripples had now developed into a strong swell better suited to surfing. Leyton's words about the weather turning earlier than the forecast stated haunted me. Had he been right?

'I think we'd better head back,' I called, hauling myself back onto my board and sitting astride it.

They were both still in the water, holding onto their boards and staring past me towards the shore. Seeing Charlee's eyes widen, I whipped round and my stomach sank to the seabed. I could barely see the shore. How had we drifted so far out in such a short space of time?

Charlee glanced at me, her fear unmistakable. She could swim, but she wasn't a strong swimmer like Matt and me.

We were wearing thick winter wetsuits with gloves and booties as well as buoyancy aids, but the right kit wasn't going to stop us being swept out further.

'I think we'd best get paddling,' I said. 'Lie on your boards and paddle with your hands as though you're going to surf.'

They did as I suggested, but our efforts were fruitless. The swell increased with each passing minute and we were getting further from the shore instead of closer. My arms were used to hard work but my muscles were already burning so I could only imagine what Charlee must be feeling.

She screamed as a rogue wave knocked her off her board.

'Charlee!' Matt yelled, frantically paddling over to her.

She clung to her board, sobbing. 'I can't do it.'

'Yes, you can. We've got this!' he said.

But I wasn't convinced we had. Looking at the waves and the darkening sky, the weather had this – not us.

While Matt continued to reassure Charlee, I lifted up the water-proof pouch attached to my wetsuit and jabbed at my phone through the plastic. No signal. No!

'Do either of you have a signal?'

'I didn't bring my phone,' Charlee said.

Matt lifted up his pouch and pressed several keys on his phone. 'Nothing.'

I looked from Charlee's pale face to Matt's stricken expression to the distant shore. For the first time ever, in the hundreds or perhaps even thousands of hours I'd spent in the water, trouble had arrived. Serious trouble and we needed help. Quickly.

6

HOLLIE

'It's the end of month three of training for Spaniel and Starfish,' Chief said as we gathered in the training room at the lifeboat station that evening. 'We're going out in the D-class tonight for a discussion followed by a practical, but I'm not going to tell you what that is until we're out on the water.'

A huge beefy man in his mid-forties, Chief could have provided the inspiration behind the design of Stormy Stan – the RNLI's giant mascot – with his bushy ginger beard and thick wavy hair. He was the classic gentle giant and I was sorry I'd lost touch with him after Dad and Isaac died but, back then, it had been too difficult for me to maintain links with the crew.

'Bart will be at the helm,' he continued. 'Mouse and I will be your crew. Get kitted up and we'll see you shortly for safety checks.'

Mouse was Jake's nickname because, when he'd first joined the RNLI, he'd been quiet as a mouse. Thirty-nine-year-old Bart – real name Finley Scott – had joined the crew aged eighteen. He'd been obsessed with *The Simpsons* at the time, so the name had stuck, and his seriously impressive party piece was doing impressions of all the recurring cast members.

Some nicknames were obvious and came quickly – like Starfish for me because of the café. It was an important aspect of the sense of being part of a family.

After kitting up, I joined the others and we walked down the ramp behind the small tractor which pushed the D-class ILB on its trailer. The shore crew guided it safely towards the sea and gave us permission to board.

'Starfish, what did you notice about the sea earlier today?' Chief asked once we'd launched and Bart steered the ILB straight out to sea. 'Even as recently as half an hour ago.'

'Pretty calm with only a gentle swell.'

'Spaniel, what are the risks with weather like that, particularly at this time of year?'

'The calm sea can be deceptive. The weather can change quickly and anyone on a kayak or paddleboard can be swept out to sea quickly and knocked off as the swell increases.'

'And the sea temperature?' The question was directed at me.

'Also deceptive. A bit of sunshine and a nice day won't have any impact on heating the sea up until later in the summer, so it's as cold as winter right now. Anyone in the water is in danger of hyperthermia pretty quickly, even if they're in the right kit.'

Chief gave us both a thumbs-up. 'Good work. This evening, we're heading south with several stops, but that's all I'm saying for now, so sit back and enjoy the ride.'

As Bart turned south to follow the shoreline and sped up, Jake glanced across at me and smiled. The first time I'd been out on the ILB in January, I'd been absolutely terrified. There were no seats and therefore no seatbelts, so crew had to kneel on the bottom. I'd tightly gripped one of the handles on the side of the boat, fighting back the growing nausea.

I'd expected to feel comforted having Jake there, but it had been worse because I was worried about him as well as myself. I kept imagining a rogue wave capsizing the boat, Jake getting knocked out and disappearing beneath the waves. I'd had a nightmare about it that night and had woken up screaming, but Jake had been there to hold me and reassure me that he wasn't going anywhere.

The next couple of times weren't much better, but I gradually relaxed as I became more accustomed to the ILB's reactions to different sea states. Last month, I had a breakthrough where, instead of fear, I felt elation. The adrenaline rush, the wind and spray against my face, and the thrill of being part of something special took hold and I knew I'd taken a leap forward in facing my demons.

'What do you notice now?' Chief shouted as we bounced across the waves.

'The wind's whipped up and it's getting rough,' I called.

'Exactly! This is the sort of weather where we expect shouts – sudden unexpected changes where the forecast doesn't match what's happening now. This is when even the most prepared water-sports fans can get caught out.'

As we approached The Bay Pavilion on our starboard side – an entertainment and restaurant complex at the far south of South Bay – Bart slowed the ILB, then brought it to a stop.

'The focus tonight is on pulling casualties from the water,' Chief said. 'I'm going to give you a number of scenarios and weather types and I want you to tell me about the different approaches we might take and the challenges that might be presented. We'll be travelling along the coast to mix it up as there'll be different hazards depending on where the casualty is found. All ready?'

'Ready!' Spaniel and I responded. I loved how training was always practical, on the ILB and out on the sea, rather than being classroom based. Chief believed it was more effective being surrounded by our 'workspace', experiencing the weather, feeling the sea state, and I had to agree. I certainly learned much faster this way than by reading my training manual.

'We'll start with what might initially seem an easy rescue. It's a bright summer's day and there's a flat calm sea. An eight-year-old girl and her five-year-old brother were playing in a small inflatable dinghy on the beach right over there.' He pointed to the beach in front of The Bay Pavilion. 'The dingy wasn't tethered because their parents were sitting nearby watching and believed their children were safe. A sudden gust of wind swept the dingy from shore with the kids inside. What happens next?'

Memories flooded back to me of rescues that Dad and Isaac had talked about. I knew exactly how dangerous inflatables were at the seaside, for adults as well as children, because of the wind and currents and how they should ideally be avoided or, if used, tethered.

Discussion complete, Bart started up the boat and steered her past the point where the sand ended and the shoreline became cliffs. We were halfway through exploring our third scenario when a call came through from the coastguard, alerting us to three paddleboarders who'd got into difficulties.

'Sounds like one of the scenarios we've just been discussing,' Chief said as Bart steered the ILB south towards Starfish Point. 'Eyes peeled. Mouse and Spaniel starboard, Starfish and me port.'

I knew that spotting casualties was a challenge, even in calm seas, as there was such a vast expanse of water and the crew were looking for a speck. In this case, it would be much easier if they were upright on their paddleboards but, with the swell this evening, it was a safe assumption that there'd be bodies in the water and we could so easily miss them with the increasing rise and fall of the waves. The fading light wouldn't help, either.

My stomach did somersaults as I narrowed my eyes, searching through the sea spray. This was my first proper rescue and apprehension blended with excitement. Hopefully all three of them had managed to stay together meaning they could be taken straight to the lifeboat station and into a waiting ambulance if needed. If they'd got separated, the stakes were much higher. Even if we found them soon and all together, they wouldn't be out of danger yet. They could be injured, hypothermic, or both.

'Come on,' I muttered under my breath. 'Please be close.'

It wasn't working. It didn't matter how hard we paddled; we were still being swept further away from the shore. I was exhausted, my muscles were on fire, my eyes were stinging, and my legs kept cramping up. And the cold. Oh, my God, the cold! I'd never felt pain like it.

I stopped my futile paddling and turned to face Charlee and Matt, cringing at Charlee's terrified expression.

'I'm knackered. What about you two?'

Matt nodded.

'Nothing left,' Charlee muttered, her teeth chattering.

Matt took a few strokes in my direction, grabbed the end of my paddleboard, and pulled me closer.

'What do you – oh, shit!' he cried as a large wave knocked us all off the boards for the millionth time. Matt managed to scramble back onto his, but it was clear that Charlee really was spent. I was running close to empty too.

'New plan,' I said, injecting all the positivity I could muster into my voice. 'I don't think we're going to stay on the boards, so how about we huddle together for a bit to stay warm and conserve energy?'

Matt slipped back into the water and wrapped his arms round Charlee from behind. 'Try to relax back against me. You're not going to sink. Trust your life jacket.'

'I'm so cold,' she whimpered.

Matt tightened his hold and I moved closer, not that I had any warmth I could give her.

'Are we going to...?' she ventured.

'Get rescued?' I interrupted. 'Of course we will! Leyton will have seen the sea change and he'll have raised the alarm. The RNLI will be here soon.' I had to believe that was true because, if it wasn't, this could be the end for us.

'I know!' Matt said, his voice overly high. 'I spy, with my little eye, something beginning with...' He looked around and released a hollow laugh. 'S.'

'Sea,' Charlee and I shouted together. At least we could still laugh. For the moment.

'I think we're going to run out of "I Spy" options quickly,' I said. 'I've got one! I went to the market today and I bought some apples. Charlee?'

'Too cold to play games.'

'Come on! It'll take your mind off it. Apples and something beginning with B.'

She sighed. 'I went to the market today and I bought some apples and bananas.'

'Brilliant! Matt?'

'I went to the market today and I bought some apples, bananas and cod liver oil tablets.'

'Random,' I said. 'I went to the market today and...'

We were on the third round when I realised that not only was Charlee struggling to remember the shopping list – a normal aspect of the game – but she seemed to be struggling to remember the order of the alphabet. Her speech had slowed and I was all too aware of what that could indicate.

The sea didn't seem quite so choppy now, or perhaps that was wishful thinking on my part. I caught Matt's eye and he nodded, clearly thinking the same as me.

'Charlee?' he said. 'We're going to get you out of the sea and back onto a board.'

'Bed?' she drawled.

'No, the board,' I called.

I'm not sure how we managed it first time, but luck was thankfully on our side. The surface temperature was still low, especially with the wind chill, but it was higher than the sea. She lay on her stomach, clinging onto the sides, pale faced and panting.

I tugged at my board. 'Do you think we should lie this on top of her to keep the wind off?'

Matt looked at the board then Charlee. 'It's worth a try.'

Trying to manoeuvre the spare board without hitting Charlee on the head with it, while trying to keep her board steady, was too ambitious.

'Where's Teddy?' Charlee murmured. 'Need to read him a bedtime story.'

'Teddy's at home,' Matt said. 'We're waiting for help.'

'Is Aria in bed?'

Matt's stricken expression was unbearable. This couldn't be it. This couldn't be how it ended for us all.

'What are you doing for Aria's birthday, Charlee?' I asked.

'Don't know.'

'Yes, you do,' Matt prompted. 'It's her first birthday a week tomorrow and we're—'

I grabbed Matt's arm. 'Can you hear something?'

The waves dipped and I spotted an orange dinghy in the

distance. The sense of relief was so powerful that I couldn't move for a moment, battling with a desire to break down sobbing.

'Help!' I yelled, pulling myself together and waving my arms in the air. 'Help!'

Matt joined in, but our voices were carried on the wind and that euphoria was replaced with panic. What if they passed us?

'Light!' I grabbed my phone. I might have no signal, but I could still activate the torch. I held it in the air and frantically waved it about and Matt did the same with his.

'Help! Help!'

And help came. An orange lifeboat and five crew pulled alongside us.

'Anyone hurt?' a large man called.

'No!' Matt and I shouted.

'Freezing!' I added. 'And so relieved to see you.'

'Ditto!' the man responded. 'We'll bring you on board one at a time. Keep hold of those boards until we tell you to let go. Who's first?'

'Charlee,' we both said, pushing her paddleboard against the side of the lifeboat.

'Hi, Charlee, I'm Chief and this is Mouse. Can you get onto your knees so we can help you into the boat?'

Somehow, Charlee found the strength to push herself onto all fours and, moments later, she was half-lifted, half-rolled into the lifeboat. With a helping shove on my backside from Matt, I unceremoniously splatted onto the bottom of the boat and scrambled to the back of the lifeboat beside Charlee so they could haul Matt over the side.

A woman who introduced herself as Hollie draped foil survival blankets round our shoulders, asked our names, and suggested we huddle together.

'Do you know how long you've been in the water?' she asked.

'About forty minutes,' I said through chattering teeth. 'Some of that time was on the boards, but we kept getting knocked off. Did my boyfriend call it in?'

'We got a call, but I'm not sure who from. We were out here doing a training exercise, so we were nearby for finding you.'

I glanced at Charlee, slumped against Matt's side, shaking, and reality hit alongside gut-wrenching guilt.

'He said the weather was going to turn sooner and I didn't believe him.' It could have been the end for all of us tonight. I should have listened to Leyton, but I'd let my stubborn streak get in the way. It wasn't the first time it had caused me problems.

Hollie crouched down beside me. 'You can't blame yourself, Tori. It wasn't forecast and we were just discussing how easily weather like this can catch people out. I bet you're frozen.'

'I can't feel my feet.'

'We'll soon have you back on shore and warmed up.' She glanced at Matt and Charlee. 'Are you sure nobody's hurt?'

'I'm worried about Charlee,' Matt said. 'Her speech is slurred and she's confused.'

Charlee was muttering something, but I couldn't make it out. Her eyes kept closing and it looked like she was fighting sleep.

'I need you to stay awake, Charlee,' Hollie said. 'Can you both keep her talking?' She stood up and spoke to Chief and Mouse, but I couldn't hear what they were saying.

Matt asked Charlee basic questions like what she wanted for tea, which fragrance of bubbles she wanted in her bath, what PJs she'd put on when they got home, but her answers made no sense. I pulled my foil blanket more tightly round me, my heart thumping. I'd done this. I'd risked all our lives because I was annoyed with Leyton for taking out his bad mood on me. I'd never forgive myself if Charlee didn't recover.

Mouse crouched down in front of us. 'Hi, Charlee, I'm a nurse. How are you feeling?'

'So cold.' Her voice was barely a whisper and I could hear her teeth chattering like mine.

'We'll soon have you warm and dry.'

Jake asked Charlee several questions, most of which Matt answered when she seemed unable to. As they spoke, I watched Hollie help Chief and the man steering the boat – Bart, I think they said – lift the paddleboards out of the water and secure them in place. I was half-tempted to tell them to leave them there. I wasn't sure I could face paddleboarding again after tonight's ordeal.

A request was made over the radio for ambulances to be waiting and soon we were on our way, bouncing across the waves back towards civilisation. The wind whipped the hair that had escaped from my ponytail across my face and made my eyes stream. I pulled the foil blanket more tightly round me, my whole body shivering uncontrollably. I tried to picture myself on dry land, wrapped in a duvet, my hands clutching a steaming mug of tomato soup, but all I could picture was the three of us all alone in the North Sea. That could have been it. We could have died tonight.

'Nearly there,' Hollie said, putting her arm round me and cuddling me to her side. 'We've got you.'

The lifeboat slowed as it entered the harbour walls, and the sea calmed. Flashing blue lights drew my attention to two ambulances backed onto the slipway. Darkness was falling and I shuddered at the thought of us still being out there, all alone, at night. Although I knew that, truthfully, we wouldn't have survived to see sunset.

'The ambulance is here,' Matt said to Charlee. 'You're safe.'

He grasped my hand. 'Are you okay?'

I couldn't let him see how terrified I was, not when he needed to focus on Charlee.

'We've had better nights out, haven't we?' I said, hoping I'd managed to sound light-hearted.

'Oh, I dunno. What about that time we did flaming sambucas and I set fire to my hair?'

I smiled at the memory.

'Your carriages await,' Chief called. 'The paramedics will check you out and get you to hospital. We'll store your boards for collection when you're back on your feet.'

Mouse jumped out of the lifeboat first and he and the youngest crew member – Spaniel – helped Charlee over to the first ambulance. She was in a bad way, barely able to place one foot in front of the other. Matt followed her and Hollie helped me out of the boat and to the second ambulance.

I scanned the slipway but there was no sign of Leyton.

'Are you okay?' Hollie asked.

'I was looking for my boyfriend. I thought he'd be here.'

'What's his name?'

'Leyton.'

'You get into the ambulance and I'll run to the top of the slipway. The shore crew usually keep onlookers back.'

She was back moments later. 'Sorry. There's a small crowd gathered, but nobody's answering to the name of Leyton.'

'Okay. Thanks for trying.' I lay back on the trolley bed, feeling suddenly alone. Where was he?

I glanced down at my phone, but I was so cold and tired, I couldn't muster the energy to pick it up. I just wanted to sleep.

'Try to stay awake, Tori,' said the paramedic in the back of the ambulance with me. 'Short ride to the hospital and you'll be able to sleep soon.'

'Tired.'

'I know you are, my love,' she said, her voice gentle and reassuring. 'I've never met a Tori before. Is it short for anything?'

'Victoria.'

'That's my middle name. My mum's obsessed with the royal family. I'm Elizabeth Victoria and my brother's George Edward. Guess what breed of dog she has.'

'A corgi,' I suggested.

She laughed. 'A King Charles Spaniel. You won't believe what she called it. Camilla Diana! How hilarious is that? Do you have pets?'

'My boyfriend doesn't like animals.'

'Aw, that's a shame.'

'Parents have two dogs, three cats...' I was finding it harder to form the words as my eyelids became heavier.

'Stay with me, Tori. Two dogs and three cats sounds like a lot.'

'Horses, three goats, two llamas...'

'Do they have a farm?'

'A castle.'

'Did you just say castle?'

'Sleepy.'

'We're nearly there, Tori. I know it's hard, but keep fighting. Two minutes. That's all.'

Two minutes. Such a short amount of time, yet tonight each minute had felt like forever. What if it had taken the RNLI another two minutes to find us? What if they'd never found us at all?

8

HOLLIE

I stood on the slipway, watching the ambulances pull away.

'First real-life rescue,' Jake said, placing his arm round my shoulder and giving me a gentle squeeze. 'How do you feel?'

'A bit emotional. I don't know if I want to cheer or cry.'

'I'm here for you, whichever you want to do and whenever you want to do it.'

I rested my head on his shoulder and put my arm round his waist, feeling a bit shaky.

Chief called us back to the ILB.

'You did well tonight, Starfish,' he said as we clambered back into the boat.

'Thanks, but I didn't do much.'

'You got the blankets out without being asked, you kept the casualties talking, you were calm and reassuring. It's a team effort and everyone has something to contribute.'

Jake, kneeling beside me, gave me a smile and a wink as Bart pulled away from the jetty. That desire to cry dissipated. I'd done it! I'd been on my first rescue and I hadn't panicked about something going wrong, as I'd feared I might. No wonder Dad and Isaac had returned from shouts buzzing. There couldn't be a better feeling in the world than knowing you'd played a part in saving a life. Or three lives, in this case.

The shore crew were waiting for us on the beach. Bart steered the ILB onto the trailer and we all clambered out, following the tractor as it towed the boat back up the ramp and into the lifeboat station for a thorough clean.

'Will you find out what happened to them?' I asked Jake as we propped the three paddleboards against the wall for collection later.

'We usually get an update from the hospital to put in the log. Casualties often drop in to thank us too, which is nice.'

'Do you think they'll be okay?'

'Matt and Tori should be. Charlee was struggling more, but hopefully we got there in time.'

'If we hadn't been on an exercise nearby...'

Jake nodded. 'It could have been a different story, but that's always the case. If someone hadn't called it in... if their information hadn't been accurate... if we hadn't spotted them when we did... What we do is full of what ifs, and it's best to stay focused on the successes. We found them and they're in hospital now. Best place for them.'

* * *

As was usual after Monday night training, we went to the pub opposite the harbour – The Lobster Pot.

Chief raised his glass when everyone had their drinks. 'To Starfish and Spaniel on their first rescue!'

I blushed as the crew toasted us and, as they shared anecdotes of their first rescues, something slotted into place for me. This group was a unique, eclectic mix of individuals of all ages, backgrounds and careers who'd joined together to do something extraordinary. Chief was right about everyone having a role to play. The tractor drivers, shore crew and a whole host of others weren't actually aboard the lifeboat, but the part they played in the rescue was just as vital as the role the lifeboat crew played. I was part of that, and it felt pretty amazing.

Some of the others decided to stay for a second drink, but Jake and I were keen to get back to Pickle. After we pulled on our coats and said our goodbyes, Chief followed us to the door.

'Just wanted to check you're okay,' he asked. 'The first rescue's a big thing.'

'I'm great, thanks. I had a teary moment but it feels amazing now.'

'It's the best. Has it convinced you to be the first female crew from the Brooks family?'

I usually shook my head and reminded him I was only here to overcome my demons, but that wasn't how I felt right now. I glanced across at the rest of the crew, laughing at something Bart was telling them and felt warmed by that feeling of being part of more than a team – a family.

'Don't get carried away but let's just say that, after tonight, I'm not ruling it out.'

'Good lass. I hope you do, but it's got to be your decision. See you next week.'

'Will do.'

After saying goodbye, we stepped out into the darkness. Over the road in the harbour, sailing boats and dinghies bobbed on the waves and I could see the silhouette of the lifeboat station just beyond them.

'Did you mean that?' Jake asked, taking my hand as we crossed the road. 'Could you see yourself becoming full crew?'

We paused with our arms resting on the metal harbour railings.

I breathed in the cool evening air, gazed at the lights on the boats, and listened to the halyards clanking against the masts – a comforting sound which always made me think of Dad and Isaac, who'd been keen sailors.

'I thought I'd understood the pull of being in the RNLI but I hadn't. Until tonight.'

'Because of the rescue?'

'It's more than that. It's being part of something that makes such a difference.' I looked up at Jake. 'Something clicked with me in the pub tonight – a sense of belonging.'

He drew me into his embrace. 'It's a special feeling, isn't it?'

'Amazing. I can't believe you were going to give all of that up for me.'

He cupped my face and gently kissed me. 'I'd do anything for you.'

We set off walking back to the car, holding hands.

'I honestly didn't expect it to happen to me,' I said. 'I thought I'd make some progress in overcoming my fears and be able to walk away.'

'There was never any chance of that. As soon as you started training, it was always going to captivate you because that's who you are. When you decide to do something, you throw yourself into it, heart and soul. It's one of the many things I love about you.'

I stopped and turned to face him. 'You know what else captivates me? Your photographs. So if you mean it when you say you'd do anything for me, I have a request. I want you to believe in yourself and your photography. I want you to see the brilliance I see. And I want you to do me a large print of that sunrise with the seal you took this morning so I can display it in the café.'

He smiled at me. 'You want a lot of things, Ms Brooks.'

'I know. Can you accommodate my demands?'

'I'll try my best.'

9

TORI

When I arrived at the hospital, I still felt drained, but I'd found a reserve of energy from somewhere to help fight the overwhelming desire to sleep. On the ward, it helped having so much activity going on round me with questions and checks.

Settled in my bed a little later, waiting for a doctor to confirm whether I could be discharged, I rang Leyton.

'You survived, then,' he said when he answered, the sarcastic tone instantly putting me on edge.

'Only just.'

'It was your decision to go out. I *did* warn you.' I hated that smug tone and now really wasn't the time for *I told you so*.

'Yeah, I know. I should have listened.'

'Are you back at the camper now?'

'No. Hospital. I'm waiting to find out whether I'll have to stay in overnight or not.'

There was the slightest pause. 'Are you okay?' It was a relief to hear him dropping the sarcasm and sounding as though he was actually concerned.

'I think so. My hypothermia's only mild and they're not

concerned about anything else. Charlee's struggling. I think they'll probably discharge Matt and me but keep Charlee in.'

'I'll grab a taxi to the hospital.'

'I need some clothes. There's some in Carrie.'

'I haven't got the spare key.'

'Then can you pick up the spare key from home and drive Carrie to the hospital?'

'I've had a couple of pints.'

I inwardly sighed, wondering why I was the one having to come up with the solutions when I'd been through a traumatic ordeal and my head was fuzzy.

'Then please can you go via home and collect some clothes and we'll collect Carrie when I'm discharged?'

'Okay. Anything else?'

'That's it. Oh, and thanks for calling the coastguard. You saved our lives.'

'Yeah, well, I said I would if the weather changed, so that's what I did. See you soon.'

* * *

By the time Leyton arrived, clutching a bin bag, I'd been seen by the doctor and my discharge was confirmed.

'I wasn't sure what to pick.' He emptied the bin bag onto the bed and I stared in disbelief at the dungarees and T-shirt in clashing colours and the winter boots. For someone who always looked immaculate, he evidently had no idea when it came to women's clothes. Not that I was that bothered. I'd have worn PJs and slippers if he'd brought them. All I wanted to do was get home, have a hot cup of tea, and wrap myself up in the duvet.

Matt, in the bed next to mine, was in conversation with a couple of medical staff so the curtain between our beds was drawn. I pulled it fully round so I could change in private.

'You shouldn't have gone out tonight,' Leyton said as I whipped off my hospital gown and got dressed, choosing not to pass comment on the lack of underwear. 'You should have come to the pub with me.'

He'd clearly consumed more than a couple of pints, judging by the slur in his speech and his inability to stand still, and I was fuming at his seeming lack of concern. Where was my hug and kiss? Where was the *thank God you're all right, I couldn't bear it if anything had happened to you*?

It wasn't the right time or place, but I couldn't help myself. 'Enjoyed your skinful while we nearly drowned?' I hissed as I stuffed my wetsuit, gloves and booties into the empty bin bag.

Red rag to a bull.

'And whose fault was that? I told you about the weather. I warned you it was going to turn but would you listen? Nooooo!'

'Sshh!'

'Don't shush me! Nobody ever listens to me.'

'I *am* listening,' I said, through gritted teeth, yanking back the curtain in the hope that the busy environment would snap him out of it. 'But this is a hospital and you're making a scene.'

'Ha! That's rich! You're the one who's made a scene this evening, taking stupid risks and putting the lives of others in danger just because you wanted to play in the sea with your friends.'

Mortified at the curious gazes from the other patients, I grabbed the bin bag with one hand and Leyton's arm with the other and marched him off the ward. Silence reigned in the taxi to the seafront, and again while I slowly drove Carrie back to the house, silently cursing Leyton that I was the one who had to drive after such an ordeal.

The moment I closed the door, he started on me again – same

slurred crap he'd come out with at the hospital. I didn't argue back, I didn't walk away but I did zone out because there was only one thought running through my head: *The transition is complete. You have turned into your father.* It wasn't quite as terrifying as our near-death experience earlier, but it was a close second.

* * *

I woke up the following morning to the sound of my mobile ringing. A FaceTime request from Charlee flashed up on my screen.

'Charlee! How are you?' I asked, rubbing my eyes as I connected the call.

'I'm good, thanks. They've discharged me so Matt's driving me home now. No lasting damage.'

'That's such a relief.'

'Have I woken you up?'

'Yeah, but it's fine. What time is it?'

'Half ten.'

Stomach lurching, I pushed the duvet aside. 'Seriously? I must have slept through the alarm. Luckily, I'm not meeting my client until twelve. How are you feeling?'

'Tired and still a bit chilly, so I can't wait to get back to Chestnut Barn for a long, hot soak in the bath.'

Matt and Charlee lived in a stunning barn conversion in the grounds of Uncle Hugh and Aunt Kathryn's farm.

'You're not going into the shop later, are you?' I asked Charlee. She made the most mouth-wateringly delicious chocolates which she sold in Charlee's Chocolates on Castle Street.

'No. Jodie's covering for me. I'll be back in tomorrow. How are you holding up?'

I scrunched up my nose. 'I feel stupid. I'm so sorry for taking you out last night.'

Charlee shook her head. 'Not your fault. We all checked the forecast and we all looked at the sea and deemed it safe. The weather changed unexpectedly. One of those things. Hang on.'

She turned her phone and I could see the side profile of Matt driving.

'Don't you dare blame yourself,' he said sternly, 'or I'll force feed you flaming sambucas and set fire to *your* hair this time. Consider yourself told.'

Charlee reappeared on the screen, laughing. 'He's a man of his word, so I hope you were listening.'

'Thanks, both of you. I appreciate it.'

Her smile faded. 'How was Leyton?' She glanced across at Matt and I knew he'd have told her about the altercation at the hospital. I'd had several texts from Matt across the evening checking I was okay.

'I've not seen him this morning, but you know that phrase about never going to bed on an argument...' I blinked back the unexpected tears. 'On the bright side, there's nothing like swallowing a ton of seawater and a mild case of hypothermia for wiping you out. I don't think I've slept that well in years.'

Charlee didn't smile at my feeble attempt at humour. 'You know where we are if you want to talk about it.'

'It's fine. Just a blip. I can't blame him. He did warn us, but he also saved us, so I shouldn't moan.'

Charlee frowned. 'How did Leyton save us?'

'By calling the coastguard.'

'Did he tell you that?'

'Yes.' My stomach clenched as I saw her worried glance towards Matt. 'What's going on?'

'Hang on, Tori,' Charlee said. 'We've just pulled onto the farm and Matt wants to speak to you. Handing you over.'

Matt's face appeared on the screen. 'Sorry, Tori, but Leyton didn't alert the coastguard. It was a cleaner at The Bay Pavilion.'

My stomach clenched again. 'How do you know that?'

'We've just called by the lifeboat station to collect the paddle-boards and thank them. The older guy was there and he told us. The cleaner saw us setting off when she arrived for work, noticed the weather change, and was worried about us. She looked through one of the viewing scopes they have on the terrace, spotted we were in trouble, and called the coastguard. Did Leyton definitely say it was him?'

I frantically replayed our phone conversation from the hospital in my head. Yes! He definitely said he'd called it in. I might have initially voiced that assumption, but he'd had the opportunity to correct me and he hadn't taken it.

'Tori?' Matt prompted.

He looked really concerned but I thought about Charlee saying how much she wanted a bath. I needed to let them get off the phone and focus on each other, so I shrugged. 'Probably me getting confused. It's all a bit of a blur. Anyway, great news that Charlee's okay. You'd better get her back for her bath and I'd better get ready for my meeting. I'll see you on Sunday for Aria's birthday.'

'Okay. See you then.'

As soon as we'd said goodbye and ended the call, I slumped back against my pillows. It was bad enough that Leyton had had a go at me for not heeding his advice about the weather, but why would he lie about his part in the rescue? That made no sense.

10

HOLLIE

Shortly after we arrived back from the pub, the rain started, the wind intensified, and a storm steadily built across the evening. Isaac and I had loved storms when we were kids and would sit by the side window in the spare bedroom – what was now my room – watching the sky illuminate over the sea, counting the seconds between the thunder and lightning. Now storms reminded me of the night we'd lost them and a melancholy always descended on me.

While Jake was brushing his teeth, I stood by that same side window, gazing into the darkness. I wrapped my left arm across my body for comfort as my right hand fiddled with my necklace, jumping each time a strong gust of wind made the rain batter against the pane with greater intensity.

What had I done? How had I let myself get so carried away earlier? Because I'd felt like part of a family again and not just any family – a family that Dad and Isaac had been part of. So many of those stories of first rescues had involved one or both of them and I'd never felt closer to them than I did a few hours ago. I'd always felt close to Mum at The Starfish Café but this evening I'd experienced that same feeling towards Dad and Isaac, and I'd wanted to cling onto it.

I shuddered at another intense burst of rain and swallowed down the ball of fear rising inside me. I'd made a mistake. I couldn't join the crew. This evening we'd executed a straightforward rescue during daylight hours in a slightly choppy sea, but not all rescues would be like that. There'd be darkness, serious swell, storms. I couldn't do it. And I couldn't bear the thought of Jake doing it either.

That fear hadn't gone. With a storm raging outside, I wasn't sure it had even weakened. What if his pager went tonight? What if he was called out to a rescue and it all went wrong?

I tried to wipe my tears as Jake returned to the bedroom but I was too late. He rushed over to the window, gathering me in his arms.

'What's wrong?'

His voice was so full of concern that I crumbled, tears tumbling down my cheeks. 'I've messed up. I can't do it!'

'Can't do what?' he asked gently, stroking my back.

'Join crew. I'm not ready. I don't think I'll ever be.'

Jake held me tightly as my body shook with sobs. Ever so slowly and gently, he steered me away from the window and lowered me down onto the edge of the bed. He passed me the box of tissues and I blew my nose and wiped my cheeks until the tears finally subsided.

'What would I do without you?'

'You'll never be without me.' He brushed my hair back from my face. 'It's the storm, isn't it?'

'Every time. I know the odds against it happening again must be ridiculously high...'

'Two billion and eighty-six trillion to one,' he quipped. 'Give or take.'

'That's impressively high,' I said, smiling gratefully at him. 'But you do understand, don't you?'

'More than anyone. The fear will probably never go, but there are ways of dealing with it and you've been doing so well.'

'I know! And that's why I'm so frustrated. I felt like I'd taken such a leap forward earlier and now I'm right back at the start.'

He took my hand in his and gently kissed it. 'It might feel that way while there's a storm outside, but it won't in the morning. You're not back at the start but the finishing line you saw earlier this evening might be round the next bend instead.'

'Round several bends,' I suggested, loving his analogy.

'Perhaps. But it's there and I'm convinced you'll reach it. As I said earlier, you throw your heart and soul into everything. I believe that becoming crew is what your heart wants, it's already part of your soul, but your head isn't quite there yet. But it will be and I'll be here every step of the way helping you.'

'I might need a lot of help.'

'I've got a lot to give.'

Even though the storm continued to rage outside, I felt calm as I settled into bed with Jake's strong comforting arms round me and soon drifted into a peaceful sleep.

* * *

Driving to work on Tuesday morning, the rain showed no let-up, although the wind had lost some of its strength. The route to The Starfish Café was littered with debris from the trees and I had to clear a couple of large branches from the car park.

Angie didn't work on Tuesdays, so I was on my own, baking, until Avril arrived at 9.30 a.m.

'It's hideous out there!' she cried, peeling off her soggy waterproof in the kitchen and running her hands through her windswept hair. 'I think they lied about spring arriving.'

'It's forecast to last all day, so I suspect it'll be a quiet one.'

'Do you want me to do a stock-take and place an order?'

'You star. That would be brilliant, thanks.'

I unlocked the door at 10 a.m., but there was nobody around. Looking at the puddles in the twig and leaf-strewn car park, I shook my head. Today was going to drag.

'It's a bit wild out there,' Kerry said when she arrived for her shift a little later, battling with an umbrella which had been blown inside out and trying to smooth down her blonde bob. 'Have we had any customers?'

'A couple of van drivers for take-outs, but that's it.'

A single mum of four primary school-aged children, twenty-nine-year-old Kerry Marsden worked a 10.30 till 2.30 weekday shift during term time only. This provided me with valuable extra lunchtime cover, gave her the flexibility she needed for the school run, and didn't leave me short during the school holidays because I had several students who worked then.

The door opened again and Betty and Tommy stepped inside.

'Good morning!' I called to them. 'I thought the rain might have put you off.'

Tommy tipped his trilby at me as always. 'Good morning, darling girl. We held off for a bit, hoping it would ease, so apologies we're a little later this morning.'

'It's always great to see you both, whatever time you make it.'

I gave them time to settle into their favourite window booth then went over to take their order.

'How was lifeboat training last night?' Betty asked.

Jake had been right about everything seeming better in the morning. Even though the storm hadn't fully blown over, my worries had settled.

'Amazing,' I said. 'We were called out to a real-life rescue.'

Betty gasped. 'Oh, my goodness, what happened?'

'Three paddleboarders got into difficulty when the weather changed, but we were nearby and got to them in time.'

'Were you nervous?' Tommy asked.

'Not that much, actually. It was good for me to have a live rescue so soon. Now I know I can deal with it.'

'You can deal with anything,' Betty said, patting my hand. 'You're the strongest young woman we know.'

'As well as the best cook we know,' Tommy added.

'You two are so lovely. Thank you.' I gave them both a warm smile. 'What will it be today? The specialist scone is lavender but, because Easter's fast approaching, I made a batch of chocolate hot cross buns this morning. I think they're right up your street, Betty.'

'Sold!' she declared. 'One of each for me please.'

'I'll give the hot cross bun a try,' Tommy said, 'and a fruit scone, please.'

'Coming right up.'

'Those hot cross buns smell divine,' Kerry said as I joined her at the counter.

'They taste it too,' I said, winking at her.

She sorted the drinks while I plated up the food. I loved her efficiency, cracking on with helping instead of waiting to be asked. As we worked, a group of four walkers arrived in the porch, shaking off their coats.

One of the men opened the inner door. 'Is it safe to go down to the beach?' he asked gruffly.

'That heavy rain will have covered the steps in mud, which makes them slippy. I'd suggest either taking it steady or avoiding it.'

The others joined him, muttering about the rain ruining their plans.

'Where should we sit?' he asked.

'Anywhere you like except Betty and Tommy's laps.'

If he had a sense of humour, the rain had evidently washed it away as he stared at me, frowning.

'There are menus on the table. Our speciality scone of the day is lavender and we have chocolate hot cross buns today too.' I pointed to a blackboard where I'd added the specials. 'Kerry will be over shortly to take your order.'

They chose one of the tables in the middle of the room and picked up menus. Kerry delivered Betty and Tommy's order then went across to the walkers' table to see if they'd like any drinks. I watched in admiration as she soon had them laughing. I didn't take it personally that the man had been off with me. Thankfully, most grumpy customers snapped out of it when they had a hot drink and a tasty treat inside them.

'Two hot cross buns, one cheese, and one lavender scone,' Kerry said, returning to the counter. 'And three flapjacks and a salted caramel brownie for the road. God, I'm good!'

'You're brilliant!' I agreed. Kerry was great at upselling and nearly always talked walkers into something sweet to take away.

She made the drinks while I plated up the food and wrapped their snacks and I smiled as she had them laughing again when she delivered their order. I was so lucky to have such good, loyal staff members.

11

TORI

I couldn't stop thinking about what Matt had said about Leyton not being the one to call it in. Why lie to me like that? In the shower, I replayed the conversation – or argument – I'd had with him over and over, wondering if I could have misconstrued it, but he had categorically said he'd been the one who phoned the coastguard.

Discovering that it wasn't him, so much else slotted into place. It explained why he hadn't been waiting at the harbour when we'd been rescued and why he'd opened our phone conversation with such a crass line as: 'You survived, then?'

There was no point dwelling on it any further as I was just going to tie myself into knots. I had a client meeting this morning and I wasn't going to let what Leyton had or hadn't done affect my business, especially when it was a project I was particularly excited to be working on.

From the moment I met her a few weeks ago, I adored Lorraine Thorpe, the proprietor of Sunny Dayz Guest House. She'd been a referral from a delighted client, and stepping into her guest house on Ocean Ravine in North Bay had been like stepping into the sunshine. Lorraine was as warm and sunny as the bright yellow décor and, although she'd joked about the cheesy 1970s spelling of the word 'Dayz', it seemed perfect for her personality and the friendly feel of the accommodation.

Lorraine would turn sixty in the summer and had decided she didn't want or need anything herself, but her beloved twelve-bedroom guest house was due a makeover. Even though that wouldn't happen until the lucrative summer season ended, she'd wanted to agree a design now.

'I'm thinking maybe less yellow,' she'd told me when I took the brief, 'but I still want it to feel like a sunny day when my guests arrive.'

I'd been relieved at the 'less yellow' brief. I wasn't against the colour, but there's a splash of yellow and there's an explosion in a custard factory and Sunny Dayz was definitely the latter. In the dining room, the crockery was bright yellow, the walls lemon, the tablecloths and curtains white and yellow gingham. The bedrooms had yellow bedding and curtains. God knows where she'd managed to source twelve bright yellow kettles. Yellow hairdryers had been an even greater surprise.

* * *

The rain was still torrential as I parked Carrie on the forecourt outside Sunny Dayz Guest House, relieved that there was a space free right by the entrance. I pulled up my jacket hood and made a dash for the reception area with my easel and portfolio.

'Tori! Wonderful to see you, my dear,' Lorraine said, beaming at me. 'I'm so excited to see your designs. I just know I'm going to love them.'

'I hope you will.' I pushed Leyton firmly out of my mind as I returned her smile. 'So the brief was less yellow but to keep the sunshine, which we definitely need on a day like today.'

'Too right, my dear. It's horrible out there.'

We moved into the dining room and I set up my easel but kept the designs covered for the moment.

'Do you know the artist Jed Ferguson?' I asked. 'He's got a gallery on Castle Street – Yorkshire's Best.'

'Oh, yes! I love his paintings. They make me so happy.'

'I'm relieved you said that because what I've designed is based on Jed's paintings. They're happy and sunny so my proposal is that the "sunny" in "Sunny Dayz" comes from the prints and we take inspiration from them for accent colours in the crockery and bedding. Let me show you what I mean.'

I removed the cover to reveal my designs. I always looked at the client to gauge their initial reaction but, even if I hadn't been looking at Lorraine, her squeal conveyed her delight.

The pine tables would be replaced by white ones, the walls would be painted white, and the yellow crockery would be gone, but the sunshine would remain in Jed Ferguson's prints round the walls, yellow placemats and coasters, and new white crockery with buttercup yellow stripes round each item.

Lorraine grabbed my arm. 'It's beautiful. Oh, Tori! I never imagined... well, I never... I'm just...' She pressed her fingers to her lips, tears welling in her eyes. 'I'm never lost for words, but this... yes, please! All of it!'

'You haven't seen the bedroom designs yet.'

'If they're anything like this, I already know I'm going to love them.'

* * *

It was still bucketing it down as I waved goodbye to Lorraine an hour and a half later, but the weather wasn't going to dampen my spirits. Another contract signed by a delighted client. I couldn't wait to order everything in, ready for September's refurbishment.

The windows had steamed up, so I sat in Carrie for a while with the heating on full blast while they cleared.

I had another proposal to work on this afternoon and had planned to drive straight home to crack on with it, but I hesitated at the edge of Sunny Dayz's forecourt. Matt and Charlee had been to the lifeboat station to give their thanks and I should really, so I headed in the opposite direction down Ocean Ravine to the seafront. As I drove along North Bay and round the Headland to South Bay, I knew I was kidding myself that my visit was only to express my gratitude. I needed to hear it from the crew. I needed to know for sure that Leyton hadn't been the one who'd alerted the coastguard.

* * *

It was nearly half seven when I heard Leyton's key turning in the lock. I gave him a few moments, but he didn't even call out a greeting, so I took a deep breath and stepped into the hall.

'Tough day?' I asked as he placed his shoes in the cabinet.

He looked up and scowled. 'The worst, although the good news is that the Durlings have agreed to meet me to discuss reinstating their business.'

'That's brilliant! That should get your father off your back.'

He rolled his eyes at me. 'As if! I'll be lectured forever more on losing the business in the first place.' He sniffed the air. 'What's cooking?'

'Stew and dumplings. Ideal comfort food for this weather.'

'Have you put swede in it?'

'Yes.'

He slammed the shoe cabinet shut and flashed his eyes at me. 'Next time, don't. I hate swede.'

'Since when?' In nearly eight years together, he had *never* expressed a dislike for swede.

No response.

'I'll be down in ten minutes.'

I frowned as I watched him run up the stairs, two at a time. Bit rude.

'Why are the dumplings so enormous?' Leyton asked a little later, prodding one with a fork.

Because they are seemed a childish answer, so I ignored him and shoved in a forkful of my 'enormous' dumpling. Observing him removing every chunk of swede and scowling as though it was a stray hair or dead fly had made me want to hurl my bowl at him. I didn't underestimate how tough a day he'd had or how much stress his father had placed on him with the Durling situation and the industrial tribunal, but why was I getting the brunt of it? And, worse than that, why was I putting up with it? I'd turned into the sort of person I swore I'd never become – someone who put up and shut up instead of addressing important issues head-on – and I hated that.

Tonight, I wasn't going to be that person.

'I spoke to Matt and Charlee earlier,' I said, keeping my tone light and conversational. 'Charlee was discharged this morning and she's fine. She'll be back at work tomorrow.'

'That's good,' he said in a tone that sounded more like *I couldn't care less.*

'Yeah, I'm so relieved. I was worried about her. If you hadn't called the coastguard when you did, she might not have made it. What was it that prompted you to make that call?'

His shoulders tensed and he shoved a piece of beef in his

mouth. Nice buying-time tactic. I stared at him while he chewed, but he didn't make eye contact.

'I looked out the pub window and saw how choppy the sea was,' he said, attempting to spear a butterbean with his fork, still not looking at me.

'But how did you know we were in trouble? How did you know we hadn't already turned back and were in Carrie having a cuppa and some Jaffa Cakes?'

'Because I had a couple of pints then wandered back along the seafront. I couldn't see you, but I could see there weren't any boards by the van.'

'Oh, right. And that's when you rang the coastguard?'

He scrunched his paper napkin into a ball and dropped it into his bowl with a sigh. 'Yes! And then I went back to The Anchor to wait.'

'Okay. You know, I genuinely believe the person who made that call saved our lives. We'll be forever grateful.'

He finally looked up at me and flashed his most charming smile. 'You're welcome.'

How could he do it? How could he sit there spinning such an elaborate lie?

'I tell you what's really lovely,' I continued in a sweet voice. 'That I got to thank that person face to face earlier.'

His smile faded. 'What are you talking about?'

'I stopped by the lifeboat station after my meeting at Sunny Dayz. I was awarded the contract, by the way. Thanks for asking. Anyway, I decided to call in to thank the crew for their help and I couldn't believe my perfect timing when they introduced me to Della Thompson. She's a cleaner at The Bay Pavilion. She saw us go into the water and then spotted us in trouble a bit later. She happened to drop into the lifeboat station while I was there. She wanted to make sure the crew had found us and we were okay. Wasn't that nice of her?'

His jaw tightened as he shoved his bowl away and fixed a hard stare on me. 'What are you insinuating?'

'I'm not insinuating anything,' I responded, a sharp edge to my voice. 'I'm telling you that you did *not* call the coastguard because Della did.'

'Yes, I did!' he snapped, a vein in his neck pulsing. 'This Della woman must have called it in too.'

'I wondered that, so I asked. The coastguard logs all calls and there was only one for our stretch of coast at that time. One.' I pushed my bowl aside with a sigh. 'I don't care that you weren't the one who made the call, Leyton. What I care about is why you lied about it.'

'Bloody hell, Tori, does it matter?'

'It matters to me,' I snapped. 'What's going on?'

He wouldn't look at me.

'Come on, Leyton. Talk to me.'

'For God's sake! I didn't sit by the window, okay! I was pissed off with you for not listening to me, so I sat in the snug. Happy now, Miss Marple?'

Pissed off with me for not listening to him? How petty could he be? I needed to know why he'd lied. I couldn't bear liars. I'd already had enough of them to last me a lifetime.

His shoulders dropped and he lowered his eyes. 'I know I warned you the weather was going to turn,' he said, his voice softening, 'but I didn't actually believe you were in any *real* danger. I thought you'd notice the change – if there was one – and give up. It was a hell of a shock when you rang from the hospital.'

He looked up at me, his expression remorseful. 'I felt guilty, okay? I said I'd keep watch but I didn't. When you thought I'd alerted the coastguard, I didn't see any reason to correct you. I already hated myself enough and I didn't want you to hate me too.'

I couldn't help feeling empathy for him. The stress he was under was obvious in his wobbly voice and defeated body language.

'So that's why you were so off with me at the hospital,' I suggested gently. 'Because you were annoyed with yourself.'

'You could have died out there.'

The strain showed in the dark circles below his eyes and the creases on his brow and, even though I was still fuming with him for lying, I understood how it had happened. I moved round the table and wrapped my arms round him from behind and pressed my cheek against his.

'But I didn't. We're all fine and we even got the boards back intact.'

He patted my hand and I waited for an apology, but none came. The silence grew uncomfortable, as did my hold on him. If he'd been that worried about losing me, why didn't he take me in his arms and hold me tight?

As I sat back down, Leyton scraped his chair back. 'I've been summoned to Fenby Heights. They want a progress report. I could be gone several hours, so don't wait up.'

Then he left. No hug, no kiss, no apology. No thanks for dinner.

I brushed my fingers across my lips, struggling to remember the last time he'd kissed me hello, goodbye or good night. We used to kiss all the time. We used to say 'I love you' too. When had that stopped?

If ever there had been a more appropriate time for him to say those three words, my brush with death was it. Although didn't that work both ways?

12

HOLLIE

'He's back,' Kerry whispered under her breath after the lunchtime rush on Thursday.

I stopped wiping the spillage on the floor and looked up at her from my crouched position behind the café counter.

'Who's back?'

'That bloke. The creepy one.'

'Which one?' We'd had a few customers over time who matched that description.

'Hello, Mr Smith,' Kerry said in what I recognised as her fake-smile voice.

Ah! That one!

'It's Smythe,' he snapped. 'Is Ms Brooks around?'

I shuddered at the confident smarmy tone, which reminded me of Alan Rickman's Severus Snape in the *Harry Potter* films. He even had an equally alliterative name – Sebastian Smythe. He detested anyone shortening or mispronouncing it and was quick to put them in their place in a way that made them feel like they'd committed a serious crime. My inner rebel wanted to deliberately call him Seb Smith just to annoy him in return for him annoying me by repeatedly turning up unannounced. He'd wanted to buy The Starfish Café for years and seemed incapable of taking no for an answer.

Wiping my hands on the cloth, I reluctantly stood up. His charcoal suit, tailored to perfection, screamed money and power. Aged maybe in his early sixties, a full head of grey hair was swept back from his forehead and sculpted into place. I doubted a single hair would dare escape from the clutches of the styling wax.

'Mr Smythe,' I said, smiling politely.

'I've told you before, you must call me Sebastian.' He flashed me a dazzling white-toothed trust-me-I'm-your-friend kind of smile that didn't reach his eyes.

'What can we get you this afternoon?' I wasn't going to invite him to call me Hollie. Our relationship was strictly professional. In fact, it wasn't a relationship at all. It was extremely rare for me to take a dislike to anyone, but there was something about Mr Smythe that made me uneasy. 'The quiche is particularly good.'

'An espresso and fifteen minutes of your time... please.' The pause convinced me that the good manners were an afterthought.

'I can help you with the espresso, but not the fifteen minutes. As you can see, we're very busy.' I swept my arm round the café to emphasise my point. The sun had finally made an appearance after two days of solid rain, bringing stacks of customers out, enjoying the last couple of days before the schools closed for the Easter holidays.

'Ten minutes, then?'

I sighed inwardly. The man was on a mission and I wouldn't get rid of him. The power suit wasn't just for show; he genuinely was one of the most powerful men in Whitsborough Bay. The Smythes – a self-made local family – ran four arcades along South Bay's main promenade, the grand casino, Pleasureland (the small fair near the harbour), several pubs, restaurants and hotels. There were rumours of backhanders and dodgy dealings which wouldn't surprise me. From the moment I met him, my gut-feel had been that he was what Angie called a 'wrong 'un'.

'Five,' I said. 'But I'd suggest that even five minutes is a waste of your time and mine. You already know my answer.' It was a fight to keep my tone light and friendly, but I had to remain on polite terms as there was a fine line between being firm and being foolish when dealing with a man like him.

The doubtful raise of his eyebrows indicated to me that he believed everyone had their price and that he was about to present me with an offer I couldn't refuse. He obviously didn't know me at all.

'Take a seat in the corner and I'll bring your drink over. But I mean it when I say five minutes. Kerry's shift finishes soon and I'm not leaving Angie on her own.'

With a slight incline of his head, Mr Smythe tucked a tan leather portfolio under his arm and headed towards the corner.

Kerry shuddered when he'd gone. 'Ooh, I hate that man. I don't know what it is about him, but he turns my stomach.'

'Mine too,' I agreed, preparing his espresso.

'You wouldn't sell to him, would you?'

'Never. Even if he offered me millions, I wouldn't sell this place. The part he doesn't seem to understand is that this isn't just a business for me. It's my heritage and it's my future.'

I placed a shot of espresso in front of Mr Smythe and eased myself into the seat opposite him.

'You're not having a drink with me?'

'There's no point. It won't cool sufficiently in five minutes for me to drink it.'

He'd already removed some papers from his portfolio and picked one up. 'I'll get straight to the point. Here's my offer.' He placed a folded-over sheet of A4 in front of me.

Slowly opening it, I glanced at the figure. *Oh, my God!* Trying to maintain a poker face, I folded the paper again and pushed it back towards him. 'Thank you, but the answer's still no.'

He narrowed his eyes at me. 'Come on, Ms Brooks. Look at that figure again. You know it makes sense.' He sounded exasperated.

I shook my head. 'Actually, it doesn't make sense at all. Why so much? It's way more than the business is worth.'

'I'm well aware of that.'

'So you'll understand my confusion.'

'Lots of things in life don't make sense. You of all people should know that.' He held my gaze and I had to look away, my stomach churning. What right did he have to bring that up? Since meeting Jake, I'd made considerable progress in coming to terms with losing my family, but it didn't mean there weren't unexpected moments like this when it was challenging.

'It's an extremely generous offer,' I said, keeping my voice low and steady. '*Too* generous, which makes me think there's more to it than you're letting on.'

He didn't flinch, although I hadn't expected him to. He was far too professional and in control. 'It's a sound business in a good location, Ms Brooks. I know that your turnover is good, but it has potential to be even better.'

'And you'd achieve that, would you?'

'You know my business portfolio. You know I've turned around every business I've owned, even those on their knees.'

'It's extremely impressive, but you won't be adding The Starfish Café to your portfolio. I'm the third generation of my family to run a café here and family businesses are an important legacy. You, of all people, should know that.'

He had a good poker face, but his anger at me throwing his own quote back at him was obvious in the white knuckles clenched round the small cup as he necked back his drink and slammed it down into the saucer.

'It's my intention to keep this as a family business for generations to come,' I continued. 'If the business was failing, I might not have much choice, but it's thriving, as you've recognised. In fact, it's doing so well that I can let you have that espresso on the house.' I pushed my chair back and stood up. 'Are you sure I can't tempt you with the quiche? Or a homemade Scotch egg? They're to die for.'

He gave me a stony look and I suspected that, despite my best intentions, I'd just crossed that line between firm and foolish.

'I have other appointments, so I'll take my leave. You'll regret this, you know.'

'Is that a threat?'

'No. It's a statement of fact.'

I gave him my most dazzling smile, although I felt far from happy inside. 'Then it's a risk I'm prepared to take. Enjoy the rest of your day.' I marched towards the counter, trying to keep my shoulders relaxed so he couldn't see how rattled I was.

Two minutes later he'd gone, but he'd left the folded offer on the table. Scrawled on the top of it he'd written:

WE BOTH KNOW YOU'LL SAY YES EVENTUALLY

I snatched up the note, ripped it into small pieces as I crossed the café and dropped it, floating like confetti, into the recycling bin behind the counter. I would *never* say yes to selling, but if ever I found myself in a situation where I needed to, Sebastian Smythe would be bottom of the list.

A few minutes later, the door opened and a woman with long auburn hair entered the café, glanced round, then made a beeline for one of the bar stools. She looked familiar and it took me a moment to realise why. Of course! Last time I'd seen her, she'd been wearing a wetsuit and shivering.

I gave her a few minutes to settle in and peruse the menu then wandered over.

'Tori, isn't it?'

She put her menu down and gave me a big smile. 'Yes. They told me at the lifeboat station that you owned this place. I was hoping I'd see you.'

'How are you feeling?'

'A bit embarrassed and very grateful. Thank you so much for rescuing us.'

'You're very welcome. How are Charlee and Matt?'

'They kept Charlee in hospital overnight, but they're both fine. The man at the station said it was your first rescue?'

'Yes, so I'm relieved it went well.'

'You were brilliant. Really calm and reassuring.'

'Aw, thank you. I appreciate that. I'm sorry I couldn't track down your boyfriend. Did he find you?'

'Erm, yes, thanks. I rang him from the hospital.'

'I bet he was worried sick.'

Tears clouded her eyes for a moment, then she blinked and cleared her throat. 'It's lovely in here. I can't believe I've never visited before.'

'Hopefully you'll like it so much that you'll become a regular. What can I get you? Our specialist scone of the day is rhubarb, and we have orange hot cross buns.'

'I'm loving the sound of a rhubarb scone. Can I have one of those and a green tea, please?'

'Coming right up.'

As I prepared Tori's order, I glanced over at her. She had one elbow resting on the counter, her head held in her palm, and she was staring at the floor.

'Do you know her?' Angie asked, following my eyeline.

'She's one of the paddleboarders we rescued on Monday.'

'She looks like she's got the weight of the world on her shoulders.'

'I was thinking the same, but I don't like to pry.'

'There's a difference between prying and caring and you know which camp you fall in. Remember how you saved Mrs Sultana? Maybe your paddleboarder needs saving again.'

Armed with Angie's encouragement, I took Tori's order over to her.

'Rhubarb scone,' I said, placing it in front of her. 'Green tea, and a listening ear if you want to talk about it.'

She looked at me for a moment as though weighing up whether I was trustworthy, then she sighed.

'My boyfriend Leyton claimed he'd called the coastguard, but it wasn't him and now he's avoiding me because I called him out on it.'

'Oh! Why did he lie?'

'Why does anyone lie?' She shook her head and gave me a weak smile. 'Sorry. That's a heavy question for a Thursday afternoon.'

'Do you live together?' I asked, keen to find a way to continue the conversation.

'Yes, although it's his house, as he often reminds me. Makes it difficult when you're being avoided.'

I glanced round the café. 'It's quietened in here and I'm serious about that listening ear. I'm bound by a solemn oath, too. What's discussed in The Starfish Café stays in The Starfish Café.'

Tori smiled. 'If you're sure...'

I sat on the stool beside her as she explained what had happened on Monday evening, how she'd discovered Leyton's lies, and how she'd barely seen him since. I got the impression she was holding back, but that was understandable when we'd only just met.

'What are you going to do about it?' I asked.

'I don't know. It's not just the lie. There've been so many other things recently. Relationships have ups and downs but when there are so many downs that you struggle to remember the ups...'

'Then you could have come to the end of the road,' I suggested when she tailed off.

'You know what, Hollie? I think we have. It's the same thought that's been going round in my head and I haven't wanted to voice it. How can you be certain it's the end and not just a rough patch? A really long rough patch?'

I thought back to my relationship with Craig and how I'd convinced myself that we were right for each other when there was so much about being with him that didn't make me happy. It was scary making the decision to end our engagement – especially when the realisation had come around the time of Dad and Isaac's funeral – but it had been the best thing I could have done.

'Listen to your heart,' I said gently. 'Your head will say things like you've been together a long time so it's a lot to throw away, it's a blip and things will get better, you've been through rough patches before and survived. But your heart will be honest with you. Do you still love him? Can you picture the two of you growing old together?'

'Really sorry to interrupt,' Angie said. 'Mrs Hibberd's on the phone. You wanted to speak to her.'

'Oh, yes. Sorry, Tori, I'm going to need to take that.'

'It's fine. You get on. That was brilliant advice, thank you.'

'Good luck.' I gave her an encouraging smile before heading to the counter to take my call. Mrs Hibberd had hired The Starfish Café for a function on Saturday night and I'd been chasing her all week trying to confirm numbers and food choices.

It was a fairly lengthy call and, when I'd finished, I was disappointed to see Tori had gone.

'She left you a message,' Angie said, handing me a piece of paper.

Hi Hollie
I've discovered 3 amazing things today:
The Starfish Café
Rhubarb scones
Listen to your heart
Thank you for the awesome advice. You are an absolute star! See you again soon.
Tori xx

'And her business card,' Angie said, passing it to me.

'Tennyson Designs, architect and interior designer,' I read. 'Very impressive.'

'I think you might have made a new friend there.'

I smiled. 'You could be right. At least one of my visitors today was lovely.'

'Smythe got to you earlier, didn't he?' she asked as she plated up a couple of flapjacks.

'He always does. I don't know why I let him, but it's exhausting repeating myself all the time. Why won't he accept my decision and leave me alone?'

'From what I hear, nobody's ever said no to him. Everyone eventually has their price.'

'Well, I don't, and I told him that, but I don't think he'll stop trying. Do you think there's grounds for a restraining order?'

'I wish there was, honey. Stay strong. He'll get bored soon.'

She took the flapjacks over to the customers and I crossed my fingers. 'Let's hope so,' I muttered, but somehow I couldn't see it.

13

TORI

After I settled my bill and left the note for Hollie, I sat in Carrie, wound down the window and put the key in the ignition, but didn't turn it. I needed a moment to mull over her advice.

Shards of sunlight filtered through the tall pine trees and a grey squirrel scampered up one of the trunks in front of me and sat on a branch, nibbling on a nut. A gentle breeze pushed tendrils of my hair across my face, tickling my nose. I could hear the chirp of birds and the distant lapping of the waves on the beach below. What a beautiful spot. How had I never visited before?

The heart versus head thing was spot on. I'd had many moments of doubt over the past months – maybe even years – and I'd always pushed them aside because I knew how messy splitting up after a long-term relationship could be. Even though Leyton and I weren't married or even engaged – been there, done that – so didn't have the legal proceedings to go through, I was still going to end up homeless. You'd think I'd have learned after Ewan, but love can be blind, and who goes into a relationship preparing for it ending?

Could I picture us growing old together? No. Absolutely not. It would be like living with his father and I couldn't do it. I was ambitious and driven, but I wasn't ruthless or wholly consumed by it. Leyton hadn't been at first, but he'd changed when Ernest retired and now every day seemed to be a power struggle to prove to his father that he was a worthy successor. I'd have supported him with that as I hated how his father looked down on him and repeatedly pulled rank as the biggest shareholder, but it was hard to support a cause you no longer believed in.

Some people turned to drink when things got tough, but I preferred chocolate and, right now, Jaffa Cakes weren't going to cut it. I needed some of Charlee's delicious creations. I started the engine and drove into town.

* * *

Charlee's best friend and business partner Jodie was restocking bags of chocolate buttons on a hanging unit when I pushed open the door of Charlee's Chocolates. She turned round and smiled at me.

'Tori! I haven't seen you in ages.'

'I can't remember the last time I came in. I normally message Charlee with my order and pick it up from the farm. How are you? All set for your wedding?'

Jodie was getting married a week on Saturday – Easter weekend – and Leyton and I had been invited to the evening do, although it was now looking like I'd be going solo. Her fiancé Dean was my cousin Tim's brother-in-law, so she'd be joining the extended family.

'I think so. Charlee and I are making the favours tonight and we have wine, so heaven help whoever gets the last few bags we make.'

The door opened and a customer stepped up to the counter where the individually made 'posh chocs' were kept.

'Charlee's in the workshop,' Jodie said, going to serve the customer.

Thanking her, I pushed through a pair of saloon doors into the workshop – the large room where they prepared the chocolates for sale and ran chocolate-making parties.

Charlee looked up from scrubbing chocolate off the table and beamed at me. 'Tori! Are you checking up on me?'

'Would I do that? I have a craving for some of your white chocolate and raspberry buttons.'

'Uh-oh, what's he done?' She pulled out a couple of chairs.

'What makes you think he's done anything?' I asked, sitting down beside her.

'You once told me you eat chocolate when you're stressed and it's white chocolate when you're super-stressed. So what's happened? I could tell you were keeping something back on Tuesday morning.'

I'd never opened up to Charlee before. In fact, I'd never opened up to anyone since it ended with Ewan. I'd only fully let three people into my life, Ewan being the third, and they'd all let me down so badly that I'd learned it was easier to keep that distance. If nobody truly knew me, they couldn't hurt me. It was why it had worked so well with Leyton. Our relationship had been very business-like and uncomplicated and that was what I'd wanted. At first.

I'd only given Hollie the basic details earlier, before she was called away, but that bit of time with her this afternoon had been the first time I'd let someone in for eight years. It felt good.

'Leyton and me. It's not going so well,' I admitted.

Over a mug of tea and a large bag of white chocolate and raspberry buttons, I explained to Charlee how things had started to deteriorate ever since Leyton took over at Clairmont Properties, how there always seemed to be tension and niggles between us, and culminated with everything that had happened this week.

'So it looks like I'll be moving out and starting over, yet again.' I held my head in my hands and released a frustrated cry. 'I'm forty next year! How is it my life is still such a mess?'

'It's not a mess. You've just had a few setbacks. As for turning forty next year, you're not even thirty-nine yet! A lot can happen in fifteen months, and I should know. That's roughly the same amount of time from me moving to Whitsborough Bay with my ex Ricky to Matt proposing. So don't give up on a happy ever after.'

'I won't. Although I'm not sure mine will involve a man. I haven't exactly got the best track record there. Maybe it's me.'

'You don't believe that, do you? Because I think it sounds like them. When are you going to end it?'

'There's no point prolonging it. Might as well have the dreaded conversation tonight. If I can pin him down, that is. He's been elusive all week.'

'Good luck! If you need somewhere to stay, we've got a spare bedroom and you'd be more than welcome.'

'That's very kind, but it's not just the bedroom space. I need an office too.'

'You could stay with Kathryn and Hugh. They've got plenty of space.' She scrunched up her nose. 'Unless that would cause problems with your parents.'

I hadn't spoken to my parents for seven years and I was fairly sure Uncle Hugh hadn't spoken to my mother – his sister – during that time either, but I didn't want to place my uncle in a difficult position. He'd fought enough of my battles over the years.

'I'll be fine. I'll organise something.'

'Could going back to the castle be an option?' she asked tentatively.

'Not after how it ended.' I shuddered at the thought of that final confrontation with my parents before I walked out of their life for good.

'That was so long ago, though. Could now be time to make your peace with them? Sometimes people make the wrong decisions. It's what makes us human.'

Could I forgive my parents for what they'd done? My gut said no. Was that because what they'd done was unforgivable or because I wasn't a forgiving person? After all, I'd never forgiven Ewan for what he did to our marriage.

14

TORI

Nine years ago

'I never thought it would come to this.' Ewan's husky voice cracked and, somewhere deep inside, I took pleasure that he was hurting too. After all, this was all *his* doing.

I glanced across at him, leaning against the doorframe, all dark and brooding, and I hated how much I still loved him and would do anything for him. Except the one thing he wanted, which had become a dealbreaker in our marriage.

'Neither did I,' I snapped. 'When I agreed "till death us do part", I meant it.' I dumped the armful of dresses still on their hangers into my suitcase.

'So did I!' he protested, as though incensed that I could suggest otherwise.

I grabbed another pile of clothes and flung them in the case. 'Yes, just like you meant it when you categorically said you *never* wanted kids.'

'That's a low blow.'

'Really? I'd say the low blow was you changing your mind about something so fundamental. We agreed, Ewan. We agreed that neither of us wanted children and you were even more vocal on the subject than me. I'm not the one who hit forty and suddenly decided I'd love to be a parent after all. Most men who have a midlife crisis buy a bloody sports car. They don't decide it's time to become a father.'

'It's not a midlife crisis.'

'Then what the hell do you call it when a person is willing to walk away from their marriage because they now want the one thing they never, ever wanted?'

He sat down on the bed. 'I don't want to walk away, and I know you don't either.'

I yanked out a drawer and tipped the contents into the case. 'No, I don't, but what choice do I have? You gave me an ultimatum. Kids and we live happily ever after. No kids and we're divorced. What happened to the no kids and we live happily ever after that we both agreed on? After nine years together, why's that off the table?'

I glared at him and he opened his mouth to speak, but I beat him to it. 'And don't you dare accuse me of being stubborn again. Stubborn is refusing to move on stuff that doesn't really matter like where to dine out, what colour to paint the lounge or where to go on holiday. Stubborn is *not* refusing to change my mind about an enormous lifelong commitment like becoming a parent.'

He stood up and threw his arms in the air in evident exasperation. 'I can't talk to you when you're like this.'

'You mean you can't change my mind. We've already given it six months after you dropped your bombshell and neither of us is going to cave, so there's no point dragging this on any longer.'

I grabbed another drawer and tipped out the contents. 'I can't live like this anymore so go ahead and initiate divorce proceedings and find yourself a suitable mother for the babies you're suddenly so desperate to have. Unless you've already found someone.'

'Of course not! What sort of person do you think I am?'

'Six months ago, I knew exactly what sort of person you were. Now, I haven't a clue.' I shoved the drawer back in the unit, slammed it closed and turned to face him. 'This is humiliating enough, Ewan. Do you really have to watch?'

'You want me to leave?'

I nodded, biting back a sob.

'Okay. How long do you need? Two hours? Three?'

I shrugged. How long did it take to pack up your whole life?

'Two.' It came out as a squeak.

'Okay. I'll leave you to it. You won't go without saying goodbye, will you?'

The tears I'd fought hard to keep back broke free. 'We said goodbye the moment you changed your mind.'

He was across the room in three paces and holding me in his arms as I sobbed. I loved him so much. From the moment I'd walked into the offices of Callaghan & Shipley Architects as a twenty-one-year-old intern and was assigned to rising star Ewan Osborne's triple barn conversion project, I lost a piece of my heart to that gorgeous man. As we worked together and discussed our shared passion for breathing new life into old buildings, I surrendered my heart fully. The ten-year age difference brought a maturity to our relationship and I loved being with a man who was ambitious, driven and focused on his career, but also focused on me and nurturing our relationship. We worked long hours but redressed the balance with date nights, weekends away and plenty of holidays.

When he said he'd love me forever, I believed him. And when he said it would only ever be the two of us, I believed him. Turned out he was as much of a liar as my two cheating exes before him.

'I'm sorry,' he whispered, his breath warm against my ear, his lips so close to touching my skin. 'I still love you.'

I pulled back and took a deep shuddery breath. 'But not enough to be content with just me.'

'I'm sorry.'

Sorry. I hated that word. I'd heard it so many times that it felt meaningless. *I'm sorry I changed my mind. I'm sorry I broke all my promises to you. I'm sorry I broke your heart.*

I straightened up, wiped my damp cheeks and stepped into business mode as it was the only way I could get through this. 'I'll post the keys through the letterbox. Your solicitor can write to me at Redamancy Castle and I'll let him know my new address when I've found somewhere.'

'Are you sure there's nothing I can say to convince you to stay?'

'There is, but we both know you're not going to say it. I need to crack on. Long drive. I want to get there before it's dark.'

His eyes were so full of pain as they fixed on mine, pleading with me to change my mind, but I retained unfaltering eye contact. With a shrug of his shoulders and a frustrated sigh, he walked out of my life.

The closing of the front door brought a fresh torrent of tears. Nine years together, seven of them married, and it was all over. Numbly, I shoved the rest of my clothes into cases and bags and carried them out to the car, where they joined the contents of my office already packed in a few boxes.

Back in the lounge, I stared at the pile of cardboard boxes, the packing tape dispenser and the thick roll of bubble wrap and couldn't muster the energy to pack anything else. We'd agreed that I wouldn't take any furniture. Most of it had been Ewan's, bought before we even met, and what would I do with the few pieces we'd chosen jointly? Shove them in one of the spare rooms or outbuildings at Redamancy Castle? I looked at the lamps, candles and pictures I was meant to take and suddenly I didn't want any of them. I didn't want reminding of how happy we'd been before the night of his fortieth birthday when he'd told me how much he loved me, how happy I made him... and how he thought it was time we started a family.

An hour later, after adding another two boxes to the car, I returned to the lounge and removed our wedding album from a cabinet. We'd flown to the Seychelles and married on the beach at sunset. No guests. Our wedding day had represented who I thought we were – a couple who only ever needed each other.

I turned the pages until I reached my favourite photo of us on a wooden pontoon stretching into the Indian Ocean. The photographer had suggested that holding hands in front of the setting sun would make a beautiful photo, but Ewan spontaneously lifted me up and spun me round, billowing my dress out. We'd been the centre of each other's world back then. I'd never imagined that would change.

After a few more deep calming breaths, I removed my three platinum rings. Propping the album up against the sofa cushions still open on the 'sunset spin' photo, as we'd called it, I laid my engagement, wedding and eternity rings in a row in front of it.

'Not eternity after all,' I whispered.

Driving back to my childhood home to start again at the age of thirty certainly hadn't been part of the plan, although nothing about the last six months had been. I still couldn't quite believe it was over.

I hadn't just lost my husband and home; I'd lost my job too. There was no way I could continue to work alongside him, so I had little choice but to resign. I needed to leave the area and start afresh, where I wouldn't have any chance of bumping into him and his new family.

The only friends I had were in Bath and they weren't really my friends anyway – they were Ewan's – which left only one place to go. The only place to which I'd sworn I'd never return.

* * *

Redamancy Castle wasn't an actual castle, but it was as grand as one. Late in the afternoon on that sunny Saturday in August, I paused outside the wrought-iron gates and closed my eyes for a moment, hoping I'd open them and this wouldn't be my new reality. But it was.

Exiting the car, I pressed the button hidden beneath the deep red ivy on the stone wall that surrounded the property. With a screech begging for a healthy dose of WD-40, the gates opened inwards.

The gravel crunched under the tyres as I edged my car through the gates and along the conifer-lined drive. I'd always admired the architect's vision, keeping the house hidden from sight until the last moment when the visitors in their carriages would have swept round the bend and gasped at their first view. Even now, despite all the cringeworthy and painful memories that had led me to flee to Bath with no desire ever to return, the house itself couldn't fail to impress. Besides, it wasn't the house from which I'd fled; it was the owners.

Nervous butterflies took flight in my stomach as I steered round the fountain to park outside my childhood home. The twelve-bedroom ivy-clad Georgian manor house was set in 100 acres of woodland and countryside in the Yorkshire Wolds twenty miles south of Whitsborough Bay. There was an estate manager's cottage, stables, and extensive gardens full of water features and follies. As a young child, it had been like a giant playground to explore on foot or by pony.

I couldn't sit in the car forever, especially when they were expecting me and had probably been watching me approach, so I pushed open the door and took a deep gulp of fresh country air.

A pair of excitable grey and white greyhounds hurled themselves at me.

'Hello there,' I said, bending down to stroke them. I knew from Mother's emails – our main source of communication since I'd left home as soon as college finished – that they were two-year-old brothers called Holmes and Watson, although I wasn't sure which was which.

'Welcome home, darling!'

I straightened up. 'Hello, Mother.'

Although her greeting was warm, her stance was uncomfortable, arms folded awkwardly across her body.

'You must be exhausted after that drive,' she said.

'I am a bit. I stopped a couple of times for coffee and a leg-stretch.'

'Very sensible.'

The dogs lost interest in our stilted conversation and trotted back inside. Who could blame them?

For the last half hour or so of my journey, I'd imagined how it might go, seeing Mother again for the first time in five years. At one point, I'd imagined her bursting into tears and rushing towards me, arms wide, but I'd swiftly dismissed that image. She'd never been particularly tactile while I'd lived at home and a five-year absence was more likely to widen the gap between us than close it.

'You've been riding?' I asked, searching for something to say and landing on the obvious. She was wearing a Victorian-style bottle-green riding habit with shiny brass buttons down the waistcoat, although she'd removed her jacket, exposing her white blouse sleeves. Her long hair was styled in a plaited chignon. The blonde had turned to grey but, from a distance, she still had a youthful complexion, despite her sixty-five years.

'Yes,' she said. 'We've not been back long.'

My father emerged from the house, wearing a waistcoat, shirt and riding breeches, like something out of an Austen novel. His dark hair and sideburns had been peppered with grey last time I saw him, but the transition was complete. His hairline had receded and, unlike Mother, he looked his age, possibly older.

He slid his arm round Mother's waist. 'Hello, Victoria. It's wonderful to see you again.'

'Thank you both for letting me stay.'

'You'll always be welcome here,' Mother said, her voice warm and gentle. 'Always.'

As I followed them into the grand entrance hall, I felt like I'd just stepped back in time to my teenage years. I'd figuratively stepped back in time too, but beyond my lifetime. My parents were still method writers living in Georgian, Victorian or Edwardian England – the time periods favoured in their bestselling historical novels – and there was still that distance between us, as though I was a guest who they politely tolerated rather than embraced.

And those were the reasons I'd left in the first place.

15

HOLLIE

Present day

I'd just run off the sales report and Angie was in the kitchen, loading the last few items into the dishwasher, when there was a knock on the door. I wandered over to the porch, laughing as I was greeted by the sight of Pickle waving his paw. Jake lowered him from in front of his face and beamed at me, turning my insides gooey.

'What are you two doing here?' I asked as I unlocked the outer door.

'Pickle had a suggestion,' Jake said, stepping into the café. 'As it's a lovely evening, he fancies a walk along South Bay and a visit to the chippy. What do you think?'

'Sounds good to me. I'll be about ten minutes.'

Angie emerged from the kitchen. 'It's my favourite two boys!' she declared. 'Who'd like a biscuit?'

'Me!' Jake joked.

Angie opened the dog biscuit jar and offered it to Jake.

'I really would, but we're going to the chippy and I don't want to spoil my appetite.'

'Spoilsport!' she said.

While I sorted the float for tomorrow, Angie got Pickle to do a few tricks in exchange for biscuits. I smiled at how good he was. It was lovely having a dog back in my life. My family had always had dogs, but I hadn't been able to bring myself to replace our beloved pale golden retriever Willow after she crossed the rainbow bridge four months after losing Mum.

Pickle was such an affectionate dog and, although I'd never forgive his owner for abandoning him the way she did on Bonfire Night last year, I would remain forever grateful that she had because I'd never have met Jake otherwise.

* * *

'Sebastian Smythe turned up again today,' I told Jake as we walked Pickle along South Bay beach after a delicious chippy tea.

'*The* Sebastian Smythe who isn't content with already owning half of Whitsborough Bay and wants to add The Starfish Café to his ever-expanding business empire?'

'That's the one. You won't believe what he offered me today.'

Jake released a loud whistle when I told him the amount. 'Why so much?'

'That's what I asked him and he wittered on about it making business sense, but it doesn't. I said no, of course, but I doubt he'll accept that.'

'Did I ever tell you what Nanna christened him?'

'I don't think so.'

'Dad and his team were convinced he was up to no good and Dad was desperate to arrest him, but he always seemed to be one step ahead of the rumours and allegations. Because they could never pin anything on him, Nanna named him Slippy Smythe. They loved it down the police station. I'd be surprised if he isn't still known as that today.'

'That's hilarious! And so perfect for him.'

We walked in companionable silence for a few minutes, watching Pickle running up and down with a piece of driftwood between his teeth.

'Did you say he'd tried to buy the café from your mum before?' Jake asked.

'It was years ago when Isaac and I were teenagers, but she turned him down flat. He'd turn up intermittently reaffirming his interest and it was always a no, but when the cancer came back for the second time, she invited him to the house to give her an updated offer.'

'She was going to sell up?'

'That depended on me. She'd got a bee in her bonnet that I'd worked in the café since I was twelve and maybe it wouldn't have been the career I'd have chosen if it hadn't been a family business, so she gave me a proposal. Either I could step up and become the permanent full-time manager and she'd return to work part-time when she was well enough, or she could sell to Smythe and give me a chunk of the sales proceeds to invest in retraining and a deposit on a house for Craig and me. There was no way I'd ever walk away from the café, so she had to turn Smythe down again.'

'I bet that went down well.'

'Like a lead balloon. He told us both we'd made the wrong decision, that it was a one-time only offer, and we shouldn't come crawling back to him when we'd changed our minds.' I rolled my eyes at Jake. 'It was him who came crawling out the woodwork again after Mum died and he's turned up every so often to try and convince me, but he's never tried twice in one month, so he's obviously on a mission right now. Not sure what's changed.'

'I bet he's got his eye on the summer trade. If you agreed a sale now, there'd be time to do the legal stuff and a refurb ready to reopen for May half-term.'

'That's a good point.'

The breeze had picked up and, when I shivered, Jake called Pickle back to us and we headed home. Sebastian Smythe wanting to pocket the proceeds from the busy summer trade did make sense, but I couldn't shake the feeling that there was more to it than that and that he'd be back again soon. I'd have to refuse to speak to him and hope he'd finally get the message that no didn't just mean no. It meant never.

16

TORI

Shortly after eleven on Sunday morning, I stood outside Chestnut Barn – Matt and Charlee's home – psyching myself up for an afternoon of saying 'no' every time a baby was thrust in my direction. What was the obsession with holding other people's babies? Every time one was forced on me, they screamed, puked or crapped themselves, or they wriggled so much that I was terrified I'd drop them. Why couldn't people accept that no meant *I couldn't be less interested in holding that baby* rather than *I know I said no, but really I'd love it and I'm just playing games and, while we're at it, let's have a conversation about why I'm approaching forty and childless.*

When Matt and Charlee invited me to Aria's first birthday party, I'd come so close to declining. The thought of a room full of screaming children gave me the heebie-jeebies, but then Charlee had added, 'It's mainly family coming and there'll be lots of cake. Carly's making it.' Sold! Carly's Cupcakes was on the same street as Charlee's Chocolates and Carly made the most delicious cakes I'd ever tasted. Her shop opened a couple of months after I'd moved back to Redamancy Castle and I swear that a combination of Jaffa

Cakes and her cupcakes were what had got me through that eighteen months – way longer than anticipated – living back at home.

'Are you thinking about going to the pub instead?' a woman called.

I turned and smiled at Jodie and her fiancé Dean, who were approaching along the drive. 'It's tempting, but I'm reliably informed that there's cake.'

'One of Carly's masterpieces,' Jodie said. 'She's making our wedding cake too. I might be more excited about that than saying "I do" on Saturday.'

She looked adoringly at Dean.

'Only might?' he asked, raising an eyebrow. 'I'm *definitely* way more excited about the cake. Five layers of different flavoured sponge cakes. I say let's not bother with the other stuff. Let's just grab a fork and dive in. In fact, ditch the fork. We can scoop. What do you reckon?'

'I reckon you're a man after my heart,' Jodie said, laughing.

I followed Jodie and Dean into Chestnut Barn and felt my shoulders relax when the sounds that hit me were mainly adult chatter and laughter. Matt and Charlee's toddler, Teddy, ran past us in the large entrance hall, clutching onto a soft dinosaur and giggling with delight as Tim's daughters Lillie and Elin, twelve and eleven respectively, chased him.

While Jodie and Dean hung their coats up, I headed into the lounge to get it over with. Charlee was on the sofa with a sleepy-looking Aria in her arms.

Aria did look adorable in a dusky pink party dress with a matching headband round her thick dark hair, but I felt nothing. No longing for one of my own. No fear that my biological clock was ticking. No regrets that I'd made the wrong decision.

'Happy first birthday, cutie-pie.' I planted a kiss on Aria's chubby cheek then swiftly backed away from them, willing Charlee not to ask me if I wanted to hold her daughter.

I'd never spoken to Charlee about why my marriage ended. It had, after all, happened before Matt even knew her, but I suspected he'd shared, which I didn't mind. One less person to have to justify myself to, not that I'd have expected Charlee to judge me for it because she wasn't like that. Shame there were so many who were. I'd had it all over the years – everything from an assumption that not having children couldn't possibly be a woman's actual choice and there had to be a medical reason stopping me from having kids, through to a suggestion that I was selfish for choosing my career and lifestyle instead of devoting my life to bringing up other humans. Why was *I don't want children because I don't want children* such a difficult concept to understand? Why did there have to be some deep reason?

'She's just been napping,' Charlee said. 'Do you want to pop your gift over there? We'll open them when she's a bit more awake.'

As I added my gift to a pile in one corner, Jodie appeared and, within seconds, she was pacing round the room lightly rocking her goddaughter, clearly smitten.

'Have you had the conversation with Leyton yet?' Charlee asked.

'I've barely seen him. He's racked up some ridiculous hours this week trying to appease his father.'

'You're sure he's...' She shook her head. 'Ignore me. Forget I said that.'

'Am I sure he's actually working and not seeing someone?' I suggested. 'The thought did cross my mind, but cheating's not Leyton's style.'

'What are you going to do?'

'Nothing much I can do. I can't interrupt him when he's working. His work's important.'

'And your relationship isn't?'

Loud voices and laughter drifted through from the hall. 'That's my parents,' Charlee said, standing up. 'We'll talk later, yeah?'

'Yeah.'

I stared into my lemonade, wishing it was something much stronger. Our relationship had been important, but it was past that now. My heart told me it was over and I just needed to find the opportunity to discuss that with Leyton. I'd let the dust settle from this latest problem but, as soon as it did, that conversation would be happening. I wasn't going to listen to my head accusing me of being a chicken for delaying the inevitable.

I shoved all thoughts of Leyton out of my head and focused on enjoying the time with my family. It was a perfect spring day. Fluffy white clouds floated lazily across a blue sky and there was a gentle warmth to the sun.

Aunt Kathryn organised us into teams for a mini sports day in the field behind Chestnut Barn. I hadn't been to primary school, my education being home-schooling by a governess, so sack, wheelbarrow, egg and spoon, and three-legged races were all new to me and I had no idea something so simple could be such fun. Afterwards, Elin and Lillie challenged me to a hula-hooping contest – something I'd done a lot as a child, although it wasn't so easy with a stitch from laughing so much.

The two girls were a delight to be around, and I hated saying goodbye when the party broke up. Another accusation I'd had levelled at me was that I didn't want kids because I didn't like them, in a tone that suggested I was a despicable human being for feeling that way. It was completely untrue. I wasn't comfortable with babies but the few kids I'd been around had been fun, inspiring, hilarious and I'd genuinely enjoyed their company. I just had no desire to have my own.

It had been an unexpectedly lovely day but, as I headed back to Leyton's, my thoughts turned to our relationship and a heavy cloud descended on me. There was no escaping from the fact that it was a disaster zone right now, but had it always been that way? During the sports day, I'd observed the playful banter between Matt and Charlee, my cousin Tim and his wife Kendal, Jodie and Dean, and even Uncle Hugh and Aunt Kathryn. They made each other laugh so much and acted like the best of friends but with the added bonus of being head over heels in love. It had never been like that between Leyton and me. Or Ewan and me, for that matter. Was it me or was it my choice of partner? Had I deliberately chosen men who were unromantic and emotionally detached because it was so different to the relationship my parents had – so besotted with each other that there was never space for anyone else?

17

TORI

Twenty-six years ago

'I'll be ten years old two months from today,' I announced as Mother, Father and I sat down for our evening meal in early May.

'What would you like for your birthday, darling?' Mother asked.

'To go to school.'

They both stared at me, eyebrows raised.

'Please,' I added.

Mother cleared her throat. 'Why would you want to go to school, darling? You have everything you could possibly need right here.'

'I don't have any friends.'

'You have Miss Pemberley and Phipps.'

Miss Pemberley was my governess – the only teacher I'd ever known – and Phipps was the estate manager. He'd taught me to ride and often accompanied me when I was out on my pony. I adored them both, but they were adults.

'It's not the same. I mean children.'

'What about Matthew and Timothy? They're your friends, aren't they?'

Even though Mother and Uncle Hugh had fallen out when they were teenagers – something to do with Grandfather planning to give Uncle Hugh the family farm when he retired, despite Mother being the oldest – she let me spend time with her family. I was really close to my cousins and particularly valued my time with them because it was the only regular contact I had with anyone my own age.

Matt and Tim sometimes stayed during the school holidays and we'd play for hours, roaming the grounds in amazing costumes made by Mother or Father – costume design and sewing being one of their shared passions – and acting out scenes from different periods of history, inspired by the many bedtime stories my parents told us.

Sometimes I stayed at Grandfather's farm, where my cousins lived. We fed the animals and he let us take turns riding in the tractor cab with him.

Miss Pemberley was a brilliant teacher. She made every lesson fun and memorable and we spent more time outside learning than we did in the schoolroom on the second floor but, the more time I spent with my cousins, the more I felt I was missing out. They talked about friends from school, clubs they'd joined, parties they'd been to, and I wanted that.

'Matt and Tim are my friends,' I said, answering Mother's question, 'but I only get to see them for a bit each holiday. I want friends I see every day.'

'I'm sorry, Victoria, but it's out of the question,' Father said gently. 'Redamancy Castle is too far from the local primary school. The daily commute would be too exhausting for a young child and I'm afraid it would eat into our working day too much to take you.'

'Please!'

'Besides,' Mother added, 'you only have one more year left of primary education. There'd be no point in disrupting everything for just one year.'

'Then can I go to senior school? Please, Mother.'

'Do you have concerns about Miss Pemberley's teaching?'

'No! She's fantastic!'

'Then we'll continue as before. Agreed? Ralph, darling, would you please pass me the salt?'

I slumped back in my chair, blinking back tears of disappointment. Not agreed at all, but I'd be sent away from the table without dessert if I argued and Cook had made my favourite – syrup sponge and custard – so I wasn't going to miss out on that. They hadn't listened to me properly. They hadn't heard the part about me wanting to have friends. That happened a lot.

* * *

Sixteen months later

'Waaahhhh!'

Miss Pemberley and I exchanged knowing looks.

'I think we'll go across to the cottage again today,' she said, scooping her books into a wicker basket. 'Gather your things together, Tori.'

I loved that she and Phipps called me that and couldn't understand why Mother and Father never would. I hadn't been able to say 'Victoria' when I was little and it had stuck. I liked it a lot better.

It was the beginning of September and the start of my secondary education. At home.

'I thought it would be fun having a baby sister,' I said to Miss Pemberley as we crunched along the gravel pathway down to the stables and Phipps's cottage. I could still hear Robyn's incessant screams, despite being some way from the house. There wasn't a single room where her screams were muted, so we'd had to hide out in Phipps's cottage several times over the past few days.

'She's only a few days old and babies cry a lot, although young Robyn does seem to cry more often and much louder than most babies I've known.'

'When will she stop?'

'I couldn't say. It won't last forever, and you'll soon be the best of friends, chasing each other round the grounds.'

We reached Phipps's cottage and Miss Pemberley placed her basket on the kitchen table with a sigh.

'I think we could do with some fresh air for our lessons. What do you say to a spot of art?'

Art was one of my favourite subjects and outdoor lessons were the best. 'Where?'

'I think you deserve a treat, so let's go to your favourite place.'

Fifteen minutes later, we arrived at the abandoned church at the edge of the woods. Although my parents had restored Redamancy Castle, they'd chosen not to restore the church. The external stone walls were intact but the roof had never been added after the original owner ran out of money. Exposed to nature, a couple of trees had grown inside it and shrubs and ivy hugged the walls. It felt like such a magical place to me and I'd passed so many happy hours in there reading, playing and drawing.

'*L'eglise des arbres,*' I whispered, turning in a circle in the middle of the abandoned building, as the sun filtering between the tall trees surrounding the church warmed my face.

Because the church hadn't been finished, it had never been given a name and Miss Pemberley had suggested that the French translation for 'the church of the trees' sounded as magical as the atmosphere. When I was there, I always felt like anything was possible.

'Do you think Mother and Father will change their minds about me going to senior school?' I asked Miss Pemberley as we sat on a picnic blanket, sketching. 'We can't work properly with Robyn crying so much. What if she never stops?'

Miss Pemberley smiled at me. 'She *will* stop eventually.'

'I could go to Matt and Tim's school. Tim and I are in the same year and he can introduce me to his friends.'

'You want this badly, don't you?'

'More than I've ever wanted anything. You're the best teacher ever, but I really want some friends.'

She ruffled my hair. 'I understand. Leave it with me. I'll see what I can do.'

18

TORI

Twenty-three years ago

Be careful what you wish for, they say. And they're right.

My baby sister was diagnosed with a rare bowel condition called Hirschsprung's disease. It was treatable but she needed lots of hospital appointments.

Mother made the surprise announcement that they agreed with Miss Pemberley that Redamancy Castle was no longer an environment conducive to learning and that I could get my wish to start senior school. I tried not to act too disappointed when they told me I'd be attending the private school in Whitsborough Bay – Whitsborough West – instead of the comprehensive school Matt and Tim attended. It was a minor setback and I needed to celebrate that I'd finally got what I wanted. I was going to school at last, where I'd mix with other children and make friends.

Then she dropped another bombshell. I'd be boarding there. So, not only did I start school at age eleven for the first time ever – a week later than everyone else – I became a boarder while my parents focused on my sister. And I hated it. As soon as the other boarders heard that my parents lived locally, the comments began. *Your parents must really hate you. They probably never wanted you. They'll forget you're here.*

Every weekend, when I returned to Redamancy Castle for Sunday lunch, I begged Mother and Father to let me stay home. I even suggested Miss Pemberley come out of early retirement to tutor me and promised I'd never complain about being home-schooled again.

'Stop whining, Victoria!' Mother snapped at me. 'You wanted to go to school and now you're going to school.'

'But I didn't want to board.'

'And Robyn didn't want to be poorly and I didn't want to spend my days traipsing to and from hospital, but your sister is seriously ill and our priority for now has to be about making her better. You've heard her cry. Just imagine the pain she's in.'

'I'm in pain,' I retaliated. 'Everyone hates me. They're all picking on me.'

'For goodness' sake, stop being so dramatic. Sticks and stones may break my bones, but words will never hurt me.'

I hated that stupid saying. Words did hurt. Especially when shouted across the dorm room in the early hours. It wasn't just my parents being local that the bullies latched onto. My auburn hair was an easy target and I'd naively shared that I'd been home-schooled by a governess, which had led to jokes about me being stuck in the Victorian ages.

Mother's voice softened. 'Boarding isn't forever. I promise you that. However, it's how it needs to be for now and I won't hear another word about it. Is that clear?'

It was clear, but it didn't resolve anything, although, by the end of that first year, I'd surprisingly made a couple of good friends thanks to the bullies. Millicent, a boarder who started after Christmas and Tracie, a local scholarship student, joined me to form the 'Red Hair Gang', sick of being teased for all having auburn locks.

The three of us grew closer and, before long, we were inseparable. We didn't need anyone else and, for the first time ever, I had friends who weren't family and it was fantastic. I couldn't imagine anything ever breaking our bond.

By the summer between my second and third years at Whitsborough West, Robyn had made a full recovery. Mother confirmed that I could return in September as a day student and she even invited Millicent and Tracie to stay at Redamancy Castle for a few nights. That news both excited and alarmed me because the three of us had talked about so much, but there were a couple of aspects of my home life that I'd never shared.

After an evening of surfing in late July, we sat on the beach drinking hot chocolate.

'Before you come to stay next week, there's something I need to tell you,' I said, nerves making my voice sound squeaky. 'It's a secret, though. You have to promise me you won't tell anyone.'

'Sounds intriguing,' Millicent said. 'I promise.'

Tracie nodded. 'Me too.'

'You know how I told you that my parents are authors and that my mother writes as Rebecca Lannister?'

'My mum and nanna's favourite author,' Tracie declared, grinning. She'd told me that, between them, they had most of her books which was impressive because Rebecca Lannister was prolific.

'I didn't give you the full story.' I took a deep breath, my stomach churning. 'My mother *is* Rebecca Lannister. But so is my father.'

'What?' they both cried.

'It's a joint pseudonym. They write the books together.'

'Oh, my God!' Tracie exclaimed. 'I can't wait to tell my mum and nanna that their favourite author is also a man.'

'No! You can't tell them. Please.'

'Why's it a secret?' Millicent asked.

'It's a marketing thing. Most of the readers are women and the belief is they're more likely to buy from a female author.'

Millicent shrugged. 'I can't see what difference it makes, but your secret's safe with us.'

Tracie nodded in agreement.

'Thank you, but there's something else.' Another deep breath. 'You know how I used to be teased for having a governess and asked whether I lived in the Victorian times? Well, I did.'

I glanced from Millicent's confused expression to Tracie's.

'The books they write are historical and, to get the details right, they...' I swallowed hard. This was harder than I thought, but they were going to discover it when they stayed, so I needed to forewarn them. 'They act like they're from that time. They dress up in the clothes and do lots of the stuff Victorians would have done.'

They stared at me for a moment, wide-eyed, then Millicent burst out laughing.

'You had me going there for a minute.'

'I don't think she's kidding,' Tracie said, nudging her.

'I'm not.'

'You do have electricity?' Millicent asked, eyes wide with shock.

'Of course! They've not gone that far, thank God. We've got electricity, central heating, running water, modern kitchen and bathrooms, a car...'

'TV?' she asked.

I grinned at her. 'Better. We've got a cinema room.'

They both squealed with excitement. As they threw out ideas for films we could watch in the cinema room, the tight knots in my stomach gradually unravelled. They fired a stack of questions at me

– What's your bedroom like? What do your parents wear? Do you dress up too? Do they have servants? Do you call your dad 'sir'? – and I answered them all, relieved that they sounded fascinated rather than freaked out.

'I was excited before,' Millicent said as we left the beach a little later. 'But I'm even more excited now.'

'You promise you won't tell anyone about the Victorian stuff, especially at school. They'd rip me to shreds if they knew.'

'They won't hear it from me,' Tracie said, giving me a hug.

'Nor me,' Millicent said.

They crossed the road to where Tracie's mum was waiting and I joined Phipps who secured my surfboard to the roof of the estate Land Rover while I peeled off my wetsuit and pulled on jeans and a T-shirt over my swimming costume.

'How was the sea?' he asked as we set off back to Redamancy Castle.

'Amazing. I love riding but I love surfing even more.'

'Don't let your parents hear you say that. Young Victorian ladies should be accomplished riders, not surfers.' His mock-stern tone made me smile. 'Are your friends looking forward to staying?'

'I've told them what to expect.'

'How did they react?'

'Really well. They were interested but they didn't think I was a freak.'

'I should hope not!' He pulled over on the side of the road and twisted in his seat to face me. 'You don't think that, do you?'

I shrugged. 'I didn't exactly have a normal childhood, did I?'

'Did you have a happy one?'

'Yes, although I would have liked some friends.'

'Yeah, I can understand that, but it sounds like you have a couple of really good friends now.'

'They're the best.'

'Glad to hear it. And what's "normal" anyway?'

He pulled away again and I smiled at his question. My upbringing might not have been conventional by modern standards, but maybe there was no 'normal' after all and my more unusual childhood made me more interesting.

* * *

The few days planned for Millicent and Tracie to stay at Redamancy Castle extended into a week and it was the best week ever, exploring the grounds, baking, having cinema nights. Phipps taught them both to ride and we chatted endlessly about our hopes for the future and what we thought of everyone at school, especially the boys.

'I can't believe you're going home tomorrow,' I lamented as we picnicked on our final day. 'I'm going to miss you both so much.'

'I wish we could stay longer,' Tracie said, and Millicent nodded in agreement.

'I wish you could too. I'm glad you've enjoyed it.'

'Your parents are so cool,' Tracie said.

'You think so?'

'Yeah! I love that they do what they do to make the books authentic, but they still live in this century with the cinema room and stuff. I wish I could tell Mum and Nanna. They'd love it. But, as promised, my lips are sealed.' Tracie did a zipping motion across her mouth and I smiled at her gratefully.

'Have they ever done anything even you've thought was completely bonkers and over the top?' Millicent asked.

'Like what?'

She shrugged. 'I dunno. Peeing in a chamber pot?'

I laughed at the thought. 'Nothing like that. It started as getting the details right like how it felt to wear the clothes and how they restricted or helped movement, but it became a thing. They find the writing flows better when they're playing the part. They often enact scenes from their books and take photos and videos.' My cheeks coloured as I thought about a couple of occasions when I'd unexpectedly stumbled across them acting out racier scenes.

'Why have you gone red?' Millicent asked.

I glanced round me then encouraged them to huddle closer. 'I've caught them acting out sex scenes in the follies.'

Tracie squealed. 'You have not!'

'Sshh! They don't know, obviously.'

Millicent clapped her hand across her mouth. 'Oh, my God! That's hilarious! What did you do?'

'Made a very swift exit.'

Even though it was mortifying reliving those experiences, laughing with my two best friends about it made me feel even closer to them. We'd known each other pretty well before the week at Redamancy Castle but now we knew everything about each other, and it felt extra special to have been able to share my deepest secrets with them both.

When we waved goodbye the following morning, we all shed a few tears and prayed the rest of the summer would fly past so we could be reunited again at the start of the school year.

Three months later

'He's on his own,' I whispered to Millicent. 'Why don't you ask him?'

It was late October and the school was buzzing with an unexpected announcement that there'd be a masked ball for all students after the half-term break. Since returning to Whitsborough West, Millicent had developed an all-consuming crush on new boy Alistair Soames. The three of us had spent hours dissecting every look, every snippet of conversation, and were convinced he felt the same about her because he was always looking in her direction. The ball was the perfect opportunity for a date.

Millicent shook her head vigorously. 'I can't do that.'

'Why not?'

Her big blue eyes were wide and fearful. 'What if he says no?'

'What if he says yes?'

She glanced across at him, her cheeks colouring pink. 'He's so gorgeous.'

'And so are you,' Tracie said. 'You'd look great together.'

'If he's really into me like you both think, he'll ask me himself.'

We worked in silence for a few minutes.

'What if I asked him?' I said.

'You want to go with him?' Millicent looked aghast.

'No! I mean what if I asked him for you?'

'Thanks, but no. I'd never live it down if he's not interested.'

A few minutes later, I sighed and glanced round the library to make sure there were no teachers watching, then picked up my books and slipped into the chair beside Alistair, ignoring Millicent's hissed protests to come back.

Alistair looked up at me and smiled, flashing a set of perfect white teeth. With his dark hair and dark eyes, I'd agreed with Millicent on many occasions that he was hot and that his smile was to die for.

'Exciting news about that ball,' I said. 'Will you be going?'

'Probably. Could be a laugh.'

'I was wondering if you'd like to go with my friend Millicent.'

We both glanced over at them and I smiled as Millicent and

Tracie quickly lowered their heads, trying to look as though they weren't watching. Alistair chewed on his lip as though contemplating it.

'No,' he said eventually, huddling a little closer to me, 'but I'll go with you.'

My stomach lurched. 'Oh! No! It's Millicent I'm asking for, not me.' I gave him a gentle nudge. 'Go on! She's lovely.'

It wasn't difficult to sing Millicent's praises for the next few minutes, but there was no changing Alistair's mind.

'Nice try, Tori, but it's still a no to your friend and a yes to you.'

Awk-ward! I returned to Millicent and Tracie, cursing myself for going against Millicent's wishes. I couldn't believe he was interested in me instead. All those smiles and glances in our direction hadn't been aimed at Millicent like we'd thought.

'I'm really sorry, but it's a no.'

Millicent's eyes clouded with tears. 'Did he say why?'

'Not really.'

'Then why were you talking to him for so long?'

I couldn't tell her I'd spent all that time trying to talk him into it. Without success. 'It wasn't that long.'

'It seemed it.' She shrugged. 'We'd better get on with our work.'

I hated hearing the wobble in her voice and seeing the tears in her eyes. As she put her head down, Tracie caught my eye and winced. How painful had that been? I hoped Millicent would get over it and not blame me for Alistair's no.

* * *

'You devious little bitch!' Millicent cried, hurling herself at me as soon as I arrived at school the following morning.

Tracie dragged her back before she could do anything more than shove me, but it didn't stop her trying to kick me.

'What the hell?' I jumped away from her flailing arms and legs.

'You know how I feel about him!' Millicent yelled. 'How could you do that?'

'Do what?'

'Tiffany says you're going to the ball with Alistair,' Tracie said, grimacing.

'Well, she's wrong because I'm not.'

Millicent glared at me. 'So he didn't ask you?'

I grimaced. 'Yes, but—'

'So you lied to me.'

'No, but I didn't see any benefit in telling you he'd asked me when I said no.'

'He fancies you instead of me.'

'But I *don't* fancy him and I'm *not* going to the ball with him.'

'You're such a liar! Tracie and I saw you chatting him up.'

'I was trying to persuade him to go with you.' I cringed, realising too late that probably wasn't what she needed to hear right now.

Millicent gave me the filthiest look. 'It was a secret. I begged you not to say anything, but you ignored me. You've ruined everything.' She stormed off across the playing field.

'You must believe me,' I pleaded with Tracie.

'I was there,' she said with a sigh. 'You looked very cosy.'

'Because I was trying not to let anyone overhear.'

'You were laughing. And you've always said you thought he was really hot.'

'I was being supportive of Millicent. Doesn't mean I fancy him.'

'That's not what Tiffany said.'

'And you believe her over me?'

'Not normally but, as I said, I was there. I saw you two together.'

'Tracie!' I called, as she ran after Millicent.

'Oh dear, is that the end of the Red Hair Gang?' Tiffany's sing-song voice cut right through me.

'Get lost!'

'You want to be careful when you spill someone else's secrets, especially when they know all of yours.' With a fake laugh, she ran off to join Millicent and Tracie, leaving me with the stomach-churning feeling that everything was about to go from bad to worse.

By lunchtime, it seemed that every single student knew that my father was also Rebecca Lannister and that my parents dressed as Victorians. By the end of the day, the rumours had escalated to them also acting out the sex scenes from their novels and that Millicent had supposedly caught them at it when she'd stayed in the summer.

Everywhere I went, there were giggles and smutty comments. Students I didn't even recognise seemed to know who I was and thought it was their place to make snide remarks.

Three more days of hell followed, and the weekend couldn't come fast enough for me. I hoped the two-day break would make the gossip die but there was worse to come.

Even I didn't know the gossip that raced round school on Monday morning. Rebecca Lannister, author of slightly racy historical novels, wasn't the only joint identity my parents held. They also wrote prolifically as Domino Blaize.

'What's this?' I demanded as soon as I got home, holding up a well-thumbed copy of one of the Domino Blaize paperbacks that had been circulating round school with the most X-rated passages marked up with bright yellow highlighter pen.

Mother glanced up from her sewing but didn't stop feeding the fabric through the machine. 'It's a book, darling.'

'And who's it by?'

'Domino Blaize.'

'Which is you and Father, right?'

She released the pedal and sighed. 'That is correct.'

'So you and Father write porn.'

'It's not porn. It's erotica.'

'Is there a difference?'

'Of course there is!' She laughed lightly, as though this was all a big game. 'There are no dodgy photocopier or washing machine repairmen in our books.'

'Mother!' I lobbed the book across the room and it skidded to a halt by the French doors. 'I'm being serious.'

'I can see that, darling. What's rattled you?'

'That!' I pointed to the book. 'And the fact that everyone in school knows that my parents wrote it and thinks it's okay to quote passages to me everywhere I go.'

I expected an expression of shock and sympathy. Instead, she took it as an opportunity to educate me.

'Pornography is all about sex, but erotica is about sexuality. You know, the Victorians used to—'

'I don't give a shit what the Victorians used to do,' I cried, a little shocked with myself for swearing in front of her. 'It's you and Father we're discussing here.'

Father burst into the room at that point. 'What's with the shouting?'

'Our daughter has discovered that Rebecca Lannister is also Domino Blaize.'

I hated how amused she sounded.

Father looked perplexed. 'And that explains the shouting?'

'Apparently *everyone* at school knows.'

How could they laugh about it? My life was in tatters and they thought it was somehow funny?

'We also write as Ashlyn Raven and Arabella Locksley,' Mother said.

It got worse. 'More porn?'

'Ashlyn's books are set during the American Civil War,' Father said. 'We haven't written as many of those as they take more research, and Arabella's books are all Regency.'

'And Domino does *not* write porn,' Mother added. 'Although Destiny Falls writes absolute filth.'

'Oh, my God! How many identities do you have?'

They were both in fits of laughter. 'I'm teasing, darling,' Mother said, barely able to catch her breath. 'I've just made up Destiny Falls.'

'Marvellous name, though.' Father's voice was full of admiration.

'Yes, it is rather. But you came up with Domino Blaize. Out of this world.'

They didn't get it. They couldn't see how screwed up this all was. All they cared about was congratulating each other on their name-creation talents, presenting the usual united front.

'They're all laughing at me at school,' I screeched. 'They think I'm a weirdo. Even Millicent and Tracie have turned against me.'

'Then they aren't the sort of people you want or need in your life,' Mother said, her tone still light.

'But they're my best friends!'

'You'll make new friends,' Father said.

'Did you not hear me? The whole school thinks I'm weird because of you two and your bloody freakish obsession with the past. It's not normal.'

'It's our normal, darling,' Mother said. 'And please don't swear. It's not ladylike.'

'I'm not a lady! I'm not a Victorian, Georgian or Edwardian and neither are you. Stop pretending to be something you're not.'

'I thought this was meant to be about you,' Father said calmly. 'Why are you attacking us?'

'Because you're the reason I'm a laughing stock and my friends hate me. Why can't you see that? What you do, how you live, how you make me live – none of it makes any sense!'

'Just because somebody doesn't understand something, it doesn't make it wrong,' Father said.

'You're not listening to me!'

'You're screeching, darling,' Mother said. 'Believe me, we're listening. We couldn't do anything else.'

'No, you're not. You *never* listen to me. I begged you for years to let me go to school and you only let me because Robyn was ill. I've asked if we can go on family holidays or even days out but you're always too busy. You *never* put me first. I might as well not exist.'

'That's unfair,' Father said. 'You've always been our number one priority.'

'Well, you've got a funny way of showing it. I hate living in the past. I hate that you write porn. I hate that I have no friends because of you. And do you know what? I hate you too and I can't wait till the day I leave home because, when that happens, I'm never coming back.'

'Victoria!' Mother called, as I stormed out of the drawing room.

'It's Tori!' I yelled.

19

HOLLIE

Present day

'I think that's enough for today, don't you, Pickle?' I said, downing tools in my workshop and stretching out shortly after four on Sunday. 'Jake'll be home from work any minute.'

The sound of the front doorbell – which I had wired into the workshop as well as the house – made me jump and set Pickle off barking. It very rarely rang.

Pickle trotted along the driveway next to me. There was nobody at the front door, but there was an obscenely enormous bouquet of lilies propped up in the sheltered entrance porch.

'Wow! That's a lot of flowers. Who do you think these are from?'

I smiled as I carefully removed the small envelope taped to the cellophane and opened it, but my stomach sank as I read the note written in capital letters:

I UNDERLINE YOU TO RECONSIDER. YOU KNOW IT MAKES SENSE

The words 'urge' and 'know' were each underlined twice.

I ran to the end of the drive and looked up and down the street, but there was no sign of Slippy Smythe, not that he was likely to have made the delivery himself. He no doubt had plenty of minions to do his work.

He'd only made his offer on Thursday. To make contact again after only three days showed more determination than ever before. Why?

I read the note again, shaking my head. 'It *doesn't* make sense,' I muttered. Anger surged through me at the audacity of the man. It was bad enough repeatedly pestering me at the café, but this was my home. And on a Sunday! How dare he?

'You know where you can shove your lilies, Slippy Smythe.'

I stormed round to the back of the house to the garden waste bin, thrust the lid open, and began ripping off the cellophane. It was a waste of beautiful flowers, but no way did I want anything from that revolting man in my house.

'What are you doing?' Jake asked, sounding amused.

I'd been so preoccupied; I hadn't noticed him pulling onto the drive.

'Destroying these.'

He picked Pickle up and scratched behind the dog's ears. 'I thought you loved flowers.'

'I do. Just not when they're sent as a bribe.'

He stopped scratching and stared at me, eyes wide. 'They're from Smythe? When?'

'They arrived a few minutes ago.'

'He's been to the house?'

His concern was touching. 'I haven't actually seen him. The doorbell rang and they were on the doorstep with this.'

I passed the card to him and he tutted as he read it. 'The man's certainly persistent.'

'Too persistent.' I closed the lid of the bin, feeling better for getting the frustration out of my system. 'How was your day?'

'Classic Sunday on A&E – lots of sports injuries.' He put Pickle down, then cuddled me to his chest and kissed my forehead. 'How was yours before the flowers arrived?'

'Good. I saw Katie and I got my orders finished. Pickle hasn't had a walk since the beach this morning, so he could probably do with one if you fancy it.'

Ten minutes later, the three of us set off along the esplanade and took one of the turnings down the cliffs through Cascade Gardens. It was my favourite route down to the sea.

We ambled down the stone steps, past the fountain, and back up the other side to sit for a moment under one of the ivy-clad shelters.

'Mum loved it here,' I said, cuddling up to Jake while Pickle explored the shelter. 'On her days off, she'd sometimes bring a flask and a book and sit here for hours. When she was ill that final time, I hired a wheelchair so I could bring her here. I thought she'd want her ashes scattering at The Starfish Café or in the sea like Dad and Isaac, but she wanted this to be her final resting place. We waited until April when the flowers were at their best, like they are now, then Angie, Katie and I came down with her flask and the last book she'd read and we sat here for a few hours reminiscing.'

Jake squeezed my shoulder. 'I bet that was a special day.'

'It was. We cried but we laughed a lot too. It was what she'd have wanted. Because she didn't have a favourite spot, we scattered her ashes all over. There's a little piece of her everywhere here.'

I'd expected the tears to fall but, instead, I felt warm with all the happy memories.

'This would have been six years ago?' Jake asked.

'Six years and four months. I can't believe it. Where does the time go?'

'I've no idea.'

We sat in companionable silence for a few minutes, lost in our thoughts.

'Was there anyone around when you scattered her ashes?' Jake asked.

'No, thankfully. We might have got a few peculiar looks.'

'Nanna wanted me to scatter hers at the castle. It was the height of summer and she wanted to fly from the keep. Can you imagine how hard it was doing that without being seen? She had such a great sense of humour and I think that was her having her last laugh.'

'Your nanna sounds amazing.'

'She was one of a kind. She'd have loved you so much.'

'And my family would have loved you too. And you, Pickle,' I added when he jumped onto the bench for some attention.

We left the gardens and continued our walk down the cliff and along the seafront towards the commercial part of South Bay. It was busier down there, as expected during the school holidays. In my opinion, it was still coat weather, but there were some hardy souls in swimming costumes or shorts on the beach, braving the waves, although the squeals told a tale of how cold the sea was.

On our left was the Golden Galleon, the largest of the dozen or so amusement arcades spread along the curve of the bay and the flagship of Smythe's seafront enterprises. The four-storey building was illuminated with red and gold flashing lights, and the ugly late-1960s cladding was mainly obliterated by an enormous poster announcing the fun to be had inside. The ground floor housed the standard penny falls, grab machines, children's rides and other family-friendly arcade games. The first floor contained the shooting and gambling games aimed at older visitors, the next one was devoted to soft play and trampolining, with a ten-pin bowling alley and café on the top.

'Slippy Central,' Jake said, making me laugh as we paused to look up at the building.

'I think you should paint that on a sheet and unfurl it overnight.'

'If only I was brave enough.'

'I haven't been in there since I was little,' I said. 'I used to love playing on the grab machines.'

'It was the penny falls for me.' Jake fished a pound coin out of his pocket. 'Not that I want to give him my business, but do you fancy a quick go while we check it out?'

We crossed the road and, spotting a sign stating that well-behaved dogs on leads were welcome on the ground floor, we stepped inside.

A wave of nostalgia hit me as I breathed in the sweetness of candy floss blended with fresh coffee. Flashing and whirling lights drew my eyes in every direction and my ears tuned into winning sirens, bursts of music, and the clatter of coins. Décor-wise, it didn't look like it had changed much over the years.

Jake handed me the pound coin, which gave me five goes on one of the grab machines. The claw, although perfectly positioned over a lilac teddy bear, failed to take hold.

'Have you got another coin?' I asked Jake, knowing I only had notes in my purse.

He handed it over and I had another five failed attempts. I was on the verge of asking for a third coin but stopped myself. With any form of gambling, there was one golden rule: the house always wins. Was that what made Smythe so arrogant, knowing he always won? Not this time. The Starfish Café was mine.

We wandered round a bit more and couldn't resist a few goes on the penny falls. There was plenty of laughter and the occasional cheer. It didn't seem right that a childhood heaven like this was run by somebody as unsavoury and unscrupulous as Smythe, and yet it also seemed the perfect front for someone up to no good.

'I was thinking about him offering you way over the odds for the café,' Jake said as we walked back through the covered walkway by The Bay Pavilion a little later. 'Do you reckon it could have anything to do with – and please don't judge me for suggesting this – Tingler's Treasure?'

His question surprised me so much that I released some sort of half-laugh-half-snort which echoed round the walkway.

'Please tell me you're joking.'

'Please tell me you didn't just make that sound,' Jake said, his voice shaking with laughter. 'Think about it, though. The Yorkshire Coast was rife with smuggling and Starfish Point was rumoured to be one of the routes.'

'Rumoured being key. There've never been any maps or paperwork found to substantiate that and I'd have known if there were because Isaac would have unearthed them. He was obsessed with finding the treasure.'

'He believed in it, then?'

'You know the wall of cork tiles on the top floor in Isaac's bedroom? Barely any cork was visible for maps, charts and photos. When you see crime programmes on TV and they've got pins in everything connected by string, that's what it looked like.' I smiled as I pictured it. 'I used to feel so sorry for his girlfriend Bex because, every time he uncovered something new, he'd be back to his old room with Kyle, looking for connections. I once asked her why she didn't get him to move everything across to their garage, but she said she'd never see him if she did that and it was better that he returned home occasionally to get his pirate-chasing out of his system. Plus, she couldn't stand Kyle – Jaffa – back then so it kept him away, too. The pair of them were massively into pirates and smuggling, but their biggest obsession was Tingler's Treasure. I dread to think how many hours they spent discussing it, researching it, and even looking for it.'

'Did they get close?'

'They thought so loads of times, but it was always a dead end. So what's your theory? Don't tell me!' I adopted a dramatic film-trailer style voice. 'Menacing businessman Sebastian Smythe has unearthed a long-lost treasure map revealing the final resting place of Tingler's Treasure. The only problem is that X marks the spot right in the middle of existing thriving business The Starfish Café. Will the beautiful but mysterious café owner be willing to accept his ridiculously high offer and surrender the café lovingly built by her late mother, or will it be a fight to the bitter end?'

I could barely get to the end for giggling.

'You may well mock me,' he said, laughing with me, 'but do you have a more plausible suggestion?'

'No. None. I'll admit that I'm baffled by the whole thing.'

'Do you know that Sherlock Holmes quote – something about eliminating the impossible and whatever remains being the truth, even if it seems improbable? My dad had that in a frame on his desk at the police station. Tingler's Treasure being buried under The Starfish Café and Smythe knowing that is improbable, but is it impossible? I'd say not.'

'If Isaac was here today, he'd be straight on the phone to Kyle and the pair of them would drag you up those stairs to The Smuggler's Key and never let you escape until you'd helped them solve it.'

'It sounds like fun.'

'It was, actually.' I pictured the pair of them, eyes shining with excitement, interrupting each other in their eagerness to tell me about a new lead or a theory they wanted to run by me. 'Abe Tingler fascinated him, which wasn't surprising when part of the legend involved the land our family owned. So you believe in the legend?'

Jake ran his hand through his hair, leaving it gorgeously dishevelled. 'I honestly don't know. The thing with myths and legends is that there's often enough truth in there to make you wonder if it could all be the truth.'

'Such as?'

He counted off the points on his fingers. 'Abe Tingler existed and was a known smuggler. He was caught and hanged for smuggling and murder and there were plenty of reliable reports about him scoping out Starfish Point. As to whether he hid some long-lost treasure in a cave there...' He tailed off and shrugged. 'I'd like to believe it, but I can't help thinking it sounds more like something out of Treasure Island.'

'Which, as you know, was Isaac's favourite book and earned him the nickname of Silver down at the lifeboat station. He and Kyle passionately believed in Tingler's Treasure, but Mum and I were doubtful. Granddad bought the land in 1955 and worked on the beach for the next twenty-five years or so. If there'd been caves or secret passages, he'd have discovered them, and I know he looked. So did Isaac. He once convinced Dad to dive the area with him in case there were caves under the water further round the cove, but they never found any. So if Sebastian Smythe has offered me some massively inflated price because he thinks he's going to find treasure on the beach or under the café, then he's more delusional than I originally thought.'

We made it back to Sandy Croft and an exhausted Pickle curled up in his bed by the fire while we prepared our evening meal. As I chopped vegetables, I couldn't stop thinking about the legend of

Tingler's Treasure. Abe Tingler's story was pretty gruesome. Smuggling had been rife on the Yorkshire Coast from the start of the eighteenth century to the middle of the nineteenth. As well as tobacco and alcohol, items such as tea, silk, lace and salt were smuggled to avoid the phenomenally high taxes.

Shipments arrived at night and whole villages could be involved in the smuggling process. In Shellby Bay up the coast, there was a tunnel under the harbour slipway and smuggled goods could travel from there to the top of the town without ever going out into the open, having passed through tunnels, trapdoors and hidden cupboards connecting a whopping eighty-seven properties. When Isaac told me that, it blew my mind.

Abe Tingler was one of the leaders, particularly prolific in the smuggling of salt, which the local fishermen needed to preserve their catches for transportation. The landlord of The Coachman on the moors stored salt in the cellar walls so coaches of fishermen rode their catch to the inn at night, salted it, then continued their journey to sell it. If the landlord spotted a taxman in the pub, he placed a warning light in a window.

One fatal night, the landlord didn't notice a stranger in the bar. He went down to the cellar with the fishermen and the stranger – a taxman – followed and confronted the men. A fight broke out and Abe Tingler hit the man with a rock, intending to knock him out, but it cracked the man's skull. They tried to dispose of the body on the moors but it was discovered a couple of days later. In an attempt to avoid the gallows, the fishermen pointed their fingers at Tingler and he hung for that and other crimes.

As for the legend of Tingler's Treasure, some claimed it was made up to add notoriety to Abe Tingler, but others swore the treasure existed, although nobody knew what it actually was. Coins? Jewels? Something else? While that element of the unknown thrilled Isaac and Kyle, it made me a little more sceptical.

'You're very thoughtful,' Jake said. 'Tingler's Treasure?'

'You've got my mind whirring, but I'm still not convinced there ever was a treasure. Abe Tingler was undoubtedly a dangerous man not to be crossed, but he was a smuggler, not a pirate. He moved regular goods like alcohol, tobacco, tea and salt. You think "treasure", you think "pirate". There *is* a difference. The beach and the cliffs have been thoroughly searched and there's nothing there. As for the treasure being buried under the café, do bear in mind that my mum bulldozed that site before the café was built. If there'd been a great big treasure chest there, I'm pretty sure somebody would have spotted it.'

Jake shrugged. 'In that case, there could be a simpler explanation for Smythe's persistence.'

'What's that?'

'His pride. He can't bear being told no. Far too humiliating for a man like him.'

'But that would mean he's never going to stop.'

'I'm sure he will, eventually. You'll just have to keep being firm with him. He's bound to give up at some point. He'll probably set his sights on somewhere else.'

I hoped he was right, but my gut told me that Smythe wasn't going to give up until he had what he wanted. But I wasn't going to give up either. Seemed I was going to have a fight on my hands.

20

TORI

We reached Thursday evening, the week after Aria's birthday party, and I'd barely seen Leyton. He'd been at Fenby Heights until late on Sunday evening and had arrived home in a foul mood, nursing a bottle of lager while he flicked through the TV channels, and refusing to talk. The next three evenings, he'd rushed in from work to shower and change before going back out to schmooze a client or strategise with his father. All I'd managed to pick up through snatched conversations while he dressed was that the rebuilding of the relationship with the Durlings had hit a snag and some accounting anomalies had been discovered. I had no idea if the two things were connected or what they meant for the future of Clairmont Properties or Leyton at the helm of the company.

He looked fraught and, even though I no longer wanted to be with him, it didn't stop me being concerned about the toll the immense pressure seemed to be taking. I wanted to help if I could but, every time I attempted to be empathetic and supportive, he turned on me. When I asked if he'd like dinner preparing so he could eat before dashing out again, he told me to stop keeping tabs on him. When I offered my help, he rolled his eyes as though it was the most ridiculous question in the world. Obviously I knew I couldn't do anything to resolve the client issues or anomalies, but I could have typed up a document, done some research or even dropped his suit off at the dry cleaners if practical help would make a difference.

When Charlee invited me to meet her for a drink after her shop closed on Thursday night, I accepted immediately, desperate to be around someone who enjoyed my company.

'How's it going with Leyton?' she asked as we settled side by side on a cushioned bench in The Purple Lobster.

'It isn't. I've barely seen him this week and when I have, he's practically bitten my head off.'

'That's not good. What are you going to do?'

I hugged my arms across my chest and gave her a half-hearted shrug. 'Move out and see if he notices?'

'It's definitely over?'

'I think it has been for a long time and we've both been too preoccupied with work to admit it. He's always said he never wanted to get married and that was fine by me. Been there, done that. But the reality is that he *is* married... to the job. It's all-consuming and there's no room for anything else.'

'Aw, Tori, I'm so sorry. How do you feel?'

'Like I've wasted the past eight years.'

'It's *all* been bad?' Charlee sounded shocked.

I took a deep glug on my wine as I pondered on it.

'No, not all of it. The early days were good but that was because he was exactly what I needed to move on from Ewan and I was what he wanted – a girlfriend who wasn't looking for anything serious. It worked at the time, but it would probably have petered out if I hadn't had that huge fallout with my parents...'

'And moved in with him,' she said when I tailed off, my stomach churning with the realisation that I should never have done that.

Here was me blaming Leyton for being so work-obsessed and morphing into his father but the cracks in our relationship had appeared long before that.

'It's my fault,' I said. 'I needed somewhere to stay, he said I could stay with him for a few nights until I found somewhere to rent, and I never left. It wasn't right but somehow it worked. Until it didn't.'

Charlee shuffled closer and drew me into a hug. 'If you need any help moving your stuff, just give us a shout. And I know you said no to moving in with us, but the room's there if you need it.'

I squeezed her back. 'Thank you. You're a good friend.'

* * *

Back at home later that evening, I stood in the open plan lounge/kitchen/diner and had a flashback to the day I moved out of Ewan's home. It felt like history repeating itself. This was Leyton's home and his belongings, and I was the lodger. Nine years with Ewan followed by almost eight with Leyton and what did I have to show for it? I still didn't own a share of a house or anything in it. When I moved out, I'd be able to fit everything in Carrie.

I sank onto the sofa, feeling empty. I was still sitting in the darkness, the door keys in my hand, when Leyton arrived home an hour later, just past eleven.

'Shit! You scared the life out of me!' he cried as he flicked the light on. 'What are you doing in the dark?'

'Nothing. Just thinking.'

A normal, caring boyfriend would have taken that prompt and asked, 'What about?' but it was as though I hadn't even spoken. He went into the kitchen and poured himself a glass of chilled water from the tap on the American style fridge-freezer, gulped half of it down, then topped it up. I quite fancied a glass of water. It would have been nice to be asked.

'I'm off up to bed. Make sure you put the lights out when you come up.'

I had to say it. Crap timing or not, we couldn't go on like this. 'Leyton?'

'What?'

One word. So much frustration. My resolve crumbled. Maybe I *would* just pack and go instead.

'What?' he asked again, his voice louder.

I had to say something. 'Jodie needs to confirm the numbers for Saturday night. I'm presuming you won't be going.'

'Why wouldn't I be going?' He sounded surprised.

'Because of how fraught things are at work.'

'It's evening, not all day, yeah? Then I think I've more than earned an evening off. But I'll need a few drinks after the fortnight from hell, so either you're driving or you'll have to organise a taxi.'

'I'll book a taxi.' I suspected I'd need a drink too. Or five.

21

TORI

On Saturday evening, ten minutes before the taxi was due, my phone rang and Leyton's name flashed up on the screen.

'He's going to cancel,' I muttered to myself before connecting the call. 'Hi. Where are you?'

'Held up at work, so I'll have to meet you there. Can you bring me a fresh shirt? My new blue one. And those cufflinks my mother gave me for Christmas.'

I sighed. 'Anything else?'

'My best black shoes.'

'How late do you think you'll be?'

'I should be there by eight. Maybe quarter past.'

'I'll check them into the cloakroom and you can get the ticket from me when you get there.'

'Okay. See you later.' He hung up before I could say anything else.

'Just as well I was ready early,' I muttered, slipping my phone back into my bag and gathering his belongings.

As I watched out for the taxi to take me to The Bay Pavilion, I allowed myself a moment to acknowledge that, although I'd felt frustrated at the idea of Leyton cancelling last minute when he called, I'd been hoping he would because I didn't relish a whole evening in his company.

* * *

Jodie was a vision in a romantic lace off-the-shoulder dress with fluttering chiffon sleeves and pale pink floral detailing, reminiscent of something a Disney princess might wear.

'You look stunning,' I said as she gave me a twirl.

'Thank you. It's not what I thought I'd have gone for, but I feel amazing. I never want to take it off!'

'I could just see you in that at work, smothered in chocolate. Although you do wear aprons, so maybe you could get away with it.'

'I'll suggest it to Charlee. She could wear her dress too.'

I glanced across the room towards where Charlee was talking to Uncle Hugh and Aunt Kathryn. She was the only adult bridesmaid, wearing a beautiful pale sage green dress.

'How's it gone so far?' I asked.

'Perfect. Better than I could have imagined.' I followed her adoring gaze across the room to where Dean was talking to a man wearing a morning suit who had to be either his best man or an usher, and two men in smart suits who were presumably regular guests. One of them looked familiar, but I couldn't place him. He was really tall – maybe six foot four or five – with a muscular build and blond hair worn long on top.

'Who's Dean talking to?'

She looked over once more. 'The one in the morning suit is his best man and best mate from school, Gary. The other brunette is Gary's husband Rob, and the blond is Finley, another school friend. Why?'

'Finley looks familiar. What's his surname?'

'It's Finley Scott.'

I shook my head. 'It doesn't ring a bell.'

'Then you'll just have to ask him. He's lovely, by the way. If I hadn't spotted Dean first...' She laughed. 'I'm kidding. But there's no denying he's hot. And completely loved up, I'm afraid.'

'Who's loved up?' Charlee asked joining us.

'Finley.'

'Which one's he?'

'Dean's school friend,' Jodie said. 'The one with blond hair he's talking to now. Tori thinks she recognises him but doesn't know where from.'

We all looked across and the poor man must have been getting a complex because he and Dean both turned to us, questioning expressions on their faces. Jodie sort of rescued the situation by blowing Dean a kiss, as though we'd all been looking at him.

'I can't help,' Charlee said. 'I don't know him.'

My mobile started ringing.

'I'd better go and mingle,' Jodie said. 'Thanks for coming.'

Charlee held up her empty glass and mouthed, 'I'm off to the bar.'

'Where are you?' Leyton snapped as soon as I connected the call. Charming.

'In the function room.'

'I can't see you.'

I turned round and spotted him in the open doorway, about five metres away, and marched over to him.

'You didn't look very hard.' I had red hair and had just been talking to the bride – the most conspicuous person in the room. Not difficult to spot.

'It's dark,' he muttered, snatching the cloakroom ticket from me.

Seeing as he'd stomped off to get his clothes and change, there was only one place for me to go: the bar.

'Have we met before?'

I looked up at Dean's blond friend and smiled. 'Apologies for staring at you earlier. I thought you looked familiar, but I can't place you.'

'Finley Scott,' he said, holding out his hand. 'Friend of the groom since school.'

'Tori Tennyson,' I replied, shaking his hand. 'A more complicated connection for me. The chief bridesmaid, Charlee, is my cousin's wife and the groom is my other cousin's brother-in-law.'

'I think I followed that. Tori, did you say?'

'Yeah. Short for Victoria, but nobody calls me that if they want to come out of the situation alive.'

'I think I may have worked out how we know each other. I have a random request. Can you pull your hair back as though it's in a ponytail?'

'That's very random, but you've been vouched for, so I'll go with it.'

I pulled my styled waves back from my face, bemused when he smiled widely and nodded.

'Got it! We met a couple of weeks ago. I can't remember if we were actually introduced but, if we had been, they'd have told you I was called Bart. I think you had other things on your mind at the time.'

'Oh, my God! You were on the lifeboat. You were the driver.'

'That's right.'

Charlee had hypothermia with no idea where she was, so it was no wonder she hadn't recognised him.

'Small world! Thank you so much for everything you all did that night. I called into the station and spoke to Chief.'

'He passed the message on and we really appreciate that. What are you drinking?'

'A large white wine, but the drinks are on me for saving my life that day.'

We gave our orders to the barman and I dug my purse out of my bag as he poured the drinks.

'You don't need that,' Finley said.

'I insist.'

He laughed – such a warm and gentle sound – as he shook his head. 'It's a free bar, although I would have bought you the drink if it wasn't.'

I clinked my glass against his. 'To saving lives. Cheers.'

'You're very welcome. I'd say any time, but I'm not sure that's appropriate.'

'What's going on?'

My whole body tensed at the clear accusation in Leyton's tone.

'Just getting a drink,' I said, smiling sweetly. 'This is Finley. He was one of the lifeboat crew who rescued us. Finley, this is Leyton.' I couldn't bring myself to add the words 'my boyfriend'.

Finley held out his hand and, to my horror, Leyton blanked him and ordered himself a pint.

'Nice to see you again, Tori,' Finley said. 'Leyton. Have a good evening.'

As he walked away, I wanted the ground to swallow me up whole.

'What was that all about?' I hissed.

Leyton necked back half his pint in one. 'What was all what about?'

'You were rude to Finley.'

'No, I wasn't.'

'Yes, you...' I stopped mid-sentence. He really wasn't worth it.

'Good evening, ladies and gentlemen, boys and girls,'

announced the DJ. 'A very warm welcome to the guests who've just joined us to celebrate Dean and Jodie's wedding day. Your bride and groom are ready for their first dance as husband and wife.'

Dean led Jodie onto the dance floor and kissed her hand before pulling her into his embrace. I turned to Leyton to tell him I was moving closer, but he had his phone pressed to his ear.

'Yes... okay... I'll be about ten minutes.' He hung up and downed the rest of his pint. 'I need to go. I've got to meet the Durlings at the casino.'

'What? Are you coming back?'

'Probably not. I'll see you tomorrow.'

Necking back the rest of my wine, I ordered another, absolutely seething. *I'm really sorry for abandoning you, Tori. Will you be okay on your own?*

I straightened up and walked to the edge of the dance floor to join the other guests watching the happy couple. Yes, I would be okay on my own. Not just tonight but also for the foreseeable future and possibly forever. I'd rather be on my own than with someone who showed me as little respect as Leyton had shown me over the past few weeks. Months. Years.

* * *

It was the best evening do I'd ever been to. The venue was amazing, the buffet delicious, the atmosphere buzzing, and the DJ played back-to-back crowd pleasers. I ate, drank, danced and laughed, but I had the strangest sensation that I was there but not really there – as though I was on the sidelines in a dream, watching the action unfold in front of me.

It was over with Leyton and any lingering doubts had gone running to the casino with him. His attitude towards Finley disgusted me. I'd introduced him to one of the crew who'd saved my life and he didn't even have the decency to shake the man's hand. It showed me how much Leyton had changed. When we met, I'd loved how friendly and approachable he was, able to talk to anyone. Actually, I'd been in awe of it. I'd never have thought he had it in him to be so dismissive of someone.

I was in no rush to leave the wedding, but I needed a little time out away from the noise to think about my Leyton-free future. French doors from the function room opened out onto Pavilion Court where the wedding ceremony had been held earlier. It was a large outdoor area facing the sea with a checked tiled floor and external 'walls' constructed from curved windows which provided stunning panoramic framed views of the coastline. A bandstand situated in the middle of the glass wall hosted musicians, singers and comedians during summer concerts and doubled up as the altar for weddings.

Guests had spilled out of the function room into Pavilion Court. Spotting Uncle Hugh and Aunt Kathryn among them, I knew there was no chance of me settling into a quiet corner without them joining me, so I grabbed my coat from the cloakroom and took the stairs to the roof terrace.

Relieved to see the area deserted, I leaned against the metal railings for a few minutes, looking down onto Pavilion Court, the chatter drifting up to me along with the muted sounds of the disco.

To my left was the curve of South Bay up to the Old Town and the harbour and I could just make out the silhouette of Whitsborough Bay Castle on the headland. Ahead of me was the beach where Charlee, Matt and I had entered the water just under a fortnight ago and nearly hadn't returned. They said that a near-death experience could change your perspective on things. Had that been the catalyst for me to wake up and question my relationship or had the events that followed caused that? Either way, there was no coming back from it. I knew for certain that not only did I not love Leyton anymore, I didn't even like him, and I feared that might have been the case for a long time. The cracks I'd mentioned to Charlee on Thursday night had evolved into gaping crevices.

I whipped round at the sound of footsteps and saw Finley Scott approaching. He stopped dead when he spotted me. 'Sorry, I thought there'd be nobody up here.'

'Great minds,' I said, smiling at him.

He hesitated. 'Do you want me to go?'

I'd come up to the terrace to get away from everyone, but found I wanted Finley to stay.

'No. There's plenty of space for both of us to have a quiet moment.'

The undersides of my arms felt cold from leaning against the railings, so I pulled on my coat, sat on one of the wooden benches, and invited him to sit too.

'I'm glad you're here actually,' I said. 'I need to apologise for Leyton's behaviour earlier. He's not normally like that. He's under a lot of pressure at work at the moment and...' I shook my head. 'I don't know why I'm even defending him. He was rude to you and there are no excuses for it. I'm sorry.'

'It's not your fault.'

'I know, but I was there and...' I shrugged, not sure where I was going with that one other than more undeserved excuses.

'Did I see him leave?' he asked.

'Yeah. About five minutes after he arrived. Turns up late, necks a free drink, then heads off to the casino to meet a client. I knew he was going to be late – found that out ten minutes before the taxi arrived – but I had no idea he was going to abandon me again. He must have known going to the casino was on the cards – no pun intended – so why bother showing up in the first place? What was the point?'

'I wish I could answer that, but I have no idea why some people behave the way they do.'

'Sounds like there's a story there.'

'There is! It's the reason I needed to escape for a bit just now.' He ran his hand through his hair, smiling ruefully. 'You wanted some peace and quiet. You don't need me offloading my woes.'

He stood up, but I didn't feel like I wanted him to leave. He had one of those voices that was so easy to listen to – the sort of deep, velvety tone where I could imagine him reading a car maintenance manual out loud and I'd be hooked.

'We could swap sad stories if you like. I'm a good listener.'

For a moment, Finley looked like he was going to decline, but he shrugged and sat down once more. 'Go on, then. You really want to hear this?'

'I'm all ears.'

'Okay. Nobody knows what I'm about to tell you, but we've been through a near-death experience together, so we've got a bond of trust, yeah? The reason I wanted some space up here was to escape from all the questions and well wishes. My girlfriend Demi is four and a half months pregnant and the baby isn't mine, but everyone thinks he is.'

His whole body seemed to deflate and it had obviously taken a lot for him to make that statement out loud for the first time, which wasn't surprising because it was a whopper.

'Go on...' I encouraged when he fell silent. 'Bond of trust.'

Finley gave me a weak smile. 'Feels weird finally saying it to someone. I'd better go back to the start. In my teens I had a really bad case of mumps and, although it's rare for it to leave men infertile, it turns out I'm a rare breed. When I met Demi four years ago, she already had two children with her ex-boyfriend Damon, and she made it clear that she didn't want any more.'

He looked down at his hands held loosely between his legs. 'It was the perfect opportunity to tell her that was fine by me because I couldn't have kids anyway but, for some reason, I didn't. Looking back, it was stupid of me, but my infertility had been the cause of several relationships ending and I was still stinging from an ex accusing me of not being a *real* man because I couldn't father a child.'

'That's awful!' I cried, incensed for him that somebody could be so cruel about something he'd had no control over.

'It wasn't the greatest experience. Anyway, I told Demi I was happy to be there for India and Roman and wasn't bothered about being a biological dad myself. It was a learning curve for me suddenly having a ready-made family, but the kids were great. They were quite young, so they took it all in their stride. They're nine and seven now.

'I wanted to make us a proper family and asked Demi to marry me several times, but she was a bit jaded by the idea of marriage. Damon had strung her along for years saying they'd get married soon. "Soon" never came.'

'He sounds like a delight,' I said.

'He's an absolute nightmare. Don't get me started on the problems he's caused over the years. He's one of those who doesn't want Demi, but doesn't want anyone else to have her, and he doesn't want joint custody of his children but resents me spending time with them.'

Imagining how exhausting that had to be, my heart went out to him, and to those poor kids for having such an idiot for a father.

'A couple of months ago, I arrived home from work to find the table laid and candles lit. Demi had packed the kids off to her mum's and said she wanted some alone time because she had some news. I'd never seen her so excited. After we'd eaten, she pushed this gift box across the table saying it was a big clue to her news. It was a pair of baby booties.'

I winced. 'Ooh. Not good.'

'Not good at all! I wouldn't say we had the perfect relationship – mainly because of *him*. But when Damon wasn't disrupting things, it was pretty good, and I'd never have believed she'd cheat on me. But what other explanation was there for being pregnant when I was infertile? Unless I wasn't infertile after all. So I acted all surprised and pleased, just in case the tests were wrong, and I booked an appointment with a fertility clinic.'

Finley looked up at me and my heart broke at the obvious pain in his eyes.

'The tests weren't wrong?'

'Conclusive proof that I could *not* father a child.'

I winced again. 'What did you do?'

'Gave her an opportunity to tell the truth, but she didn't take it. Got mad with me for accusing her of being unfaithful so, of course, I had to explain how I knew without a shadow of a doubt that the baby was someone else's. She then went off on one about me lying to her. She was right about that, and that was on me, but I didn't see why I should be the bad guy when she was the one carrying another man's baby.'

'I'm so sorry. What a situation to be in.'

'And we're still in it. When we'd both calmed down, we talked about it and she told me it had been a drunken fumble at her work Christmas party. He'd been her first boyfriend when she was a teenager and the catching up on old times went a bit far. She swore she'd never done anything like that before and could only offer Christmas, nostalgia and too much prosecco as the explanation.'

'Did she know the baby was his when she told you she was pregnant?'

'She'd convinced herself it was mine, and it could have been if I hadn't been infertile. Prosecco had a lot to answer for that night.'

His rueful expression confirmed his meaning and I couldn't

help judging a woman who could have sex with her boyfriend on the same night she'd been with her ex. What sort of person did that?

'If I'm the first person you've told, you're hiding from the well-wishers, and you say you're still in the situation, would I be right in thinking you're still together?'

Finley sighed and nodded. 'She got upset, claimed she loved me and it was a one-off stupid mistake which meant nothing. She said I was already raising two children that weren't mine and doing a brilliant job of it so why not a third? And do you know what? It kind of made sense. So I went with it. We had the scan at the start of last month and I'll admit I got swept away with the excitement of it. When she talked about the baby as though it was mine, I could almost believe it. We told the kids, who loved the idea of a new brother or sister, and we started planning the future as a happy family of five. I kept thinking *I can do this!* Like Demi said, I was already bringing up two children that weren't biologically mine, so what difference did a third make?'

'But it did make a difference, didn't it?' I asked gently.

'How could it not? India and Roman were born before I even knew Demi. They came as a package deal and I knew that and embraced it right from the start. The new baby was the product of a drunken quickie with an ex while she was in a relationship with me. It doesn't matter to me whether it was a one-off mistake or a ten-year affair. At the end of the day, my girlfriend had sex with another man and, if I hadn't been infertile, she'd have been ready to lie to me for the rest of my life. Now that the truth is out there, she has us *both* lying to everyone we know, including her own children. That's a lie of epic proportions. I can't help thinking that my omission about my infertility isn't on the same scale as this.'

'I agree. Two very different things. So what happens now?'

'I have an enormous decision to make. We went for the twenty-week scan last week, which is how I know it's a boy. She wants to discuss names for *our son*, but all I can think is *he's not mine*. Then I hate myself for thinking that. He's completely innocent in all this, but she's guilty and that's what I keep coming back to. So, to bring a very long story back to your original question, what am I hiding from? *How's Demi? How's the baby? Are you excited about being a first-time dad? What do India and Roman think? Are you planning to get married?* I couldn't muster any more fake excitement, so I came up here and have just managed to put a massive downer on your evening by telling you my life story. You were right about being a good listener, though. Thank you.'

We sat in silence for a few moments. Bursts of laughter drifted up from Pavilion Court and I raised my gaze to the white lanterns across the top of the glass wall and the dark sea beyond that. Considering how much turmoil our lives were in right now – especially Finley's – all felt calm with the world. I was still amazed at how much better I'd felt sharing my concerns with Hollie and Charlee. I hadn't opened up to anyone like that since sharing all my secrets with Millicent and Tracie. Millicent had hurt me so badly that I'd never felt able to trust anyone since. Not even Ewan if I was completely honest with myself. And nobody had opened up to me like Finley had done just now either. I really wanted to help him if I could.

'I'm so sorry for what you're going through,' I said eventually. 'I can imagine what a jumbled mess your thoughts must be, especially as this isn't just about you and Demi and the baby. It affects India and Roman too.'

'Tell me about it. I love those kids.'

I thought about Hollie's head-versus-heart advice and how helpful it had been. 'Do you want some advice?'

'I'd love some.'

'Your head is no doubt telling you all sorts of things. You'll feel differently when the baby arrives. Nobody needs to know he isn't yours. You'd better stay together in case Demi stops you from seeing India and Roman.'

'Are you a mind reader?' he asked, smiling at me.

'No. Just someone who's done a lot of thinking recently. All those thoughts you're having are compelling reasons for staying, but what's your heart telling you? Is there any chance you can still have a relationship with Demi knowing what she's done? Can you trust her not to do it again? I know it's hard, but you have to stop the voices in your head and listen to your heart.'

He exhaled as he ran a hand through his hair. 'That's really good advice.'

'I can't claim credit. It's something I heard recently and from a friend of yours, actually – Hollie at The Starfish Café.'

'Starfish said that?' Finley smiled. 'She's such an inspiration. What happened to her family makes my problems seem a bit trivial.'

I had no idea what he meant about Hollie's family, but I wasn't going to probe. I liked her and planned to visit the café again and hopefully make a new friend. If she wanted me to know, she'd tell me herself.

'I'm assuming Demi isn't here tonight?' I asked.

'No. She was coming, but her mum's ill and couldn't have the kids. Does it make me a bad person to say I was relieved?'

'I'd say it makes you human. I felt the same when I thought Leyton wasn't coming tonight and I feel it now that he's gone.'

'Which brings us onto your story. Why do you need to listen to your heart?'

'You can probably guess, having had the pleasure of meeting him earlier...'

I'd no sooner spilled it all out to Finley when Lillie and Elin appeared on the roof terrace.

'Aunt Jodie says you need to come back inside,' Elin announced, grabbing my hand.

I smiled at her. 'Does she now? Did she say why?'

Lillie took my other hand. 'She's going to throw her bouquet and she says all the single ladies have to try to catch it. Come on.'

'And all the men and married ladies have to watch,' Elin told Finley.

'We'll pick up our conversation later,' he said, laughing as the two girls dragged me towards the stairs. There was no point protesting that I wasn't single because, to all intents and purposes, I was. Leyton just didn't know it yet.

'Found her!' Lillie and Elin cried, pushing me onto the dance floor with a crowd of women of various ages, some looking hopeful, others looking mortified to be there.

Jodie, at the end of the dance floor, turned her back on us, but I didn't miss the wink she gave to Charlee first. It was therefore no surprise when the bouquet landed in my hands. Laughing, I thrust it in the air like a trophy while everyone applauded. I caught Finley's eye and shrugged.

'Nice catch!' Charlee said, putting her arm round me. 'You next!'

'I doubt it. I think you'll find that Lillie or Elin have more chance than me of getting married next.'

'The flowers have spoken. Never say never.'

* * *

It was the early hours of the morning before Finley caught up with me again and asked if I wanted to go for a walk so we could finish our conversation in peace. I picked up my bag and Jodie's bouquet from a table and retrieved my coat, pulling it on as we stepped into the cool evening air.

'Not much of a dancer?' I asked as we ambled through the

covered walkway. I'd caught his eye several times while I'd been on the dance floor and he'd smiled, but he hadn't joined us.

'Usually I am, but the last time I was on a dance floor was at my cousin's wedding last summer, before the baby, before the lies. I could vividly picture all four of us and it struck me we might never do that again.'

I lightly touched his arm. 'Aw, Finley, that's so sad. I'm not surprised you didn't feel like dancing.'

'Thank you. Anyway, we came for a walk to talk about you. What's your heart telling you about Leyton?'

'My heart knows it's over and my head has nearly caught up too. I just need to get a few things straight in my mind. My biggest head problem is that I'm struggling to stop thinking of myself as a failure.'

We paused by the steps down to the beach and sat on the wall, facing each other with our backs resting against the stone columns. The tide was in, gently lapping against the wall below us, and the full moon bathed us in gentle light.

'In what way?' Leyton asked. 'A failed relationship doesn't make the person who ends it a failure.'

'I know and, weirdly, I never felt like a failure when my marriage ended. I hadn't personally done anything wrong.'

'And you haven't done anything wrong with Leyton either.'

I sighed. 'Maybe I'm the problem. Maybe my expectations are too high.'

'Hit me with them. What are your expectations from a relationship? I'll tell you if I think they're stratospheric.'

I laughed as he raised his hand high into the air.

'I want a partnership. An equal one built on trust, respect and loyalty. I want to admire my partner and be passionate about the things that are important to him, and to have him feel the same way towards me. Every relationship will have some give and take, but it should be a balance, instead of all take from one and all give from another. I want...' I paused and laughed as I realised what I'd just described. 'I can't believe I'm about to say this. I want what my parents have. Or at least what I thought they had before I...' I shook my head. 'Another story for another time, perhaps.'

I ran my hands through my hair, stunned at the realisation that my parents were my relationship role models. For all their quirks, eccentricities and the challenges they'd caused me over the years – and even after what had happened seven years ago – they were a true partnership. The care, respect, support and passion they showed for each other was second to none, and that was the reason I felt like a failure. I'd seen what an amazing partnership looked like and I hadn't been able to replicate it.

'Those things you've just described,' Finley said, bringing my attention back to the present. 'Those aren't unrealistic expectations. They sound like the blueprint to happiness.'

'You think so?'

He pulled a leg up and rested his elbow against it, gazing out to the sea. 'Here's a scary thought. Demi, as far as I'm aware, has only recently messed up on the trust thing, but all those other things in the blueprint, they've never been there. I thought we were happy, but I've realised that was only because I always gave and she always took, so there wasn't any conflict. I used to love watching *The Simpsons*. It was how I got my RNLI nickname, Bart. She hates it so I haven't watched a single episode since we met. I used to surf on a weekend, but Demi likes to go shopping so that's what we do. The only thing I've clung onto that was me before her is the RNLI, and that's a bone of contention. She's already using the baby as an excuse for me to resign.'

I pulled my knees up and hugged them against my chest, the bridal bouquet dangling from my clasped hands. 'Then you know what you have to do, don't you?'

'I do. And you?'

'I'm ending it tomorrow and, if he won't even give me five minutes of his time, I'll leave a note. I can't keep dragging it out. What's your plan?'

'I'll talk to Demi tomorrow, but I'm not hopeful of it going well.'

'Do you think she'll let you see the kids?'

'I don't know. I'd like to think she'd be reasonable and recognise that keeping us apart would hurt them, but my gut tells me she'll refuse just to hurt me. And, unfortunately, I'll have no legal leg to stand on.'

'I'm sorry.'

We sat for several minutes, just listening to the sound of the waves.

'You probably already know this if you're a surfer,' Finley said, 'but it's a spring tide tonight, which is why the sea's higher than usual. During a spring tide, the moon and the sun are in alignment and I think it's pretty obvious from our chat tonight that Demi and me, and you and Leyton, are anything but aligned. Isn't it weird how you can think everything is good and then suddenly realise that, not only is that not the case, but it hasn't been the case for a long time?'

'Kind of creeps up on you, doesn't it?' I agreed. 'Something else about spring tides, which you probably know too, is they happen on a new or full moon. Tonight there's a full moon – the energetic high point of the lunar cycle. It's said that the light from the moon draws attention to the things in our lives that are giving off negative energy and which we need to deal with, and we're urged to face up to and eliminate them. Spooky timing, eh?'

'Very spooky. Are you into all that stuff about the moon and the zodiac?'

'Not really. I never read my horoscope or anything like that. I'm actually a morning person and love being up and about at dawn, but I'm also a selenophile.'

'A what?'

'Selenophile. Isn't that a gorgeous word? It's someone who loves the moon. I was brought up in the countryside with no properties anywhere near us, so it was incredible for stargazing. I had a telescope and I learned all the constellation names, but my favourite thing in the sky was the moon. I could gaze at her for hours.'

A car horn beeping in the distant suddenly reminded me of the time and I glanced down at my watch.

'We'd better head back. I've got a taxi booked for two.'

'You were right about being a good listener,' Finley said as we walked back towards The Bay Pavilion. 'You've really helped me tonight.'

'And you've helped me too. Good luck with that conversation tomorrow.'

'Thanks. Good luck with moving out, with or without the conversation first.'

We reached the entrance and I felt an overwhelming urge to give him a hug but fought it off.

'I think my taxi's here,' I said, spotting a couple of cars from the company I'd booked. 'It was really good to meet you tonight. See you around.'

'And you. Bye, Tori.'

We smiled inanely at each other for a moment, and I couldn't help noticing how attractive he was with his tie loose, the top button of his shirt open and his hair dishevelled. He saved lives in his spare time, cared passionately about two children as though they were his own, was a great listener, and seemed like an all-round lovely man. Demi had to be mad to have turned elsewhere.

'Right, best be off,' I said. 'Good luck again.' I set off towards the taxis.

'Tori!' he called, running up to me. 'I feel like it was more take and less give from me tonight. If you ever want to redress that balance and talk about what happened with your parents, you can find me in The Lobster Pot most Monday evenings after lifeboat training.'

'Thanks. I might just take you up on that.'

* * *

It was 2.22 a.m. when the taxi dropped me outside Leyton's house. I couldn't think of it as 'home' anymore because it wasn't. Not wanting to disturb him, I removed my shoes by the door, avoided putting any lights on, tip-toed into the kitchen where I slowly filled a vase with water for Jodie's bridal bouquet, and was as quiet as a mouse creeping up the stairs. I needn't have bothered. The bed was empty.

I'd not long settled down to sleep when I heard a key turning in the lock. The door slammed open and there was a clatter like a set of keys being dropped on the floor, followed by several loud curses. The door slammed closed and I lay rigid on my back, listening to him banging about in the kitchen. Such a contrast to how considerate I'd been earlier. Spoke volumes.

How one person could run up one flight of stairs and sound like a stampede was beyond me. He switched the main light on and the glare stung my eyes.

'Leyton!'

'You're back then.'

'About twenty minutes ago and I'm trying to get to sleep. Put the big light out.'

He ignored me. 'Why were you so late?'

'Because I stayed till the end.'

'On your own?'

'I wasn't on my own. I was with friends and family.'

'And that blond geezer.' He sounded like a jealous teenager and, at that moment, my head finally caught up with what my heart had been telling me for some time.

It was late and I only had to glance at him swaying in the doorway, his tie in a low knot and red wine stains on his shirt, to know he was drunk. It wasn't great timing, but was there ever an ideal time to end a relationship?

I pushed back the duvet and pulled on a pair of loose sweatpants over my pyjama shorts. 'You knew you were meeting the Durlings tonight and you used me for a change of clothes, didn't you?'

'So what if I did? You didn't need me there. You were with friends and family.'

No idea why he felt the need to mimic my voice and add air quotes for 'friends and family'.

'Yes, I was,' I snapped. 'I was with people who care about me, which was a refreshing change.' Anger surging through me, I grabbed a hoodie and pulled that on too. 'We both know this isn't working anymore and it hasn't been for a while.'

I paused, giving him the opportunity to protest. There was no way he'd be able to talk me round, but it would have been nice if he'd shown the teeniest bit of effort to challenge me. Instead, he thrust his hands in his trouser pockets and glared at me.

'So I'm going to grab some spare bedding and sleep in Carrie tonight and I'll move my stuff out tomorrow.'

'Suit yourself.' He sounded like a mardy teenager.

'That's it?'

He shrugged. 'What do you want from me?'

I winced at the coldness in his voice.

'You want me to beg you to stay?' He curled up his lip. 'Because that's not my style.'

'No!' I cried, horrified at the thought. 'But after nearly eight years together, I thought you might at least want to talk about it.'

He shrugged off his jacket and tossed it onto the bed, where it slid to the floor.

'What's there to talk about? You've made your mind up and I agree with you. It isn't working, so why prolong the agony?'

Agony? Bit harsh.

'I'm expected at Fenby Heights at nine so you can come back in when I'm gone.' He unfastened his tie as he spoke. 'I'll arrange for a locksmith to meet me here at two, so you'll have five hours to pack your stuff. And *don't* take anything that's mine.'

He narrowed his eyes at me with that final sentence, the hard expression on his face and the stiff business-like manner just like his father.

'I wasn't going to,' I snapped, giving him a harsh look in return.

'Good. And don't forget you have no investment in this place, either.'

'I know. I have the legal document telling me that.'

* * *

Ten minutes later, I lay on the bed in Carrie the campervan on the drive of my ex-home and gazed out of the window at the full moon. Time to get rid of the negative energy? I'd just done that, and it felt amazing.

It had been so different from my break-up with Ewan. I'd been devastated when my marriage ended, but the best word to describe how I felt now that it was finally over with Leyton was elated.

It was strange to think that something that felt so good had arisen from the most traumatic of experiences. If I'd taken Leyton's advice and not gone out paddleboarding that evening, would I have ever woken up to how bad things were between us? I'd never have known Leyton could tell such whopping lies, or felt how little I mattered to him. I'd never have met Hollie or Finley either, who I couldn't help thinking had both come into my life to physically but also metaphorically save me.

I smiled across at Jodie's bridal bouquet which I'd retrieved from the kitchen. I was convinced that Charlee and Jodie had hatched the plan to deliberately throw it to me to make me think of a future without Leyton. Well, now I was about to start a future without him and I didn't feel anxious or worried about being alone. I felt free.

22

HOLLIE

I billowed out a bin bag on Sunday morning and passed it to Jake along with a litter-picker, ready to clean the beach at Starfish Point. Jake had bought a harness for round his waist to which he could attach Pickle's lead, leaving his hands free. I was certain Pickle wouldn't bother the seals, but I needed to set a good example to visitors and not make any exceptions to the dogs-on-leads rule.

'I'll go north and you can go south,' I told him. 'And I've got a challenge for you while you're at it.'

'See who can find the most litter?'

'No. See who can find the entrance to the cave where Tingler's Treasure is hidden.'

He laughed. 'I bet you're only sending me south because you know the cave's at the north end of the beach. I think I should take the north instead.'

I grinned at him. 'But what if it's a double-bluff because I knew that you'd challenge it?'

'But what if you knew that I knew that you knew I'd challenge it? Then where would we be?'

'Very confused!'

We both laughed as we set off in opposite directions.

An hour later, we'd gathered four bin bags full of rubbish – predominantly plastic bottles – and placed them beside the steps.

'Did you find the treasure?' I asked him.

'Not today. You?'

'Oddly enough, not a sniff of it.'

'There's lots of seals on the beach today,' he observed.

'Yeah. More than usual. Some of them will move out to Starfish Arc when the visitors come down.'

It was half nine, so another half hour until Angie as Sunday manager opened the café, although I was surprised we were still the only ones on the beach. It was a mild sunny morning, which usually brought visitors out in droves, coming down to the beach early and rewarding themselves in the café for the climb back to the top.

'I spy some rubbish I've missed.' Jake unclipped Pickle's lead from his waist and passed it to me. 'Back in a minute.'

I shielded my eyes from the sun, watching him crunch across the pebbles and sand towards something blue sticking out from behind one of the boulders. It looked like it could be a jumble of fishing lines.

Jake crouched down for a moment, then waved me over. He had his back to me so I couldn't see anything as Pickle and I approached, but I gasped when he moved aside. A small common seal lay on its side with a mass of netting and fishing lines tangled round its right flipper. I could clearly see the belly so could tell she was a female. She had a beautiful cream coat covered in pale grey spots with a darker grey band across her head like an Alice band.

'There's blood,' Jake said.

I moved round him and grimaced at the streaks of red blood across the pale fur.

'I don't like the way she's holding her flipper,' I said. 'I think it might be broken.'

Her dark eyes seemed so mournful, as though begging us to help her.

'I'll call it in.'

We were lucky to have the Sea Rescue Sanctuary at the far tip of North Bay who specialised in rescuing and rehabilitating sea creatures, some of whom stayed permanently in the facility if their injuries or rescue circumstances meant they'd be unable to survive in the wild after treatment.

'Hi, Mitch,' I said. 'It's Hollie. Any chance of a rescue from Starfish Point?'

'What have you got?'

'A female common seal tangled in some fishing nets. The rope has cut into her right flipper, and I think it might be broken from the way she's holding it. We're on the beach with her now. She's calm and lying on her left side, so we haven't touched her.'

'Okay. Sea's calm here. How's it looking at Starfish Point?'

'Calm here too. The seal's only about a metre from the shore but the tide's going out.'

'We're on our way. If she tries to move into the sea, head her off, otherwise just stay on guard without touching her.'

I relayed what he'd said back to Jake. 'He'll need to gather a team so it could be anything from forty minutes to an hour if you want to take Pickle home and get your camera.'

'You don't mind me taking photos?'

'No, and neither would Mitch. It's a great way to spread the message about what to do if a member of the public finds a seal in this state, and it can raise some donations for them too.'

As he headed off, I knelt in the sand near the seal.

'It'll be all right,' I said gently. 'Help's on its way and we'll have you all fixed up soon. How about a name for you? I'm thinking Alice because of your Alice band. You like that? Good girl.'

I wished I could stroke her, but it was an absolute no-no. It was essential to keep human contact to an absolute minimum, restricted only to the actual rescue and medical attention.

* * *

'Three humans and one seal rescued in the space of a fortnight,' Jake said as we settled into a booth in The Starfish Café a couple of hours later with large cappuccinos. 'You're racking up the saves.'

'So are you! I'm so glad you spotted that bit of litter.'

'Me too. Alice must have just hauled herself out the sea because she definitely wasn't there before.'

Jake scrolled through the photos on the screen on the back of his camera. 'I've got some great shots.'

'We'll wait to hear from Mitch as to whether her flipper is broken and then we'll share a post about it.'

'You were so calm earlier,' he said, smiling at me.

'Alice was a great patient today. She must have been terrified, but it was like she knew we were there to help and didn't put up too much of a fight.'

The approach to beach rescues was to get the stretcher ready then lay a towel over the seal's head, covering their eyes, as soon as possible. Not being able to see what was going on round them took some of the stress out of the situation while they were lifted onto the stretcher and transported into the dinghy. There'd been a couple of moments when Alice had tried to get away but, as soon as the towel was placed over her, she relaxed.

'What will happen if her flipper is broken?' Jake asked.

'They'll keep her at the sanctuary until it heals. Everything depends on how badly broken it is and where, but their work is all about minimal human intervention and getting the seal back into the wild. Hopefully they'll be able to return her to the beach here. We're so lucky to have the Sea Rescue Sanctuary so close. I can relax now, knowing Alice is with the experts.'

Jake took my hand and ran his thumb over mine. 'Pickle and I think you're amazing and we love how much you care about everyone and everything.'

'Thank you. We think you're amazing too, although you're useless at treasure hunting. Can't believe you didn't find any on the beach this morning.'

He laughed. 'I'll admit I ran my hands along the cliff face a few times and pressed a few stones but didn't find anywhere that could be a cave entrance or a secret passage. Shame.'

'You sound like Isaac. One of his many theories was that the cliff face was one of those optical illusions where the rocks look solid, but there's really a passage. I dread to think how many hours he spent running his hands along them, half-expecting to find some hidden entry point.'

Jake jumped up and took a few paces away from the table before stamping his foot on the floor. 'This is it! It's buried right here.'

I rolled my eyes at him. 'I guarantee you, there is *nothing* buried under the café and there are no hidden caves anywhere on the beach. Tingler's Treasure is a legend. End of.'

* * *

Later that afternoon, we were relaxing on the sofa in front of a film when Mitch called with the great news that Alice's flipper wasn't broken but some of the wounds were infected, so they would need to keep her in for treatment. And she was pregnant.

'I've never seen a baby seal,' Jake said, after I'd relayed the conversation.

'They're adorable. You're in for such a treat when they start arriving, although the grey seal pups which arrive in November are even cuter because they have white fluffy coats. It's fascinating watching the mums with their pups. They're so caring and attentive.'

'I bet you'd be a really caring and attentive mum,' Jake said, his voice husky as he weaved his fingers between mine.

Butterflies fluttered in my stomach. It had all moved very fast between us, so we'd not actually had a conversation about starting a family. Jake hadn't declared that he didn't want children, but he'd never categorically said he did either.

'We should probably talk about that,' I said. 'How do you feel about having children?'

'Until I met you, it wasn't even on my radar. I avoided relationships so I expected eternal bachelorhood, as Irene would call it. And that meant no children.'

Irene had lived in Seafarer Lodge next door to Lighthouse View all of Jake's life and had been good friends with his nanna and a great support to Jake. She'd moved into Bay View Care Home just before Christmas and we regularly visited together or separately, depending on how Jake's shifts fell.

'And now?'

'And now everything's different. I've found the person I want to be with forever and that changes things. Moving in together is a huge step, but it didn't feel that way because it's with you. Marriage and children are huge steps too, but they feel like steps I want to make thanks to you. But only if that's what you want.'

'I'd always wanted children but, like you, I'd given up on that ever happening. I would still like children, but if you didn't want a family or we both wanted one and it didn't happen, I'd accept that because I'd got used to the idea of a future without being a mum.'

'So we've agreed we'd both like a family?' Jake asked.

'I think we have. How soon?'

'I'd love to say let's have five years together first, but I'm conscious we're both thirty-five...'

'I know!' I grimaced. 'Tick tock.'

'Would you want to get married first?'

'Is that a proposal?'

Jake laughed. 'It's an expression of intention. When I propose – and I *will* do that – it'll be something special, not a Sunday afternoon conversation on the sofa.'

'I don't mind.'

He shook his head. 'You deserve better. Besides, you told me how disappointed you were with how Craig proposed. The bar hasn't been set very high, but I can definitely do better than that.'

It had been disappointing – a completely unromantic suggestion in the pub that, because we'd hit our two-year anniversary, we might as well make it official, followed by the presentation of an ostentatious engagement ring.

'Thank you. I'll look forward to that happening. As for wedding or babies first, I don't have a strong opinion on it either way. Maybe we should leave it up to nature and see what happens. If I happened to fall pregnant this afternoon, so be it.'

'That would mean...'

I was already up and heading towards the door. 'Yes, it would!'

23

TORI

I stood beside Carrie at lunchtime on Sunday and sighed. Same set of three suitcases from when I'd moved out of Ewan's house nine years ago. Same bags. Different house, different ex, different vehicle. And different feeling. That sense of relief was still there and the only thing that stopped me from leaping in the air and whooping was what I needed to do next. Something I should have done many years ago.

The jangle of keys as they hit the tiled floor in the hall was satisfying, like the clang of a bell signalling the end of a difficult relationship.

I made a final check on the bungee cords securing my paddleboard and surfboards to Carrie's roof then clambered into the driver's seat and pulled off the drive for the last time. Another new chapter.

The urge to drive to the seafront and go surfing was strong, but I couldn't procrastinate any longer. It was time to visit Redamancy Castle. I'd thought about phoning first but what would I say? *Hi, it's me, long time no speak. Will you be in just after lunch if I stop by for a cuppa?* Easier to turn up and face the music.

The RNLI rescue had made me challenge my relationship with Leyton, but it was also making me challenge my relationship with my parents – or lack of it. Lying awake last night, staring at the moon, thoughts had whirred round my mind. What if we hadn't been rescued? What if a couple of police officers had turned up at Redamancy Castle to give my parents the news that I'd drowned? How would they have felt, knowing that my last words to them were hostile and that we'd never had the chance to make amends? Would they blame me for that, or would they be consumed by guilt? Perhaps they were already riddled with guilt. I had no idea.

I'd thought about what I'd said to Charlee about wasting the past eight years and realised it didn't just apply to my relationship with Leyton; it applied to Mother and Father, too. I'd always thought we had time and we'd speak again eventually, but what if we didn't? What if I'd been the one who'd had the unexpected visit or phone call with bad news? They were both seventy-four now and, while they hopefully still had a couple of decades ahead of them, none of us came with a long-life guarantee. I had no idea whether they had any health problems. How could I when I wasn't in touch with them or my sister?

They'd tried to get in touch for the first six months or so after I stormed out. They'd phoned, written, and even turned up at Leyton's house, but I'd refused to see them. I'd never dreamed that, just like my two best friends from school and my ex-husband, they'd hurt me by their lies and deception.

My stomach clenched with nerves as I drove out of Whitsborough Bay and headed into the Yorkshire countryside, ever closer to my childhood home.

After the Domino Blaize episode when I was thirteen, my relationship with my parents rapidly deteriorated and I was back to being friendless and bullied. I repeatedly asked my parents if I could change school and it was always a no. Whitsborough Bay wasn't that big and, if all the students at Whitsborough West knew about my parents' identities and Victorian lifestyle, the students at other schools would too.

I threw myself into my studies, determined to secure an education that would enable me to get away and stay away. Riding and surfing helped release my frustrations but, otherwise, I spent the rest of school and sixth form in my suite, barely speaking to my parents, ignoring my little sister. It seemed like my only friend was the moon. Every night, I sought her out and shared my hopes for the future as well as my woes. She felt like the only constant, reliable thing in my life.

I left home right at the start of the summer, shortly after my eighteenth birthday, having secured a seasonal job in a museum in Bath. My parents never seemed bothered that I'd be living so far away from home, although they barely seemed to notice my presence when I was there, so why would my absence affect them?

Academically, I found university a breeze. Socially, I struggled. I'd spent so many years on my own that I had no idea how to make friends. Afraid of being hurt again, I found it difficult to let anyone in, so it was only during my internship where everyone was older and the focus was on work rather than relationships that I found my place. And the love of my life.

I stayed in touch with my parents, mainly by email, but they never visited me in Bath. They didn't even attend my graduation ceremony, which hurt. Weren't they proud of me? Didn't they care?

It was exhausting hearing the same excuses that had been reeled out throughout my whole life – impending deadlines and big commitments – so I stopped asking them. That way, they couldn't keep disappointing me.

Ewan and I visited Redamancy Castle twice, the first time shortly after we'd moved in together when we were at a friend's wedding in the area. The second time was eighteen months later and it was a disaster.

I wanted them to know we'd eloped. They were definitely surprised but I had no idea if they were hurt. We hadn't done it to hurt anyone – it was what we'd both wanted – and it was a route they'd gone down themselves, so I thought they'd understand. They'd both had difficult relationships with their own parents and had married in secret when they were nineteen.

I don't know what had possessed me to do something so spontaneous but they'd both turned sixty that same year and I'd decided it was a milestone to be celebrated alongside our marriage. I booked a restaurant and invited Uncle Hugh and the family and some of my parents' friends... and had to cancel the lot. Edits going badly, no time to spare. Never any time to spare for me.

When I'd returned home with my tail between my legs after it ended with Ewan, I was touched by how concerned they were. I even got the impression that, with Robyn away at university, they were grateful for the company. For the first time ever, they made time for me, walking round the grounds, accompanying me on rides and encouraging me to talk about what had happened with Ewan and my plans for the future. I didn't feel ready to open up to anyone – least of all the two people who'd never listened to me before – so conversations were superficial, but at least we were talking.

Where they really made a difference was in helping me establish myself as a freelance architect, using their local network and recommending me to their friends and contacts. It was thanks to them that I had an epiphany about the future. Interior design had never been part of the plan, but they'd recommended me to a friend called Giles Tilley who wanted to expand his restaurant in a village called Little Fraisby. We'd agreed to a discounted plan in return for me using the extension as a showcase to help establish my business in the area.

The Country Tavern, a Grade II listed coaching house, was stunning but I felt the dated décor let it down. Giles had made a throwaway comment about his clientele predominantly being elderly regulars or visitors to the area who stumbled across the tavern. That didn't strike me as a future-proof strategy and, while I was designing the extension, I couldn't stop thinking about how much better The Country Tavern could be, attracting new customers by bringing it into the modern world while still retaining the period charm.

I didn't know Giles well enough to know if he'd appreciate my meddling or the feedback that his décor needed a rethink, but I had to try. I was convinced that showing him designs on a laptop wouldn't cut it. I invested in an easel and a huge grey artist's portfolio and created my designs on boards. I positioned the easel at the entrance to the restaurant and unveiled the first board.

A first-class degree, distinction in my Master's, professional awards and glowing client feedback confirmed I was an excellent architect and I'd only ever felt the slightest flutter of nerves when presenting a client proposal. But did that validate me as an interior designer? My legs shook as I stood beside Giles that day, terrified I might have offended him and taken advantage of the kindness my parents had extended by setting up the opportunity.

Giles didn't speak for several minutes. He stepped back from the easel and studied my face, his expression unreadable.

'This isn't what I asked for,' he said eventually, and my stomach sank. 'We agreed you could submit your plans for the extension and I'd pay a reduced fee.'

My stomach sank even further and I forced myself to stand straight and maintain eye contact. Trust me to run before I could walk.

'I wasn't sure when Vivienne and Ralph recommended you. Mixing friendships with business can be awkward, but they sung your praises so highly that I decided to make an exception.'

I prepared to thank him for his time and pack away my work, but he surprised me by thrusting out his hand and shaking mine.

'I'm so glad I did. This is exceptional work, Tori. Your parents were right about you. You *do* have a gift. So I will pay you in full and my only question is: when can you start?'

I wasn't sure what shocked me most – securing the work, being paid in full, or that my parents thought I had a gift. They'd always seemed so wrapped up in their own little world that I didn't think they'd even taken any notice of my designs or accolades.

So Tennyson Designs was established. I'd continued my professional development as a practicing architect but, where I could, I leaned more towards interiors. It didn't pay as well but it gave me far more satisfaction. I often worked collaboratively with Uncle Hugh, Matt and Tim who had a construction business and all specialised in different trades. I hadn't realised quite how much I'd missed my cousins until I'd moved back home, and it was a joy to be able to work alongside them.

* * *

I pulled up outside Redamancy Castle beside a smart silver Audi displaying a sticker for a vehicle hire company in the back window. I still had no idea what I was going to say to them. One thing for sure was that I wasn't going to ask if I could stay. It would be rude and unfair to have repeatedly spurned their attempts to reach out to me, then expect a welcome home and a roof over my head just because another long-term relationship had ended.

Did I want to apologise or hear their apology? Did I want to address our problematic past or draw a line in the sand and focus on the future? All I knew was that the full moon symbolised a time to face up to and dispel the negative energy. I had a phenomenal amount of latent negative energy about the situation with my parents and it was finally time to address it because it was taking up way more head space than my split with Leyton.

I exited Carrie, looked round me, and took several deep lungsful of fresh country air. Being here always made me feel conflicted because, among the bad memories, there were so many that were good. Except that last one – the one that had driven the wedge between us and sent me running. If it hadn't been for that, would I ever have moved in with Leyton? Had I really fallen for him or had he been convenient when my life was in a mess?

I glanced at the hire car again. A reunion with my parents after so long wasn't going to be easy and I didn't want to play it out in front of a visitor, so I pulled on my coat and set off walking down the drive towards the stables.

The familiar scent of ammonia hit me, mingled with hay and manure, and instantly transported me back to happy days from my youth, mucking out the stables with Phipps, grooming the horses, and riding. Galloping across the fields gave me a similar buzz to surfing. I hadn't ridden since walking out and I'd missed it.

A stallion with a gleaming chestnut coat and a diamond of white on its forehead whinnied and I slowly reached out my hand and stroked it.

'Hello, there. You're a beauty, aren't you?'

There were four horses in the stables, none of them familiar, but seven years had passed and a lot would have changed during that time.

'Can I help you, miss?'

I jumped at the man's voice. He looked about a decade older than me and was wearing an estate fleece so presumably he worked here.

'I'm Tori Tennyson. Victoria. I'm Vivienne and Ralph's daughter.'

He glanced towards a gallery of photos on the wall, which showed me in the saddle of various ponies during my youth.

'You haven't changed much,' he said.

'I hope I've grown taller.'

He laughed and strode towards me, hand outstretched.

'Great to finally meet you, Miss Victoria.'

'Please call me Tori. And you are?'

'Charlie Bovis, estate manager.'

'What happened to Phipps?'

'Retired.'

'Oh! I didn't know.' Although why would I? 'When did he retire?'

'About seven years back, I think. Maybe eight.'

My stomach churned at the timings. I wonder if he had really retired or whether he'd been pushed. Had I caused a good man to lose his job and his home?

'It's all change here,' I declared brightly, not wanting to go down that path. 'I don't know any of the horses anymore.'

'That's Apollo,' he said, nodding towards the chestnut stallion. 'He's your father's. Your mother alternates between Stardust, the grey mare at the back, and Tango, the black one. Jazz belongs to a friend of theirs.'

'They're all gorgeous.'

'Aye, they are that. If that's everything, I'll be getting on.'

'Thank you. Oh, I don't suppose you know whose hire car that is outside the house?'

'Yes, it's—'

'It's mine,' a woman said, her voice strong and confident.

I peered past Charlie at a young woman standing in the entrance with her hands planted on her hips. She wore a red jumper dress over tan boots, with long blonde hair tied in a side fishtail plait. The last time I'd seen her, she'd only been fourteen.

'Robyn?'

'Oh! So you've remembered who I am, have you? It's only our parents you seem to have forgotten.'

Looking embarrassed, Charlie made a swift exit, nodding to Robyn as he passed.

'That's not fair!' I protested.

'Really? When was the last time you visited or even spoke to them? Last month? Last year? Year before?' Her voice was dripping with sarcasm and it was obvious she knew the answer.

'That's rich! You moved to the other side of the world to get away from them.'

'But at least I stayed in touch. You only turn up when you want something, like a place to stay or some business contacts. I spotted the cases in your camper. Split up with the boyfriend? Again.'

I lowered my head, stung by the truth in her words. I'd accused Mother and Father of being terrible parents, but my behaviour had been pretty deplorable, especially after they'd supported my education, helped me establish my business and provided me with a home.

'They knew where to get hold of me if they needed me.' My voice lacked conviction. They'd tried and I'd ignored them.

She looked me up and down, her lip curled in disgust. 'They don't want to see you, so you've had a wasted trip.'

'I only want ten minutes of their time.'

'Why should they give you ten seconds when you've blanked them for seven years?'

'You don't understand. You don't know what happened back then.'

'Of course I do! You came crawling back from Bath and, as soon as things didn't go your way, you had a massive strop and stormed out.'

'You don't know what you're talking about.'

'I think you'll find I do! It's how it's always been with you, Tori. You think the world revolves round you and you can't bear it when you're not the centre of attention or things don't go the way you want them to. Look at us! You've always resented me, right from when I was a baby.'

'That's not true!'

'Oh, purlease! Have you heard yourself? You hated that I was ill and Mother and Father's focus had to be on me.'

'That wasn't how it was. I hated that I had to go to boarding school. It wasn't about you.'

She glared at me, shaking her head. 'You ignored me my whole life, just like you've ignored our parents for the past seven years. Now the tables have turned, so you can take your campervan and your failed relationship or business or whatever it is that's made you turn up here, and go and bother somebody else. Because nobody here cares.'

And with that parting shot, she stomped across the yard and out of sight. I sank back against the stable door, feeling quite shaky. Apollo nudged my head and I stroked his muzzle, drawing comfort from the softness.

'What the bloody hell was that all about?' I whispered to him. Robyn and I had never been close, but it hadn't been anything to do with her illness as a baby. It had simply been down to an eleven-year age difference, meaning we were at very different life stages growing up. I'd left home when she was seven. Perhaps I should have made more of an effort and I could see now why a lack of big sister's interest could have hurt a little girl. But that stuff about needing to be the centre of attention? That wasn't true. Was it?

24

HOLLIE

'We could have just made a baby,' I said to Jake as I lay against his bare chest. 'Does that blow your mind?'

He made a noise like an explosion as he stroked my hair back from my face.

'You won't get upset if it doesn't happen for us quickly?' he said. 'Or even at all?'

'If losing my family has taught me anything, it's to live in the moment. Right here, right now with you, I'm happier than I've ever been. If this is how it remains with just the two of us and Pickle, I'll still be incredibly happy. You can waste so much time worrying about the future that you don't enjoy the here and now.'

He drew me into a gentle kiss, which soon intensified. But his pager sounded.

'I'm so sorry.' He stroked my cheek then sighed as he pulled back the duvet.

I jumped out of bed and ran along the landing, retrieving his clothes that we'd discarded en route to the bedroom earlier.

'I'll grab your bike,' I said, pulling on my dressing gown and running downstairs to fetch it from the workshop.

'Stay safe,' I called as he cycled down the drive. 'Call me later if you want picking up.'

Standing on the edge of the drive, with Pickle by my feet, I watched until he disappeared from view.

'You know what's weird,' I told Pickle as we went back inside. 'I wish I was going with him. That's a turnaround, isn't it?'

I'd still felt that flicker of nerves and fear when his pager buzzed, but it had been swiftly replaced by a rush of excitement. I'd wanted to pull on my clothes and race down to the lifeboat station with him. I never in a million years imagined I'd feel that way.

I warmed up a pan of milk, made myself a hot chocolate and took it over to the sofa in the snug area at the end of the kitchen. Pickle curled up beside me as I blew on my drink, my thoughts wandering. There was still a knot of anxiety in my stomach around Jake's safety, but it was surrounded by excitable butterflies as questions raced through my mind: *What's happened? Who's in danger? Where? What skills will the rescue require?*

Chief had taken us out on the ILB again on Monday night and we'd picked up from where we'd stopped the previous week to rescue Tori, Matt and Charlee. Towards the end of the session, Bart steered us into the harbour to complete the final part of that lesson – hauling a casualty into the boat.

'We're in the harbour as I want to do this in a safe, controlled environment and so that young Mouse here can get straight in the shower afterwards.'

We discussed different methods, then Jake slipped over the side into the water.

'Quick demo from Bart and me,' Chief said, 'then he's all yours.'

Although it couldn't beat the adrenaline rush from the real-life rescue, it was pretty close. Jake made it feel so realistic by demonstrating different behaviours we might encounter, ranging from a calm casualty who needed little assistance to get on board to a terrified one who was shouting and flailing. It brought home to me how important people skills were in remaining calm and reassuring throughout the rescue, but it also made me reflect on Isaac and Dad's final rescue when they'd encountered drunk, violent casualties. They'd done everything right when they'd boarded the stricken vessel that day, but they'd been battling a storm, a fire, and unpredictable human behaviour. Occasionally – and thankfully rarely – things could go wrong.

I finished my drink and my gaze fell on the paint colour charts I'd picked up during the week so we could plan our refurbishment of the top floor.

'Might as well keep ourselves occupied while he's out,' I told Pickle, gathering them up.

He followed me upstairs and into my former bedroom at the back of the house which had become a dumping ground. In a feeble attempt to keep myself distracted the Christmas after Mum died, I'd decided to clear the attic and had carried down about half the boxes stored up there. Nothing was labelled so I had no idea what I'd find. I'd opened the first box and discovered it was full of mine and Isaac's childhood toys and the tears started. The next one was full of mementoes from my parents' wedding day and the tears intensified. The boxes had remained untouched ever since.

I held up different pages from the first colour chart against the wall, hoping something would pop, and sighed when it didn't.

Pickle looked up at me, his head cocked to one side, and I couldn't resist picking him up for a cuddle. My heart warmed as I gazed round the room, picturing how it used to look when I was a little girl. If Jake and I had a girl, would this be her room too? It was weird to think that we'd already started that process. It was possible that, right now, I was in the earliest stages of pregnancy. A thrill of excitement ran through me.

'Mustn't think like that,' I muttered to myself. 'As I said to Jake, what will be will be.'

Carrying Pickle, I wandered into Isaac's old bedroom at the front of the house. When Angie, Martin, Katie and her boyfriend Trey helped me clear and re-decorate my parents' room and relocate mine four months after Mum died, we'd also tackled Isaac's. I hadn't known what to do with it, so I'd kept the furniture and gone for a neutral warm cream paint.

The wall opposite the window was still covered in cork tiles. We probably should have removed them but I'd been worried about pulling the plaster off. Darker shapes on the cork showed where my brother had pinned things for the longest. Pickle started to wriggle so I put him down and ran my fingers across the tiles, feeling the indentations where pushpins had punctured the cork. I could visualise it full of maps, photos and newspaper articles connected by string. Colourful Post-it notes had posed questions in Isaac's neat capitals and if I concentrated hard, I could smell Sharpies from when he'd been on a questioning frenzy.

'Do you think Jake could be right about Smythe being after Tingler's Treasure?' I asked Pickle. 'I know he was joking, but it does make you wonder.'

Pickle glanced up at me then continued his exploration under Isaac's bed, scratching at something.

'What have you found?' I knelt on the floor and peered under the bed.

'It's just crates,' I told him, but his tail kept wagging as he scratched at the floor with one paw. 'Okay. I hear you. I'll look behind them.'

I pulled out a couple of plastic crates and spotted an old blue tugger toy of Willow's.

'Is this what you're after?' I held it up in front of him and he bounced about excitedly so I sat cross-legged on the floor and played a few rounds of tug with him.

When he lost interest, I adjusted position to shove the crates back under the bed but stopped and stared at them, chewing my lip thoughtfully. The two I'd pulled out contained the contents from Isaac's noticeboard. When we'd cleared my brother's room, it had felt wrong to dispose of so much dedicated research, especially when it also belonged to Kyle. I'd planned to pass it on but, in the same way that I hadn't been able to deal with Bex's grief at the loss of my brother on top of my own, I hadn't been able to face Kyle's. He'd repeatedly rung and left messages begging me to get in touch, but I'd ignored them.

I removed the lid from the crate nearest to me and rifled through the contents before looking towards the noticeboard and experiencing the same surge of excitement I'd felt each time Isaac and Kyle had rushed into my room, faces aglow, telling me they had a new lead. Should I? I'd snapped several photos before taking it down so that Kyle wouldn't have to start from scratch when I got round to handing it over. Since we'd reconnected, he hadn't asked about it and it hadn't crossed my mind to ask him if he wanted it.

I scrolled way back through the photos on my phone and found the ones of The Smuggler's Key. The map of Starfish Point – resting on the top of the pile of papers – had been the central piece. I lifted it out and reached for the tub of pushpins slotted down the side. Maybe I'd pin the map up, just for fun, and then text Kyle to see if he wanted the crates.

* * *

Two hours later, I rubbed my stiff shoulders and stepped back from the cork tiles, a sense of achievement making me smile. I made a final check against the photos on my phone and nodded. I'd done it! I'd recreated The Smuggler's Key.

I sat down beside Pickle who'd curled up for a nap, a warm feeling of nostalgia hugging me as I gazed at the board. I could vividly picture my brother pacing up and down in front of it, muttering to himself. Occasionally he'd stop and scribble something on a Post-it note or grab one of his reference texts. I'd often sat cross-legged on his bed, rapt by his latest piece of evidence or a new theory. If Kyle was with him, they'd be like a pair of detectives dramatically presenting their findings.

I glanced down at the Sharpie pens and Post-it notes – the only items left in one of the crates. I had three new questions which I scribbled down on a Post-it note each and added to the board:

WHY DOES SMYTHE WANT THE CAFÉ SO BADLY?
DOES TINGER'S TREASURE REALLY EXIST?
DOES SMYTHE KNOW WHERE THE TREASURE IS?

Seeing them written down, I chuckled to myself. The idea that a phenomenally successful and powerful businessman like Sebastian Smythe was willing to pay over the odds for The Starfish Café because he was hunting for some long-lost potentially fictional treasure was absurd. Far more likely to be the more plausible explanation that his pride was wounded and he wasn't used to anyone saying no.

Oh well, it had been an enjoyable trip down Memory Lane recreating The Smuggler's Key. I'd show it to Jake when he got home and we could leave it up for a bit, but then I'd ask Kyle if he wanted it, although Bex probably wouldn't thank me for getting him hooked on that again.

'How about we go for a walk, Pickle?' He leapt off the bed,

wagging his tail. 'I need a stretch after putting that together. Then hopefully Jake will be back.'

* * *

Pickle and I walked along the esplanade. It was Easter Sunday and the weather was warm and bright, so Sea Cliff was busy. There was a lengthy queue at the ice cream van. As kids, Isaac and I loved having an ice cream van parked so close to the house and were always gutted when the season ended and it stopped coming.

There were only buildings on one side of Sea Cliff, the road which ran parallel to the wide esplanade. Mum and I had loved speculating about the families who'd lived in the grand houses in the Victorian era when Whitsborough Bay secured its place on the map as a spa town and a must-visit for anyone with money.

Pickle and I paused on the grassy area by the wooden rowing boat. I couldn't imagine ever growing tired of that view. I loved how I saw something different each time depending on the light, the weather, the season.

My eyes scanned across the sea. 'What sort of rescue do you think it is?' I asked Pickle, but he was too busy sniffing out scents on the grass.

I was sure I'd heard the air sea rescue helicopter earlier. The sea looked calm, although that didn't mean it wasn't full of dangers, but bank holiday weekends – particularly warm ones like this one – attracted tourists in their droves and there were often call-outs to walkers or their dogs who'd got too close to cliff edges and taken a tumble, or to visitors unfamiliar with the tides who'd wandered too far along a cove and got trapped by the rising tide. Mind you, locals did that too on plenty of occasions.

My phone buzzed in my pocket with a text. I thought it might be Jake but I didn't recognise the number.

✉ From Unknown
Did you like your flowers? The offer's still on
the table

I shuddered. Urgh! Slippy Smythe. Or should it be Slimy Smythe? Smarmy? Any of them worked for him.

My mobile number was on our Facebook site for enquiries about functions but I didn't appreciate him using it. I'd have to block him if he kept pestering me on it. I bet he was seething that a whole week had passed and I hadn't been in touch.

I thought about the conversations with Jake about Tingler's Treasure and smiled to myself as I saved the number under 'Abe Tingler'.

✉ To Abe Tingler
Thank you for the flowers last Sunday but there
was no need to go to that trouble. My decision
still stands and nothing will make me change
my mind

I half expected some reiteration of everyone having a price or a comment that I would change my mind but my phone remained silent while we were out.

I was unclipping Pickle's lead in the kitchen when another text arrived.

✉ From Abe Tingler
I am willing to increase my offer by £5k but
that's it. Absolute final offer. I urge you to
think very seriously about this, Ms Brooks. You
are an intelligent businesswoman and, with that
sort of money, you could open a chain of cafés

```
and build your own empire in Whitsborough Bay.
Let me know by 8pm tomorrow night after which
this exceedingly generous offer expires and will
never be on the table again
```

'Ooh, that man! What part of "not interested" doesn't he understand?' I ground my teeth as I typed in my response.

```
⊠ To Abe Tingler
I can tell you my answer right now and it's the
same as it has always been. Thank you but no
thank you
```

```
⊠ From Abe Tingler
I suggest you start thinking with your head
instead of your heart
```

I started typing in a *who the hell do you think you are?* message but stopped halfway, deleted it, and switched my phone to silent. I wasn't in his good books but there was no benefit to making an enemy of him.

'I can't believe he added another five grand to his offer,' I said to Pickle as he lapped up his water. 'It really feels like he knows something we don't.'

But what could it be? I still wasn't buying the Tingler's Treasure theory.

25

TORI

I clambered back into Carrie and started the engine, feeling the intensity of Robyn's angry stare the whole time. She kept her arms crossed and had a face like thunder.

'Well, that went well,' I muttered to myself as I pulled away.

I'd had no idea Robyn hated me so much. I'd objected to being a boarder at Whitsborough West, but I'd never blamed or resented her for it. When she'd had her diagnosis, I'd even asked to come home so I could help. By the time she was fully recovered – and it took a second surgical procedure to get to that point – I was in the Red Hair Gang and busy with my friends. When that fell apart, I was angry with my parents – not Robyn – but perhaps I was tunnel-visioned. All I wanted to do was study hard and get out of there where nobody knew me and nobody would quote passages of pornography penned by Domino Blaize.

I steered Carrie towards the coast and paused by the turning to Kellerby Cliffs Holiday Park near Fellingthorpe. It was Easter Sunday. The chance of them – or any of the other holiday parks in the area – having a pitch available was slim, but it was worth a try.

Where else could I go? I didn't want to drag Uncle Hugh into it and I had no close friends. I really needed to change that.

'It's a long shot,' I said to the receptionist, 'but I've found myself unexpectedly homeless. I don't suppose you have a pitch for a small campervan for tonight?'

'Sorry, but we're fully booked with it being Easter.'

Her tone was kind, but I could tell she was thinking I was stupid for asking.

'Thanks anyway. How's it looking for the rest of the week?'

'Nothing until after the school holidays.'

'Could I maybe book in for a week then?' I was going to need to look for somewhere to rent, but it could be weeks before I could move in. 'Actually, can you make that a fortnight?'

An older man who'd been standing nearby flicking through some paperwork stepped forward.

'Did you say a small campervan?'

'Yeah, it's just a vintage VW.'

'I'm Chris, the Duty Manager. If you don't mind being near the road and a bit of a traipse to the shower block, I can let you have a pitch for this week only in one of our old fields. It would be discounted, of course, and then I'd need you to move onto the main site at the normal fee next Sunday evening.'

'That would be perfect, thank you.'

He gave me a sympathetic smile, evidently picking up on the relief in my voice.

'Mindy will get you booked in. Welcome to Kellerby Cliffs.'

After taking my details and payment, Mindy showed me on a colourful map how to get to the pitch. My stomach rumbled loudly as I walked back to Carrie, reminding me that I hadn't eaten all day. There was a mini market next to the reception building, so I headed back to that.

Half an hour later, I tucked into a ham salad bun and gazed out of the window at the passing traffic. As I finished eating, a few droplets of rain intensified into a full-on downpour and I pulled on a hoodie, shivering.

My phone buzzed with a text:

✉ From Leyton
Locks are changed. I'll text you if I come across anything else of yours. When are you planning on returning the spare bedding?

✉ To Leyton
Never

✉ From Leyton
But it belongs to me

✉ To Leyton
So call the police and have me arrested for stealing it and see how seriously they take it

✉ From Leyton
Hilarious. I'll let you have it but you'd better not have taken anything else

I switched my phone to silent. Good grief! What had I ever seen in him?

Resting the back of my head against the side of the camper, my eyes scanned round the pile of boxes and suitcases. I might have embraced the symbolism of the full moon and addressed the negative energy. Would I have to wait for a month for the new moon, symbolising new beginnings? I hoped not. Much as I loved Carrie, I wasn't sure I could live and work in her for very long.

26

HOLLIE

The Easter holidays passed with no further contact from Smythe and it had been lovely to see The Starfish Café so alive with visitors. A fortnight later – a week into May – we had a special occasion to celebrate.

'Are you taking me to The Country Tavern?' Irene asked as Jake steered his car off the main Fellingthorpe Road into the village of Little Fraisby. I loved hearing the excitement in her voice.

'We might be,' Jake said.

'Oh, you two! What are you like? It's too much!'

'It's your birthday and we want to spoil you,' I said from the back seat.

'My Derek and I used to come here all the time,' she said as we pulled into the car park. 'That extension's new.'

'My friend Tori refurbished it several years back, so I don't think you'll recognise it inside,' I said. Tori had visited the café several times, sometimes bringing her laptop and doing some work. She'd reported that she'd listened to her heart and the boyfriend was no more. Although she sounded happy about it, she looked tired, so I suspected she was struggling to adjust. Eight years was a long time to be in a relationship.

Irene linked my arm as we walked across the car park. Widowed for thirty-four years with no children, Jake was her only 'family' and she'd swiftly adopted me as another surrogate grandchild when we'd started dating.

'Oh, my goodness, it's beautiful,' she gasped as we stepped inside.

We were led to our table by the window in the main building and I felt so proud of my new friend as I gazed round the room. What a talent Tori had! She'd introduced modern colours and furnishings in a way that perfectly complemented the old building and made them seem like they'd always been there. The space was light while also maintaining a cosy feel.

'The last time I dined here with my Derek, this is where we sat,' Irene said once we'd placed our orders and drinks had been brought over. 'It almost feels like he's sitting right beside me, celebrating with us. Is that silly?'

'Not at all. I often feel Mum's presence in the café, particularly when I put the Christmas tree up on Bonfire Night. I don't think the ones we love the most ever truly leave our sides.'

Jake gently squeezed my leg under the table, showing that he understood.

'Happy eighty-third birthday, Irene,' he said, raising his glass.

We all clinked drinks then laughed as we held them towards the empty chair where Derek would have sat.

'Do you want to talk about him?' I asked.

'Goodness, Hollie, don't make an invite like that! We'll still be here past midnight.' She laughed as she took another sip of her drink. 'He was a wonderful man but, as is often the case, the good ones get taken too soon. I was eighteen when I met him and he was ten years older. My mother didn't approve of the age gap. She was convinced he'd lose interest, but not my Derek. It was true love. Mother could see how happy we were so she finally relented and we married after four years together. Just as well because she dropped dead of a heart attack the following year.'

'I'm sorry to hear that,' I said.

'She'd had a tough life. I was born just before war broke out. My father joined the army and went missing in action in forty-one. They were never able to confirm anything and she worked herself into an anxious wreck over the years. She kept thinking she could hear him at the door or she'd see a man on the street and run after them, thinking it was him. I don't think her heart could take the strain in the end.

'My Derek and I moved into Seafarer Lodge and got ready to start a family, but it never happened for us. We were content, though. Lots of dogs over the years to give our love to. Then he developed this cough that he couldn't seem to shift. He was always tired and breathless. When the weight started falling off him, I finally managed to persuade him to see a doctor, but it was too late by then. Terminal lung cancer. Blummin' annoying for a man who'd never smoked a single cigarette in his whole life. We've got Sebastian Smythe to thank for that. Still, at least we had thirty-one happy years together, which is more than many manage, and I'd do it all again in a heartbeat.'

'How's Sebastian Smythe to blame?' Jake asked, voicing the question burning in my mind.

'My Derek worked for him. Did I never say?' Irene frowned. 'Probably never came up. You were two when he died. He worked for the Smythe family from the age of sixteen. He could turn his hand to anything and did all sorts for them over the years – handyman, bookkeeper, security. When Smythe was twenty-one, he took the helm and, being a young man about town, his big push was adding pubs and clubs to the business. There was a holiday camp called Marvel's not too far from your café, Hollie, which Smythe took over. I'll give the man his due. It was failing and he turned it around. The big draw was the clubhouse. He tripled the capacity with a nightclub upstairs and nightly entertainment downstairs – comedians, singers, cabarets, the works. He made my Derek head of security there and, when he'd finished a shift in the clubhouse, he went upstairs to the nightclub, so it was years of passive smoking killed him. Forty years he'd devoted to that family and do you know what they did a few months before he died? Sacked him for having too much time off sick.'

'That's horrendous!' I said. 'Especially when it was their fault.'

'To be fair, they didn't know it was lung cancer when they sacked him, but even so. His attendance record was immaculate before that so they should have given him some slack and realised it was serious.'

Our starters arrived, naturally pausing the conversation.

'Did Derek talk to you much about Smythe?' Jake asked Irene when our plates had been cleared away.

'Oh, yes! The things I heard. Enough to make your hair curl.'

'He wants to buy The Starfish Café,' I said.

'Don't sell him it. He's a wolf in sheep's clothing, that one. Dresses impeccably, schmoozes the right people, makes out he's really family-orientated with his Golden Galleon and his Pleasure-land, but it's all a front. Strip that away and you'll find a devious, back-stabbing criminal whose business empire is built on bribes, corruption and deception.'

'I'm getting the impression you're not his biggest fan,' I said laughing. 'I've got no intention of selling, but he's being so persistent and his offer is too generous, so I can't help thinking he knows something we don't. I don't suppose anywhere in your conversations with Derek, he'd have mentioned a reason why Smythe or his family might have wanted the café or the land?'

Irene scrunched her forehead, as though deep in thought. 'Now you're asking. My mind's still as sharp as a tack, but I don't recall anything about Starfish Point. The persistence thing's familiar, though. He was like a dog with a bone when it came to buying Marvel's. It was rundown but the family were trying to turn it round so they repeatedly rejected his offers. Then the financing they'd secured mysteriously fell through, leaving them with no choice but to sell up.'

'And you say it was all about the clubhouse?' Jake asked.

'Seemed to be. Don't get me wrong, they cleaned up the site and invested in new caravans, but the clubhouse was the big thing. The existing building wasn't in a bad state and could have been extended but he flattened it and started over. Took long enough, mind. They seemed to be digging forever and missed an entire summer season which was crazy. Why would you miss the summer?'

Jake nudged me and I began laughing. 'You can't be serious.'

'Why not?'

'Am I missing something?' Irene asked.

'Jake has a theory that the reason Smythe is so desperate to buy the café is because he thinks Tingler's Treasure is buried there and, if I'm reading him correctly, he thinks what you've just told us is connected.'

'It could be!' Jake exclaimed. 'Marvel's was close to Starfish Point and it sounds like he spent a long time digging there. Why miss the lucrative summer season unless you're digging for treasure?'

'Or you've discovered the foundations are shot and the project needs a lot more work than originally suspected,' I said, offering a more plausible explanation.

'Jake's theory's more fun,' Irene said.

'Thank you, Irene,' Jake said. 'I knew there was a reason why we'd remained friends.'

I clapped my hand over my heart, as though mortally wounded. 'Two against one. I'm devastated. Humour me, then. Why Marvel's in the early eighties and The Starfish Café today? I concede that the two places aren't a million miles away from each other, but I can't see a connection otherwise.'

'What if his treasure map had X in the wrong place?' Jake exclaimed, clearly enjoying this. 'And he's since discovered that the treasure's really buried at Starfish Point.'

'How?'

'Perhaps he discovered something in his recovered family archives,' Irene suggested.

Jake and I both stared at her.

'What family archives?' I asked.

'It was in *Bay News*. Remember that horrendous storm we had in early January? The roof at the Maritime Museum lost several tiles so they had to clear the attic to prevent anything from getting damaged. They found several archive boxes with "on loan from the Smythe family, please return" written across them and a date from the late fifties. Smythe was in the paper looking smug as ever and waxing lyrical about how delighted the family were to have documents from their long-lost heritage returned to them. Apparently, the boxes were full of old photos, papers and newspaper articles, some dating back several hundred years.'

'Including a treasure map?' I asked doubtfully.

'I've no idea,' Irene said, 'but you mentioned Tingler's Treasure earlier so you never know.' She grinned at our bemused expressions. 'You don't know the family connection, do you? Oh, how wonderful! The rumour is that Abe Tingler was the great, great, great – however many greats you need – grandfather of Sebastian Smythe. The Smythes apparently changed their family name to detach themselves from Abe Tingler's legacy so they could build their empire.'

Jake raised his eyebrows at me. 'I was only winding you up about the treasure before, but this is new information and it's pretty compelling stuff. Come on, Hollie. Do you really think it's a coincidence that Smythe made you an offer within a week of getting those documents back or that he's never stopped pestering you since?'

I looked from his excited face to Irene's. The pair of them had completely bought into this.

'If Isaac was here today, his nose would be twitching with a fresh lead,' I conceded.

'And what about yours?' Irene asked.

I twitched my nose and sniffed a bit, like Pickle did while out walking. 'Just as well Bex banned Kyle from taking The Smuggler's Key home because we have some more Post-its to add to it.'

'Ow!' I squealed, catching my already badly bruised shins on the corner of a cardboard box yet again.

I locked Carrie's door behind me and stomped over to the shower block. It was Saturday morning and I'd now spent twenty nights at Kellerby Cliffs Holiday Park and was a woman on the brink. Much as I loved my campervan, she wasn't designed as a semi-permanent home and office combined, especially when she was full of boxes and cases.

The search for somewhere to rent wasn't as easy as I'd antici-pated. Anywhere with just the one bedroom was either a tiny bedsit, giving me little more room than I already had in Carrie, or it was in an area giving off seriously dodgy vibes. I'd tried to secure three different two-bedroom flats or houses so far and all of them had fallen through for various reasons and I was beginning to think I might have to ask Uncle Hugh and Aunt Kathryn if they could put me up after all.

Brushing my teeth, I stretched out and winced as my joints cracked. My body never used to do that. The seat padding I'd bought when I made the soft furnishings for Carrie's refurbishment was comfortable enough for the duration of a cuppa and a box of Jaffa Cakes, but it absolutely wasn't right for sleeping on and, boy, did my body know it!

Picking up my toilet bag and towel, I stepped into a shower cubicle, then stopped. I knew something that would sort out those stiff joints even better than a shower, and it would leave me feeling more alive, ready to work on a new client proposal later this morning.

* * *

Forty minutes later, I ran along the beach at Whitsborough Bay's North Bay with my surfboard tucked under my arm. The slap of my feet on the wet sand filled my weary body with joy. I'd missed this.

There were a handful of other surfers, all of whom I recognised. Sometimes we'd bob on the swell and have a catch-up, but today I had frustration and tension to work out of my system, so I needed to keep surfing.

Feeling exhausted but fulfilled, I decided to catch one final wave then call it a day. As I stood upright, I glanced towards the shore. On the esplanade above the beach, a solitary figure was leaning against the railings next to the giant statue of Stanley Moffatt. I squinted. Was that Finley? Next moment, I tumbled into the surf. Wipeout. Served me right for losing my concentration.

When I'd caught my breath and stopped spluttering, I looked up to the esplanade, but the figure had gone. It could have been anyone, especially at that distance. I coughed once more – damn salt water.

'Are you okay, Tori?'

I twisted round at the woman's voice. 'Hi, Jemma. Yeah, fine. Thought I spotted someone I know up there and, well, I'm guessing you saw the result of that.'

'It was an impressive wipeout,' her husband Sam said, smiling at me. 'Reminded me of my early attempts.'

Jemma laughed. 'What do you mean, your *early* attempts? You still do that now! Are you coming back in, Tori?'

'No. That was my somewhat unstylish finale for today. I've got to do some work. Surf's good, though. Have fun out there.'

They smiled and thanked me as they ran into the sea. I stood by my board for a moment, watching them. They were such a lovely couple. Jemma ran Bear With Me, the specialist teddy bear shop next to Charlee's Chocolates and Sam was a neurologist at the hospital. They were great friends with Jodie and Charlee.

I watched them bobbing on their boards, chatting to the other surfers, and shook my head. I knew I shouldn't compare myself to other people, but I'd been comparing my relationship with Leyton to other relationships a lot lately and questioning why we'd stayed together so long when we were so clearly incompatible. If anyone who didn't know us saw us together and was asked to guess our connection, no way would they think we were a couple.

I couldn't deny that there'd always been a physical attraction, but there'd never been that deep friendship the other couples I knew seemed to share.

'That was a big sigh.'

'Oh, my God! Finley? So it was you on the esplanade earlier.'

'You spotted me?'

'Yeah. And wiped out spectacularly because of it.'

'That was my fault? I'm so sorry. I saw you go splat and wanted to check you were okay.'

'It wasn't your fault,' I reassured him. 'It was mine for not concentrating.' I picked up my board and walked back along the beach beside him. 'Not surfing today?'

'I wish. Just a walk and a think.'

'Fancy turning it into a cuppa and a chat?' I asked.

'Best offer I've had in weeks.'

* * *

'Ooh, that looks good,' I said as the waitress placed a couple of large hot chocolates and teacakes on our table at Waterfront Lodge.

I'd stripped off my wetsuit in Carrie and pulled on some clothes, ignoring that my hair was wet and messy and my skin was dry with salt.

It was so good to see Finley again. For the past couple of Monday evenings, I'd toyed with taking him up on the offer to drop by The Lobster Pot after he'd completed his RNLI training, but I'd managed to talk myself out of it. Making casual chit-chat with him now while we tucked into our teacakes, I had no idea why I'd done that. He was great company.

'Tell me the latest with Demi,' I said, wiping my buttery fingers on my napkin when we'd finished eating.

'The day after the wedding, I thought we could have a proper talk, but she was in a really weird mood. "Fine" seemed to be the answer for everything and she wouldn't look at me. The softly-softly approach wasn't getting me anywhere, so I had to spell it out for her. I was expecting an argument or tears, but all I got was stony silence.'

'Ooh! Bit awkward.'

'You're not kidding! She said she was tired and wanted to watch a film so she shoved the telly on and ignored me. The kids arrived back from her mum's and, when they went to bed, she had a bath then went to bed too. Every evening I asked if we could talk and she refused. It was the weirdest thing. The tension was horrendous and India and Roman even separately asked if something was wrong, but Demi wheeled out the "everything's fine" lie.'

'Please tell me you've managed to have a conversation since then? The wedding was three weeks ago.'

'She finally agreed to talk last night while Damon had the kids for a rare overnighter. I say talk, but it was basically her yelling at me for two hours.'

'Oh, Finley.'

'I've never seen her like that. It was as though she'd spent three weeks building up this anger against me and she just unleashed it all. The upshot is an ultimatum. I either "grow a pair" and raise the baby as if he's my own, or I never see India and Roman again.'

'No!'

'Yep! I'd hoped for better from her. It feels low to use the kids like that. I have until the end of the weekend to decide and, when I spotted you, I was asking myself the heart versus head question. My heart says walk away from Demi and so does my head.'

'But not from the children,' I said, my heart breaking for him. 'That's really tough.'

'So do I stay for the kids?'

'Not seeing them again would be hard, but would staying be easier on any of you? You said they both picked up on the tension at home when Demi wasn't speaking to you. Imagine the vibes between you if you stay. That could be even more destructive.'

'What would you do?' asked Finley.

'Honestly? I'd still walk away. The closest comparison I have – and I know it's not the same thing – would be when I left my ex-husband Ewan. I never wanted that to end, but having a family was *not* for me. I've always known that and I could envisage a scenario where I went along with it just to keep Ewan and it drove us apart anyway, not to mention any damage I might have inflicted on any children we had. This is *your* life, Finley, and you only get one shot at it. Hollie told me what happened to her family and I've had my own near-death experience. Those things show how important it is to seek out happiness because we don't know when our time's up. Do you genuinely believe that you and Demi could make a go of it and live happily ever after?'

'No. I can't forget what she did and I'm not sure I'll ever forgive her either.'

'Then you have to walk away and hope she changes her mind about the kids.'

'I guess I'll be packing my stuff later, then.' He ran his hands through his hair and smiled ruefully. 'Anyway, I promised you a listening ear next time we met, so do you want to tell me the story about your parents or do you need to rush off?'

'I'm free for a bit longer if you are. Have you heard of the author Rebecca Lannister?'

'Yes. Local author. My mum's a huge fan. Reads all her books.'

'Rebecca Lannister is my mother.'

'Wow! Famous mum.'

'Rebecca Lannister is also my father.'

'No way! So they write the books together? That's amazing!'

He gave me a gentle smile and I loved that I'd been able to say something to wipe away the frown, although I wished I could say something to take away the pain and make him smile properly. He was so lovely and he deserved to be happy.

'They're in their mid-seventies now and have been writing together since they were eighteen, so we're talking hundreds of books, several films and a small fortune. They met while studying History and English at Oxford and bonded over their shared passion for women authors of the Georgian and Victorian eras such as the Brontës, Jane Austen and Elizabeth Gaskell. One of the reasons they're so good at writing historicals is that they're passionate about history and they live and breathe the era they write about.'

I paused, stomach churning, my mind casting back to the first time I'd ever shared this with anyone who wasn't family. Millicent had taken the information and used it against me, but this was different. Finley was different. He'd let me into his most personal secret and I was still the only one who knew, and I somehow knew I could trust him wholeheartedly with mine.

'When I say live and breathe, I mean literally...'

Over another coffee, I told Finley about my childhood and everything that happened once I started at Whitsborough West, finishing with the recent disastrous trip to Redamancy Castle and my new residence at Kellerby Cliffs.

'Here was me about to ask if I could rent your campervan for a few days while the dust settles, but I guess that answers that question. I'm so sorry it didn't go well.'

'Thanks. I haven't given up. When I'm settled somewhere, I'll try again. As for you staying in Carrie, you'd have been welcome to her, but she's not the most comfortable. I need to find somewhere to rent pretty urgently.'

'That makes two of us.'

We looked at each other, a moment of understanding passing between us, and we spoke at the same time.

'We could always...'

'What if we...?'

'We'd be doing each other a favour,' I said.

'And splitting the rent and bills would save us both money,' he agreed.

'I'm game if you are. I know we've only just met, but we know each other's secrets, so I'd say that makes us friends.'

Finley nodded enthusiastically. 'And I think we could both do with a good friend right now. Let's do it.'

'You're on! I work from home so I need some space I can use as an office like a third bedroom or a dining room. What about you?'

'Similar. I need some space to study, although I don't mind

sharing it.'

'What are you studying?'

'Architecture.'

My jaw dropped. 'You're not! I'm an architect, although I try to focus more on interior design.'

For the first time that morning, Finley smiled properly, flashing a beautiful set of straight white teeth at me. 'Sounds like we have a lot in common.'

'It does! A friendship made in heaven. Are you studying full-time?'

'Part-time. I'm actually a dentist – following in my dad's and granddad's footsteps – so we're talking big career change, but it's exciting.'

'That feeling there,' I said. 'Hold onto it. You look and sound so happy. That's how life should feel.'

We exchanged phone numbers before settling the bill, an agreement made that Finley would contact me once he'd spoken to Demi, at which point we'd start house-hunting.

'My car's near Hearnshaw Park,' he said as we stepped outside, 'so I'm heading that way. Thanks for all the amazing advice. If you ever fancied a career change, I'm sure you'd make a brilliant counsellor.'

I laughed. 'I think I'll stick with interior design. See you soon for a spot of house-hunting and good luck today. Stay strong. I'm sure she'll come round eventually when she sees how much the kids are hurting.'

'Fingers crossed.'

We parted and I'd only taken a few steps when he called my name.

'Tori! I'm glad I fled to the roof terrace at the wedding.'

I smiled. 'So am I.'

But as I walked back to Carrie, my smile slipped. I hadn't been completely honest with Finley. I'd managed to carefully gloss over the reason why I'd left Redamancy Castle and moved in with Leyton so soon. He'd shared an enormous confidence with me, but I hadn't done the same. It wasn't that I didn't trust him. It was more that I still hadn't come to terms with it. Would I ever? Especially now that my parents were refusing to see me and my angry, bitter baby sister was their gatekeeper. I might not have had a plan about what to say to my parents, but I had assumed I'd actually be able to see them, even if it had been an unpleasant but deserved *you've got a nerve turning up after all these years*. I wasn't sure what to do next.

* * *

I stood at the back of Carrie early that evening, rubbing my shin again, and surveying the clutter. There had to be a way I could make the campervan more liveable until Finley and I found somewhere to rent and could move in.

I already had a box on the passenger seat and another in the footwell but I might be able to squash the contents of the one I kept tripping over into the space round them. Anything was worth a try.

Pulling the heavy box out from under the table, I studied it for a moment. My name was written across it in marker pen, but there was no mention of what was inside and I couldn't for the life of me remember, which probably meant the contents could be chucked or given away.

I ripped off the packing tape. Textbooks from my degree sat alongside some DVDs. The books were seriously out of date – no use to me or to Finley – and I didn't own a DVD player so I could sling all those for a start. I piled them on the table and dug deeper. There was a wooden box containing some costume jewellery that I thought I'd lost, and a couple of framed photos from my university days.

At the bottom, there was a large purple box. I lifted it out and was about to remove the lid when a knock on the window startled me. Finley was outside holding a bottle of wine in one hand and a paper bag in the other.

I yanked back the door. 'Hello!'

'Hi. Sorry for turning up unannounced, but you're still the only one who knows what's been going on. The deed is done, it was awful and she's thrown me out. Have you eaten? If not, do you like Indian food?' His voice was overly high and fast and he looked as though he might burst into tears at any moment.

'Curry's great. Come in. Let me clear the table.' I piled everything back into the box. 'As you can see, space is at a premium. How about you shove this box and a couple of my cases in your car to give us space to eat?'

'As long as I can bring them back in later. My car's my bed for the night.'

'You can't sleep in your car,' I cried, taking the food and wine from him and placing them on the table.

'It's only for one night. I'll book into a B&B tomorrow and stay there till we find somewhere to rent.'

'You'll sleep in here tonight. It's the height of luxury and who needs space? Completely overrated.'

He smiled gratefully. 'Has anyone told you lately that you're the best?'

'Actually, no, and it feels good to hear it.'

We hugged each other. I could feel the tension in his body and suspected he was dying inside after this afternoon, particularly if he'd had to say goodbye to the kids. For me, it felt so good to be held in a strong pair of arms after months of neglect and I bit back a sob for me and for Finley.

'It'll be all right,' I whispered.

'I hope so. It doesn't feel it right now.'

28

'Let's see it, then,' Jake said on Saturday evening, stepping out of the shower following a twelve-hour shift at the hospital.

'You're sure you don't want to get dressed first?'

'I'm too intrigued about this new information you've uncovered.'

'Don't get too excited. I haven't solved it.'

Jake followed me up to the top floor and Pickle chased after us. When we dropped Irene back off at Bay View Care Home last night, she'd invited us in for a coffee.

'I keep the paper in case I fancy doing the crossword,' she said, rifling through a pile of newspapers in search of the article about Slippy Smythe getting his family's documents back. 'The storm was late January. Let's see.'

I'd been surprised to find my heart racing as she tossed several editions aside before she found the right one. 'Bingo! Front page news. Here you go.'

It had been late when we returned to Sandy Croft with the copy of *Bay News* so I'd only added the article to The Smuggler's Key this evening, but I'd also done further digging.

'Smythe purchased a derelict pub about a mile down the coast a decade ago.' I pointed to the new information I'd printed off the Internet. 'You can read it yourself later but, in brief, the plan was to refurbish the pub but he knocked it down instead. There were rumours of asbestos but the previous owner swore there wasn't any. There was a lot of excavating of the site and then nothing.'

'I'd forgotten about that pub,' Jake said. 'There's nothing there now.'

'Exactly. I couldn't find any explanation for him not rebuilding it, so that's a lot of money down the drain. From what I've seen, Smythe doesn't make bad business decisions like that.'

'Interesting.' Jake scanned his eyes across the Post-it note questions I'd added. 'Very interesting. Although I see what you mean about it not solving anything.'

'It's so frustrating. It's like clue after cl—'

My phone ringing stopped me mid-flow and my stomach lurched as 'C&L Alarm Systems' appeared on the screen.

'It's the alarm company,' I told Jake as I connected the call. 'Hello?'

'Is that Ms Brooks?' a man asked.

'Yes. Is everything all right?'

'We've received a notification that the alarm is sounding at The Starfish Café at Starfish Point and we've linked into the CCTV system but I'm afraid nothing's showing.'

'There's no CCTV?'

'Either there's a fault in the system which we're checking now or somebody has deliberately damaged it. There's a police patrol car in the area and they should be there within five to ten minutes.'

I closed my eyes and pressed my hand against my scrunched-up forehead. 'Thanks. I'll go there now.'

Feeling sick, I hung up. 'It sounds like there's been a break-in at the café. I need to meet the police there.'

'I'll drive.'

'Would you? Thank you. I'm shaking.' I held my hand out to show him and he drew me into a hug, helping calm me.

* * *

The police patrol car was parked in my usual place when we arrived, blue lights flashing, but no sirens blaring. The alarm company would have centrally deactivated the alarm once the police confirmed they were on site.

I stepped out of Jake's car and made my way towards an officer relaying something over her radio.

'Hi, I'm the owner, Hollie Brooks,' I said when she'd finished. 'The alarm company called me.'

'I'm PC Dawkins and my colleague, PC Kramer, is checking the perimeter.'

'Is it a break-in?'

'There's a broken window, but we haven't been inside. We were told the keyholder was on the way so we didn't want to cause any further damage.'

'What about the CCTV? Is that smashed?'

'We spotted three cameras and they all seem to have something covering them. We noticed a sign saying there's no money left on the premises overnight.'

'There's some change for the float, but that's in a hidden safe. The till drawer is always left open. The only reason I—'

I paused as her colleague radioed through that the perimeter was clear. 'The keyholder has arrived,' she told him before turning back to me. 'Sorry. You were saying...?'

'Just that I only keep it alarmed as a deterrent with it being so remote out here. We've never had any trouble before.'

'It's often kids messing about, although that's less likely given the remote location and the covering of the CCTV. We'd better not speculate until we've looked inside. Here's my colleague.'

After the introductions, Jake and I were asked to hang back while PC Kramer unlocked the door and they checked there was nobody still inside. I told them where the light switches were and, as soon as light flooded out of the café, my heart sank.

'Look at the state of that!' The window to the side of the entrance porch was completely smashed in, only a few fragments of safety glass clinging onto the frame.

I stepped closer to the building and clapped my hand across my mouth as I saw through the open door the upturned chairs and tables, the legs smashed off the chair closest to me.

'Jake! They've trashed it!'

Jake put his arm round me and gently tugged me back a few steps. 'We'd better not get too close in case there's any forensics.'

I gratefully leaned against him, fighting back the tears. Who'd do this to my beautiful café? But a name immediately sprung to mind.

'I'd bet my life on Sebastian Smythe being behind this,' I said, clenching my fists.

'I was thinking the same. Will you tell the police?'

'I have to, but I'll have to be careful about it. An outright accusation won't do me any favours and, of course, if he is behind it, he won't be the one who actually did it. He'll have an airtight alibi. Probably photographed attending some big function with hundreds of guests while his minions sent me a message.'

PC Dawkins opened the door. 'There's nobody inside, but the place is a mess. It would help if you can come in and see whether anything has been stolen, but I'll need you to be careful where you stand and please don't touch anything. Are you ready to do that?'

Having already seen a flavour of it from outside, I had some inkling of what to expect, but nothing could fully prepare me for the senseless vandalism inside. Nothing was left unscathed. Squiggles of spray paint covered the walls and floor. Legs were smashed off the freestanding chairs and tables and there were chunks out of the booths and counter tops, as though they'd been attacked with a sledgehammer. The upholstery on the booths and cushions had been ripped and I could see dirty footprints on some of the cushions where the vandals must have stamped on them. The glass display cabinets on the counter were smashed and so was every last piece of crockery. The trays of cutlery had been emptied over the floor and jars of tea and coffee tipped on top of them. My precious driftwood photo frame depicting the café's evolution was broken on the floor, face down. I'd been instructed not to touch anything and that was fine. I didn't want to turn it over and see the smashed glass and damaged photos.

Taking a deep breath, my legs shook as I followed PC Dawkins into the kitchen. A mist of flour hung in the air, and it seemed the entire contents of my pantry and fridge had been emptied onto the floor. Mixing bowls were broken, utensils snapped and cupboard doors hung off their hinges or had chunks smashed out of them. The double doors to the large fridge hung at an awkward angle and the glass on the oven door was cracked.

I pressed my head into Jake's chest as a small sob escaped.

'That's a lot of damage in a short space of time,' Jake said, voicing what I'd been thinking.

'You'd be surprised at how quickly these things can be done,' PC Kramer said. 'My guess would be that there were several perpetrators and this was planned rather than spontaneous.'

'What makes you think that?' Jake asked.

'They couldn't do this level of damage without having tools with them and the covering of the CCTV would also suggest its premeditated. Do you know anyone who might have wanted to do this, Hollie?'

I swallowed down the lump in my throat and straightened up. 'We don't tend to attract angry customers and there are no aggrieved former employees. Everyone loves working here. The only thing I can possibly think of is that there's someone who has wanted to buy the café for a long time. He's visited a lot recently and has made me an unexpectedly high offer and wasn't impressed when I still said no.'

PC Dawkins dug out a small black notepad. 'What's the name of this person?'

'It's Sebastian Smythe.'

She stopped, pen poised against the paper, and exchanged a look with PC Kramer. '*The* Sebastian Smythe who owns half of Whitsborough Bay?'

'That's the one. I'd like it on record that I'm not accusing him of anything. But you asked who might have wanted to do this and he told me that I'd change my mind about selling the café to him.' I swept my arm round the room. 'This sort of thing could certainly make somebody change their mind.' But not me. I wasn't going to be driven out of a business that had been in my family for three generations.

'We could do with taking a full statement from you, but perhaps not here.' PC Kramer glanced round at the mess. 'In the meantime, are you able to tell if anything's missing?'

I picked my way across the floor to the pantry. There was a removable bottom in one of the cupboards where we kept the safe, but that was intact and the coins were still inside.

'Have they trashed upstairs too?' I asked.

PC Dawkins shook her head. 'It looks like the focus was purely on the café and the kitchen. There's no damage in the toilets either.'

'What happens now?' Jake asked.

'I'd suggest you get an emergency glazier to board up that window and then get yourselves home. Because there's a considerable amount of damage, we'll get a team out first thing in the morning to check for forensics. Your insurance company will likely want to send out an assessor too. I presume you're insured.'

'Yes. Fully covered. I'll call their emergency line now. When do you want a full statement from me?'

'In the morning.'

'But you won't visit Sebastian Smythe in the meantime and tell him I've said anything?'

PC Dawkins narrowed her eyes at me. 'You seem particularly concerned about that. Has Mr Smythe or anyone else threatened you?'

'Not directly.'

I didn't want to say anything more in case it sounded like I had a vendetta against him. When I gave my official statement, I knew I'd need to be factual and keep my emotions and speculation out of it, which wasn't going to be easy when I was absolutely 100 per cent convinced he was behind it. Mindless acts of vandalism didn't happen in remote locations like this which needed access by car, had an alarm, and were covered by CCTV. Yobs like that attacked town centre locations they could easily reach on foot, by bike or skateboard.

I was still trembling when the police left.

'Let's get you back to the car,' Jake said gently. 'I'll put the heating on and we can ring the insurance company to organise getting the window secured.'

'I've got cover for the smashed window, so they'll sort that straightaway. I'd better let Angie and the team know too. I don't want them to hear it from anyone else.'

I held my head in my hands for a moment as reality hit me about what this meant for the business. 'Oh, my God, Jake! We'll have to be closed for ages while we do a complete refurb. All that lost custom.' I shuddered at the thought.

'I'm sure the insurance company will act fast and you'll be open again in no time. I know it's not much consolation, but we're only a week into May. You'll definitely be open again before the summer.'

'But not before half-term.' I heard the defeat in my voice and hated it. I'd faced far worse than this. If it was Smythe and this was a dirty tactic to get me to sell, he'd underestimated me. Stunts like this might make others sell up, but it made me even more determined not to. There was no way that man was getting his greasy mitts on my business. I'd rather flatten the café and let the land become derelict than sell to him.

I took a deep breath and straightened my shoulders. 'I'll make that call and we'll take it from there. You're right. We'll be open in plenty of time for the summer trade and we'll come back fighting.'

My insurers said they'd send an emergency glazier straight out. I texted Angie to ask if she was still awake. She FaceTimed me back immediately and looked as shocked as I felt.

'Obviously, don't come into work tomorrow,' I told her. 'I'm going to message the others to tell them the same.'

'I'm so sorry, honey. Give me a call in the morning when you've spoken to the police. I'll help with the clear-up and I'm sure everyone else will too.'

'Thanks, Angie. Sorry to be the bearer of bad news at such a late hour.'

She smiled gently. 'I'm the one who's sorry. Absolute thugs. You try to get some sleep and we'll catch up tomorrow but don't worry about it. We'll pull together and sort it all out. Version three of The Starfish Café will be even better than its predecessors.'

I thanked her again and disconnected, then typed the news into the staff WhatsApp group. I didn't have the energy to speak to anyone else so I made it clear that I had no more news for tonight but I'd speak to everyone at some point tomorrow after I'd given my statement to the police.

When the glazier arrived, I felt tearful once more as I stared at the ugly board he fitted where the glass had been, but I swallowed back the lump in my throat. Tomorrow, the board would be replaced by glass and the clear-up would commence. As Angie had said, the third refurbishment would be even better.

'How are you feeling now?' Jake asked as he drove home.

'I'm upset and I'm furious, but I've been through a hell of a lot worse. On the scale of horrendous things I've experienced in my life, this is nowhere near losing my family. It's just stuff. It's upsetting, it's inconvenient and it's unfair but nobody got hurt, everything can be repaired or replaced, and I'm insured. It's nothing compared to what I've already been through and I got through that... am getting through that... so I'll get through this.'

I believed every word I said. It had been a hell of a shock and I was sure I'd shed plenty of tears, especially when I saw the damage in the light of day tomorrow, but it was also an opportunity for a fresh start and that was a good thing.

29

HOLLIE

I was wide awake by half five the following morning, my mind racing with everything I needed to do to get the business up and running again. I was itching to drive straight to The Starfish Café and start tidying up, but I had to wait until the police had finished their investigations before I could go inside.

Jake was asleep on his stomach, but with his head turned towards me. Taking care not to nudge him, I reached for my phone and started a list. The operator on the emergency helpline last night had registered the insurance claim, but said someone would call me to take more details this morning. I'd have a better idea of the damage when I had more time and fresh eyes today, but my initial assessment was that everything would need ripping out and starting again and we'd be closed until at least the end of June.

As well as finding a construction team, I'd need to source new furniture, equipment, crockery and so on. Awaiting delivery of everything would take time, so even late June might be ambitious. Last time I'd refurbished, I'd allowed the entire summer for sourcing and ordering before closing at the end of the season.

I slumped back against the pillows and couldn't help releasing a frustrated sigh. I didn't want to be closed at this time of year. From Easter onwards, trade steadily grew. May half-term was nearly as busy as the summer holidays but there was no chance of reopening for then. Pups season for the common seals in June and July brought an increase in visitors to the beach and most of them visited the café. We might open in time to catch some of them, but definitely not all.

My insurance policy would cover the team's wages but it wouldn't cover any lost sales of Hollie's Wood while the café was closed because that was a separate entity. My two best times of the year were Christmas and summer and I didn't want the charities to lose out so I'd need to do a major online push, but would I manage to find time for that – and for posting the stock – around the refurbishment?

Aside from the practicalities, there was no escaping the emotional toll this was going to take. Shortly before we lost Dad and Isaac, Mum had announced that it was time to refurbish the café. It was out with the pine and in with a fresh New England theme. Katie and I had been tasked with creating mood boards, but the refurb took a back seat after losing Dad and Isaac and then Mum's third cancer diagnosis. When she died, I really struggled with the idea of changing what she'd so lovingly created. It was Angie who'd made me see sense, although the mounting repair bills from the café falling apart round us also helped.

Now I was much stronger, but there'd still be memories swirling round me and I had some big decisions to make. This was an opportunity for another fresh start, which meant goodbye to the New England theme. But that was a theme Mum had approved so, even though she hadn't seen the changes, she'd been involved in the decision-making process. What the next incarnation of The Starfish Café looked like was all down to me. My eyes teared up at the thought of there being nothing left of Mum in the café and I feared this could end up being more emotionally challenging than last time.

Jake snuffled beside me and I glanced down at him. He'd be there for me, as would Angie and the team, and Katie and Bex. I wouldn't be going through any of it alone.

I opened my bedside drawer and removed the two cards that Mum had asked Angie to give me after she died. I smiled at the little girl in the pink tutu and red wellington boots on the front of the first one, dancing in the rain with her dog. I turned to the second one with the same little girl on the front alongside a teddy bear with its arm in a sling. Mum had asked Angie to give me it when I'd lost my way and needed some help. That moment had been when I ended my fledgling relationship with Jake last November.

In the first card, Mum had written one of her favourite phrases: *Keep dancing in the rain*. In the second, she'd shared an extension to it: *If you stumble, make it part of your dance.*

What had happened at the café was simply another stumble and I *would* make it part of my dance. My eyes fell on the quote she'd included from Sir William Hillary, founder of the RNLI: *With courage, nothing is impossible.*

That was so true. Yes, this was going to be emotional, but that's how life was. I'd be brave, I'd take some risks and we would be open in time for summer because nothing was impossible. Nothing at all.

30

HOLLIE

The same two police officers from last night arrived at about 9.30 a.m. to take a full statement, so Jake took Pickle for a walk along the esplanade.

'How did it go?' he asked, joining me in the kitchen when the police had left.

'Good. I gave them the full history of Smythe's offers to Mum and me. I kicked myself for ripping up the obscene offer he wrote down, but I still had the note that came with the flowers and I had his texts, although I think they were a bit bewildered by me saving them under the name of Abe Tingler.'

'What happens next?'

'The CSIs are at the café and should be done by lunchtime. I'll get a call when they're packing up. The insurance company called and a claim assessor is meeting me there at one, so I'll drive up when I get the call from the police and hang around for the assessor. Then the clear-up starts, which will be fun.'

Jake gave me a hug. 'I'm here to help and I'm sure Angie and your staff will help out too. Coffee?'

'Please. I need it to stay awake.'

'I've just found out something interesting,' Jake said as he handed me a mug of coffee a few minutes later. 'Irene rang while I was out. She'd been thinking about Smythe and she's remembered a few things.'

Jake plonked himself down on one of the sofas in the snug area and I sat on the one opposite so we could talk.

'You know Bean Cuisine, the vegan restaurant on the seafront.' Jake said. 'It used to be a café called the Harbour Tea Parlour. Irene says it was run by a husband-and-wife team, the Bensons. Smythe decided Whitsborough Bay needed a vegan restaurant and the Harbour Tea Parlour was the site he wanted for it. He made an offer and the Bensons said no and that's when things started to go wrong.'

'What sort of things?' I asked.

'Repeated visits by the health inspectors during busy periods, a burst pipe in the toilets leaking sewage into the café, the freezer breaking down, an allegation of food poisoning...' Jake scrunched up his nose. 'I can't remember everything that Irene said, but you get the picture. Trade dipped and they struggled to pay their bills. When it all got too stressful, they turned to Smythe and he was still keen to buy, but his offer had decreased.'

'Ooh, how devious! Could they trace any of that stuff back to him?'

'Irene says nothing got investigated. The Bensons claimed they'd been the ones to originally approach Smythe because they were struggling and he'd said no because the price was too high. When a few more things *coincidentally* went wrong, they allegedly begged him to reconsider at a reduced price.'

'She thinks he'd threatened them to change their story?'

'She's convinced of it. The café was thriving and they'd run others successfully so they weren't novices. She says there was no way they were struggling but they were only a few years from retirement, so the rumour is they accepted his pay-out instead of risking him destroying their business and them losing their retirement nest egg.'

'That's horrendous, but I can completely imagine him doing that.'

'Irene said Smythe doesn't normally target successful businesses like the Harbour Tea Parlour and The Starfish Café. His usual style is to cause major problems for already struggling businesses and then swoop in with a silly offer that they have no choice but to accept. Of course, the problems could never be traced back to him and he's hailed as some sort of saviour instead for bailing them out.'

We spoke for another twenty minutes or so, each new tale that Jake relayed from Irene turning my stomach. Smythe clearly stopped at nothing to get what he wanted.

'I bet he'll be back as soon as *Bay News* cover the break-in,' I said. 'He'll offer his condolences and renew his interest – at a reduced price, of course. And when I say no, how long before something else happens? It wouldn't take long for repeated visits from health inspectors and allegations of food poisoning to destroy The Starfish Café, just like it destroyed the Harbour Tea Parlour.'

'Hopefully it won't come to that if the police have him on their radar.'

I held up my crossed fingers. 'If only we had some evidence. We'll just have to hope that the CSIs find something that can link back to him because rumours and hearsay aren't going to cut it. Did you tell Irene about the break-in?'

'No. I wasn't sure if I should until the police have finished and I didn't want to worry her.' Jake took out his phone. 'Let's see if we can find what he was up to last night. I bet you're right about him having some major alibi.'

While Jake investigated, I thought about the Bensons having to close the Harbour Tea Parlour. To Smythe, places like that and The Starfish Café were just buildings that he could take over and turn into whatever took his fancy but, to the owners, they were never 'just a business'. And to the customers, they were so much more than somewhere to grab something to eat. They were a place to feel safe and warm, to go with friends, and to meet new friends. They were a community. Mum had worked hard to create a place where everyone was welcome and made to feel like part of the family and people like Sebastian Smythe would never understand that.

'I've found it!'

Jake passed me his phone and I curled my lip at the photos of Smythe on the socials, grinning and shaking hands at some business event last night which had ended way after the café alarm sounded.

'An airtight alibi, just as you predicted,' he said.

'Urgh! I hate that man!'

I stared at Smythe's smug grin and shuddered. He could do what he liked, but he wasn't taking my community or my family away from me. If it was a fight he wanted, so be it.

31

TORI

I'd already been over to the shower block on Sunday morning and was dressed and checking my emails when Finley awoke. I couldn't help smiling at the groan he emitted as he sat up in his sleeping bag and rubbed his eyes.

'Morning,' I said, lowering my phone. 'I'd ask if you slept well, but I think that groan says it all.'

'I actually slept like a log, but...' He rolled his shoulders, grimacing. 'Still, it would be a lot worse if I'd spent the night in the car. I'm so grateful to you for letting me stay.'

'Pleasure. I enjoyed the company. Bodes well for us renting together, assuming you're still up for that.'

'More than ever.'

While Finley went to shower and change, I boiled the kettle and made a couple of strong coffees. Outside, I opened out two deckchairs and placed the drinks on a plastic table I'd found in a charity shop.

'Nice view,' Finley said, sitting beside me and sipping his drink. 'That's good coffee. Thank you.'

'You're welcome. So, what's your plan for the day?'

'I'm not sure. At some point I'll be summoned by Demi to collect my stuff so I can't go far or do much. I'll need to find a B&B and we should probably start our rental search too.'

'How about we go to The Starfish Café for brunch after we've had these? There's decent WiFi, so we can search online for rentals and find you a B&B. Once you've collected your stuff, there's a storage place on the industrial estate which is open seven days a week. I'm happy to go halves on it and shove some of my things in there too.'

'You've got yourself a deal. I've never been to Hollie's café.'

'I hadn't until recently but I go there quite often now. It's lovely, just like her.'

It was just after half ten when we pulled into the car park at The Starfish Café. The café would have been open since ten, so I was surprised to see only one car outside. I'd have thought a sunny Sunday would have brought loads of visitors out.

Hollie was standing outside holding a chair and there appeared to be more pieces of furniture piled up nearby.

'I think something's wrong,' I said to Finley.

32

HOLLIE

When the insurance assessor left, I stood in the middle of the café with my hands on my hips, shaking my head as I turned in a slow circle, taking in the destruction. It was all so senseless. In some ways, I'd have preferred to find the safe empty because at least there'd have been a reason for the break-in rather than mindless vandalism. Well, a reason other than Smythe trying to get me to sell him the business. How long would it be before he turned up, acting all smarmy and sympathetic?

'Where do you want to start?' Jake asked, putting his arm round my shoulders.

'The skip won't be here for an hour and a half but we can't do much with broken furniture all over the floor, so I suggest we start by dumping the chairs and tables outside.'

With the internal and external double doors propped open for ease of access, we set about piling up the broken pieces outside. We were only on our second load when a car pulled into the car park. I steeled myself for another 'sorry, we're closed' conversation, having had several of those while the insurance assessor was here.

'I'm sure that's Bart's car,' Jake said.

I paused with a chair in my hands and squinted at it. 'It is! And Tori's with him.'

'What's going on?' Tori asked, frowning as she approached us.

'Break-in last night.'

'Oh, my God! No! You weren't here, were you?'

'No, thankfully. It was quite late.'

'Did they take anything?' Bart asked.

'No, but they've completely trashed the place. There's not much we can do about organising a refurb on a Sunday so we're clearing out what we can for now. I need to feel like we're making some sort of progress.'

'Could you use some help?' Bart asked.

'Do you have time?'

He and Tori exchanged looks.

'We have a lot of time,' she said, 'although Finley will need to head off if he gets a call.'

'Thanks.' I put the chair down. 'How come you two are together? I didn't realise you knew each other.'

'We have mutual friends,' Tori said. 'We met at their wedding a few weeks ago and recognised each other from the rescue.'

She glanced across at Bart and I sensed there was more, but they clearly didn't want to share it and there was work to do so I wasn't going to waste time quizzing them.

Within an hour, the café was teaming with people. Angie and Martin arrived with Katie and Trey, followed by staff members Avril and Kerry and the team who usually worked alongside Angie on a Sunday: Javier, Joey and Maya.

I'd posted earlier on the WhatsApp group not to worry about their jobs or their wages as they'd still be paid. Offers of help had come rolling in and I'd said there was no need, but here several of them were and those who couldn't make it today had said they'd be available during the week in whatever capacity I needed them. That meant the world to me.

* * *

Javier and Maya went down to the beach to collect litter for me and Joey stood at the entrance of the car park, turning customers away. In theory, the customers could have gone down to the beach, but I didn't want anyone to see the café in such a horrific state or to have to repeatedly explain what had happened, so it felt more comfortable closing the whole site.

The rest of us made light work of clearing out the café. When the skip truck arrived, the driver and his colleague expressed their disgust at what had happened and mucked in too.

I'd brought a wheelbarrow and shovel from home which was ideal for transporting the broken crockery, which I started on while the others continued to load the skip with furniture and smashed equipment. I paused midway between the counter and the door, frowning at the colourful chunks of plates, mugs and bowls.

'Are you okay?' Jake asked as he stepped back into the café.

'Yeah. I was just thinking what a waste this is. Everything was in good condition before last night and would have lasted several more years and now it'll be tipped into landfill. That doesn't sit well with me. Poor environment. Unless...' I picked up a chunk of turquoise plate and a piece of deep blue and held them against each other. 'Unless I repurpose them.'

'A mosaic?' Jake asked, peering over my shoulder.

I nodded. 'I've never done it before but I'm sure I can learn. I'm thinking pictures of starfish and shell mosaics to add to the Hollie's Wood website. Or maybe I could make a big one to hang on the wall after we refurbish to show how resilient we are. They can try to break us, but we'll rise again even better than before and here's the proof.' I could picture it already: a bright colourful starfish risen from The Starfish Café's previous life.

'You're amazing. You do realise that?' He bent down and kissed me tenderly.

I'd always been a strong and confident person – probably as a result of being surrounded by such positive, confident role models – but when my role models were so cruelly taken from me, it had hit me hard. Last year, I'd felt that old strength surging through me again and it had grown severalfold this year. I would not be defeated. I had a successful business which would thrive again, great friends on my staff who'd be there every step of the way and I'd unexpectedly found love with an amazing man who, if nature was kind to us, would father my children. Life was pretty damn good right now.

Angie and Martin drove to the supermarket at lunchtime and came back with a box full of sandwiches, drinks, crisps and fruit. They dumped the box on one of the picnic tables with the instruction for the workers to help themselves when they were hungry.

Feeling ready for a break, I sat down beside Tori and ripped open the packet on a tuna mayonnaise sandwich. The phone call she'd said Bart was expecting had come through half an hour earlier. Although I hadn't been close enough to hear it – and wouldn't have been rude enough to listen in even if I had been – I didn't miss Tori calling 'good luck' as he ran over to his car.

Tori and Bart seemed really close, chatting and laughing together while they worked, but I couldn't think of a way to ask how come they'd arrived together without it sounding like an accusation that there was something going on between them. I knew Tori had just split up with Leyton but, as far as I knew, Bart was in a long-term relationship and about to become a dad.

'There's nothing going on between Finley and me,' Tori said, as though reading my mind.

'Oh, I didn't think...'

She gave me a warm smile and I knew she wasn't offended at all. 'I'm going through some stuff, as you know, and he's going through some stuff too so we've bonded over it. He's a great guy.'

'I don't know him that well myself, but my dad and brother really rated him. I'm glad you've found each other. It's great when people come into your life just when you need them.' I glanced across at Jake, who was failing abysmally to chuck something into the skip because he was laughing too much at whatever Martin had had just said to him.

'You've got a good one there,' Tori said, her voice full of warmth.

I turned back to her and smiled. 'It'll happen for you when the time's right. These things usually do. Jake and I had a rough start, but then everything seemed to just fall into place as though it was always meant to be.'

'I love that idea.'

When we'd finished eating, Kerry asked if I wanted her to get some plastic storage crates from a nearby retail park to load the pieces of broken crockery into. I joked about the mammoth task ahead of me sorting it out into colours and Kerry and Avril immediately offered to return tomorrow to do it for me. When I said I couldn't expect them to do that, they retaliated that they wouldn't accept their pay if I didn't accept their help, so we had a deal.

At around three, I sent everyone home. We'd made great progress and my muscles were aching, so I suspected everyone else's were too.

'I'm really sorry I can't help next week,' Maya said as I hugged her goodbye and thanked her.

'Please don't feel guilty,' I assured her. 'You've got university and I wasn't expecting any of you to help. This isn't part of your job description.'

'Maybe not, but I hope you know we'd all do anything for you.'

I hugged her again, not trusting myself to speak in case I started crying. The situation wasn't making me tearful because I refused to let it, but the kindness everyone had shown today was.

'I'm free for my usual hours next week and will do whatever you need,' Avril said after she'd hugged me goodbye. 'Cleaning, painting, varnishing. I could help with the mosaics. I'm no expert but I went on a weekend course a couple of years ago and I've dabbled a bit since.'

'Avril, that would be perfect. Thank you.'

'And then there were three,' I said shortly afterwards, waving off the final carload of Angie, Martin, Katie and Trey.

Tori looked up from her phone. 'Finley will be here in about twenty minutes. Do you mind if I stick around?'

'No problem.'

'Thanks.' She lowered her head and typed something into her phone.

I looked towards the skip, biting my bottom lip. It was such a waste.

'You're thinking you can repurpose that wood, aren't you?' Jake asked.

I grinned at him. 'Can you read minds?'

'When we first met, you told me there were three things you were passionate about – dogs, the café and wood. And I know how much you love repurposing damaged wood.'

'You don't mind hauling it all out again? I can't believe I didn't think about it earlier.'

'It never entered my head either. Where should we put it all?'

Leaving Tori on her phone outside, we stepped into the café to assess the best space to store it, and I snaked my arms round Jake's neck.

'There's actually a fourth thing I'm passionate about,' I said.

'Oh yeah? What's that then?' he asked innocently.

'You,' I whispered before drawing him into a kiss.

We'd stacked a fair bit of the wood up in the porch and were taking a breather outside when Bart returned. His car was jam-packed with boxes and bags, and it didn't take a genius to work out that his relationship had ended and he'd moved out, especially when Tori had said that they'd bonded over going through some 'stuff'.

I grabbed Jake's hand and pulled him into the café so Tori and Bart could have a moment alone.

'What's going on?' he whispered.

'I'm not sure yet.'

We watched as Tori wandered over to his car. They exchanged a few words, Bart shrugged and shook his head, then they hugged.

'Are they together?' Jake asked, looking surprised.

'No. But something's going on with Bart. Look at his car. I think he might have just moved out.'

'But isn't his girlfriend pregnant?'

'Yeah. Don't say anything. He'll tell us what's going on if he wants us to know.'

As they walked towards the café, we stepped outside.

'Sorry for abandoning you,' Bart said. 'There was something I had to do.' He glanced across at Tori, who gave him what looked like an encouraging nod. 'There's something you might as well know...'

33

TORI

Finley and I stood in the middle of the top floor room a couple of hours later, looked at each other wide-eyed, and started laughing.

'How amazing is this room?' I released a low whistle. 'The space! The light!'

'An architect's and designer's dream,' he agreed. 'I can't believe it. It's a yes from me.'

'And me. Easiest decision I've ever made.'

'Are you two okay up there?' Jake shouted up the stairs.

We ran down the two flights and joined him, Hollie and their dog in the hall.

'It's ideal,' Finley said. 'Where do we sign and when can we move in?'

'I told you they'd love it,' Hollie said, lightly nudging Jake.

'You're sure you don't want to sell it?' I asked. 'Because I don't imagine it would take long to find a buyer.'

Jake shook his head. 'I'm not ready to part with it yet, but I didn't want to let it out to strangers either, so this is perfect for me.'

'Any chance we can stay here tonight?' I asked, conscious that the day hadn't worked out as expected so Finley hadn't had a chance to look for a B&B.

'I could probably do with buying new mattresses,' Jake replied.

Finley smiled at me. 'After a night in Tori's camper, I'd happily sleep on the floor.'

'Me, too,' I said. 'Honestly, Jake, an old mattress would be heaven after the past three weeks sleeping in Carrie. Unless you'd rather sort out paperwork and money first. Don't want to rush you.'

'Tonight's fine, then. How about Hollie and I help you empty the car and then we get out of your hair? We'll call this week a favour to some mates and, if you like it and circumstances haven't changed by the end of the week, we can sort the business stuff at the weekend.'

Finley's eyes glistened as he shook Jake's hand and hugged Hollie. I suspected the week's grace would be invaluable for him in detangling his finances from Demi's. Leyton and I had held separate bank accounts, so that aspect had fortunately been straightforward for me.

It didn't take long for the four of us to empty the car and dump Finley's belongings in the dining room to sort later. It struck me that he could pack his whole life into roughly the same number of boxes and cases as me. We hadn't acquired much stuff between us over the years.

'What are your thoughts on refurbishing the café?' I asked Hollie while the men brought in the final load.

She sighed. 'I don't know. The builders I used last time were the same ones who did our extension at home, but they've retired since, so I don't have any contacts. Design-wise, I haven't a clue. I did it myself then and it was something that had been planned a couple of years previously. This is your area of expertise, yeah? If you have any contacts or bright ideas, I'm all ears.'

She looked and sounded exhausted, which wasn't surprising.

She'd already done so much for me – saving my life, giving me the best piece of advice ever, never making me feel like I was taking up space when I stayed for several hours at the café, and now providing somewhere to live. I owed her so much and now I had an opportunity to repay her.

'That thing you said earlier about people coming into your life right when you need them seems to be the theme of the moment. You and Jake have just done something amazing for Finley and me and I'd love to return the favour. Will you be at the café tomorrow?'

'Yes.'

'I've got a client meeting first thing, but would it be okay to drop by around late morning? We can throw a few ideas around about the design and I'm confident I can help you. And, as for you having no contacts, the great news is that I do. You know my cousin Matt who you rescued? He runs a business with his dad and brother and they can do all the trades between them. They're always booked solid, but they've got a great team they can call on so I'm sure they can help too.'

'Really? Oh, my God, Tori! You're a life saver!'

'Not quite on the same scale as what the three of you do, but happy to help where I can.'

34

HOLLIE

I stood behind the damaged serving counter on Monday morning, trying to visualise how the third incarnation of The Starfish Café might look, but I had nothing. Did I want to go for the same layout but different colours or did I want to completely change it? Thank goodness Tori was both an architect and an interior designer because I had no idea where to start and would be relying on her expertise.

Javier, Kerry, Angie and Avril were expected, as was the glazier to replace the broken window, so soon the café was a hive of chatter and activity.

Kerry and Javier took charge of transporting the salvageable wood back to Sandy Croft to stack against the garage wall. I'd found a couple of old A-frame advertising boards in the stock cupboard upstairs, so I painted 'Café & beach closed' on them and Javier and Kerry displayed them at either end of the approach road on their first trip to Sandy Croft to deter potential visitors and customers. I just hoped they didn't stay away for good.

Angie, Avril and I sat on one of the picnic benches sorting the broken crockery into plastic crates, organised by colour. I'd drawn a few sketches of what we might create with the pieces, which they both loved.

'Looking very productive out here,' Tori said, arriving shortly after the glazier left, looking fabulous in a maxi dress covered in ladybirds and bees. She'd told me she made most of her own clothes and I was in awe of her talent with a sewing machine. Definitely not my forte.

'Getting there!' I said. 'How was your first night at Lighthouse View?' She looked a lot brighter this morning than she had yesterday.

'Amazing. Honestly, Hollie, it was the best sleep I've had in months. We're both so grateful.'

'Glad we could help.'

I left Angie and Avril to the sorting and took Tori inside. 'How's Bart... Finley holding up?'

'Putting a brave face on it, but he's devastated. He loves those kids. Demi's punishing them because she's angry with him for her whopper of a mistake. Doesn't seem right.'

'No, it doesn't.' Someone as kind as Finley didn't deserve that at all. I hoped that, when the anger subsided, Demi would change her mind.

'So, let's talk about plans for the future of this place,' Tori said. 'Right now, I'd imagine you're feeling angry and hurt and all over the place as to whether you want to replicate what you had before, go extreme with something completely different, or settle somewhere in the middle.'

'Spot on! And I've not got an answer.'

'You don't need one for now. My advice is to push all those thoughts of what it will physically look like out of your mind and let's think practicalities. Imagine for a moment that I'm the designer of your previous concept and I've given you and your team a unique opportunity to try it out for a few weeks. I've promised you I will change anything that niggles, no matter how big or small. What would you want me to change and why?'

She opened up a colourful notebook and poised a pen over it.

I thought for a moment. 'The obvious one would be to widen the space behind the counter. I know a bigger counter area potentially means less seating, but it also means more efficiency. We might have three people behind it at once – making coffee, taking a payment and serving up cake – and it's so tight that a queue builds while we're wasting time shimmying round each other.'

'That's really helpful. Anything else you'd want to change?'

For the next hour and a half, we wandered round the café, Tori occasionally knocking on walls, peering behind doors and taking photos as I talked about how we'd previously used the space and where the niggles had been. She asked some great questions which made me realise other inefficiencies in the way we'd worked. Angie and Avril chipped in with their feedback too and I posed a question on the WhatsApp group which generated more really helpful suggestions.

'I think I've got everything I need,' Tori said, scanning the information she'd scribbled in her notebook before putting it away in her bag. 'I'll work on some ideas ready to present to you on Friday. In the meantime, I've provisionally secured Uncle Hugh, Matt and Tim. If you like what you see, they can make a start next week.'

'That would be such a weight lifted. Thank you.'

I handed her a thick envelope containing the architect's drawings for the building and the designs from the refurbishment so she had all the accurate measurements.

'The Starfish Café looked gorgeous before,' she said as I walked her out to her campervan. 'With these new designs, we're going to crank up the awesomeness level. I'm so excited about this. If you think of anything else in the meantime – niggles you had, things on your wish list, colours you love – drop me an email or give me a call.'

I waved her off and returned to the picnic bench.

'The crockery's sorted,' Avril declared. 'Anything else we can do to help?'

'Not that I can think of. You can both head off if you want. I'll wait for Javier and Kerry.' I smiled as I spotted Kerry's car on the approach road. 'Speak of the devil.'

Javier walked towards us with a tray of hot drinks and a large paper bag. 'We thought you might be ready for a break.'

I grinned at him. 'Thank you. Your timing couldn't be more perfect.'

We took the crockery crates into the café and I locked the door behind us so we could enjoy our drinks out the back on the terrace, which had thankfully been spared any damage.

'Thank you all so much for your help yesterday and today,' I said once we'd settled round a table with our drinks and brownies from The Chocolate Pot in town. 'You've been absolute stars.'

'We wouldn't be anywhere else,' Angie said, followed by murmurs of agreement.

'I'll need everyone's help when we're preparing to reopen, but it looks like you'll spend the next five to six weeks on paid leave.' I smiled at them ruefully. 'Please don't find other jobs in the meantime.'

I was reassured by their protests that they'd never abandon me and loved working here. There was going to be a sea of change and I could do without the ripples reaching my staff too.

* * *

On Thursday morning, I sat on the steps on the way down to the beach at Starfish Point with Pickle curled up on my knee, watching another sunrise. This one was serene and understated with gentle lemon, peach, gold and orange hues, but still stunningly beautiful.

I yawned, several restless nights taking their toll. Lack of sleep was understandable after what had happened to the café – so much to think about – and Jake working night shifts for the last two nights hadn't helped. I was always a little unsettled without his warmth beside me. But I knew deep down that my lack of sleep was about more than that.

I felt out of sorts. Lost. So I'd come down to the beach this morning hoping that I could work out why I felt that way.

As the sun steadily rose behind the lighthouse, brightening the beach, I clipped Pickle onto his lead and walked down the final flight of stairs onto the pebbles. I paused for a moment, looking left and right, seeking out the named seals hauled up on the sand and rocks.

Tank was easy to spot, as usual, his enormous body stretched out beside a triangular-shaped boulder. Near him, I clocked Panda. Also a grey seal, she had distinctive dark grey circles round her eyes.

The temperature had dropped last night, so a walk should warm me up. Near the southern tip, I found Edison – a female common seal with a dark grey marking strongly resembling the shape of a lightbulb – lounging on one of the rocks. She moved her flipper as we walked past. I liked to think she was waving at me and couldn't resist waving back.

In a month's time, adorable common seal pups would appear. I loved pupping season and, because the common seals gave birth at a different time of year to the greys, we had a bi-annual treat.

I looked down at my stomach. There hadn't been much baby-making going on recently. Another thing Slippy Smythe had messed up. But I was relaxed about that happening or not, so that wasn't why I felt low.

'Why do you think I'm feeling like this?' I asked Pickle as we made our way back up to the café. Not being able to put my finger on it was almost as unsettling as the feeling itself.

I let myself into the café and switched the lights on. Walking into the empty graffitied space still shocked me. It wasn't like I hadn't seen the café as an empty shell before, but that last time had been through choice. This had been forced on us. Besides, last time it hadn't been empty for long and the site had been buzzing with the trades, quickly and efficiently pulling version two together.

That's when it struck me why I was feeling so out of sorts. It was the downtime that was killing me. I was used to being constantly on the go. If I wasn't at the café, I was beachcombing or in my workshop and, since the start of the year, walking Pickle and spending time with Jake too. When we'd refurbished before, the build had commenced the moment I closed the café, I'd checked on progress a couple of times a day, and had spent the rest of my time in my workshop or in my office preparing for the reopening, creating a new logo and fresh menus.

This time round, it was different. I'd been busy on Monday and I'd had crew training on the evening, but I'd had little to do since then. Any new menus needed to fit in with the look of the café and I wouldn't know what that was until tomorrow. I'd been into the workshop several times, but hadn't felt inspired. I'd stared at The Smuggler's Key but found no answers. Poor Pickle had never been walked so much!

I still hadn't shared the reason for closing on social media – merely posting a notice that we were closed and I'd let customers know as soon as there was more detail – but it would be out in the open today as it was publication day for *Bay News*. A reporter had met me on Tuesday to take photos and ask questions. I'd had to bite my lip hard not to blurt out my suspicions as to who was behind it.

'That could be another reason why I feel so down today,' I said to Pickle. 'Everyone will know soon. I wonder how long it will take Slippy Smythe to crawl out of the woodwork. Will he rush over today or wait until tomorrow?'

I checked the time on my phone and sighed. It was only just past seven and the only thing in my schedule for today was meeting Jim from The Hope Centre at the café at ten. The vandals had tipped the cutlery all over the floor, but it wasn't damaged. There'd also been some pots and pans that had survived. It was important to me to start over completely, the only reminders from before being the rising-from-the-ashes mosaic and a new café evolution photo frame. Jim said he'd be delighted to take the items for use at the centre or to distribute among families struggling to set up in a new home after a crisis.

There was no point in me moping around the café for three hours, especially now I'd realised that lack of activity was a reason for my melancholy.

'We'll be home before Jake gets back from his night shift,' I told Pickle as I locked up. 'You can stay and have a nap with him when I meet Jim later.'

* * *

I was back at The Starfish Café by 9.40 a.m. in case Jim was early. Although not windy, there was a chill in the air, more reminiscent of autumn than spring, so I stayed inside.

A vehicle pulled into the car park and I assumed it would be Jim, but my stomach lurched. Big, shiny, expensive and with a private number plate, that car could only belong to one person.

There was nowhere to hide, not that I really wanted to hide from him in my own café as that would prove to him that he'd won and there was no way I'd give him the satisfaction.

I grabbed my phone from my bag, switched it on to record

mode then slipped it into the pocket on the front of my hoodie. Best to be prepared.

Deep breath. Shoulders back. You are *not* scared of this man. He cannot hurt you. Even so, I was relieved that Jim's arrival was imminent.

'You'd better not have more flowers for me,' I muttered under my breath as I opened the inner door. 'And you can leave your stupid portfolio in your car too.'

I flung open the external door when he was a few paces away and leaned against it. I didn't want him in my café. I didn't want him to secretly gloat at the destruction his minions had caused. Unfortunately, I could do nothing about the skip, to which his eyes were now directed. He shook his head and actually dared to look like he was devastated.

'Ms Brooks! I heard what happened and wanted to offer my condolences. Are you all right? Was anyone hurt?'

'Just the café,' I said, nodding towards the skip. 'It was night-time, so there was nobody here.'

'Oh, thank goodness. Was it theft?'

'Vandalism.'

'That's despicable. Have they caught anyone?' His expression was one of shock, his tone full of contempt. Impressive acting skills.

'They're pursuing a few lines of enquiry. The good news is the CSIs had a lot to work with. I think the vandals may have been a bit careless.' I watched his face for a flicker of something, but he was good. I hadn't actually heard back from the police but there'd been footprints in the flour and on some of the seat cushions which I knew the CSIs had removed, so I couldn't resist trying to rattle him.

'Were you able to salvage anything?'

'Not much.'

His eyes flicked to the sign taped to the window beside me for the benefit of anyone who'd decided to drive past the A-boards. 'Not open until the summer? I'm so sorry. That must be tough.'

I shrugged, refusing to give him the satisfaction. 'Not ideal, but one of those things.' I added a smile.

He stared at me for a moment and I detected the slightest curl of his lip and, despite the concerned-businessman routine, I could feel the contempt emanating from him at how easily I was taking this in my stride.

'You know you could save yourself a lot of time and hassle,' he said, his eyes flashing. 'My offer still stands.'

'What offer is that?'

'Don't play games. You know exactly what I mean.' He took a couple of steps closer. 'Although I would, of course, need to reduce it significantly.' He dragged out the last word.

It echoed of the stories that Irene had relayed to Jake about the way Smythe conducted business.

'Why a reduced price?' I asked.

'Why do you think? Look at the place. You've barely got a business left. No assets. No customers. It's just a worthless bit of land and a scabby building.'

'Then why would you still be interested in buying it?'

He took another step closer and I pressed myself back against the door, my heart racing. I could smell the coffee on his breath, see every pore on his nose, feel the hate in his words as he leaned closer and placed his hand on the frame behind me.

'Has anyone ever told you you've got far too much attitude, Ms Brooks? And you ask too many questions.'

He put his other hand up, blocking me. 'You know what happened to the curious cat, don't you?'

I swallowed hard, fear gripping me, followed by relief as I spotted a small white van with the branding for The Hope Centre on the side slowly pulling into the car park. Jim! Thank God for good timing.

'He got killed?' I answered, keeping my voice confident.

'Exactly.'

'That sounds like a threat, Mr Smythe.'

'Get over yourself. You wouldn't be worth the effort.'

'You need to step back.'

'And you need to see sense.'

'I mean it! You're scaring me. Step back and let me go!' I tried to duck under his arms, but he grabbed my wrist.

'Don't hurt me!' I cried, as Jim opened the van door, but my stomach plummeted when he didn't see or hear me, distracted by the phone he held to his ear.

'I'm not interested in hurting you. Just your business. And I promise you this. I *will* have it.'

'You won't! Why can't you understand that no means no?'

'No? That word doesn't exist in my vocabulary. Sooner or later, I always get what I want.'

'Leave me alone!' I shouted even louder, and this time Jim *did* hear.

'Oi!' He ran towards us. 'What the hell are you doing?'

Smythe immediately released me and stepped away. He plastered a smile on his face and turned round. 'We're just talking.'

'Didn't look that way to me.'

'Jim, isn't it? This is none of your business, Jim.' He emphasised Jim's name in a tone that said to me: *I know who you are and I could make trouble for you.*

'You've just made it my business, Sebastian.' Jim drew out the syllables of Smythe's name and I got the full meaning of that too: *And I know who you are and you don't scare me.* 'Are you all right, Hollie?' he asked, his voice softening.

I nodded, completely shaken by the whole thing. What would

Smythe have done if Jim hadn't turned up? Was he the sort who'd resort to violence to get his way? Irene hadn't mentioned it, but it didn't mean it hadn't happened.

Jim glared at Smythe. 'I think you'd better leave.'

'Whatever you think you saw, you're wrong. Hollie and I were discussing a little business. That's all.'

'Really? I often discuss business too, but I usually find a hand-shake is more effective than gripping my client's arm.'

I'd never met Jim before and we'd only spoken on the phone recently, but I loved him already. What a line!

Smythe pushed back his shoulders and straightened his tie. 'We'll talk again, Ms Brooks.'

'No, we won't! I've said no and I mean no.'

With a withering look at me then Jim, he stormed back towards his car. I slumped against the door, shaking.

'Did he hurt you?' Jim asked.

'Just my arm, but he scared me. He wants the business and he won't take no for an answer and I think he...' I stopped myself in time. It wouldn't do any good me starting a rumour, but Jim glanced at the skip and the empty café and sighed.

'Sounds about right, from what I've heard about the way that man conducts his business. People like him make me sick.'

'You won't say anything, will you?'

'I wouldn't jeopardise anything for you. I presume you've shared your thoughts with the police.'

I nodded. 'I'd better give them an update. If they can come over, would you be able to stick around and tell them what you saw?'

'Absolutely.'

'I don't want to keep you from your work. You were only meant to be picking up a few boxes.'

'I've been working flat out since seven. That picnic bench there looks like a good spot to take a well-deserved break and I'd love some company if that's okay with you.'

'That would be great. I can't offer you a drink, though. They destroyed everything.'

'Then it's just as well I've got a flask of coffee in the van and a spare cup. Can I interest you?'

'That would be amazing. And thank you for what you said to Smythe.'

I switched off the recording as Jim went to the van and released a long, shuddery breath. I couldn't help feeling that Smythe was an extremely dangerous man who really would stop at nothing to get what he wanted. That thought terrified me.

* * *

Jim and I had loaded up the boxes into his van by the time PC Dawkins and PC Kramer arrived. We sat on the picnic bench and they took a statement from Jim first so he could get back to The Hope Centre. When he left, they took my statement and I played the recording on my phone.

'We'll pay Mr Smythe a visit when we're done here,' PC Kramer said. 'Do you mind emailing that to the station?'

'Already done.'

'Let us know if he makes further contact but, until this is all resolved, you might not want to be here on your own.'

'I'm heading home now. Thank you.'

They returned to their patrol car and I retrieved my bag and locked up. It was a relief to see them still sitting there when I pulled away, but that sense of relief made me hate Smythe even more. How dare he make me feel like that in my safe haven? I refused to let that man and everything he'd done bring me down. I might not be as busy with this refurbishment as I had been last time round, but there were still things I could do to prepare for the grand reopening and my starting point would be sorting through the box of recipe books we'd brought back from Lighthouse View. I'd look through Jake's nanna's recipes and try some out to see which we could add to the menu. Angie would help me. I wasn't going to focus on what we'd lost. It would be all about the future and what we'd gained instead.

'Tori? I'm home,' Finley shouted up the stairs at Lighthouse View on Thursday evening.

'In the office,' I called.

I heard his footsteps on the stairs, but was in the middle of a delicate tweak to my designs, so I called 'hello' but didn't turn round.

'Are these the designs for Hollie's café?' he asked, peering over my shoulder as I sat at my drawing board.

'Yes. Just doing the finishing touches before I present them to her in the morning. Give me a sec.' I added in the final flourishes. 'All done! Let's hope she loves it.'

'It looks fantastic.'

'Thank you. I really want to get this one right. Hollie doesn't deserve all the crap that's happened to her.' I leaned against my chair back. 'Speaking of crap, how did it go with Demi?' Finley had texted to say he'd be late home because he'd been summoned to the house after work.

'Crap.' He pulled up his chair. 'She didn't want to talk after all.

She'd found some more of my stuff and didn't want it littering the house.'

'So why did she say she wanted to talk?'

'God knows. I asked if there was any chance she'd reconsider me seeing India and Roman and was treated to another *over my dead body* lecture before she slammed the door in my face.'

'Charming.'

'As ever. When I loaded the boxes into my car, I heard knocking. I looked up and India was at her bedroom window in tears. She pointed at me and made a heart with her fingers. I barely held it together.'

I felt a sudden lump constricting my throat at the thought of how much that little girl had to be hurting. I understood that Demi was angry and hurt that the relationship had ended, but why was she taking it out on her kids when she was the reason it had ended?

'At least you know India still loves you,' I said, the words coming out husky. 'Hang on in there. I'm sure she'll see sense eventually.'

'I hope you're right.' He stood up. 'Have you eaten?'

'Not yet. I wanted to finish this first. Do you—'

But I didn't get to finish the sentence as his pager went off.

'At least I don't have far to go. I used to envy Mouse his quick sprint down the hill. See you later.'

'Happy rescuing!'

I wandered over to the front window and watched Finley tugging on his jacket as he ran down Ashby Street. It would probably do him good to have a rescue to focus on, doing something that was normal for him after his world had been turned upside down.

For me, I was steadily finding my new normal at Lighthouse View and liking it very much. Even though it was Jake's home and we were renting it – or we would be when he let us hand over some money – I already felt more relaxed than I'd ever felt at Leyton's place and, if I was honest, at Ewan's too.

Of course, the company helped. Finley and I had spent such a good week together so far, with lots of laughter. We'd discovered we had loads in common and I felt confident that I'd found a good friend. I'd remembered what he said about Demi banning him from watching *The Simpsons* and put it on while we ate our tea one evening and were soon giggling at it.

There'd been no awkwardness as we'd discovered each other's good and bad habits. Like me, he was a morning person, so we'd been up at dawn twice to surf – such an invigorating way to start the day. Leyton had taken forever to get going in the morning to the point where I'd learned it wasn't worth trying to speak to him as I'd either get snapped at or ignored.

I put the lights out and wandered down to the kitchen but couldn't be bothered to cook so took the lazy way out with a plate of cheese and crackers which I took into the lounge. I switched on the TV and flicked channels while I ate, but nothing held my interest, so I turned it off again.

Feeling too tired to do any more work, I stood up and scanned along the paperbacks on the bookshelves in the alcove. Jake said they'd belonged to his nanna and he could soon clear the shelves if we wanted the space, but most of my books related to design and architecture and were more use to me displayed on the shelves in the office to refer to while I was working.

His nanna had evidently loved historicals and read them more than once, judging by the broken spines and battered corners on the large collection by the likes of Catherine Cookson, Josephine Cox and Val Wood. I ran my fingers along another shelf and couldn't help smiling. Rebecca Lannister. So my new landlord's nanna had been a fan of Mother and Father's books. Small world. I scanned to the end and was relieved there were no Domino Blaize books.

I'd unpacked most of my things but there were still a couple of boxes in the dining room and now seemed as good a time as any to tackle them.

The first one I opened was the one I'd started unpacking in Carrie the night Finley showed up. I piled everything onto the dining table, curious as to what the purple box at the bottom contained. Removing the lid, I peered inside.

'A birthday present,' I exclaimed, frowning at the pale pink wrapping paper covered in birthday cakes and balloons. The paper had been ripped at one end, but smoothed back into place, and I had a sudden flashback to my thirty-second birthday. It had been my first birthday since moving in with Leyton and I'd been intrigued when he'd appeared with a mysterious package after already giving me my gifts.

'Is this from you too?' I'd asked.

'You'll have to open it and find out,' he teased with a mischievous twinkle in his eyes.

I'd made one rip of the paper then reeled back in horror. 'Is this a joke?' I cried, pointing at the paperbacks.

He took a closer look and held his hands up in surrender. 'Nothing to do with me, I swear! I found them on the doorstep. Your parents must have put it there.'

I hastily re-covered the books with the wrapping paper and thrust the parcel at Leyton. 'Please put them somewhere out of sight.'

'Do you want me to throw them out?'

I shook my head. Hurling them in the bin might give me a moment's satisfaction, but growing up with parents for authors in a house bursting with books I had too much love and respect for literature to do that.

'No. I'll maybe give them to charity at some point. Just put them somewhere I won't find them and don't tell me where.'

And that somewhere turned out to be a purple box buried under a bunch of my belongings, out of sight, out of mind. I'd forgotten about how Leyton had initially reacted to the find, giving off the suggestion that they were from him. If it had been a good gift, would he have maintained that pretence? Probably. Just like he'd done with the coastguard call. How many other times had he taken credit for something that was nothing to do with him?

He wasn't worth any more of my time, but this gift was. I ripped off the rest of the wrapping paper to reveal a collection of twenty or so paperbacks. The names of my parents' various pseudonyms – including Domino Blaize – leapt from the colourful spines. I recognised some of the titles as their biggest sellers, but others were unfamiliar.

Freed from the wrapping paper, the neat pile slid apart and, nestling between two Rebecca Lannister books, there was a cream letter.

My heart raced as I tentatively lifted it out. On the front, in Mother's immaculate calligraphy was my name but, significantly, it was Tori rather than Victoria. I couldn't remember her *ever* calling me that. A red wax seal with the Tennyson family crest sealed the letter closed and I ran my fingers over it, remembering being fascinated as I watched Mother at her writing bureau, placing her quill back on its stand and melting the stick of wax in the candle flame. She loved writing letters and would sometimes let me stamp the seal.

I sank down heavily on the chair, butterflies taking flight. She'd sent me this letter five months after I'd found out the truth but I'd had no idea it existed. Up until that point, I'd ignored phone calls and returned any letters I received unopened. Then they'd stopped and, until now, I'd never correlated that with the arrival of the books.

Gulping back my nerves, I split the seal and opened the letter.

My darling Tori

It is perhaps a little underhand to enclose a letter with your birthday gift, but I am not sure how else to contact you. I hope and pray that this letter and gift do not return to us like the others, although my heart tells me to prepare for this.

Your father and I have failed you in so many ways. You have no idea how desperate we were to have a child. Or perhaps you do, given what you now know. Having difficult relationships with our own parents, we were determined to be the best and most wonderful parents in the world if we were blessed with children, yet we have managed to be the worst.

Not revealing the truth is clearly our biggest failing and we will regret that forever. You were correct. You had a right to know. It remains our wish that you will grant us an opportunity to explain. Even if you then wish to remain detached from us, you will at least know the full story.

I therefore want to address a couple of our other failings in this letter. The first is a refusal to address you by your preferred moniker. This was not a wish to be obtuse and merely a habit. We longed for a baby girl and chose the name Victoria for you when we married, seventeen years before we were finally blessed with your arrival. Reflecting on it now, it shows a lack of respect for your wishes and an imposition on you of ours. Tori, we are sincerely sorry.

The second failing is how we've made you feel throughout your life. We assumed you knew how incredibly proud we were of everything you've achieved and the exceptional woman you have become. Hindsight being marvellous, we see that this was a careless and foolish assumption.

This brings me onto the reason for the gift. Let me reassure you that this isn't some random collection of author copies we have cobbled together. These are very special first edition books that we have been saving for you. They're not special because they're first edition – they're special because they're about our first edition!

You believed we weren't proud of you and we thought we'd made it clear that we were, but we've realised that we made it clear on the page and not in person. Every single one of these books is dedicated to you, our beautiful, talented, incredible daughter. Not only are they dedicated to you, but every one of the heroines in these books is inspired by you. If you read them, you will be left in no doubt as to how much you mean to both of us.

We wish you the happiest of birthdays and, as an additional gift to you, we are going to (finally) respect your wishes and stop making contact. We desperately hope you will one day be able to forgive our many failures and find a way to rebuild our relationship – or perhaps that should say to build a fresh one.

You know where we are when you feel ready, no matter how long that takes. In the meantime, you'll remain forever in our hearts, our truly wonderful first edition.

Love and respect always
Mother & Father

I hadn't realised I was crying until a tear splashed onto the page, smearing the ink. Gently placing the letter on the table to prevent further damage, I removed one of the Rebecca Lannister books and flicked to the dedication at the front:

*For Victoria, whose strength and resilience conquers the highest
mountains.*

And another:

*For Victoria, whose smile lights up the darkest room and whose laugh is
like sunshine.*

I picked up a third, but I could no longer see through my tears.
Slumping forward onto the table, I rested my head on my arms and
sobbed. Years of pent-up frustration spilled out in anguished wails.
All those wasted years and it was all my fault! I'd clung onto my
virtue as the truth-teller, unwavering in my disregard for those who
lied, like Ewan, Leyton and my parents, yet I'd been lying to myself
for most of my life.

I'd never recovered from the scars left by the malicious gossip at
school or the loss of the two closest friends I'd ever had. The years
of loneliness that followed had taken their toll and affected all my
subsequent relationships. It had been easy to blame my parents for
it all, to direct all the hurt and pain at them, to shut them out of my
life like Millicent and Tracie had shut me out of theirs. But it wasn't
their fault and I couldn't keep telling myself that it was.

The truth was that I'd been the one to blow on the tower of
cards and send the whole pack tumbling to the ground. I'd been the
one who'd approached Alistair Soames and told him Millicent
wanted to be his date to the ball after she'd expressly asked me not
to. I was the one who'd brought humiliation and embarrassment on
my best friend by revealing her secret, so she'd retaliated by doing
the same to me. I was the one who'd tried to get Tracie to take sides,
losing her friendship too. And I was the one who'd been so
wrapped up in how it was affecting me that I didn't pause to step
back and consider ways of handling it differently. Several sprung to

mind now. I could have laughed it off or even joined in, finding the raciest passages possible. I could even have involved my parents, asking them to direct me to their riskiest books.

Life was all about choices and I'd chosen to wallow. I'd chosen to blame my parents because that was easier than blaming myself.

When Ewan first dropped his bombshell and our relationship continued on borrowed time, I'd initially blamed my parents for that, telling myself I didn't want children because I'd had such terrible role models from whom I hadn't learned what it was like to be a parent. Not true. By the time I'd moved back home, I'd managed to accept that it was all my choice and not influenced by my own childhood.

As for my parents being terrible role models – something I'd so cruelly levelled at them before cutting them out of my life – that hadn't been true either. They were passionate about what they did and so dedicated to it that they wholeheartedly immersed themselves in that world and, deep down, I admired them for that. I'd harnessed those behaviours when approaching my own career and had been attracted to Ewan and Leyton because they demonstrated the same traits.

Were any of us really, truly honest about everything?

Reading Mother's words just now, I had to acknowledge the truth around why I'd really fled from Redamancy Castle both times: because I didn't feel like I mattered. Robyn had been scarily accurate with her insights. I *had* wanted to be centre of my parents' world, but it wasn't because I resented my sister, as she believed. I wanted us *both* to be the centre of their world, but they'd been so devoted to each other, and their fictional, historical world felt impenetrable. I thought I'd been a mistake, coming along so late in their marriage and, with the eleven-year age difference, I'd believed Robyn had been too.

When I was little, Miss Pemberley, Nanny, Cook and Phipps had

spent more time with me than Mother or Father. If I fell over and
hurt myself, Miss Pemberley or Nanny kissed it better. If I did well
in my studies, Miss Pemberley was the one who expressed delight.
Cook taught me how to bake. Phipps taught me to ride and cheered
me on at my gymkhanas. What had my parents done? They read
me bedtime stories. The couple who were so wrapped up in their
devotion to each other that they'd given their home a name that
means 'loving the one who loves you' managed to break away from
their research and their deadlines to do the one thing they did day
in day out anyway. And, of course, that stopped when I became too
old for bedtime stories, and nothing took its place. When I started
at school, there was no more Miss Pemberley either.

My remaining years at Whitsborough West were friendless and
lonely and I didn't even see much of Matt and Tim anymore.
They'd shown an interest in construction and spent their holidays
labouring for Uncle Hugh. So I threw myself into my studies so I
didn't have time to wallow in how alone I felt at home. That's when
I became a selenophile because, unlike my parents, the moon was
ever-present in my life. I talked to her, asked her questions, wished
on her.

I'd be forever grateful for the financial support my parents gave
me. I knew how lucky I was and had never taken that for granted,
but I'd have traded it all for an emotional connection, to feel like I
mattered to them and they were proud of me. When it was clear it
would never happen, I took my opportunity to get out of there, and
I grabbed at the first relationship that came along. And the second.
Always seeking out the love and attention I'd craved, but never
quite finding my own redamancy. Not even with Ewan because if
he'd truly loved me, he'd have been willing to sacrifice his desire for
a family. And the same worked for me in reverse. Clearly neither of
us had loved the other deeply enough.

The sound of the door opening and Finley calling out slowed

my sobs. I sat up and swiped my hands across my cheeks, trying to regain control of my breathing, but I was still too emotional. The tears kept tumbling and I couldn't stop shaking.

'What's happened?' Finley cried.

I tried, but I couldn't seem to form any words.

Next moment, I was lifted from the chair and pulled into his embrace. His arms were strong and comforting. He stroked my hair and back and whispered that he was here and it would be all right.

I have no idea how long we stood there, holding each other, but the sobs eventually subsided and my body relaxed enough for me to step back.

Finley gently ran his thumbs across my cheeks, capturing the final tears – a movement so tender, it made me want to cry once more. We weren't a couple. We were only just getting to know each other. But at that moment, I finally felt that I was at the centre of someone's world and that they were fully focused on me.

'Do you want to talk about it?' he asked gently.

I nodded. I suspected there'd be more tears to come, but it was time to open up.

'You know when I told you about my parents?' I said, my voice catching between words. 'I missed a part out…'

36

TORI

Seven years ago

Impressed by my refurbishment of the Country Tavern, a friend of Giles Tilley's commissioned me to work on Oyster Pearl, a restaurant she'd bought on Fellingthorpe seafront.

My parents hadn't been able to attend the grand reopening of The Country Tavern due to a prior commitment for Rebecca Lannister. Giles had invited them to visit for a complimentary meal at any time so that they could see my work but, so far, they hadn't taken him up on his offer. I'd mentioned it several times only to be met with a myriad of excuses, and I began to suspect that either Giles had overplayed their enthusiasm about my abilities when they'd recommended me or they'd overplayed my strengths in the hope of securing me the work and getting me out of the house.

As far as I was aware, the grand reopening of Oyster Pearl didn't clash with any prior commitments and I was excited about finally showcasing my work to my parents.

'What are you going to wear tomorrow night?' I asked Mother as I poured myself a coffee in the kitchen on Thursday morning.

She loaded her empty cereal bowl into the dishwasher and looked up at me, frowning. 'What for, darling?'

'For going to Oyster Pearl.'

She stared at me blankly.

'The grand reopening?' I prompted. 'The project I've been working on? Fellingthorpe seafront?'

'Oh, that! It's tomorrow, is it? Drat.'

She wasn't coming and the excuse would be the one word that made me want to shudder. 'Deadline?' I suggested, my tone flat and dripping with sarcasm.

'Sorry, darling. We barely have time to breathe just now. Your father's trying to iron out a tricky plot point and I've just eaten standing up and...'

I zoned out. I'd heard it so many times before. I understood deadlines – I worked to them all the time myself – but the great thing about deadlines was that you knew them in advance and could plan round them. I also understood that creativity wasn't a tap that could just be turned on, but my parents lived and breathed creativity. They could create a character or reel off an intricate plot at the click of their fingers so I refused to accept that they were always right on the wire with their deadlines and couldn't spare any time for me.

Mother was still talking when I slammed my mug on the side, spilling hot coffee onto the worktop, and stormed out of the kitchen and up to my room. I paced the floor for several minutes, my fists clenching and unclenching, my breathing coming fast and shallow and suddenly I had to get out of there. I stripped off my jeans and pulled on my jodhpurs. A gallop across the estate would help release that tension.

Phipps was in the stables.

'I didn't realise you were planning to ride today,' he said. 'Would you like me to saddle Taffi up for you?'

'I'll do it. Thank you.'

'Are you all right?'

'Not really. Mother has just revealed that she and Father are not coming to Oyster Pearl's grand opening tomorrow because they're on – surprise, surprise – a deadline. When are they ever not on a deadline? When will they ever find time for me?'

I knew Phipps wouldn't say anything negative about my parents – too much loyalty and respect for his employers – but I also knew he'd be supportive and listen to me offload which, right now, was exactly what I needed.

'I was thinking of taking Merlin out,' he said. 'Would you care for some company?'

I gave him a grateful smile. 'I'd love some, Phipps. Thank you.'

* * *

Later that afternoon, I couldn't find my phone. I wandered down to the stable block, wondering if it might have slipped out of my pocket when I'd removed my jacket after the ride.

Taffi was lying down in her stable. She did that more than any horse or pony I'd ever known, reminding me more of a dog than a horse. It was an indication of feeling relaxed and safe which made me happy, especially when I'd only met her six months ago.

I searched the hay around her. Either my phone wasn't in the stable or Taffi was lying on it.

'Might as well give you some more attention while I'm here,' I said, unhooking a brush. I'd only just knelt down and made two strokes of the brush when I stiffened at the sound of raised voices.

'I don't see what all the fuss is about,' Mother said.

'That's your problem! You never do!' I reeled back in shock at Phipps's angry tone. I'd never heard him raise his voice before, and would not have expected him to speak that way to his employer.

'Especially when it comes to Tori.' I jolted once more at the sound of my name.

'It's Victoria,' Mother snapped.

'And she prefers Tori. Do you realise that you and Ralph are the only ones who don't call her that?' He released an exasperated sigh. 'That's not the point. The point is that it *is* a big deal. She wants you to go.'

'How do you know that?'

'How do you think? You led her to believe you were going and suddenly you have a deadline.'

'We *do* have a deadline, Jack!' she exclaimed.

'You *always* have a deadline. Your life is full of them and you and Ralph bounce from one to the next. Jesus, even having children was a deadline for you! Especially Robyn.'

'Yes! Nature's deadline! It's all right for you men. You can sire a child till goodness knows what age, but it becomes harder for a woman once they hit their forties.'

'Don't I know it!'

I squirmed inwardly, hating that I was listening to a private conversation and knowing it was too late to alert them to my presence. But I was also bewildered. It was the weirdest conversation and ricocheting all over the place.

'I never heard you complaining,' Mother said, sounding hurt.

I gulped. What? *What?*

Phipps's voice softened. 'That's unfair, Vivienne.'

'I'm sorry you think that, but you suggesting that Ralph and I have no time for the girls is unfair too.'

'It's the truth. Search your heart and you'll realise it too.'

My heart raced. I didn't want to keep listening, but it was compelling. Phipps had it spot on. How had he picked that up and my parents hadn't?

'Are you suggesting we don't love them?'

'No, but I am suggesting you don't show it. Not in the ways they need to feel it. Why do you think Tori disappeared to Bath and we barely saw hide nor hair of her for gone a decade? Why do you think she eloped? Why do you think Robyn moved to New Zealand?'

'For their studies! Their careers! Love!' Mother's voice had raised in volume once more.

'You go on believing that. But ask yourself if missing Tori's special event tomorrow night is really demonstrating your love and support.'

'We're back to that, are we? Crikey, Jack, you're like a stuck record.' I'd never heard Mother sound so angry. She snapped occasionally when stressed, but this was something else.

'Better than being stuck in a different bloody century. She's your daughter, Vivienne! She's a beautiful and talented young woman and you should be proud to stand by her side tomorrow night.'

'If it means that much to you, why don't you go?'

'Fine by me. If you have yet another more pressing engagement, then I'd be delighted to go and support my daughter.'

The world stopped and, for a moment, I couldn't breathe. Daughter? Had Phipps just said I was his daughter? That wasn't possible!

'And maybe I'll tell her while I'm there,' he added.

My heart was now thudding at such an alarming rate, I thought I might pass out.

'You wouldn't dare!' Mother cried.

There was a pause, then Phipps's voice softened. 'I wouldn't hurt her or you like that but, mark my words, secrets rarely stay hidden. I said all along you should tell them the truth and I stand by that.'

'Yes, well, that's not your decision to make. This conversation's over.'

'Vivienne!'

I'm amazed I could hear the crunch of the gravel as she walked away over the sound of my heartbeat. What. Just. Happened?

I wanted to stand up, but my legs wouldn't move. I wanted to shout or scream, but no sounds came out when I opened my mouth. Phipps was my biological father, and Robyn's too, by the sound of it. Did Father know? Did Robyn? Was that why she'd gone to New Zealand?

All that time I'd spent with Phipps over the years, thinking how lovely he was to take the time to teach me to ride – something that wasn't part of his job description – and he hadn't been doing it because he was kind. He'd been doing it because I was his daughter.

I wrapped my arms across my stomach, feeling nauseous.

Phipps was still in the stables. I could hear him breathing and wondered if he could hear me. I didn't want to confront him, but I desperately needed some air and there was no way I could escape without being seen.

'Is it true?' I called, my words coming out squeaky.

Moments later, he peered into Taffi's stable, his eyes wide, his face ashen.

'Is it true?' I repeated, still rooted to the spot.

'Yes,' he said, holding my gaze.

He hadn't really needed to respond. It was written all over his face – not just the guilt but the similarities to me. Robyn, with her blonde hair and sapphire blue eyes, was the spit of Mother. People said I was more of a blend of my parents, with Mother's heart-shaped face and high cheekbones and hazel eyes like Father. Only they weren't his eyes. They were Phipps's, as were my full lips.

'And Robyn?'

'Yes.'

'Does Father know?'

He swallowed and nodded.

'Has he always known?'

'I can't say anything more,' he said gently. 'You need to speak to your parents. Are you all right?'

'Would you be?' I asked, struggling to avert my gaze, recognising more and more similarities between us.

'Probably not.'

My legs had gone numb from kneeling for so long. I held my hand out to him so he could help me to my feet, and I stamped them in an attempt to get the blood flowing once more.

'I'm so sorry,' he said.

'The red hair?' I asked. It had remained a mystery where it had come from as there'd been no redheads in Mother's or Father's families, but Phipps was blond.

'My mother,' he said. 'You look a lot like her. She'd have...' He hung his head. 'Sorry. For everything.'

So was I.

* * *

Present day

'That must have been a hell of a shock,' Finley said, his eyes wide.

'I was completely blindsided by it. As soon as I knew, I could see those similarities, but it wasn't obvious. You'd have to have been looking. It wasn't like we were at gymkhanas together and people were mistaking us for father and daughter. Phipps was lovely to me, but so were Nanny, Cook and Miss Pemberley. He never said or did anything to make me question my heritage.'

'What did your parents say?'

'Not a lot, although I didn't give them much of a chance. I wanted to confront them straightaway, especially after Phipps confirmed that Father knew about their affair. I was determined to be calm and adult about it but, by the time I got back to the house, I'd worked myself up into such a rage. All those lies! Years and years of them. And for me to have spent so much time in Phipps's company with no idea he was my biological father seemed so unfair to me and to him. It was like I'd been paraded in front of him. *Look what you can't have.*

'I found them in the sewing room. They were supposedly on such a pressing deadline that they couldn't attend my big night, but they had time to knock up a new riding habit. I exploded. I'm not proud of myself, but it all tumbled out – what I'd heard, how shocked I was, how accurate Phipps was about the lack of love and attention from them, how much I hated them for lying. Mother begged me to let her explain, but I didn't want to hear it. I told them I didn't want anything to do with any of them again – Phipps included – then I packed my stuff, drove to Leyton's, and seven years later...'

I passed Finley the note I'd found among the books. 'I've just found this. Read it.'

His expression kept changing as he read it, and he sighed as he passed it back to me. 'Your sister said they didn't want to see you. Do you think she was lying?'

'From what Mother wrote, it's highly probable.'

'Are you going to try to see them again?'

'I think I owe it to them and to myself to hear them out. But

there's something I need to do first. I need to read those books.' I
ran my fingers across some of the spines. 'The letter states I'll
discover how proud they are of me between the pages of these
books. I've already seen they're all dedicated to me. I think it's time I
tried to understand who my parents really are and whether they
really did care about me like they claim.'

37

HOLLIE

When I pulled into the car park at The Starfish Café shortly before ten on Friday morning, Tori was already there, sitting at one of the picnic benches chatting to someone on her phone. A large grey portfolio – the sort used by art students – was propped up against the bench along with an easel.

'I've had an absolute blast working on these this week,' she gushed after greeting me with a hug.

'Then we'd better get inside and take a look. Do you want a hand with anything?'

'If you could grab the easel, that would be great.'

'How's it going at Lighthouse View?'

'Couldn't be better. The house is gorgeous, the location is perfect, and Finley's the dream housemate. We're both so grateful.'

The words were positive and delivered with enthusiasm, but she looked tired, and her eyes had lost their usual sparkle.

'Are you all right?' I asked.

'Marvellous. Are you ready to see what your future could look like?'

'I can't wait.' Whatever was bothering Tori, she clearly didn't want to talk about it and I knew that feeling well. I wouldn't push.

She erected the easel and unzipped the portfolio, but didn't remove anything.

'Before I show you the designs, I want to explain more about my inspiration. When I'm designing anything, I listen carefully to my client. What's their personality? What excites them? What would make them love being in that lounge, bedroom, hotel or café? How do they want to use the space? My proposed design often deviates from what the client tells me they want because I fill in the gaps in a client's imagination and it usually turns out to be exactly what they want but hadn't realised. I always present within budget too. I'm not here to talk a client into something they can't afford.'

Tori's passion for her work was obvious. Her eyes shone and the words bubbled with excitement, making me wonder if I'd imagined the darkness earlier.

'You'd wondered whether to keep the New England seaside theme because of the freshness of it and the relevance to the café name and your location, but I've deviated from that a little. We're still capitalising on the seaside but, instead of New England, the emphasis will be on the café's name and something that came across to me strongly from our conversations. Would you mind indulging me by closing your eyes for a moment so I can get the eyeline just right with this?'

Smiling, I did as she asked. I could hear the flapping of paper and the movement of the easel.

'I'm excited and delighted to present you with... open your eyes... Operation Driftwood.'

My jaw dropped as I took in the design propped on the easel, angled as though I was looking at the serving counter.

'Oh, Tori. You're good!' I exclaimed. She'd done exactly what she said – listened – and it was beyond anything I could ever have come close to imagining.

As she talked me through the various features, I could see how she'd addressed the niggles and was astonished at all the practical ideas to save space and make everything flow better. Driftwood featured heavily, along with railway sleepers, tea chests and pallets.

Tori moved the easel towards the door and revealed another image looking towards the main seating area. I'd told her the customers loved the booths and she'd kept those, but the tables were made from rustic reclaimed wood supported by one sturdy metal plinth, giving customers more legroom to ease into the padded seats.

'The central seating area has the same style of tables,' Tori pointed out, 'and the wooden chairs are painted with a distressed look in white, blue, turquoise and teal so you're still getting your seaside colour palette.'

She turned the easel again and produced the final image of the other end of the café.

'I've kept the breakfast bar like you wanted using driftwood or sleepers and this shelving unit made from pallets would go in front of the porch. It's for your Hollie's Wood stock which, by the way, I have completely fallen in love with. As well as being an amazing cook, it appears that you're ridiculously talented with wood.'

'That's so lovely. Thank you.'

'Credit where credit's due. You can showcase your products here for people inside the café but, because there's no solid back on the unit, people can see them when they first come into the porch – particularly good for parents parking buggies who might have missed them otherwise.'

'You've thought of everything. These designs are incredible. And definitely all in budget?'

'All in budget. Certain aspects are pricey like the tables, but that's offset by other items I can source for practically nothing. My friend Jamie owns a reclamation yard. I put a lot of business his way, so he lets me know when he gets in sleepers and driftwood and gives me a hefty discount as a thank you. The pallets are free from another friend who has a factory. They're ones that have got damaged and can't be used anymore. I don't charge for them.'

'That's very honest of you.'

'If a client feels like I'm giving them a fair deal and I'm open and honest about the pricing, they're more likely to recommend me.'

She took me into the kitchen next and talked me through her ideas for there. 'So, what do you think?'

'I think that whoever trashed this place has done me a favour because this is outstandingly amazing. Thank you. I want it all. I can't think of anything I'd want to change.'

She beamed at me. 'I still get so nervous when I ask a client if they want to greenlight a design. I think I've understood who they are and what makes them tick, but there's always this fear that I'll be completely wide of the mark.'

'You've hit bullseye.' She really had. My love for apothecary drawers had only been a passing comment when she'd asked me where I made my driftwood products, but she'd incorporated a set as behind-counter storage. I'd joked about it being a challenge to showcase my Hollie's Wood products near Christmas, but I hadn't asked her to build in any sort of display, yet that's exactly what she'd done.

'I'll email you some paperwork this afternoon to confirm the designs and prices. As soon as you sign it online, I can start sourcing everything.'

She glanced towards the staircase. 'You definitely don't want upstairs touching?'

'It wasn't trashed and we've never really used it. Mum had it built as an overflow space for the summer, but we didn't need it when she had the terrace added on. I was going to use it for functions, but we held one down here in February and it worked so much better.'

'I'm so relieved you liked the ideas,' Tori said as we loaded everything back into her campervan. 'I was anxious to get this right after everything you've been through.'

'I love them, thank you. You didn't quite seem yourself this morning. Was that because you were anxious?'

'No. I came across something unexpected in one of my boxes last night – a blast from the past – and it threw me. It was on my mind when I was driving over this morning, so sorry if I seemed a bit distracted.'

'No need to apologise. Just wanted to make sure you're okay.'

She smiled. 'I will be. It was a shock, but I believe good things will come from it. It's just going to take some time and patience before they do.'

'A bit like the café getting trashed,' I said. 'Traumatic at the time, but look how amazing it will be when it returns. Sometimes when things appear to be falling apart, they may actually be falling into place.'

Her smile widened. 'Exactly that! I'm going to write that down before I drive away. Thanks, Hollie.'

I left her scribbling in her notebook and returned to the café, excitement bubbling in me as I envisaged how it would look with Tori's designs in place.

'It was just a stumble, Smythe,' I said, 'and I've made it part of my dance.'

A warm feeling like a hug enveloped me and I had the strongest sensation of my mum standing right beside me, holding my hand.

'With courage, nothing is impossible, is it, Mum?' I whispered.

38

TORI

On Saturday evening, with Hollie's sign-off on Operation Driftwood, I drove up to the farm to go through a schedule of works with Uncle Hugh, Matt and Tim. I'd already given them a heads-up as soon as I took the brief, so they'd had a chance to shift a few things round and contract in some extra labour. They'd been disgusted to hear about the break-in and were willing to move heaven and earth for Hollie. After all, she'd been part of the team to save our lives and they saw this as their chance to play a part in saving her business.

Hollie gave me two spare sets of keys – one for Uncle Hugh and one for me – so we could start work whenever we were ready on the Monday. I set up a table on the first floor so that I was on site to project manage everything and answer questions. It was a bit noisy trying to work inside but a warm and sunny week meant I could make phone calls on the terrace or on one of the benches on the way down to the beach. I could get used to working outside. Shame my pale skin wasn't so keen as I slapped on the factor fifty.

Slipping in Hollie's refurbishment as an extra project meant I needed to work some long hours to keep on top of my other work, but there was no way I wasn't going to help her.

Each evening during week one of Operation Driftwood, I worked on my other projects in the office at Lighthouse View while Finley studied. We'd agreed to take it in turns to cook, but he'd insisted on being chief chef every night so far, saying I had a busier week than him. His only condition was that I had to join him at the kitchen table to eat. The proper break and an opportunity to chat about something other than work was most welcome.

Finley was so considerate and easygoing that I couldn't get my head round why Demi would even glance at another man when she was living with someone like him. Oh well, Demi's loss was my gain. It was official now. Finley and I had signed a three-month lease with Jake on Sunday and I couldn't have had a better housemate.

'How's the workload looking tonight?' Finley asked when he arrived home on Thursday night.

'I need to do a couple more hours, but I'll take the rest of the evening off if you fancy a walk or a film.'

'I've got a better idea. Are you any good at disco bowling?'

'What the heck's that?'

He grinned. 'Ten-pin bowling but with loud music and disco lights. I'll book us a lane.'

* * *

Disco bowling at the Golden Galleon was exactly as Finley had described. Bit cheesy, but there was such a fun vibe. Laughter, cheering and the occasional groan punctuated the music. The thud of the bowling balls hitting the tracks and the scattering of pins all added to the tension and excitement.

Finley was brilliant at it, scoring strikes and spares galore. I was shockingly bad. I managed two foot faults, a ball in our neighbour's lane and several balls down the gutter.

'Close match!' I said, laughing as the final score flashed up on our first game. Finley had scored a whopping 268 out of a possible 300 points, and I'd scored an embarrassingly pathetic twenty-three.

'Beginner's luck,' he joked. 'Come on, admit it. You're a hustler.'

'Oh yeah, you should be afraid. Very afraid!'

I stood at the end of the alley at the start of our second game, bowling ball in hand, steely determination flowing through me. I was usually brilliant at learning new skills. I'd quickly mastered riding, surfing, paddleboarding, and kayaking. I was an expert on the sewing machine and I was an architect, interior designer and project manager. A ten-pound ball and ten pins were not going to defeat me.

Except they were.

I turned to Finley, shoulders slumped, after both my balls ended up in the gutter. He'd offered some coaching during the last game, but I'd been convinced I could master it myself. I couldn't.

'Help! I can't score less than twenty-three on my second go. I do need a coach after all.'

On my next attempt, Finley stood beside me, talking me through the body position, encouraging me to relax, explaining that the little triangles in the lane weren't decorative and were actually arrows called 'dovetails' helping the bowler direct the ball.

'I'm still doing something wrong,' I said, although knocking down three pins was a thrill.

He tried to explain how to adjust my arm position, but I wasn't getting it. 'I need a demonstration, please,' I said in a playful whiny voice.

Finley stepped behind me and pressed his arm against mine. He said something, but I have no idea what it was. The music seemed to soften and, for the briefest moment, it felt like we were alone and

I was being held by him. I closed my eyes and inhaled as he guided my arm backwards and then forward.

'And release,' he said.

The ball rolled down the lane and I grabbed his arm as it got closer and closer, looking to be on course.

'Yes!' he cheered as I scored a spare.

He picked me up and swung me round laughing. 'You did it!'

'*We* did it!'

My pulse raced at the word 'we'. Finley and me. We.

I returned to the sofa and sat down heavily, grabbing my drink and taking a big gulp. Where was my head at? There was no 'we', or at least not in that way. Friends. Good friends. The only reason my pulse was racing was the excitement of actually hitting the pins. Nothing to do with Finley.

39

HOLLIE

Thursday nights were my night with Katie and had been for years. Even when she'd travelled the world with Trey last year, she'd Face-Timed me on a Thursday whenever she was able. Since I'd started seeing Jake, we'd got into a routine of double-dating once a month and tonight was one of those nights, timed to celebrate Trey's birthday.

We'd arranged to meet in Ruby Fizz, a 1930s-style art deco bar in a side street off Whitsborough Bay's main pedestrianised precinct. Katie and I had been there a few times this year, but I hadn't returned with Jake since the awful night when our fledgling relationship ended.

'It feels weird to be back,' Jake said as we sat down at a table in the back room, not far from where we'd sat before. 'I thought I'd lost you that night.'

'And now look at us. It was meant to be.'

Our lips met, his kiss warm and tender.

'Should we come back later?' Katie asked, laughing.

'Sorry,' I said, giving her and Trey hugs and wishing him a happy birthday.

'Don't apologise for the kissing,' she said, sitting down. 'I can't tell you how happy it makes me to see you like this.' Her voice turned serious and she scowled. 'Although, if you ever hurt her, Jake, I will hunt you down and...'

She couldn't finish her sentence for laughing. 'Sorry. I'm a bit giddy today. I can't wait! We have news!'

She glanced at Trey who grinned and nodded, then she thrust out her left hand.

'Oh, my God!' I cried, grabbing it and gazing at the stunning engagement ring. 'Congratulations! When did this happen?'

'Yesterday,' Trey said. 'I couldn't think of a more perfect birthday present.'

They smiled at each other and my heart melted. They'd been together for nearly nine years and I had wondered if they'd return from their travels engaged – or perhaps even married – but Katie had said neither of them were particularly bothered about walking down the aisle.

'I need to hear all about the proposal,' I said after another round of hugs. 'Where did you do it?' Trey was known for his romantic gestures, so I was expecting an impressive response.

'In the car park at Whitsborough Bay General Hospital,' Trey said, grinning.

'Oh! That's, erm... really romantic?'

Katie laughed again. 'It was, actually. He did it properly! Bended knee, gorgeous speech, beautiful ring, promise to be a brilliant dad.'

'What?' I squealed.

'It was a big day for birthday gifts,' Trey said, passing me a baby scan photo.

'The baby's due on 15 November,' Katie added, 'and we want to get married before then. No date in mind yet, but lots to plan.'

'I need more hugs!' I cried, rushing round the table once more.

Jake hugged them both too. 'That's amazing news! Happy birthday, happy engagement and happy baby news!'

I couldn't be more thrilled for them. Trey was so perfect for Katie. I'd had a good feeling about them when they first got together, but I'd known he was a keeper when Isaac and Dad died. He'd been so supportive of Katie spending time with Mum and me, being there for her while she was there for us. She'd been in love with my brother for years in her teens and early twenties and, even though she'd since moved on, Trey had understood her need to grieve for him.

'I've got something very important to ask you,' Katie said. 'Will you be my chief bridesmaid?'

Tears rushed to my eyes. 'Aw, I'd love to. Thank you.'

'Trey's sister will be a bridesmaid too and I'm going to ask Avery.'

She looked a bit uncertain, but I smiled at her. 'Good choices.' Avery was Craig's younger sister. She worked with Katie and Trey and was good friends with them both. We'd never particularly gelled, but I suspect that was more to do with Avery and Craig's difficult relationship.

We chatted more about the specifics of Trey's car park proposal, their tentative thoughts about when and where they might hold the wedding, and how they felt about becoming parents. I hadn't told Katie that Jake and I were trying for a baby. Because we were taking the *if it happens, it happens* approach, I didn't want the pressure of anyone knowing and enquiring, even my best friend. Now that I knew she was expecting, I drifted off into a little fantasy about us being pregnant together. If it happened for me any time in the next six months, our children would be in the same school year. They might even attend the same school and be best friends – just like we'd fantasised when we'd been younger and she'd decided she'd marry my brother and I'd marry Kyle!

'Do you know any good wedding photographers?' Katie asked Jake, turning my attention away from babies and back to weddings.

'No, sorry.'

'I don't suppose you'd consider being ours?'

'It's not my speciality,' he said. 'I do landscapes and I know some people would say *it's all photos* but, believe me, it's a different set of skills. I wouldn't want to screw it up and ruin your big day.'

'I'm sure you wouldn't screw it up,' I said gently, hating his lack of confidence in himself. Nothing I said seemed to eradicate the damage his sister had done. When that seal photo he'd printed off for me got trashed, he'd said: 'Seems the vandals share Larissa's verdict on my work,' but now I suspected he hadn't been joking.

I understood what he was saying about wedding photography not being his area of expertise, but I wanted him to believe that he was brilliant at his landscape work. If he wouldn't take my word for it, might he believe a photography expert? I searched my mind for the names of the local photographers he'd seen at the library several years before we met. Their talk had inspired him to pick up a camera again. Philip and Michael something or other. I'd make it my mission to track them down and see if they ran workshops or provided critiques. I believed in Jake and I was determined he'd believe in himself.

The conversation turned to the café and an update on the work there.

'What did the police do after Smythe threatened you?' Trey asked.

I shuddered at the memory from a week ago. 'They visited him and he pleaded innocence and tried to make out it was all a big misunderstanding. They had Jim's statement backed up by CCTV footage from the doorway camera, but they couldn't use my recording. It's a grey area and he'd have claimed entrapment or something like that. So all they could do was have a strong word with him and tell him to stay away from me.'

'A strong word?' Katie cried, clearly as incensed as I'd been when they told me. 'Is that all?'

'The police asked if I wanted to press charges, but he's a powerful man and we've already seen how he behaves when he doesn't get what he wants. Imagine what might happen if I crossed him like that.'

Katie banged her fist on the table. 'Hollie! You can't let him get away with that! He'll do it again to you or to someone else.'

'I did consider that. I know it's attitudes like that which mean he keeps getting away with things, but I'd personally rather pick my battles. If he's still determined to have The Starfish Café, Slippy Smythe will slip up in a more significant way.'

She sighed. 'You're probably doing the right thing in the long run, but I hate that he doesn't have to answer for what he did.'

'Me too. But one day he will.' I had to believe that. I couldn't bear the thought of him never having to pay for everything he'd done. As well as for me and all the other business owners he'd targeted, I wanted this for Irene and her husband Derek. And I wanted it for Jake's dad, who'd always believed Smythe belonged behind bars.

We'd visited Irene at Bay View earlier in the week and she'd shared more stories about Smythe's dodgy dealings which she'd heard from other residents. I'd told her I wasn't pressing charges and had given the same rationale I'd just given Katie.

'There's a quote I love from a Chinese general and philosopher called Sun Tzu,' she'd told us. 'It's "If you wait by the river long enough, the bodies of your enemies will float by". Pretty apt, wouldn't you agree?'

I would, so I'd sit and I'd wait and I'd celebrate when it happened.

40

HOLLIE

Tori asked me to meet her at the café on the Monday of week two of Operation Driftwood, saying she had an idea she wanted to run by me. I'd begged her to give me a clue, but she kept schtum.

'We'll see you on the beach later,' Jake said, heading towards the steps with Pickle, a roll of bin bags and a litter-picker.

As I waved them goodbye, Tori stepped out of the café. 'You know how I said we'd crank up the awesomeness level? I've thought of a way to crank it up even further.'

Intrigued, I followed her inside. There wasn't much progress yet as most of week one had been spent ripping out the kitchen and the fixed furniture, such as the serving counter, breakfast bar and booths. The focus for the start of this week would be re-plastering and first-fix electrics.

'Come upstairs,' she said.

The first floor was empty except for the table and chair Tori had been using when onsite and her easel erected in the far corner.

'I do listen to my clients and I know the brief was not to do anything up here, but it's such a gorgeous space. Look at those windows! That view! That light!'

The upstairs was double height and light flooded in from three large windows.

'I love it up here,' I admitted, 'but the café is so spacious downstairs that we don't have enough customers to justify using it.'

'I completely get that and there's no point spending money on putting seating up here when the space isn't needed for customers, never mind all that extra time spent traipsing up and down with orders and cleaning the place. But what if you used the space for something completely different?'

'I'm listening.'

She led me over to the easel and flipped round the design on it. I scanned over the display cabinets, shelves and tables, excitement welling inside me.

'A shop?'

'A shop and a gallery,' she declared, the passion for the idea obvious in every word. 'Over the weekend, I was fiddling with the design of that display case for your Hollie's Wood products. I went onto your website again to get a feel for the dimensions of some of the items so I could create different sized spaces and it struck me we were thinking far too small. You have an immense talent and it should be showcased on more than a piddly little shelving unit by the door. It needs an entire floor!'

She swept her arm across the room dramatically, making me laugh.

'I spotted the photos of the snowy village you created up here before Christmas and it blew me away.'

'I knocked that together really quickly. We were struggling to find space for the houses and Angie said I should create a snowy scene.'

'And Angie was right. Your showpiece can be a wooden seaside village with a backdrop that changes with each season. You can display buildings on it that are recognisable from round the coast and others that are more generic like the gorgeous houses on your website. I bet that, when people see them all together, they'd be tempted to buy more than one building.'

'That happened at Christmas. They'd see a few pieces together and want to recreate the scene.'

'I knew it! And you could even take commissions. Create some-body's house for them in wooden format. I'm going to stop there because I'm over-stepping and telling you how to run your business here.'

'No! Keep going! That's a genius idea. I make bespoke driftwood products, but I never thought to extend it to the houses, even though I made a Lighthouse View for Jake and a Seafarer Lodge for Irene.'

'You made Lighthouse View?'

'Yeah. It's in our lounge at home so Jake will always have a piece of his home with him.'

'Aw, that's so adorable. You do realise I'm going to need one of those for Finley and me?'

'Consider it done.' I glanced down at her drawings again. 'I'm sold on the shop, but what's your vision for the gallery aspect?'

'Well, I was thinking...'

* * *

We were outside on the terrace drinking coffee when Jake returned from the beach with Pickle. Angie had stopped by to check on progress and we'd filled her in on Tori's suggestion for upstairs, which she loved as much as I did.

'Tori has had the most amazing idea for upstairs,' I told Jake. 'We're going to use the space to display and sell my Hollie's Wood stock. Brilliant idea or what?'

'Genius. I reckon you'd sell loads.' He scrunched up his nose.

'But would you have time to keep up with the demand, especially during peak season when you're working six days a week?'

'We had the same thought. Angie and I are going to look at the rota and see whether we can shuffle some shifts round to give me a couple of days a week in the workshop, although I think we'll probably have to recruit instead. We might also need someone upstairs permanently to keep the shop sales separate from the café.'

'Lots to think about, but nice one, Tori. I'd say you're onto a winner.'

'Thank you,' she said. 'It won't just be a shop upstairs. It'll be a gallery too.'

'But not paintings,' I added. 'It'll be photographs of the local landscape.' I frowned and placed my hand against my face like the thinking emoji. 'Hmm. If only I knew an amazing local landscape photographer.'

Jake looked horrified. 'Me? You're kidding, right?'

'Yes, you!'

'My photos are nowhere near good enough for a gallery.'

'I beg to differ.'

'You should get in touch with Philip Heslington or his son Michael. They're professionals and they're local.'

'Thank you, but it's you I want.'

'Sorry, Hollie, but it's a no,' he said firmly. 'I'm going to grab a coffee.'

As soon as he closed the door behind him, Angie and Tori both turned to me, eyes wide.

'What was that about?' Angie asked.

'When he was little, somebody very wrongly told him he had no talent and it's hung over him ever since.'

'But the photos you showed me are phenomenal,' Tori exclaimed.

'I know! And there's an expert who agrees with me, although Jake doesn't know that yet.'

I'd found Philip Heslington online and had emailed him to enquire about workshops or critiques. Jake didn't have his photos displayed anywhere online but I had a few he'd emailed me, so I'd passed them to Philip to give him a feel for Jake's abilities. He'd emailed back immediately and I'd released a squeal of excitement when I read his response:

Thank you for sending over the photos. My son Michael has seen them too and the verdict is that we think we have ourselves some serious competition. There are a couple of small tweaks I'd suggest in his processing technique but the talent is there. He's far better than many professionals I've encountered. I don't run workshops anymore but it would be a privilege to spend some 1:1 time with Jake.

I was waiting for Philip to confirm some dates and then I'd need to think about how to present the gift to Jake. His birthday wasn't until November and I didn't want to wait that long. I was convinced he'd be so thrilled about spending time with a professional photographer who he admired that he wouldn't see it as me going behind his back. But the mortified expression on his face and his swift exit just now made me wonder whether I should have talked to him first before contacting Philip.

'I might check he's okay,' I said, rising from my chair, but the door from the café was flung open and he poked his head out.

'I've just been paged. Can I take your car?'

'I can drop her back home,' Angie said.

I went inside and handed over my keys. 'Let me grab my hoodie off the back seat.' It was forecast to cloud over this afternoon, so I'd probably need it later.

'Are you okay?' I asked. 'I'm sorry for pushing.'

'Yeah. It's not you. It's a great idea. It's just...' He shrugged. 'You know what it is, but I love that you keep trying.'

His lips brushed mine and he smiled as he got into the car.

'Stay safe,' I called as he pulled away.

I watched him, waving, until the car was gone from view, feeling reassured that I hadn't done the wrong thing in contacting Philip Heslington after all.

* * *

'Do you need to rush off or do you fancy another cuppa?' I asked Angie when she pulled onto the drive at Sandy Croft a little later.

'A cuppa would be lovely. It's not often we get time for a proper chat.'

I made drinks and we took them into the lounge, where Pickle stretched out on the rug in front of the fireplace.

'Brilliant news about Katie and Trey,' Angie said. 'I didn't think they'd ever tie the knot or have babies.'

'Me neither, so that was a lovely double surprise.'

'None of us are getting any younger and a decision to have children can't be put off forever.' She raised her eyebrows at me knowingly and, even though I'd intentionally not said anything to Katie to take the pressure off, I couldn't help myself. I'd have told Mum, and Angie was the next best thing.

'Jake and I are trying for a baby.'

Angie squealed and pressed her fingers across her mouth, her eyes glistening. 'Oh, my goodness! I'm so thrilled for you both.'

'It's a very recent decision and we probably wouldn't be going down that route so soon after getting together if it wasn't for the age thing but, as you say, time is ticking.'

'Do you want me to keep this to myself?'

'Would you? You never know how long these things will take or if it'll even happen at all. We'd love to be parents, but what will be will be and we're not going to get stressed about it.'

'That's a sensible approach but I'd suggest it's easier said than done, especially when your best friend is pregnant.'

'I did have a little fantasy about us being pregnant at the same time and our kids going to school together and I had to stop myself from getting too carried away.'

'Remember what you've just said to me and keep coming back to that because it's easy to lose sight of it when things don't happen, or when they happen but it goes wrong.'

I narrowed my eyes at her, picking up the sad tone. 'You sound like you're talking from experience.'

She released a long sigh. 'I am. Martin and I wanted a family but, after five miscarriages, we had to accept that it wasn't going to happen for us.'

'Five? Oh, Angie!' I clasped my hand round the rings on my necklace. 'I'm so sorry. I had no idea.'

'Long time ago now. People seem to talk about it more these days, but it felt like a taboo back then.'

'Do you want to talk about it now?'

She studied my face for a moment then nodded. 'We lost two early on in the pregnancy and two at around twelve to thirteen weeks. Then we made it to twenty-one weeks and dared to believe we had our miracle baby who'd make it to term. She used to move such a lot and we were convinced that was a good sign then, one day, I couldn't feel her moving and I knew.'

Her eyes filled with tears, but mine brimmed over. That must have been terrifying for them both.

'I had to be induced and go through full labour knowing that she was already gone. She was so tiny. Perfectly formed. Stunningly beautiful. Just not breathing. We called her Bella. And after that, we both agreed no more. Far too hard and heartbreaking.'

'Put that tea down,' I whispered, hugging her tightly as soon as she did. 'I'm so sorry.'

Angie had brought me so much comfort and strength as I'd grieved for my family and now it was my turn to be strong for her as she grieved for the family she'd been unable to have. I fought back more tears so I could focus on Angie's pain, rubbing her back as the tears shook her body.

'Ooh! That was unexpected,' she said, wiping her eyes when we eventually parted. 'I haven't cried about it in years. Decades, even! I still think about my little angel babies every so often, but I made peace with what happened a long time ago so I'm not sure where that came from. I obviously needed that.'

'If you want to talk about it again, I'm here for you.'

'Thank you. That means a lot.'

I thought about her comment about being pregnant at the same time as your best friend. 'Were you pregnant at the same time as Mum?'

'My first and second were when she was carrying you. Heather and Joe were unbelievably supportive and Martin and I never felt envious that they had what we couldn't. Our friendship wasn't like that. I loved spending time with you and Isaac, my beautiful godchildren. And, of course, I have nieces and nephews, so I've still been blessed with children in my life. I'm very fortunate.'

'And so am I to have you.'

I sipped on my tea, taking a moment to absorb what I'd just learned.

'Did that contribute to you and Martin separating?' I asked.

'No. If anything, it bought us closer together. We had many happy years before things turned sour.'

'How's it going now?'

'It's nice. We're friends.' She was trying to look and sound casual, but I could hear the disappointment in her voice.

'Who are still madly in love with each other but too scared to admit it.'

'We're not still in love!'

'You keep lying to yourself like that, but anyone who has seen the two of you together lately can see you're smitten.' I nodded towards the dog. 'Even Pickle noticed. He's been FaceTiming Felix and Pixie. They're already planning a vow-renewal ceremony for you and debating what they should wear.'

The idea of my dog and her cats dressed as bridesmaids tickled Angie, and soon we were wiping away tears again, but from laughter this time.

'Oh, gosh, Hollie. You certainly inherited your mum's silly sense of humour. And I admit it. I still love him. Satisfied?'

'I will be when you tell him.'

'What if I tell him and he doesn't feel the same?'

'You know what Mum would say.'

'If you stumble, make it part of your dance,' we said together.

Angie smiled at me. 'It's like she's here with me. Thank you. I will tell him.'

'When?'

'Soon. I promise.'

'We need to do this more often,' I said. 'It's been a good conversation.'

'It has,' she agreed. 'But every conversation I have with you is good. You're a very special young woman, Hollie Gabrielle Brooks, and I'm so proud of you.'

41

TORI

'What are you looking for?'

I jumped at Finley's voice. I'd been so preoccupied with my search that I hadn't heard him arrive home.

'My phone,' I said, continuing to rifle through the papers on my desk. 'I wanted to show Jamie photos of the progress and realised I didn't have it.' Jamie, my friend who owned the reclamation yard, had excelled himself with some awesome pieces for Operation Driftwood so I'd taken him out for a few drinks tonight to thank him.

'I'll ring it,' Finley suggested. 'Is it on silent?'

'I can't remember.'

'It's connecting.'

We both cocked our heads to one side. There was no sound of ringing in the office or anywhere else in the house, but we still crept from room to room, just in case.

'Sorry,' he said, shrugging.

'It was worth a try. Thanks.'

'You had it at lunchtime because you replied to my text about food. Did you use it after that?'

I thought for a moment. 'I know where it is! It was about to die after I replied to you and there were so many trades in and out of the café today that I put it on charge upstairs out of the way. At least I know I haven't lost it. I'll get it tomorrow.'

Finley smiled at me. 'You know you're not going to settle until you have it.'

'Argh! You already know me too well. But I've had a few drinks.'

He jangled his car keys at me. 'Come on. I'll take you.'

'Why are you so late anyway?' I asked him as we drove across town.

'I'll give you one guess.'

'Demi? What was it this time?'

'She had a proposal for me. Literally! After turning me down three times, she said she thought we could make a go of it as a married couple. She even got down on bended knee, which can't have been easy at twenty-seven weeks pregnant. I said no, obviously.'

'Crikey! If it's not working when you're not married, how would being married suddenly fix everything?'

'I'm not convinced she believed it would. There was no real conviction behind her proposal, like she was going through the motions because it was something different to try, while already knowing it had no mileage.'

'Then why propose?'

'I think she's scared of bringing up the baby on her own. When she had India and Roman, Damon wasn't around all the time – constantly in and out of their lives – but at least there *was* someone. This time there isn't. Even though it's clear to me now that she doesn't love me and probably never did, I know the way her mind works, and she'll see being with me as better than being with nobody.'

'You really think she never loved you?'

'Convinced of it. You don't notice these things when you're in a relationship but, when you step back from it, it seems so obvious.'

'I can relate to that. How are you feeling?'

'Relieved. It feels like she's finally accepted that it's over and it was all very calm and civilised. I'm also hopeful. If she's stopped being angry with me, maybe she'll let me spend some time with the kids. She didn't say anything to suggest she would, but she did talk about them. Told me how they were doing at school. It's a start.'

I placed my hand lightly on his leg. 'I'm glad for you. I hope she does see sense.'

I gazed out of the window into the darkness as Finley pulled off the main road and onto the approach road to the café, and did a double-take as I noticed a beam of light in the woods north of the café.

'Did you see that?' I asked Finley.

'What?'

'A light in the woods. There it is again! I think it's a torch.'

'I saw that one. That's weird.'

We pulled into the car park and I felt an uneasy sensation in my gut at the sight of a lone white van. Finley parked between the van and the skip and voiced what I was thinking. 'Why would anybody be out here at night with a torch unless they were up to no good?'

As we peered out of the front windscreen into the woods, there was another flash of light in the distance.

'Do you think it could be connected to the break-in?' I asked.

'No idea. But it wouldn't hurt to take a photo of the van's registration plate.'

'Shouldn't we just grab my phone and leave?'

'I think we should get photos, just in case. Wait here.'

'Okay, but knock your flash off first,' I said, as he reached for the door. The security light activating when we drove into the car park would have alerted the person in the woods that they weren't alone but that was easily explained. Several flashes weren't.

As Finley moved round the van taking photos, I kept my eyes firmly fixed on the dark woods ahead. Was it my imagination or was that light getting closer? My pulse raced and I could feel the sweat pooling under my arms. I didn't like this one bit. I feared I'd read too many crime novels because all I could picture was a man emerging from the woods with a shovel over one shoulder. *Don't think about buried bodies!*

I wound my window down. 'What's taking so long?'

'I'm looking for dents and marks in case the plates are cloned.'

'Please hurry.'

That torch beam was really close now and my heart raced as a dog barked – a deep and angry sound. *Please let it be on a lead!*

'He's coming,' I hissed.

'Whatever I say, just go with it,' he replied. 'I want to suss why he's here.'

He walked round the back of the car to the skip as a bearded man wearing dark clothes, a black beanie hat and a large backpack emerged from the woods. A white bull terrier with black markings round its left eye strained at a halter and barked at Finley.

'Down, Krueger,' shouted the man.

'Evening!' Finley called jovially, lifting a couple of metal bar stools out of the skip.

'What are you doing?'

The man's voice was gruff and sent a chill down my spine. *We could ask you the same* sprung to mind, but being a smart arse wasn't going to do us any favours, especially when there was a bull terrier called Krueger snarling at Finley.

'Skip-diving,' Finley replied, his voice strong and confident as he placed the stools on the ground.

He glanced furtively round him as though he was letting the

man into a secret that he didn't want anyone else to hear. 'Girl-friend's obsessed with getting stuff for nowt. Says it's fair game if it's been dumped in a skip. I've got these stools, but I'm not sure. The seats have been slashed.'

'Look knackered to me, mate,' the man said, curling his nose up at them. He had dark eyes and his beard was unkempt and predominantly dark, but there was a small white patch on the right side near his jawline. I couldn't place his age – anywhere from mid-twenties to late-thirties.

'Don't say that! No action for me tonight if I don't find summat decent.'

It was weird hearing Finley speak like that, his voice more York-shire and gruff than usual. He'd said to go with it, so presumably he knew what he was doing.

The man took another couple of steps closer to Finley and I held my breath, terrified of what he might do. He picked up one of the stools and twisted it from side to side, then peered into the skip and laughed. 'You might want to pick up a lad's mag on the way home. Nowt decent in there.'

He opened the back of his van, secured Kreuger in a cage and ditched the backpack. I stared at Finley, silently pleading with him to get back in the car so we could get the hell out of there. My phone could wait until morning.

The man opened the driver's door on his van. If he went first, I could retrieve my phone after all.

'Are the woods any good?' Finley asked.

The man paused, stiffened, then turned. 'For what?'

'Dog walking. I've got a shih tzu. Well, the girlfriend has. Point-less dog. It's like a walking teddy bear.'

He laughed again. 'You need a man's dog like Kreuger.' He turned his gaze to me. 'And you need to keep your missus in line.'

I gulped as he sneered at me.

'I pick my battles,' Finley continued, 'but she knows who the real boss is.'

I breathed again when the man looked back at Finley, evidently delighted by the misogynistic remark. 'Should think so too.'

'So is it any good?' Finley persisted. 'I always thought it looked a bit... woody.'

'It's dense in parts. There's no tracks. No pretty views. Ideal for us. Folk round here don't like Kreuger and they don't like me telling them I'm not interested in their opinions. Sometimes I can't be arsed with the gyp, so I bring him here. He can run round without the temptation of chasing walking teddy bears or ratty things dressed in designer clothes that live in handbags.'

He clambered into the driver's seat. 'Stupid twat face-plants the occasional tree, so I'd suggest you avoid it.'

'Yeah. You haven't sold it to me. I'll stick to the beach.'

'Have fun in your skip.'

'Cheers. See ya.'

He reversed his van out of the space and it was only when he left the car park that I released a shaky breath.

'What the bloody hell was that all about?' I asked Finley. 'Were you not intimidated by the scary man with the dangerous dog?'

'Hell yeah! I might need to change my jeans when I get home.'

I couldn't help laughing. 'So why did you keep him talking?'

'Because I found the whole thing suspicious. Did you buy his story, because I didn't? Who lets their dog run round in a dense wood and who takes a huge backpack on a dog walk that only takes them a maximum of a quarter of a mile from their van?'

'What do you think he was up to? Because he obviously wasn't trying to break into the café.'

Finley looked towards the woods, as though searching for the answers between the trees. 'I don't know. It's probably completely innocent and I'm trying to make a connection that isn't there.' He winked at me. 'Searching for criminals instead of cavities.'

I opened the door, groaning at his feeble attempt at a joke. 'I'm off to get my phone. I'll leave you to your sleuthing.'

'Sorry about the trash talk,' he said, catching my hand as I passed. 'I panicked.'

Butterflies stirred in my stomach at the feel of his hand in mine. 'Forgiven. Only because I know you didn't mean it.'

'I hated it.'

He squeezed my hand then let go. The butterflies were still there as I unlocked the café door. Adrenaline. That had to be why.

When I returned to the car, clutching my phone and charger, Finley was carefully placing one of the bar stools in the boot, using a couple of tissues like gloves.

'Dare I ask?'

'He touched the stool, so we have his fingerprints now, and I took a photo and marked on that exactly where he'd touched. Valuable evidence. And I noticed a scar like a sideways Y above his right eyebrow and pockmarks on his cheeks. Nice distinguishing features.'

He closed the boot and laughed at my raised eyebrows. 'Yeah, I know. You're going to ration my crime viewing, aren't you?'

'No more police dramas for you. Or episodes of *Scooby Doo*.'

I settled into the car and we set off.

'Although, I have to admit,' I said, glancing across at him. 'With that floppy blond hair of yours, you do look a little like Fred from *Scooby Doo*.'

'And with that gorgeous red hair of yours, you could be Daphne.' He glanced across at me, smiling. 'And we could turn Carrie the campervan into the Mystery Machine.'

I already knew that his party trick was impersonating the characters from *The Simpsons*, but it transpired that the *Scooby Doo* characters were in his repertoire too. By the time we arrived back at Lighthouse View, I had a pain in my side from laughing so much at his impressions.

As I settled down in bed a little later, I'd expected my mind to be active after tonight's events, but there was only one thing I could focus on. He'd said my hair was 'gorgeous' and, when he'd turned to smile at me, his eyes had twinkled, which made my heart race. And what about those butterflies when he held my hand? What was that all about?

42

TORI

I released a contented sigh as I reached the end of another one of Rebecca Lannister's novels on Saturday afternoon.

'How many is that you've read now?' Finley asked, looking up from his textbook.

'I've only got two left.' The books were a fairly quick read. 'Can't put off the Destiny Blaize one for much longer.'

'And how was that one?'

'Phenomenal.'

He smiled at me. 'You say that after every one.'

'That's because they are. I had no idea. I hear people being dismissive of romance novels, but I wonder if they've ever even read one. The plots, characters and settings are as well-developed as any crime or thriller I've ever read but what sets them apart is the emotion. I feel everything the characters feel. It's just...' I shrugged. 'I'm in awe. I really am. They're so talented.'

'Will you tell them that when you see them?'

'Definitely.'

'What were the Tori traits in that book?'

'Honesty. The heroine had—'

Finley's phone ringing cut me off. His brow creased as he glanced at the screen.

'It's Demi. I'd better get it.'

I gave him a reassuring smile as he stepped out of the lounge and connected the call. I'd felt so relaxed and contented moments ago and now I felt all churned up. I always felt on edge when Demi made contact because I felt bad for Finley. He missed India and Roman desperately.

'I've been summoned,' he said, stepping back into the lounge. 'She wants to meet me at The Chocolate Pot.'

'Has she got the kids with her?' I asked hopefully.

'No. They're with their dad. I'd better see what she wants. Is there anything you need while I'm in town?'

'Not that I can think of, but thanks. Good luck.'

I waved him off then returned the book to the dining room and added it to the 'read' pile. I'd decided to tackle them in publication order. If I'd inspired the heroines, it made sense to read them chronologically, seeing which traits they'd picked out at different times of my life. The only one I'd be reading out of order was the Domino Blaize.

Considering my parents had spent such a limited time with me during my teenage years and barely any in adulthood, it appeared that they knew me better than I knew myself. They'd clearly paid more attention than I'd given them credit for, which made my heart swell, but also made me sad. Had the criticism Robyn had levelled at me been founded after all? Had I been self-centred?

When I finished one of their books, I didn't like to dive straight into another, preferring to let the characters linger with me for a while first. Which left me at a loss for what to do now. I'd had a vague notion of asking Finley if he fancied ambling down to the seafront to get an ice cream when I'd finished the book, but Demi's call had scuppered that. It was the bank holiday weekend at the end of May half-term so the seafront would be heaving and I didn't feel like being all alone in a sea of people.

I made a mug of tea and took it up to my office, looking round for inspiration. My eyes fell on my silver drawing tube leaning against my desk. I unscrewed the lid and removed the blueprint inside.

'L'eglise des arbres,' I whispered, unfurling it onto my drawing board. I smiled as I lightly traced my fingers across the plans. It was a long time since I'd worked on my fantasy project and I was itching to add to it.

A couple of hours passed before Finley returned.

'I'm in the office,' I shouted down to him. 'How did it go?' I asked when he appeared up the stairs.

'Weird news and brilliant news. Which do you want first?'

'Ooh, sounds intriguing. Brilliant please.'

He wheeled his chair over to the drawing board but didn't sit down. 'Demi's letting me see the kids. I can spend the day with them on Monday.'

'Oh, my God! Finley! That's amazing!' I jumped off my chair and hurled myself at him.

'How do you feel?' I asked when I stepped back.

'Elated. I don't know times or plans but I don't care. I just want to see them. The past six weeks has felt like six years. If it hadn't been for you, I don't know how I'd have got through it. You've kept me sane.'

He moved in for another hug, but kissed me on the cheek first. The touch of his lips against my skin set my heart racing. I clung to him again, my throat suddenly dry. I could feel his strength and masculinity, inhale his delicious scent like cocoa beans and pine trees. I felt his breath warm against my neck and longed for his lips to brush it. A longing stirred within me and... and I had clearly been reading far too many of Mother and Father's novels.

His arms tightened and I wondered for a moment whether he was feeling what I was feeling. I swiftly dismissed the idea. He was relieved and excited about seeing India and Roman and it would be a huge mistake to turn that into something it wasn't. We were tactile with each other all the time – always hugging and touching – and it didn't mean anything.

'And what's the weird news?' I asked, stumbling over my chair in an attempt to create some distance between us.

'Are you okay?' he asked, reaching out to steady me.

'Yes! All good. So, ahem, weird news…'

I plonked myself down heavily on my chair and, looking bemused, he sat down too.

'You know how she told me the baby's father was an ex-boyfriend she'd hooked up with at her work Christmas party? The ex-boyfriend bit was the truth. What she'd failed to mention was that it was Damon.' His voice was a little high, as though he was still struggling to process the information.

'As in India and Roman's dad?'

'As in the man she has always and will always love, which is why she turned me down the three times I asked her to marry me. Apparently the on-off thing they had going before she met me has been a continuous on-off thing. She didn't even go to the Christmas do. She was with him.'

'Aw, Finley.'

'I thought it would be tough hearing that and, don't get me wrong, I wasn't delighted she'd had an affair and had lied to me, but I'd always known she still held a torch for Damon. I knew it was why she let him run rings round her with the kids and, deep down, I knew it was why she said no to me. It actually felt better knowing the baby was his than a seedy drunken hook-up with some random guy she'd known as a spotty teen.'

'Why did she tell you all of this?'

'Because she told Damon last weekend that the baby was his and he had until last night to consider three options – her and their three children, the children only, or to piss off out of their lives. He turned up on Wednesday night and said he chose the latter. Told her she was bad for his mental health and he was moving to Stockport anyway so good riddance.'

I shook my head in disgust. 'Wow! Smooth operator.'

'It was a wake-up call for Demi that he was the waste of space I'd always known he was. She admitted that the proposal to me on Thursday was a bit desperate, but she'd panicked about being alone, as I'd suspected, and she's full of respect for me for making the right decision by saying no. She's given notice on the house she rents and is moving in with her mum to start afresh. She asked India and Roman if they'd like to see me on a more regular basis and got a resounding yes, so it starts on Monday and we'll work out something more structured going forwards.'

I rested my hand on his thigh. 'I'm so pleased for you.'

'So am I! You know, as she was telling me all this, all I could think of was you.'

'Me?' My heart started racing once more.

'That thing you said the night we met about the spring tides and the moon and sun being in alignment. Demi and me in a relationship with the kids were not in alignment. Demi and me *not* in a relationship but with the kids, that's aligned. And I even include the new baby in that. There'll be no more pretending that I'm his dad, but I'm happy to be the father figure. There's no way I could take his brother and sister out for the day and leave him on his own.'

'I think you might just be the kindest man I've ever met.'

'Believe me, when she first mentioned it was Damon, the thoughts going round in my head were anything but kind, but then I realised we all make mistakes. Not me, of course.'

I laughed. 'Of course not, Mr Finley I-might-have-made-the-wrong-decision-to-be-a-dentist Scott.'

'Very good point, Ms Tori I'd-rather-be-an-interior-designer-despite-seven-years-of-study-as-an-architect Tennyson.'

If I'd had a cushion nearby, I'd have whacked him with it.

'Who's the house for?' he asked, nodding towards the drawing board.

'This? It's erm... it's not for anyone as such. It's kind of...' I shrugged. 'It's my fantasy house, if you must know. Little project I've messed with on and off since university. It's daft, really.'

He stood beside me, studying my drawings, and I breathed in his scent again, butterflies swooping in my stomach. It was the book! It had heightened my emotions. Finley was a good friend and my housemate. Nothing more.

'It's about taking an old building and blending the old with the new,' I explained.

'Is the building fantasy or real?'

'Real. It's a derelict church next to the woods on my parents' estate. It never got finished so it's never actually been used as a church. Miss Pemberley and I christened it *l'eglise des arbres*. I used to play in it when I was little. If anyone was looking for me, they knew to look there first. The light is simply stunning, the way it filters through the trees and the windows. So peaceful. Anyway, I add to it occasionally. I haven't quite got the inside space right but, as I'll never live there, it doesn't really matter.'

'Do you realise that, whenever you talk about your parents' place, you get all animated?'

'Really? That's probably because I never had beef with the estate. It's beautiful. What are you laughing at?'

'You never had beef with it? What are you? A teenaged gangster?'

As I laughed with him, a warmth flowed through me that I

hadn't felt in... maybe forever. I'd finish the last two books over the weekend and, while Finley was with India and Roman on Monday, I'd drive over to Redamancy Castle. There'd be a new moon on Monday evening – a time for new beginnings.

'I think we should go out to celebrate,' Finley said, pulling me to my feet. 'Get yourself sorted and let's go to the pub.'

* * *

Forty minutes later, we secured a table on the outside terrace at Poseidon's Bar, overlooking the harbour, and clinked our drinks together.

'I meant what I said earlier,' Finley said. 'I honestly don't know how I'd have got through all this without you. I came so close to skipping Dean and Jodie's wedding. I think that would have been one of the biggest mistakes of my life.'

'And I was that pissed off with Leyton that I nearly went home instead of up to the roof terrace to calm down. That would have been a huge mistake too. I feel like we've been friends forever, which is pretty special because I struggle to make friends.'

He frowned at me. 'I find that hard to believe. You were so warm and friendly from the moment I met you.'

'Aw, thanks, Finley. That means a lot to me. It's the next step I struggle with. I have lots of people I get on well with like Jamie from the reclamation yard and my surfing pals but it's taking it to that next level that I find hard. I can't keep blaming my friend Millicent for my trust issues when I was the one who let her down first.'

'I'm not having that.' Finley fixed me with a hard stare. 'You thought you were doing her a favour and there was no way you could have predicted how that would go. What she did to you was deliberate and vindictive and she'd have known exactly what the outcome would be. You were a good friend who did something misguided with good intentions.'

A couple of hours later, we walked slowly back up Ashby Street.

'I had a great time tonight,' Finley said as we stepped into the hallway at Lighthouse View.

'So did I. Thank you.'

We gazed at each other for a moment, silly grins on our faces thanks to a few rounds of drinks.

'Oh! I've got something for you,' I said. 'Well, it's for both of us. Jake dropped it off while you were in town.'

I dipped into the dining room, retrieved the wooden Lighthouse View Hollie had made and gently placed it in his hands.

'Starfish made this?'

'She's amazing, isn't she?'

'Even if it didn't have the house name on it, I'd have recognised it immediately.'

'Look on the bottom.'

He flipped it over. Hollie had written:

Finley & Tori's home
Where friendship begins & heartbreak ends

'Did you ask her to put that?'

'No. It's lovely, isn't it?'

He ran his thumb across the inscription then caught my eye and smiled.

'Absolutely perfect.'

Those crazy butterflies in my stomach swooped and soared and, for the briefest of moments, I felt as though he was talking about me and not the house.

He held my gaze and I imagined what it would be like to feel his lips against mine, his hands in my hair, his... And I had to stop thinking about him like that. I was being ridiculous, creating something that wasn't there and risking putting the best friendship I'd ever had in jeopardy.

'Night, then,' I said, laughing as I squeezed past him to reach the stairs.

'Night, Tori. Sleep well.'

I smiled at him then ran up the stairs. Sleep well? No chance of that, not while my mind was whirring with thoughts of being with Finley.

In my darkened room a little later, I stood beside the window seeking out the moon. She was the thinnest of crescents ahead of Monday's new moon, but I still drew comfort from my old friend.

'What do you think?' I whispered. 'Could we ever be more than friends?'

As I curled up under the duvet, I thought about the laughter and banter I'd had with Finley in Poseidon's Bar earlier. The couples I knew and admired all had that, but how could you tell whether it was friendship or something more? It was so different from what I'd experienced with Ewan and Leyton. Had that been love and this was a strong friendship, or was this the real thing? I was so confused right now.

43

TORI

'New moon, new beginnings,' I said to myself as I drove Carrie towards Redamancy Castle on Monday afternoon. 'You can do this.'

I'd broken my thinking-space rule and had read the remaining two books back to back yesterday. I remained completely in awe of my parents' talent and felt ashamed that it had taken me until now to read any of their work. I'd criticised them for not being there for me, for not supporting me or showing me they were proud of me, and I'd been worse. I'd never shown any interest or asked any questions. I felt like I'd missed out on so many conversations we could have had about exciting plots, feisty heroines, dashing heroes, and vile villains. Whatever the reception today, I'd make sure I wouldn't leave without telling them I was proud of them.

The Domino Blaize book, saved until last, had been a particular surprise. I recalled that argument with Mother years ago when she'd tried to explain the difference between erotica and porn, and now I understood. The heroine in that story had flame-red hair like mine and was feisty on the outside but, on the inside, just wanted to be loved. As with all of the books, the way they'd conveyed an aspect of my personality within their heroine showed me how well my parents really knew me.

I noted with relief that Robyn's hire car wasn't parked outside Redamancy Castle. It would be easier if she wasn't home for now, although I recognised I also needed to make peace with my sister. I knew nothing about her or her life, which was remiss of me.

I stood beside Carrie, looked up at the house, then glanced down again at Mother's letter, clutched in my hand:

> *We desperately hope you will one day be able to forgive our many failures and find a way to rebuild our relationship – or perhaps that should say to build a fresh one. You know where we are when you feel ready, no matter how long that takes.*

I hoped those words still applied today and not the message Robyn had conveyed last time.

One more deep breath by the door and I pulled the chain, listening to the bell jingling inside. Moments later, through the stained glass panels around the door, I watched Mother crossing the hall, smoothing down the skirt on a beautiful pale blue, lilac and lace Edwardian day dress. That was another thing I hadn't given them credit for. They were both exceptionally talented costume designers and I had them to thank for passing that skill down to me. A unique offering of my interior design business was that I didn't have to source any of the soft furnishings as I could make them myself. It also meant that bedtime stories hadn't been the only time I'd had my parents' attention like I'd previously thought.

Mother looked up and stopped dead, her hand fluttering to her neck, her mouth open. For a horrifying moment, I thought she might turn her back and leave me on the doorstep but, regaining her composure, she took the final steps and opened the door.

'Tori!'

She'd never called me that to my face and that one word told me Robyn had been wrong and I was welcome.

She smiled warmly and I noticed her hands twitching by her sides, as though she wanted to embrace me but wasn't sure she should.

'What a lovely surprise.' Her voice was full of warmth and, again, I felt reassured that the bridges hadn't been fully burned.

'I brought you some flowers,' I said, passing her a bouquet I'd picked up from Seaside Blooms this morning, the florist's opposite Charlee's Chocolates.

'They're beautiful.' She sniffed the bouquet. 'And very Victorian. Thank you. That means a lot. Do come in.'

'Is Father home?'

'He's gone for a walk with Robyn and the dogs. She's back from New Zealand to help him...' Her expression darkened for a moment as she tailed off, then she smiled once more. 'Let me put these in some water. I can't tell you how wonderful it is to see you again, darling. You look wonderful.'

'Is there something wrong with Father?' I asked, following her down the corridor towards the kitchen, barely noticing whether anything had changed since I walked out. My gut told me something was wrong.

'He's doing well now, Tori. Nothing to worry about.'

'But something has happened?'

We'd reached the kitchen and she laid the flowers by the sink, her shoulders slumping before she turned to face me. 'Your father had a stroke.'

My stomach plummeted to the floor. 'What? When?'

'A couple of months ago. He was about to go out on Apollo when he took ill. It's fortunate it happened when it did because Bovis, our estate manager, was in the stables. His speech is a little slurred and he's lost some movement down his right side, but he's improving each day.'

I slumped against the worktop, my heart thudding. What if he'd been out riding when it had happened? He'd likely have fallen and, if he'd been alone, he might have been found too late.

'I know what you're thinking, darling, because my mind took me there too. There's no point in dwelling on the could-have-beens. Bovis was there and your father is recovering nicely. Oh! That's them.'

'Mother!' Robyn called. 'We're back!'

I could hear the sound of dog paws clicking on the tiles.

'Stay here for a moment,' Mother said, rushing out of the kitchen.

'How was your walk?' I heard her say.

'We managed a bit further today,' Robyn replied. 'He's making brilliant progress, aren't you, Father?'

I strained my ears, but could hear no response. Had Mother underplayed his symptoms? Was he struggling to speak or was it just that I couldn't hear him over the scampering of the dogs?

I wouldn't have thought Father was at high risk of a stroke – non-smoker, limited alcohol intake, good diet, active – but who knew how much their lifestyle had changed since I last saw them? They'd been in their late sixties then, but they were seventy-four now. I didn't even know if they were still writing, although I assumed they were as I couldn't imagine that not being part of their lives. It was a stressful job, especially with their output, so perhaps high blood pressure had been the trigger.

'I have a surprise for you, Ralph,' I heard Mother say. 'Let's get you settled into the drawing room first.'

Several minutes later, I heard footsteps along the corridor, but it was Robyn who appeared in the kitchen.

'I thought I told you they didn't want to see you,' she said, looking me up and down, her eyes narrowed.

'And I found a letter from Mother telling me I was welcome back at any time. I decided to go with that instead.'

'Father's ill.'

'I didn't know.'

'You would have if you'd bothered to stay in touch.'

I sighed. 'I don't want to fight, Robyn.'

'Neither do I, but you can't have expected the red-carpet treatment. You abandoned us, you came back when things went tits up and you needed help, then you left again. You broke their hearts. You broke mine. And then you turn up with a campervan full of suitcases and expect to stay again. Seriously? Talk about selfish.'

'I didn't expect—'

'Had I finished talking?' she shouted, making me jump. Her tone before had all been very matter of fact.

'Sorry.'

'So I sent you away with a flea in your ear and, surprise-surprise, you're back.' She jabbed her finger towards the flowers. 'Do you really think those can make up for how you've treated this family?'

I wasn't going to even try to justify myself to Robyn – not before I'd spoken with Mother and Father – and none of it seemed that important right now when there was something far more pressing on my mind. My sister evidently wasn't one to mince her words, so she was likely to give it to me straight.

'How bad is Father?' I asked.

She stared at me and I braced myself for some sarcastic comment, but none came. She filled the kettle and set up a tray with a pot of tea, cups and saucers. Four of them. That boded well.

'He's not about to die, if that's what you're worried about,' she said eventually, her voice softer. 'Bovis was with him when it happened and he got help fast. He's having physio with me and he's making good progress.'

'That's good news.'

'Yes, it is. Very good news.'

She added a jug of milk to the tray. I noticed that she was wearing a wedding and engagement ring. I'd also picked up a slight New Zealand twang when she spoke.

'Were you here anyway?' I asked, hoping it was a broad enough opener.

'Oh! So you're suddenly interested in me after all these years of silence, are you?' The anger had returned and I was losing my patience with her.

'Robyn! It works both ways. Mother and Father have always had my address and phone number so you could have contacted me just as easily.'

'Fair enough,' she said, her voice calming. 'Potted history. I'm a physiotherapist, specialising in sports injuries. Through that I met Brett, a professional rugby player from New Zealand. I moved to New Zealand to be with him and we got married in February five years ago. He's retiring from professional rugby and, when I fell pregnant, we decided we wanted to raise our family in Yorkshire. I'd arranged to stay here and start house-hunting while Brett finished his contract, so I was already here when Father had his stroke.'

'So you're pregnant?'

'I'm pretty certain that's what I said.'

'I'm going to be an auntie?'

'Biologically, yes.'

That hurt, but it was justified. Mother's letter talked about them failing me, but I'd failed my whole family, especially Robyn. Yes, she could have contacted me, but I was the big sister. I should have led by example.

'Congratulations. When's the baby due?'

'Early September. I'm twenty-six weeks gone and, yeah, I know I'm not showing much.'

She didn't seem to be showing at all, but when she pulled her T-shirt across her stomach, I could see a clear baby bump. My sister had been married for five years, was expecting my baby niece or nephew and had made a life-changing decision to move to the UK and I knew none of it.

'I'm sorry we don't know each other.' I struggled to force the words out over the lump in my throat.

Her eyes glistened and she blinked a few times then picked up the tray. 'Father'll be parched. You can come through now.'

'Do you want me to carry that?'

'I'm pregnant, not incapable,' she snapped.

I wondered if she was always this feisty or if it was me who brought out her colour.

I followed her along the corridor and into the drawing room, trepidatious about what I might find. As we approached, the grey-hounds Holmes and Watson ran out and jumped up at me. They'd be about ten now.

'Hello, you two,' I said, giving them each a stroke. 'Down! Good boys.'

They trotted alongside me into the drawing room and I took a deep breath.

I needn't have worried about Father. He was dressed in a smart grey Edwardian-style suit. He'd lost weight but he had colour in his cheeks.

'Hello, Tori,' he said. 'What a wonderful surprise.' His voice did carry a slight slur, as Mother had said – as though he'd just woken up or had a few drinks – and his smile was a little lopsided, but he looked surprisingly well.

'Hello, Father.'

His smile widened. He'd probably wondered if I'd ever call him that again.

'Sit down, darling,' Mother said. 'Holmes, Watson, lie down.'

The dogs settled in front of the fireplace as Robyn poured the tea and handed out the cups.

'How are you?' Mother asked. 'We're desperate to hear your news. How's Leyton?'

I glanced across at Robyn and saw a flush of colour on her cheeks. I'd already suspected from several things Mother had said that my parents had no idea I'd visited six weeks ago, and this confirmed it.

'Leyton and I split up in April.'

'Oh, darling! I'm so sorry. Are you still in Whitsborough Bay?'

'Erm, yes, I'm renting with a friend, but I can tell you more later.' I looked back at Father. 'How are you feeling?'

'Don't worry about me. Plenty of old life in the old dog yet. How's business?'

I shook my head. 'I can tell you that too later. I've only just found the letter you wrote – the one with the first editions. You asked for a chance to explain, and I want to give you that, if you're still game, but there's something important I need to say first.'

I looked from Mother to Father and they both nodded.

'I've spent the last few weeks reading the books and I have to say I'm blown away. Your talent is exceptional and I'm now hooked. I'm truly sorry it took me so long to read anything you've written. I've missed out on a lot.'

Mother pressed her fingers to her lips. 'Do you really mean that?'

'Completely. I loved everything about them and the incredible dedications and inspiration made them extra special.'

'That means the world to us both,' Father said. 'Thank you.'

'I should have stayed in touch,' I said. 'I was so angry with you. I don't need to tell you that – you were on the receiving end of it – and I let it fester and build a wall between us that I couldn't see a way to break down. I'm still not sure what hurts the most – that you kept my true parentage from me or...' I searched round for words that wouldn't sound judgemental.

'Or what?' Mother asked gently.

I gasped, suddenly realising that Robyn might not know. I threw a worried look in her direction.

'Robyn knows,' Mother said. 'You were saying...?'

I sighed. 'Or that you'd had an affair lasting God knows how long if Robyn and I were both the result of it, and that Father stood by you. I thought you loved each other. I thought it was all-consuming.'

'Oh, darling, it was, it is, and it always will be.' She smiled across at Father and the expression of love passing between them was unmistakable.

'She needs to know,' Father said. 'All of it.'

Mother nodded then turned to face me. 'Your father and I believe that there are three ingredients to the perfect relationship and these certainly aren't unique to us. The first is love and we were blessed with an enduring love. The second is shared passions – for us, that was history, writing, costume design, this house, and our two beautiful children. As for the third, many would say it's compromise. For us, that has deepened into sacrifices that we've made for each other.'

She glanced across at Father.

'Your Mother and Phipps didn't have an affair,' he said. 'It was a business arrangement. We wanted children but discovered that I couldn't have them so, if we were to have the family we longed for, we needed a third-party intervention.'

'Phipps had become a good friend,' Mother continued. 'He was widowed quite young. Theirs was a love like ours and he knew his wife could never be replaced. She was taken before they'd tried for a family and it seemed like an arrangement that could work for us all. It was only meant to be one child, but we wished for a sibling for you to play with.'

'It took Phipps a while to come round to the idea,' Father said. 'Three years to be exact, but he finally agreed. You were four at the time, Tori.'

'But there are eleven years between us,' I said.

Mother sighed. 'After a few unsuccessful liaisons and two miscarriages, Phipps said no more, but I wore him down and he agreed one more time, which is just as well because we were then blessed with our little Robyn and now we're expecting a grandchild. Did she tell you?'

'Yes, she said it in the kitchen. Sorry, I'm trying to get my head round this. You're saying this wasn't an affair, but you just used the word 'liaisons'. Am I right in thinking that we're not talking about insemination here?'

'I know that part might be harder to understand,' Mother said. 'But it was something we all agreed on from the start. Modern medicine can do wonderful things, darling, but all three of us are Victorian at heart. Do you want more details?'

The hesitation in her voice and the crinkle of her nose would suggest she'd prefer not to give it and I certainly didn't want to hear it.

'Er, no. I'm good, thank you.'

Mother's shoulders relaxed. 'Robyn thankfully went to term, we got our family and Jack got to take on some sort of fatherly role, teaching you both to ride, being part of your lives. He went into the arrangement with his eyes open and it was enough for him while you were children, but he struggled with it when you left home, Tori. He blamed us for driving you away and rightly so. He thought you had a right to know once you turned eighteen.'

I looked at Father. 'That *is* an impressive sacrifice.'

'It was worth it to have both of you. I won't pretend it was easy, but I loved and trusted your mother. And she'd made such enormous sacrifices for me already.'

'Ralph, you don't have to...'

'No, I do. Best to get it *all* out in the open. We realise your childhood was different to most, Tori, and I don't just mean the historic aspects. You and Robyn spent all your time on the estate. We never went on holidays or days out. We never even went out for meals and there was a reason for that. Robyn doesn't know this either.' He took a deep breath. 'I'm agoraphobic. I can't leave the estate.'

Mother walked across the room and grasped Father's hand. 'We used to do personal appearances together. As you know, I was the face of Rebecca Lannister and we presented your father as my agent. When we'd made it big and bought the estate, we were very much in demand with interviews and book signings all over the country. The signings attracted enormous queues. I thrived on it, but your father was beginning to struggle.'

'There were so many people,' he said. 'All pushing and shoving with no sense of personal space. I was on edge every time someone got too close, worried something might happen to your mother.'

He gazed at Mother and the pain and fear was clearly still there.

'What did you think was going to happen to her?' Robyn asked gently.

'Anything! They could have had a knife or a gun or...' He shook his head as his voice cracked. 'I was right to be worried.'

'We attracted a stalker,' Mother said. 'He called himself Harris after a character in one of our early books who was obsessed with our heroine. Harris sent flowers to each signing and the message would be a different quote from one of our books which, taken out of context, read as a little scary and obsessive.' She shuddered, evidently wrestling with difficult memories.

'We had no idea who Harris was,' Father said. 'Every time we were at a signing, I found myself scrutinising all the men, wondering if they could be him, and then I wondered if it might be a woman. I was so tense all the time, I couldn't eat or sleep for fear of him hurting Vivienne.'

'Did the police know?' I asked.

Mother nodded. 'They couldn't do anything. Harris was clever. He hadn't made any threats. He'd sent flowers and quoted from our books, which looked like a superfan expressing his gratitude and admiration.'

'We were leaving a signing one evening and he was waiting.' Father's cheeks paled. 'He had a pair of scissors and lunged at your mother.'

'Oh, my God!' Robyn and I cried in unison.

'We found out later that he wasn't trying to hurt me,' Mother said. 'All he wanted was a lock of my hair, but he wasn't well and didn't realise this was not the way to behave. It was a truly terrifying experience which haunted me for a long time but the real damage was to your father.'

Father ran his hand through his hair and sighed. 'When I saw the scissors that day, I froze and I was so ashamed of myself that I couldn't protect the woman I loved.'

'He could have turned on you if you'd tried anything,' Mother said, her voice gentle and reassuring. 'As far as he was concerned, I was Rebecca Lannister and you were an obstacle in his way.'

She turned her gaze back to me and Robyn. 'After that, your father didn't think it was safe for me to meet our public. I felt the same way for a while, but the panic eased for me and I began missing that interaction with our readers. I didn't want to let thousands of wonderful fans down because of one obsessed individual. Your father tried to support me but leaving the estate brought on panic attacks. I went to several engagements on my own, but it wasn't the same. *I'm* not Rebecca Lannister. *We* are. Thanks to Harris, the magic had gone. The public adulation meant nothing without your father by my side experiencing it with me.'

'Your mother made the ultimate sacrifice for me,' Father said. 'She stepped back from the limelight she loved. No more travelling for interviews. No more signings. No more public appearances.'

'And I wouldn't have it any other way,' Mother insisted.

I pressed my hand to my chest. 'I can't believe you went through all of that.'

'Me neither,' Robyn added. 'What happened to this Harris guy? Did he go to prison?'

'I believe he got some psychiatric help,' Mother said. 'Anyway, that's all in the past but, to join some dots for you, that's the reason we never visited you in Bath, Tori, or you in Manchester, Robyn. That's why we never came to one of your restaurant openings, Tori. It was never that we weren't proud of what you two girls had achieved. We couldn't be more so. It was just very difficult.'

So much fell into place. 'When Robyn was poorly when she was a baby—'

'Your father stayed here and I did the hospital runs. If you hadn't been boarding, you'd have questioned things, rightly so, and your father didn't want—'

'I was ashamed,' he interrupted. 'I was a grown man who couldn't protect his wife from an obsessed fan and who couldn't do his share when his baby was ill.'

Mother stood up and topped up Father's tea. 'So now you have it. All of our skeletons are out of the closet, and I suspect you have a lot of questions.'

I did, but there was something far more pressing. I crossed the room and wrapped my arms round my father and held him tight. I understood it now. I understood it all.

'Thank you for sharing,' I whispered. 'I know that was hard.'

'Not as hard as losing you.'

'I'm back now, if you still want me in your life.'

'I always wanted you, right from the very start. You're my baby girl.'

I hugged Mother while Robyn hugged Father. Robyn and I nodded at each other, a shared understanding between us now. We'd explore our relationship another time. For now, the important thing was that our unconventional little family was reunited and there were no more secrets.

* * *

It was after 9 p.m. when I left. Robyn followed me out to the campervan.

'So we'll see you again?' she asked.

'Very soon. Maybe you and I could go out for a drink sometime and get to know each other.'

'I'd like that.'

I opened Carrie's door then paused. 'I lost it when I found out about Phipps being our biological father but you seemed to take the news really well.'

She shrugged. 'Don't get me wrong, it *was* a shock. I really hadn't seen that coming, but I maybe reacted differently because I've experienced something similar with Brett's family. He's adopted. He's in touch with the woman who gave birth to him and they get on really well, but she's not his mum. His mum's the woman who raised him. Phipps was part of our family so he means a lot to me, but he's not my dad, no matter what the biology says.'

As I drove back to Whitsborough Bay, I finally felt like I knew who I was. I was Vivienne and Ralph's daughter and they were the most inspirational, dedicated and devoted parents anyone could ever wish for. I wished I'd realised that sooner, but I wasn't going to get bogged down with regrets. Now was our time.

I glanced up at the gradually darkening sky. I couldn't see the moon but I knew she was there – a new moon who'd be smiling down at me and my new beginning. It was a long time coming, but it was the best new start so far and I couldn't wait to tell Finley all about it.

44

HOLLIE

Chief had warned Spaniel and me that the chances of a rescue during our training session tonight were high. Calls to the coastguard always increased during the holidays, thanks to a combination of the better weather enticing locals to the beaches and the increased numbers of day visitors and holiday makers. Today's sunny bank holiday Monday in May half-term had attracted as many visitors as the height of the summer.

Sure enough, we hadn't even made it out of the training room when we got a shout.

'Couple of teenagers trapped on the beach by the rising tide,' Chief said as we ran down to the changing room to pull on our all-weather gear.

It was the same crew as Tori's rescue – Chief, Finley, Jake, Spaniel and me – and, as we sped south, my heart raced with a mixture of trepidation and excitement. My second real-life rescue!

Given the direction we were heading, I suspected it had been a case of the teenagers thinking they could walk from the far south of South Bay round to the next cove instead of taking the clifftop paths, ignoring the warning signs.

We anticipated a straightforward rescue. One of the casualties had alerted the coastguard, so we knew exactly where they were and that neither of them were hurt. But that wasn't what we found.

There was still the tiniest bit of beach left – just enough for them to have huddled together without even getting their feet wet – but both teens were in the water. One of them was lying on his back and the other appeared to be frantically treading water beside him. Fortunately, the swell was fairly gentle.

'He fell!' shouted the one treading water. 'He's hurt his back.'

'Where did he fall from?' Jake asked.

'He panicked and tried to climb the cliffs.'

We all looked at where he was pointing. There was a significant overhang about eight feet above the beach and nothing about the rockface looked safe. I could understand that the approaching sea was scary but found it hard to believe that anybody would even attempt the cliffs as an alternative, especially when they'd already called for help.

'What's your name?' I asked him while Jake and Chief prepared the spinal board.

'Harry, and that's Alec. I can't swim very well!'

'Okay, Harry, don't panic. We'll be with you in a moment.'

Seconds later, Chief and Jake were in the water with the spinal board for Alec and a life jacket for Harry, while Finley called into the station to request an ambulance on standby for suspected neck and back injuries.

As before, it was thrilling to watch Jake working. Getting a casualty onto a spinal board was challenging as any movement could cause further damage but the sea was on our side and the lack of swell meant the transfer was uncomplicated.

Harry was exhausted from trying to stay afloat, so Spaniel and I had an opportunity to use our recent training on a real casualty as we brought him onboard.

'Oof,' I said as he kicked me in the stomach with his flailing legs.
'I'm so sorry! Are you hurt?'

'I'm fine. Don't worry about it. Sit down at the back here and
hold this round you.'

He took the emergency blanket from me while a pale-faced Alec
was secured and we headed back to the harbour at a slightly slower
pace to avoid jolting him.

'I'm so sorry,' Harry kept saying. 'I messed up.'

'It's all right,' I reassured him. 'It's what we're here for.'

Jake conducted an examination of Alec as best as he could in
the limited space. Alec cried out and Harry shot a terrified look in
his friend's direction. 'Have I killed him?'

'No. He's just a bit uncomfortable. The ambulance will be waiting. Are you friends?'

'Cousins.'

'And how old are you?'

'I'm fourteen and Alec's thirteen.'

I kept him talking to take his mind off his cousin and the cold.
The two families were on holiday at Kellerby Cliffs Holiday Park,
where Tori had been staying, and it was their first ever visit to the
seaside. They'd been allowed to wander off together for a couple of
hours as long as they didn't try to walk along the coast because it
was dangerous. Harry had convinced Alec that their parents were
being overly dramatic and, with no clue about the dangers of the
tide turning, they'd walked round the cliffs and realised they were
trapped.

Their parents, who Harry had rung after alerting the coastguard, were waiting on the slipway beside the ambulance, frantic
with worry.

By the time Finley steered the ILB back round to the lifeboat
station, Alec was sitting up in the back of the ambulance and laughing. He'd told Jake en route that he didn't think he'd seriously

injured himself after all. Jake was inclined to agree but preferred to remain cautious until he could be properly assessed on dry land. It was such a relief that they'd both emerged from their ordeal relatively unscathed and hopefully they'd learned a valuable lesson about warning signs being there for a very good reason.

'You were brilliant again this evening,' Chief said as we disembarked on the beach and walked up the lifeboat station ramp. 'I loved how you made the points about the importance of knowing the tide times and always telling someone where you're going without sounding like you were lecturing young Harry.'

I could feel my cheeks glowing as I basked in the compliment. 'Thank you. It seemed like the ideal opportunity for him to learn from the experience.'

'That information will stick and, with any luck, they'll both pass it onto their friends. Got to keep chipping away.'

'So proud of you,' Jake said, putting his arm round my shoulders and kissing the top of my head.

I was proud of me too. I'd been part of the RNLI for five months now, attended twenty-one training sessions and participated in two live rescues. I'd faced my fears, experienced new things, and learned so many new skills. I'd initially told Chief I wanted to stick around for five or six months which meant my time was almost up. But I didn't want to leave. I was part of something amazing that made a difference and I wanted to take that to the next level.

'Can we have a chat before we go inside?' I said, steering Jake towards the harbour railings a little later and letting the others go on ahead to The Lobster Pot.

'Everything okay?' he asked, his dark eyes full of concern.

'I've got a dilemma which I want to talk through with you.

Tonight, I made a big decision about my future with the RNLI. You and Chief were right about me. My heart and soul were already in and my head just needed to catch up. It has now and I would absolutely love to complete my training and become the first female Brooks to pass out as crew.'

'That's brilliant news! And the dilemma?'

'How that sits with our recent decision to try for a family. I haven't looked into the RNLI's policy on it, but I don't need to because my personal view would be that, if I fell pregnant, rescues would be a no-no. There are too many risks. Harry kicked me in the stomach today when he came on board. That can happen so easily and I wouldn't be prepared to put our baby at risk or have the rest of the crew worrying about me as well as the casualties. That wouldn't be fair on them. I also don't think it would be fair of me to commit to going through full training then have to drop out straightaway.'

'You're thinking we should hold off on trying for a baby until you've passed out?' His voice was gentle, no suggestion of disappointment or disagreement.

'I think so. I don't know.' I twiddled with my necklace. 'What do you think?'

'I think you should follow the advice you gave to Tori.'

'Listen to my heart?'

'What's it telling you?'

'To follow in my family's footsteps.'

'Then that's the right thing to do.'

'Even if it means a delay in trying for a baby?'

Jake drew me into a hug. 'We have no idea how long it will take or whether it'll happen at all and it's not like we're putting it off for years. We're only talking another seven months or so, and we both agreed we'd have ideally had longer together before having a baby, so let's make the most of that time. We'll focus on getting the café up and running again and getting you fully trained and think babies again next spring.'

'Thank you for making that easy,' I said, tightening my hold round his waist.

'Are you going to tell Chief tonight?'

'He'll probably ask me directly. You know what he's like.'

'Ready to tell him?'

'Ready.'

* * *

We could see Chief outside The Lobster Pot on his phone as we crossed the road and, with perfect timing, he ended the call as we reached him.

'Stragglers!' he declared, smiling at us.

'Have you got a minute?' I asked. 'Tonight's rescue – and the one before – were amazing. Seeing what you do first-hand has been a humbling experience and I completely get why it becomes part of who you all are because it's done the same to me. You called it right. I *do* want to become the first woman in my family to become crew.'

Chief ran his hands down his beard, his eyes glistening, and I thought for a moment he was going to burst into tears, but he suddenly grabbed me in a bear hug and bounced me up and down.

'Yes! My day is made!'

He released me, but kept his hands on my shoulders, smiling. 'I'm chuffed beyond words, and I know your dad and Isaac would be too. Welcome aboard, Starfish. Can we announce it tonight?'

'That depends. I want to be completely honest with you. Jake and I aren't getting any younger and, next year, we'd like to start a family. If things happen quickly, I might not be crew for long, so I'd understand if you'd rather not fully train me.'

Chief went all dewy-eyed once more. 'It would be a pleasure to fully train you and it would be an even greater pleasure to welcome the fifth generation of the Brooks family as future crew. That's a lot to toast tonight!'

'We want to keep the family thing quiet,' Jake said.

'No one'll hear it from me. Just let me know next year, even if it's just a suspicion you could be expecting, so we can keep you safe.'

'I will. Thank you.'

Everyone was delighted at my news with hugs all round. The pub was heaving – typical bank holiday – and we couldn't all sit together so Jake and I only stayed for one celebratory drink before heading home. Finley left at the same time and we were outside, about to say goodbye to him, when Tori came running up to us.

'Are you just arriving or leaving?' she asked.

'Leaving,' I said.

'Oh no! I thought I might have just caught you.'

'How did it go?' Finley asked.

She beamed at him. 'Better than I could have imagined. I've only just got back. I've got so much to tell you.'

'It's packed in there,' Finley said. 'There's some lagers in the fridge and I have all your favourite snacks.'

'Jaffa Cakes? Chipsticks? Giant cashews?'

He nodded at each suggestion and I watched, bemused, as they hugged each other, laughing.

'Ooh, did you tell Jake and Hollie about the man in the woods?' she asked when they broke apart.

'What man in the woods?' I asked.

'We're probably suffering with seriously overactive imaginations...' Tori started.

Between them, they outlined what they'd seen on Thursday night. Jake and I agreed that it sounded suspicious and I asked Finley to email me the photos he'd taken.

'My Uncle Adrian is a retired police sergeant,' Jake said. 'I'll see if he still has a contact who can run the plates. If you're ever passing and see anything else weird, let us know.'

We said goodbye and walked back to the lifeboat station to collect the car while Finley and Tori headed up Ashby Street.

'I think they fancy each other,' I told Jake.

'Nah, they're just good friends.'

'But all that snack stuff and the hug.'

He put his arm round my shoulders. 'You just want to pair everyone off and have them as happy as us. I honestly think it was nothing. Bart was on a rescue high and Tori has had a good day. That's all.'

I glanced back at them, giggling together. Maybe I was reading too much into it, especially as they'd both been through break-ups so a relationship was probably the last thing on their minds right now. They were clearly doing each other the world of good and it warmed my heart to see it, although I couldn't help hoping there might be something more for them – maybe not now but at some point down the line.

45

HOLLIE

'Are we crazy, doing this?' I asked Jake as I parked my car facing the woods at The Starfish Café the following morning.

'Do you think the man with the dog sounds dodgy?'

'Yes.'

'And will it be preying on your mind if we don't explore?'

'Yes.'

'Then we're going on a bear hunt.'

Next to the car park, there were pine trees with some spaces between them in which there were picnic benches. Beyond that, there was a row of dense trees and shrubs. The lack of pathways meant visitors didn't tend to explore the woods.

Jake and I pushed through a narrow gap and entered the woods – home to a mix of evergreens, deciduous trees and shrubs – and weaved in and out of the trees in a northerly direction following the compass on his phone.

There were some extremely dense parts and a few openings where the sunlight filtered through onto a soft carpet of pine needles and bark. Some trees had tumbled but, with no space to fall, they'd hugged those beside them.

At night, it would be extremely spooky but on a bright day like today with the chirp of birds and the rustle of wildlife, it felt almost magical.

'I've never actually been in here before,' I whispered, 'but it's not somewhere I'd walk a dog. Far too dense.'

'I agree. Especially at night.'

We searched as best we could but couldn't see any signs of disturbance. No shallow graves. No outbuildings. Nothing.

'Coffee?' I asked when we made it back to the car park an hour or so later.

'Definitely. Being a detective's thirsty work.'

We greeted Matt and the other workers onsite, then made ourselves drinks and took them out onto the terrace.

'It's gorgeous today,' I said, breathing in the fresh air. With the warm sun on our faces and the twinkling of the sea, it felt like we were in the Mediterranean.

Jake's phone beeped with a text. He frowned and handed it to me:

✉ From Uncle Adrian
Heard back from my contact. Plates are cloned.
You didn't hear that from me

'No surprise there, then,' I said, handing his phone back. 'But what can we do with that information? If we went to the police, what do we have other than a belief that the woods aren't suitable for dog walking?'

We finished our drinks and headed back through the café to the car. I paused in the car park, looking up at the security cameras.

'It's another long shot,' I said, 'but I'm going to forward those photos Finley took to the security company. I'll ask them to see if the dog walker did anything unusual when he arrived.'

'Do you know how long they keep recordings?'

'I'm pretty sure it's a fortnight for easy access with up to three months on the back-up so, if it was Thursday last week, that won't be a problem to find.'

'Bart said the main claimed to walk his dog here often so, if there's nothing that stands out from last Thursday, they could always scroll back.'

'I can't help thinking it's all connected,' I said.

'Me too, but how?' Then he nudged me, a silly grin on his face. 'Maybe Krueger the dog was trying to sniff out Tingler's Treasure.'

* * *

Late the following morning, I picked up an email from the security company. They'd scrolled back through the CCTV recordings and had found the same van visiting on other evenings so had sent me a link to access the relevant clips. I sat at the kitchen table watching them on my laptop. The routine was the same each time.

'Van pulls in,' I muttered to myself. 'Man in beanie hat gets out, looks round, opens the back of the van, pulls on backpack, releases dog, walks into the woods and...' I checked the time stamp '... returns forty minutes later, puts dog and backpack in van, drives away.'

That sensation that I was missing something gnawed at me. Even though the police had drawn a blank so far, I was convinced the break-in was connected to Smythe and, much as I'd initially laughed about Tingler's Treasure, I couldn't completely dismiss the idea. Smythe knew something that I didn't.

'You know what we should do?' Jake said when he arrived home from his shift to find me in Isaac's room, studying The Smuggler's Key. I'd printed off one of Finley's photos of the van and a couple of CCTV stills and added those to the board.

'Enlighten me,' I said.

'Get Jaffa to take a look. If this was his obsession as much as Isaac's, maybe he can see a connection to Smythe that we can't. Do you want me to ring him?'

'Might as well. Tell him there's a piece of chocolate cake with his name on if he's free tonight. It's his favourite.'

'You temptress,' Jake joked.

The chocolate cake inducement worked and, within twenty minutes, Kyle was sitting at the kitchen table, greedily forking it in while we updated him on the mysterious man in the woods with the cloned plates.

'How often does he visit?' Kyle asked when he'd finished his enormous slice.

'Every week on a Thursday. It's the same routine each visit and roughly the same length of time in the woods. We can't decide if that makes it more normal or more suspicious.'

'He never checks out the café?' Kyle asked.

'Barely even looks at it. Let me show you the clips.'

'Tell you what is different,' Jake said after we'd watched a few. 'The time. We've got 20:15, 21:46, and 22:27. If everything else is consistent, why does the time change?'

'Good point.' I randomly selected another clip. 'Especially when it's always a Thursday.'

'Stop! Scroll back a minute,' Jake said.

'What have you spotted?'

'His backpack.' Jake pointed to the screen. 'You see the way he grabs it here. It looks like it's empty.'

'Oh, yeah.' I clicked onto the corresponding return to the van. 'Now it's full and, from the way he moves it, it's heavy.'

We checked the other clips and would be hard-pressed to tell whether the backpack was empty on arrival or not, but the difference in his movements before and after did suggest it went from light to heavy.

I tapped my fingernails on the table. 'Man goes into the woods with an empty backpack and comes out with a full, heavy one. Do you think he meets someone who gives him something? Stolen property? Drugs?'

'Bart said there was only one torch beam?' Kyle asked Jake.

'Yes, and there was only one vehicle. If he was meeting someone to pick up a stash of whatever, that person must have had a vehicle somewhere. They said the roads were deserted and they didn't pass any parked cars or vans.'

'An earlier drop-off?' Kyle mused. 'But you said there was nowhere to hide anything in the woods and it would be too risky to leave stolen goods for later collection, especially when we're talking enough booty to fill that backpack. Unless...' He leapt up, scraping the chair across the titles. 'Can I see The Smuggler's Key?'

'It's upstairs.'

Jake and I ran after him up the stairs, exchanging bewildered looks as Kyle stood about a metre away from the cork board, his left hand running across his stubble while his outstretched right index finger floated from one Post-it note to the next.

'That's it!' He grabbed a yellow note and handed it to me.

'Tide times,' I read.

'What if...?' The excitement shone from his eyes as he steepled his hands against his lips – a gesture I'd seen him and Isaac doing so many times when they thought they'd made a breakthrough. 'What if he was meeting someone and that person *did* have a vehicle, but theirs was at the bottom of the cliff instead?'

'You mean a boat?' Jake asked.

He nodded vigorously and jabbed a pink Post-it note labelled 'Tingler's Treasure'.

'Starfish Point was connected with smuggling and in some ways it was ideal – remote, dark, with lots of rocks, meaning only those in the know would access the beach by sea. In other ways, it was a nightmare because there were no steps and handrails back then. Scrambling down the cliffs then carrying smuggled goods back up would have been risky and it would have taken too much time so there were two theories on this. One was that there was a cave where the booty was left and collected by a small fishing boat or rowing boat. The other was that there was a secret passageway from the beach to the cliff top.'

'Which is what you and Isaac were searching for but never found,' I said.

'Exactly. But what if both those theories were wrong? What if there was no cave or secret passage but a much smaller access point instead? Just small enough for a bucket which could hold a couple of bottles of rum which would only be accessible as the tide's going out...'

'...for someone to winch up from the woods,' I finished. 'That's genius!'

'And it could be used for a haul of treasure or, these days, drugs which then get stashed in a dog walker's backpack.'

'But there isn't a well or anything like that,' Jake said.

Kyle shook his head. 'It wouldn't be visible. They'd have it well hidden, excuse the pun.'

Jake stepped forward and tapped the Post-it notes I'd added about the connection of Smythe to Abe Tingler. 'In that case, what if a box of lost documents has recently been recovered which includes a real-life treasure map showing exactly where to find the secret winch at the top and bottom of the cliff?'

Kyle didn't know that part of the story, so Jake filled him in while I stared at the board, my heart racing. I felt as though we'd just found that missing piece of the puzzle. Was this how a detective felt when they'd just solved a case?

Jake turned to me. 'I bet if you were to go further back with the CCTV, you'd find the man in the woods first visits the woods shortly after Smythe gets his documents back.'

'I bet you're right. Which coincides with when he started making noises about buying the café again. But why would he need the café? His minion can visit whenever he likes and not be seen because the café's usually closed on an evening.'

'Usually,' Jake repeated. 'But you put an advert on Facebook after Betty and Tommy's anniversary party promoting evening events at the café.'

'Meaning the café could be busy on an evening, messing up their system,' Kyle said, his voice full of excitement. 'I think you need to let the police know.'

'I agree,' Jake said.

And that was the moment reality hit. I slumped down on Isaac's bed. 'And say what? We think the most powerful man in Whitsborough Bay is a direct descendent of the area's most notorious smuggler and the apple doesn't fall far from the tree. We think he wants to buy my café so he can smuggle goods up a hidden well without being seen.' I rolled my eyes at them. 'And he would have got away with it if it hadn't been for those meddling kids.'

'It does sound a bit like a *Scooby Doo* episode,' Kyle admitted. 'But I'm convinced it's true. You're not the only ones who've heard rumours about Smythe. I've heard his name connected with drugs and money laundering and he's got the perfect set-up for that: an empire of predominantly family-friendly businesses with a stack of cash passing through them.'

I ran my fingers through my hair and released an exasperated squeal. 'It feels like we have all the puzzle pieces and we even have some evidence, but it's not good enough. If we're right about the pattern, the man in the woods will be back on Thursday and the only way we'll get the evidence is to catch him in the act, but if we're talking drugs and money laundering, I bet that dog of his isn't the only potential weapon he carries with him.'

Kyle grimaced. 'Do either of you know anyone in the police who'd take this seriously? I don't.'

'My Uncle Adrian,' Jake said. 'He's retired, but he still has contacts. I'll go and see him first thing tomorrow.'

'Do you have any more of that cake?' Kyle asked. 'Because I think we've got some work ahead of us to pull together everything we've got and make sure they take it seriously.'

Over the next ninety minutes or so, we compiled a portfolio of evidence. We had the full timeline worked out with different colours capturing facts versus rumours. We checked the tide times and predicted the arrival time for the man in the woods on Thursday night.

I emailed the security company to ask them to check further back. With the aid of the tide tables, I was able to give them a time window to check. A speedy reply confirmed that the first visit absolutely coincided with the discovery of the missing documents and me advertising the café's availability for evening events.

'Keep me posted,' Kyle said, heading off shortly after midnight with a cake tin containing the rest of the chocolate cake. 'Good luck.'

* * *

The following morning, I accompanied Jake to see his Uncle Adrian and Auntie Maggs. Adrian fired a stack of questions at us, but he didn't laugh once.

'I know it's a much bigger ask than checking a number plate,' Jake said, 'but we're hoping you still have contacts who'll be interested. We don't think anyone would take us seriously, even the officers handling the break-in. We're aware it sounds far-fetched.'

'I've got contacts. Good contacts. Your dad was convinced Smythe was a wrong-un, but that man was clever. Nothing stuck. We all tried over the years. I can't say anything more about it, but I can assure you they *will* be interested. I think you'll be surprised at how positive a response this information will receive. The three of you need to leave it alone now. Don't tell anyone and don't go there tomorrow night. I'll get it sorted.'

46

We'd reached the end of week three of Operation Driftwood and I was delighted with progress. The first coat of white emulsion had been applied, instantly brightening the interior, the booth seating structures were in place, the flooring had been laid and about a third of the kitchen units had been installed.

Overnight, I'd had a couple of ideas for small tweaks in the shop and gallery upstairs, so I wanted to visit the site first thing to stand in the space and confirm my thoughts before running the changes by Hollie.

As I drove along the approach road, my stomach churned at the sight of several police vehicles in the car park. No way! They couldn't have broken in again and destroyed three weeks of work.

I parked Carrie alongside a police van and my heart leapt as I noticed police tape strung between the trees. Had the dog walker been back? Had they caught him?

I opened the door and stepped out.

'Sorry. Café's closed,' a police officer said.

'It's okay. She's with me,' Hollie responded, appearing by his side.

Judging by her enormous smile, there clearly hadn't been another break-in.

'What's happened?' I asked. 'Did they catch the dog walker?'

'Even better than that. We'll go on the terrace while the police finish in the woods. Have I got an interesting story for you! Do you know the local legend of Tingler's Treasure?'

'No, but I like the alliteration. Do tell!'

I listened, fascinated, as Hollie shared a tale of historic smuggling on the Yorkshire Coast, the downfall of the notorious Abe Tingler, her brother's fascination with it all and how it connected to Sebastian Smythe.

'We're so grateful to Jake's Uncle Adrian and his contacts because it got taken *very* seriously,' she said. 'The man in the woods is called Colt Baggott and he's no stranger to trouble. Our theory was right. There *is* a hidden passageway down to the sea with an elaborate pully system in place and, last night, they caught Baggott red-handed and also his accomplice below. They couldn't tell me what the goods were due to an ongoing operation, but I'm thinking it has to be drugs.'

'I'd have thought so. Wow! Who'd have thought it? Drug smuggling at The Starfish Café!'

'I know! Crazy, isn't it? The police confirmed that Baggott was not the criminal mastermind and they're pursuing other lines of enquiry, but they can't confirm whether or not those are connected to Smythe. They believe that Baggott will want to make a deal in return for giving up the names of those further up the chain. And I'm pretty certain we all know who the boss is.'

'That's such good news.'

'It's all down to you and Finley. If it hadn't been for you two seeing the light in the woods and sticking around to ask some questions, we'd never have put that final piece of The Smuggler's Key together.'

Butterflies surged at the unexpected mention of Finley's name. That was happening with alarming regularity.

'It was all Finley,' I said. 'I spotted the light, but he was the one who asked the questions while I was quaking in my boots.'

'We owe you both several drinks.'

'Here's an idea. When they get that Slippy Smythe, how about the four of us go on a big night out to celebrate?' As I said it, an image sprung to mind of us huddled round a table in the pub, toasting to Smythe's downfall, Jake with his arm round Hollie, and Finley with his arm round me. Our eyes met and, next moment, his lips were crushed against mine and we were lost in a moment of passion and... seriously! No more romance novels for me.

'Did you come here for something specific?' Hollie asked.

'Yes. I just want to check something upstairs. I've had a couple of thoughts and I want to measure up to see if they'd work.'

'I'll leave you to it. I'm going down to visit the seals. There could be pups appearing any time now. See you later.'

She clipped Pickle's lead on and left. I stayed on the terrace, a light breeze tickling my hair across my face. I imagined Finley beside me, gently pushing it back, my heart racing as he cupped my face and drew me into a deep and tender kiss and...

I stood up and pressed my hands against my flaming cheeks as the action turned X-rated. I could try to keep kidding myself that it was Mother and Father's books, but I needed to accept this for what it really was. I had a massive crush on my new best friend and I was going to have to get a grip. We were friends and housemates and he'd never given any suggestion that he might feel or want anything different. Best keep my wits about me and hope my feelings would disappear as quickly as they'd crept up on me.

47

HOLLIE

Five days had passed since Colt Baggott's arrest. To my knowledge, he was still 'helping the police with their enquiries' but, disappointingly, there'd been no news about Smythe. We'd visited Jake's Uncle Adrian and Auntie Maggs for Sunday lunch and Adrian had assured me that they'd be busy building the strongest possible case so they could throw everything including the kitchen sink at him.

I reminded myself of the quote Irene had given me: *If you wait by the river long enough, the bodies of your enemies will float by.* Hopefully, that wait was almost over.

In the meantime, I had something else to take my focus. I'd checked Jake's shifts at the hospital against the dates Philip Heslington had come back to me with, and I'd secured three consecutive days in Philip's diary. I'd also thought of the perfect moment to present the gift, which I was sure would resonate with Jake.

Today, Tuesday, 7 June, was the seven-year anniversary of his nanna's death and I'd asked him if he'd like to mark the occasion by visiting Whitsborough Bay Castle where he'd scattered her ashes.

'This was a lovely idea,' he said, leaning forward to peer over the castle keep. 'Nanna loved it here. Remind me when we get home. I've got a photo on my computer of Nanna and Irene sitting on those cannons down there in absolute hysterics. I wasn't with them. Their friend Kay took it, and the story went that they told Nanna not to try to clamber on it as she'd never get off, but she insisted she'd be fine. She got her leg over and promptly got stuck. They had to get a couple of the groundsmen to help her off it.'

I loved hearing the laughter in his voice as he relayed that story.

'She was always getting herself into predicaments like that.'

He leaned against the wall and I stepped back, allowing him time to lose himself in his happy memories.

A little later, after we'd walked round what was left of the castle walls, we ambled round the perimeter. The ruined castle was on a clifftop and the buildings closest to the cliff edge hadn't survived various battles and world wars, leaving a wide-open space to wander round. Because the headland jutted out between Whitsborough Bay's North and South Bays, visitors were rewarded with breathtaking views of both.

'You know that photography evening at the library?' I ventured as we sat on one of the benches, taking in the scenery. 'You went with your nanna, didn't you?'

'Yes. Nanna and Irene. A neighbour dropped out so they thought I'd like her ticket.'

'And it was seeing Philip and Michael Heslington's talk that got you back into photography?'

'Yes.' He drew the word out, eyeing me suspiciously. 'Why all the questions?'

'I have a little gift for you to commemorate your nanna on her anniversary. You reckon you're not a talented photographer and I say you are, but I realised that I'm no expert on the subject. If you want to improve anything, you turn to the experts, and who better to turn to than the ones who inspired you in the first place?'

I slipped an invitation out of my bag and passed it to him to open.

'Three days with Philip Heslington!' His eyes widened and he grabbed my arm. 'How did you swing this? He doesn't do tutoring anymore.'

The excitement in his voice filled my heart with happiness.

'I asked nicely. I checked your shifts so these are dates you can make and he's hoping Michael will be able to join you for at least one day too.'

'Hollie! I don't know what to say!'

'There's only one thing I want to hear you say. When you've spent your three days with Philip, I want you to come back and say *I can take amazing photos. I am a talented photographer. I believe in myself.* Because if you can say that with conviction, my work here is done.'

I thought for a moment that he was going to cry, but he did a whoop and flung his arms round me, showering me with kisses. Seems his heart was filled with happiness too and, when we finally chased away those demons caused by his vindictive sister, it would be brimming over.

48

TORI

I stopped by The Starfish Café on the Wednesday of week four of Operation Driftwood to check on the painting. The largest sections of wall were staying white to keep the café light and bright, but we'd chosen blue and teal accent colours for the columns and some smaller sections of wall, and I wanted to make sure they looked right now they were dry. As well as adding warmth and vibrancy, the touch of colour would complement the upholstery and the stunning mosaic which Hollie and Avril were making from the broken crockery.

Stepping inside the café, I grinned. Each time I visited, significant changes could be seen as the vision came together. I always felt such a buzz as a project approached the end. The kitchen was now complete, the serving counter and breakfast bar had been fitted, and some of the booth tables had been installed. By the end of the week, all of the tables and chairs would be in place and the lighting finished.

We'd confirmed an opening date of Wednesday, 29 June, three weeks away. Although if Jake's time spent with a local professional photographer didn't succeed in convincing him that his artwork was saleable, there'd be some bare walls upstairs on opening day, as Hollie's pebble and sea glass art wouldn't cover much space.

Tim was on site today so I had a quick catch-up with him then drove to Fellingthorpe to meet Jack Phipps. I wanted to hear his side of the story, but I also wanted reassurance that I hadn't cost him his job. It wasn't that I didn't believe Mother, but I needed to hear it from the horse's mouth. And I needed to apologise to him. I'd never paused to think about how me storming out might have affected him. It was important he knew I'd left because of the lies and not because I was disgusted by the thought of him being my biological father.

I hadn't wanted to get into a discussion over the phone, so I'd texted him asking if we could meet for a long overdue catch-up.

Nervous butterflies stirred in my stomach as I drove towards the twenty-acre smallholding just outside Little Fraisby where I'd refurbished The Country Tavern. Would it feel any different seeing him now that I knew the full story of my heritage?

Phipps was leaning against the garden fence as I pulled up outside the stone and slate cottage. He was dressed casually in jeans, a maroon polo shirt and wellington boots. His hair was messy, as always. He used to jokingly call it 'pitchfork chic', saying it looked more like he'd run a pitchfork rather than a comb through it. In his late sixties now, he could easily have passed for mid-fifties.

'Tori! Good to see you,' he said as soon as I stepped out of Carrie. He smiled warmly and stretched out his hand to shake mine.

'After eight years, I think we can do better than that.' I opened my arms and his smile widened as he accepted the hug.

'You look well,' he said, stepping back.

'So do you. Have you found a way to stop the ageing process?'

'A daily cleansing routine of pig muck. Smells a bit ropey, but it's kind to the skin.' He laughed at my shocked expression. 'Joking! Cuppa or tour first?'

'A tour would be great.'

He released a low whistle and a Border Collie came running over. 'This is Mabel.'

I crouched down and Mabel immediately offered me her paw to shake. 'Aw, Phipps, she's gorgeous.'

Mabel trotted alongside us as we wandered round, with Phipps pointing out what he'd done and the plans he still had. If my departure had spurred on his decision, it was obvious it had been the right move for him. He seemed so relaxed and settled, as though he'd always lived there.

'You love it here, don't you?' I said when we settled at his kitchen table after the tour with giant-sized mugs of tea and a packet of Jaffa Cakes. I was touched that he'd remembered.

'I do. There's only one thing that would have made it better and that would be if Nancy was here with me. This was her dream too and, when she fell ill, she made me promise I'd still do it when I was ready to retire. So here I am, living the dream.' He smiled at me and I could tell he meant it.

'It's an amazing place. It's a relief to see you settled. I was worried I'd driven you out.'

'Not at all. Vivienne and Ralph wanted me to stay, but this place came up for sale and it was exactly what I was looking for, so it was time to move on. I stay in touch with your parents. We're still good friends.'

'That's good to hear. Thank you for what you did for them. That was a precious gift.'

'They're good people and they deserved to have a family. My chance for my own family was taken from me when Nancy died. I loved her too deeply for there ever to be another woman for me, so it was in my gift to help your parents have the children they longed for.'

'How was it for you, seeing Robyn and me every day and not being able to say anything?'

'We didn't go into it lightly, any of us. We talked about it for nearly a year, throwing round the pros and cons and what ifs. When we were all on the same page with how it would work, we decided to go ahead. You – and later Robyn – wouldn't be my daughters and I knew and accepted that. I didn't want a family without Nancy, so that worked for me. The bonus was that I got to be part of your lives, spending time with you, teaching you to ride, watching you grow without having the worry or responsibility. Or at least that was the theory. I never stopped worrying about you both!'

He paused to sip on his drink. 'The relationship worked for me during your childhood but, when you got older and your relationship with Vivienne and Ralph deteriorated, that was hard. I wanted to intervene so many times, but that went against everything we'd agreed on. All I could do was listen as you offloaded and have a quiet word with your parents when I could, not that it did any good.'

'I appreciated you listening. You were the only one who did.'

'I'm sorry I didn't do more.'

I shook my head. 'No regrets, Phipps. Please.'

'Okay. I can't tell you how happy I was when you moved back home. They were supportive about your business and I thought that the time apart had given you all the space to grow and move on. Then it all went wrong and my biggest fear came to pass – that I'd never see you again.'

'I'm sorry I stormed out that day without saying goodbye. You do know it was about them and never about you?'

'I understand.'

'And I'm sorry if I caused you any problems.'

'You really didn't, Tori. It was always going to come out at some point and I'm only sorry you found out the way you did. I still kick myself that I didn't check we were alone in the stables.'

'But if it hadn't been then, it would have been some other time.'

'True.' Phipps picked up a Jaffa Cake and sat back. 'Tell me about yourself.'

'Not much to tell. Still running my design business, recently split up with Leyton...'

His eyebrows shot up. 'You've been with Leyton all this time?'

'Yeah, why?'

'I'm just a bit surprised. I'd have put money on that not lasting. Mind you, I'd never have put you with Ewan either, so what do I know?'

'What makes you think they were both wrong for me? Please be honest. I won't be offended.'

He put his mug down and sighed. 'They're not you. You're ambitious, driven and passionate about what you do, but you're also full of love, laughter and life. Just like Vivienne.'

My expression must have conveyed my surprise at hearing Mother described in that way because Phipps leaned forward, his eyes crinkling with mischief.

'When you think about your relationship with your mother before you moved to Bath, what do you think of?' he asked. 'First three things that spring to mind.'

'Erm, deadlines, being pushed out, stress.'

'I thought you'd say something like that, and I understand why. The tough stuff tends to stick in our minds and it's easy to forget the good things. You know what I picture when I think about your last few years at home? Your school leaving party, blowing bubbles in the church, that pair of enormous dungarees.'

I pressed my fingers against my lips as buried memories surfaced.

'I do remember the tears and arguments,' Phipps continued. 'What you say about deadlines and being pushed out was absolutely true – and I called Vivienne out on that so often – but there was plenty of light in the darkness and lots of fun. I appreciate that Ewan only visited twice and I didn't know Leyton that well either, but I couldn't help feeling that they were only a match for work-Tori and not fun-Tori. You're a straight-A student and an award-winning architect. You're also the person who dances in an abandoned church and hosts Jaffa Cake eating contests. I always imagined the man who'd steal your heart would be your best friend rather than a work colleague. That probably makes no sense at all.'

'Actually, Phipps, it makes perfect sense. I might have found him, but I don't know how he feels.'

'You could always ask him.'

'Because that's not embarrassing at all, especially when I share a house with him.'

He raised his eyebrows at me. 'It's only embarrassing if you let it be.'

'You used to say that to me when I moaned about Mother and Father's costumes.'

'And was that really embarrassing?'

'No.'

'There you go, then.' He picked up two more Jaffa Cakes but didn't eat them. 'Are you still a selenophile?'

'You remembered!'

'I remember everything about you and your sister,' he said softly, his eyes glistening.

He held up one of the Jaffa Cakes, sponge side towards me, then placed the other one over it, chocolate facing me, leaving the slightest crescent of sponge showing. 'It was a new moon at the start of last week so you have roughly three weeks until the next new one. Be brave and go for your new beginning and, if he doesn't feel the same, don't feel embarrassed. Feel proud that you tried.'

He wagged the Jaffa Cakes to emphasise his point then shoved one of them in whole, closely followed by the other.

'I could still beat you in a Jaffa Cake eating contest,' I said, laughing at him.

Unable to speak with his mouth full, he put both thumbs up to indicate I should bring it on. I certainly would. It was good to see him and I wanted to do it again very soon.

* * *

There was so much to mull over following my visit to Phipps that I decided to take Carrie for a drive while I processed everything.

I hadn't planned to drive to Redamancy Castle, but my autopilot had taken me there. Mother was kneeling on a gardening mat, pulling up some weeds from round the fountain. She waved as I drove past her and parked.

'What a pleasant surprise,' she said, hugging me.

She was dressed in black cropped trousers and a pale lemon floaty blouse with a black headband keeping her loose hair out of her eyes.

'Your father thinks I look like a bee in this outfit,' she said, misinterpreting me looking her up and down. 'Is he right, darling? Is it too much?'

'No, it's just that I'm not used to seeing you wearing n...' I stopped myself from saying it. I hated the word 'normal'.

'You can say it. Normal clothes. I have a couple of wardrobes full of them. Far more comfortable and practical for a spot of gardening. I sometimes write in my pyjamas.'

'I thought you always wore your costumes at home.'

'We go through phases depending what we're working on. Always have. Cup of tea?'

'Yes, please.' I followed Mother into the house, frowning. What was going on? I'd have sworn the only times I'd seen Mother out of costume were when she left the estate. But I'd also forgotten about all of those happy times Phipps talked about. What was wrong with me? Had I been so annoyed with them that I'd blanked out all the good stuff?

'I saw Phipps today,' I said while she prepared a tea tray.

'Oh, that's wonderful. How did it go?'

'It was good to see him. He seems happy and settled. Hasn't aged a day.'

'He comes from good genes, that one. I feel bad that I haven't visited him. Your father has always trusted me implicitly, but I've been conscious of trying not to spend time alone with Jack. I'd have hate to give your father any reason to suspect there was anything more than friendship and a business arrangement between us.'

'I could come with you if it made you more comfortable,' I suggested.

'I'd like that. Thank you.'

'Where's Father?'

'In the estate cottage with Robyn and Bovis. He's keen to ride again but he'll need a slower steadier horse, so they're looking through some videos of potential options.' She filled the teapot. 'You keep looking at my outfit. Is it the bee thing?' She pulled off the headband.

'No! I swear you don't look like a bee. It's just that, whenever I picture you and Father, you're always in costume and I'm experiencing a bit of a disconnect to discover that's not the case. And Phipps mentioned a few things earlier that I swear I'd completely forgotten about. It's like I've somehow blanked out parts of my past without realising it.'

'Come with me,' she said, striding out of the kitchen. 'There's something you need to see.'

I followed her down the corridor and across the grand entrance hall to the library in the east wing. It was a stunning room with floor to ceiling bookshelves and a ladder on a rail to reach the higher shelves. Victorian writing bureaus overlooked two of the three side windows with a padded window seat across the middle bay one. A pair of chaises, a sofa and several high-backed chairs provided a range of seating preferences for reading.

'We cleared out some of the books to make way for photos,' Mother said. 'Take a look.'

They kept their own books in their office, so the library shelves had always been home to authors they loved, including different editions of their favourites, and books they planned to read.

I paused by the first set of photo frames: my parents on their wedding day, graduation photos from their undergraduate and Master's degrees, them toasting their first publishing deal. I ran my fingers down the frame of the latter. Little did they know back then that their success would have such an impact on Father's mental health.

'The family photos are a little further along,' Mother said, picking up a book and settling on the window seat. 'I think you might be surprised.'

There didn't appear to be any logical order to the family photos – a photo of me as a toddler shared shelf space with baby Robyn and the last Christmas before I left home – and Mother was right about me being surprised. In the vast majority of the photos, my parents were dressed in modern attire.

I picked up a photo of Mother and me in fits of giggles, wearing the same enormous pair of dungarees. I'd been fifteen at the time and it was one of the memories Phipps had reminded me of earlier. I'd wanted to make the dungarees oversized so I'd cut more material than the pattern required, but I'd measured with inches instead of centimetres and they'd ended up so big that Mother could fit in one leg and I could fit in the other. Father had been laughing so much, he'd struggled to take a photo that wasn't blurred.

'That's one of my favourites,' Mother said. 'I've still got the dungarees somewhere.'

'I can't believe I'd forgotten about it.'

Returning it to the shelf, I moved along and found a photo of Matt, Tim and me at the mini school leaving party Mother had organised. Being friendless, I hadn't wanted to go to the Whitsborough West one, so Mother had decorated one of the follies with balloons and fairy lights and invited my cousins over.

The final occasion Phipps mentioned – the bubbles – was also captured in a frame. It was my last Christmas at home when I was eighteen and Robyn was seven. On our annual Boxing Day ride across the estate, we'd stopped at *l'eglise des arbres* for hot chocolate and Mother had produced some bubbles which had been a stocking filler for Robyn. I'd commented on how much fun it looked and she'd laughed and produced bottles for everyone. Blowing bubbles at each other in that magical place and watching them float heavenward had been such a special moment. How had I forgotten?

'Are you all right?' Mother asked as I placed the bubbles picture back on the shelf. 'You look confused.'

'I feel it. These photos are full of happy memories and, now that I'm looking at them, I remember them all vividly – except the ones when I was really young, of course. But when I look back...' I bit my lip. I couldn't find a way to say it without hurting her.

'The bad times are all you remember?' she suggested, closing her book and patting the cushion beside her.

I joined her on the window seat and we sat facing each other.

'I'm sorry. I know that sounds so bad.'

'No, darling, it's understandable and I'm sorry we let you down. We thought you'd have the best possible start in life with a governess, but we didn't appreciate how important early friendships were. Your father and I didn't keep in touch with any friends from school or college and, when we started at Oxford and found each other, we didn't need anyone else, but we realise we were unique in that. Friends come and go as we grow and develop into the people we're meant to be and you didn't get the chance to experience that at a young age so, when things went wrong with Millicent and Tracie, you didn't have the tools to deal with it. We should have taken how hurt you were – and the part we played in that – far more seriously.'

'Thank you.'

'As for the memories, it's how our brains are wired. When something bad happens to us – an injury, failing an exam, a break-up, a bereavement – the emotions can be stronger than when something good happens, which makes them more vivid. That's a small selection of photos on the shelves. If ever you want me to go through the albums with you, I'd be more than happy to.'

'I might take you up on that.'

'The tea will be stewed,' she said, standing up. 'I'll brew a fresh pot.'

When Mother left the room, I stayed where I was. I would take her up on the offer to look through the albums another day but, for now, I'd seen enough. What she said about the brain made sense, but I couldn't blame that completely. I'd chosen to be angry. I'd chosen to focus on the bad memories and shut out the good times – and my family. What did that say about me? No wonder I'd struggled to make friends. It *was* me, after all. I'd allowed one experience from the past to shape my interactions with everyone I met and maintain a distance.

I gazed out of the window, over the raised flower beds, and

thought about Finley. There'd never been a distance between us and hopefully there never would be. Everything had changed the day I could have died, and I was going to grab that second chance at life with both hands. I'd visit my parents regularly and do my best to make up for pushing them away, I'd pin down a date to go out with Robyn so we could get to know each other, I'd stay in touch with Phipps and take Mother to visit him, and I'd take a chance on the new moon and tell Finley how I felt.

49

HOLLIE

Jake was between shifts on Friday and, with a sunny morning forecast, we'd decided to visit Starfish Point before the visitors arrived. A couple of the common seals had delivered pups and I was eager to check on them. Jake was going to capture photos with his zoom lens, which meant a close photo while keeping a good distance from the mum and pup.

'Are you okay?' Jake asked as he drove us towards The Starfish Café. 'You seem a bit quiet this morning.'

'Am I? I didn't sleep very well again. I know your Uncle Adrian said it might take time, but I was hoping they'd have arrested Slippy Smythe by now.'

'Me too. I'm sure it will be soon. Hang on in there.'

'I'm trying to but I feel unsettled with him still on the loose. I keep having bad dreams about him doing something else to the café. Last night, I dreamed he hurt the seals.'

As soon as he parked outside the café, Jake drew me into a hug. 'It'll be sorted soon. We just need to wait by that river a little longer.'

I smiled at his use of the proverb Irene had cited, but I wasn't sure how much more patience I had inside me. Jake was such a calming influence, but I could feel my stress levels rising.

Jake wanted to see the progress with Operation Driftwood before the team from Richards & Sons arrived, so I unlocked the door and we stepped inside, Jake holding Pickle in case there was anything sharp on the floor.

A week had passed since I'd last been inside and the progress since then was considerable. The storage units had been fitted behind the serving counter, the booths were finished, the chairs and tables were in place, and there was a pile of seat cushions at the far end of the café, protected by clear plastic wrapping.

'It looks so different!' Jake exclaimed.

Panic gripped me at his words.

'It's not Mum's café,' I whispered, reaching for my necklace. 'I've stripped her out.'

I clapped my other hand over my mouth, feeling suddenly nauseous. I couldn't picture Mum. Even though she'd never been in the New England version, I'd seen her reaction to those designs – her smile, her enthusiasm, her passion – but there was nothing of her here in this imposter café.

'What have I done?' I cried, gripping onto the driftwood counter as my legs threatened to give way.

'Hey, it's all right.' Jake placed Pickle down on the counter and gathered me in his arms. 'Your mum's still here. She'll always be here. She broke the ground. She built the café. She created the warm and friendly space you have and none of that has gone. When it's all finished and you have your café evolution picture back in place, you're baking using your mum's and granny's recipes, and you're welcoming back the customers who knew and loved your mum, it'll all fall into place and you'll see and feel her here again.'

I didn't know what had come over me. I couldn't seem to stop crying. I clung onto Jake, fat tears rolling down my cheeks. What he was saying was right. I knew that. And yet I felt such overwhelming sadness, the likes of which I hadn't felt in quite some time.

'How about a change of scenery?' Jake suggested, stepping back and taking my hands in his. 'Although I think cute seal pups might make you cry too.'

'Probably,' I said, smiling through my tears. 'But I'll take that chance.'

* * *

The sadness eased with each step closer to the beach.

'How are you feeling?' Jake asked.

'Better, thanks. I had no idea that was building up.' I breathed in the salty, fishy aroma. 'I always feel so alive down here. Let's find the pups.'

I don't think it's possible to feel sad looking at a seal pup. They really are the most adorable creatures, with the biggest, most mesmerisingly beautiful eyes.

There were still only two pups as far as we could see – a mainly white one with a pale grey head and a darker grey one with even darker spots.

Jake set up his tripod well away from them, then showed me close ups on the back of his camera.

'They are soooo cute,' I gushed.

We stayed down at the beach for a couple of hours while Jake took photos of the seals, Starfish Arc, and Starfish Lighthouse.

'That did me the world of good,' I said as we set off back up the steps.

'And me. I've never seen a seal pup. What a special place this is.'

We were about halfway up when my phone rang: Mitch from the Sea Rescue Sanctuary.

'I've got some good news for you,' he said. 'Alice became a mum in the early hours this morning and the pup is suckling and doing really well. We've named him Lewis.'

'Aw, that's brilliant news! Thanks so much for letting me know.'

'Pleasure. I'll send you some photos and we'll keep monitoring them and then let you know about a release. We'll wait until Lewis can fend for himself before we do that, though, just in case Alice finds the transfer stressful and abandons him.'

'Keep me posted and thanks again. I needed some good news today.'

* * *

We'd only just returned to Sandy Croft and put the kettle on when PCs Dawkins and Kramer knocked on the door.

'We have some news for you,' PC Dawkins said.

My heart thudded as I prayed for good news.

'Sebastian Smythe has been arrested and charged with a series of offences including possession with intent to supply class A drugs, receiving and handling stolen goods, and money laundering. He was also behind the break-in and sabotage of The Starfish Café, but we haven't had confirmation of the exact charges there.'

'He will be charged, though?'

She smiled. 'Definitely.'

I released a long shaky breath. It was over. 'I can't thank you both enough.'

'Full team effort,' she said. 'We'll keep you posted on any further developments.'

Jake hugged me when they left. 'You waited by that river and the body of your enemy *did* float past.'

'I'm so relieved.'

'Me too. And you know who else will be?'

I picked up my phone, called Irene and put her on speaker phone.

'The police have just been and—'

'They've arrested Slippy Smythe,' she interrupted, making Jake roll his eyes at me. 'I was about to call you to see if you'd heard. What did they tell you?'

'Not a lot,' I said. 'They ran through a string of charges and there's more to come.'

'Apparently that Colt Baggott made a deal for a lighter sentence. They had an insider but they needed Baggott's extra detail and they got it. Singing like a canary, he was. Stacks of names and, of course, the top dog was Smythe.'

'How do you know all this?' Jake asked.

'I know people who know people. Tell you what, you two, my Derek will be up in heaven right now doing a happy jig. Payback at last.'

Irene regaled us with more details – likely to be some truth generously peppered with speculation, gossip and exaggeration – before heading off for her lunch.

'Singing like a canary,' I said, shaking my head at Jake. 'I think Irene's been watching too many gangster films.'

Jake called his Uncle Adrian who also already knew and confirmed that the police had indeed had someone 'on the inside' who'd been able to provide them with access to some interesting ledgers showing his legitimate and not so legitimate business trans- actions. That was how he'd been so certain they'd take what we'd discovered extremely seriously as it strengthened the case they were already building.

'It's finally over,' Jake said, pulling me into his arms. 'How do you feel?'

'I can't stop smiling. I'm so relieved.'

'I know someone else who'd love this news. Do you fancy taking Pickle for a walk along North Bay?'

The sunny morning had given way to grey skies with the threat of drizzle, but that wasn't going to dampen our spirits as we walked along the promenade towards the old slipway early that afternoon. There were still plenty of folk about, but not in the same quantities the sun attracted.

Jake heaved himself onto the giant-sized bench beside the rusted steel sculpture of local fisherman Stanley Moffatt. Set back from the slipway where Jake had been swept into the sea and his dad had drowned trying to rescue him, it was the place he felt closest to his dad.

He patted the bench beside him. I lifted Pickle up then heaved myself into position and we cuddled together as we watched the waves rise and fall.

'Happy birthday, Dad,' he said, looking across the promenade and over the seawall. 'It's happened. You were right about Smythe. They've finally got something to stick. Not so slippy anymore.'

I swallowed down the lump in my throat.

'I've just had a thought,' Jake said after a while. 'There's another huge positive to this whole thing. You've proved that, all along, your brother was right. There *was* a hidden passage. We might never find out the truth about Tingler's Treasure but, if it did exist, we've found out how he moved it.'

My lip trembled and tears pricked my eyes.

'Hey! I didn't mean to make you cry. This is meant to be a happy day.'

'I may not look it right now,' I said. 'But you have just made me so happy by saying that. All those hours with The Smuggler's Key were worth it. I can't wait to tell Kyle.'

'Are you okay?' Finley asked, frowning at me across the kitchen table as I pushed aside my half-eaten bowl of cereal on Tuesday morning.

'I'm not sure. I feel anxious this morning and I can't pinpoint why.'

'Everything going well at the café?'

'Completely on track and looking good. I'm not behind on anything else. I've even checked my diary and emails and there's nothing I've forgotten about. Weird.'

'It's a spring tide again tonight.'

I smiled at him. 'Full moon. That could be it! Maybe there's still some negativity to remove from my life.'

'Maybe Leyton will decide he absolutely cannot live without his spare bedding and will demand you return it after all.'

That made me laugh. 'Honestly, Finley, I wouldn't put it past him.'

When Finley left for work, I made another coffee and took it upstairs to my drawing board. With Operation Driftwood now in week five, I wasn't needed at The Starfish Café every day and I had more time to focus on other projects.

The past few days had been exceptionally busy. Robyn and I had finally gone out together. She'd suggested lunchtime on Friday and I'd been left in no doubt that she'd gone for lunch rather than evening to keep it short. Conversation was stilted and I saw plenty of her feisty side, but I also felt the ice thawing. If she'd been returning to New Zealand, I wouldn't have held out any hope, but her plans to settle and raise her family in the area did give us a chance of slowly building a relationship and I was willing to take a few digs to make that happen.

On Saturday night, Finley and I had met Hollie and Jake in Ruby Fizz to celebrate Sebastian Smythe's arrest. It had been a great evening and had felt like a double date. It had taken considerable restraint not to slip my hand into Finley's as we walked home.

The following day, I'd visited Redamancy Castle for Sunday lunch while Finley spent the day with India and Roman. My family had looked through the photo albums with much laughter, which I could tell had been a tonic for my parents, particularly Father. It also helped my relationship with Robyn take another step forward. I wasn't the only one who'd remembered my childhood less favourably. There were loads of photos of me cuddling my sister, pushing her round the estate in her pram, leading her on her first pony, proving I had been around more than she'd thought.

So with everything going well, why did I have this niggling feeling in my gut?

'Best stop daydreaming and crack on with some work,' I muttered, opening my emails.

An hour or so later, a rap on the door knocker made me jump. I peered out of the front window and my stomach lurched as I saw a police patrol car outside.

'Hello, we're looking for Ms Victoria Tennyson,' a female police officer said when I opened the door.

'That's me.'

She introduced herself and her male colleague, but I wasn't paying attention to their names, fearful as to why the police were on my doorstep. At her request, I invited them inside and perched on the edge of an armchair in the lounge.

'I understand you used to live with a Leyton Clairmont. Is that correct?'

'Yes. He's my ex-boyfriend. We broke up about two months ago. Why?'

'We're interested in Mr Clairmont's movements over the past year,' the male officer said. 'We'd appreciate any information you can provide.'

'Should I get my diary?'

'That would be helpful. Thank you.'

I ran upstairs and grabbed my iPad. *Oh God, Leyton, what have you been up to?* The phrases 'accounting anomalies' and 'unmitigated disaster' swam round my mind.

'Got it,' I said, holding up my iPad as I stepped back into the lounge. 'What do you need to know?'

* * *

I closed the door behind the police officers a little later and released a low whistle.

'Leyton Clairmont, you absolute idiot.'

Although the police couldn't give details, they'd shared enough for me to connect it all. Leyton had developed a gambling problem. A serious one. A regular at Smythe's casino, he'd got into trouble with the wrong people. Losing the Durling account had been about them distancing themselves from Leyton's connection to Smythe and those accounting anomalies at Clairmont Properties had been Leyton defrauding the family business to cover his gambling debts. No wonder he'd been so snappy and distant with me when his life was on a downward spiral.

I felt sorry for Eveline and Ernest. For all their faults, they had run an honest, successful business which they'd built from scratch. How devastating would it be for them to witness their only child destroying it and himself? Would they bail him out or would they leave him to fend for himself? I hoped they'd support him – he had nobody else if they didn't – but I couldn't help thinking they'd walk away.

Back in my office, I picked up my phone and clicked into my text thread with Leyton, my thumbs poised to type in a supportive message. I scanned up the last exchange we'd had about the bedding and thought about the conversation I'd had with Finley this morning about my feelings of anxiety and the full moon symbolising a time to free myself of all things negative. Leyton was one of those things. I deleted his number from my phone instead.

'Bad news?' I asked when Finley disconnected his call from Demi on Sunday morning.

'Roman's definitely got chicken pox and, because India didn't get it when it went round her class, Demi's keen she stays home with him.'

'What are you going to do instead?'

'Eat a vat of ice cream and sulk all day,' he said solemnly, then laughed. 'I'll probably do some study.'

'You'd be welcome to join me. There's always too much food.'

'Your parents wouldn't mind?'

'They'd love to meet you.' That was absolutely true. Mother had said he'd be welcome at any time, but I'd never invited him because he usually saw the kids on a Sunday. 'I'll ring her now.'

I'd left my phone on my desk which was a blessing as that meant I could have a conversation out of earshot of Finley and ask her not to attempt any matchmaking as it wouldn't be appreciated.

* * *

Mother and Father warmly welcomed Finley into their home later that morning, but I felt a pang of guilt that they were dressed in smart twenty-first century clothes when they always dressed up for Sunday lunch. I knew they'd done it deliberately not to embarrass me, but it felt wrong. They shouldn't have to change who they were for fear of upsetting me again.

'Do you ride, Finley?' Mother asked when we finished taking our morning tea.

'I haven't been on a horse since I was about thirteen.'

'Lunch won't be served until two, so why don't you and Tori saddle up and take a ride round the estate? She can show you her favourite places.'

Mother caught my eye and I knew what she was up to, but it was subtle enough for me not to make an issue of it.

'I'm up for it if you are,' Finley said, smiling at me.

'Bovis is running a clay pigeon shoot later but he'll be in the stables now,' Father said. 'He'll get you sorted.'

Mother stood up and started loading the cups and saucers back on the tray.

'I'll help you with those,' I said, fixing her with a look that said *don't object*.

'I wasn't interfering,' she said in hushed tones as we neared the kitchen.

'It's not that,' I said, gently. 'It's what you're wearing. This is your home and you should dress how you want.'

'We didn't want to embarrass you in front of Finley, especially when we know how important he is to you.'

'You're important to me too and I don't want you to change who you are and what you do for me. If any of my friends can't accept you the way you are, then they're not people I want or need in my life.'

She smiled at me, no doubt recalling saying something very

similar to me back in my teens. 'Thank you, Tori. We appreciate that.'

* * *

'I can see why this place captivates you,' Finley said, turning in a circle in *l'eglise des arbres*, his eyes darting everywhere. 'It's stunning. I'm trying to remember everything on your blueprint. You had the staircase here, yeah?'

I stepped closer to him and pointed to where I envisaged the different rooms and the various design features.

'It would make an amazing home,' he said, his eyes shining. 'There's something about this place that's so...' He paused as though trying to find the right word.

'Magical?'

'Yes. Magical. As though anything could happen here.'

We were so close together, our eyes locked, and it really did feel as though something magical could happen. I was in the place of my dreams with the man of my dreams who was gazing at me with an intensity that sent the butterflies in my stomach soaring. The air round us seemed to fizz with tension as he stepped a little closer.

'Tori,' he said, his voice low.

'Yes?'

'I was thinking about...'

As he spoke, it felt as though everything in my world was aligned. This magical place, peace with my parents, all of my negative energy gone, and this wonderful man right in front of me, perhaps about to say the words I longed to hear. Perhaps about to kiss me.

Two gunshots in quick succession made us both jump and suddenly the sky was filled with squawking pigeons and crows, disturbed from roosting in the church and surrounding trees.

'What were you going to say?' I asked, turning my attention back to Finley, knowing full well that the magical moment had gone, thanks to Bovis's clay pigeon shoot.

'Erm, yeah, it was about your design problem. I was thinking about that and I have a couple of ideas developing. Would you mind if I take a look at your blueprint again?'

'Be my guest.' I winced as another couple of shots rang out. 'Ready to see some of the follies?'

'Lead the way.'

An hour later, we returned to Redamancy Castle and I couldn't help feeling disappointed that the clay pigeon shoot had ruined what could have been a key moment, but my spirits lifted when I saw Mother and Father had changed into their Victorian finest. They soared even higher when Finley complimented their outfits and asked questions about the specific era. He had them eating out of the palm of his hand and it wasn't because he was a charmer like Leyton, buttering them up because he wanted something; it was because he was genuinely interested.

'You're welcome back any time,' Father said, shaking Finley's hand as they bid us goodbye late that afternoon.

'I hope Roman's not too ill with his chicken pox,' Mother added. 'You'd be very welcome to bring the children to explore the grounds. Lots of space to run free and exciting places to explore.'

'It's brilliant for kids,' Robyn said, stroking her hand across her baby bump. 'Can't wait for this one to explore. Come back soon, Finley.'

Mother and I exchanged looks. Even my feisty, spiky sister had warmed to Finley.

I'd briefly met the children a couple of times so I could picture them dressing up, having sword fights on the lawn, playing in the follies, learning to ride, and I longed to be part of that. Another ridiculous conclusion that people had drawn in the past about my decision not to have children was that I didn't like them. That wasn't the case. I simply didn't have the maternal instinct or desire to have my own, but it didn't mean I couldn't enjoy time in the company of somebody else's children. India and Roman were great kids and it was an absolute credit to Demi and Finley that, despite the problems with their dad and the current changes in their lives, they were really positive and well-adjusted.

Seeing Finley with them had been fascinating. He was so attentive towards them, showing me a side to parenting I'd seen at Uncle Hugh and Aunt Kathryn's farm, but never at Redamancy Castle. Until now. And while spending time with them still didn't make me want children of my own, it did make me want to be part of their lives.

* * *

A couple of nights later, I was invited to Chestnut Barn for a Chinese takeaway with Matt and Charlee.

'Is there any more news about Leyton?' Charlee asked as we tucked into our food.

'Nothing. We cut ties when we split up so I wouldn't expect to hear from him. I thought about reaching out after the police visited but I deleted his number instead.'

'Good move,' Matt said. 'Sounds like you had a lucky escape from him. He didn't owe you any money, did he?'

'No. We'd kept our finances completely separate and he never asked me for money. The alarm bells would have rung if he had. I had no idea he was a gambler. Makes me wonder what else I didn't know.'

Matt and Charlee exchanged looks.

'Matt needs to tell you something,' she said.

Matt visibly squirmed. 'I tried to get on with Leyton because I thought you were happy with him, but it wasn't easy.'

'Leyton didn't make it easy,' I said. 'I appreciated you making the effort.'

'I could probably have tried harder but I found it difficult to trust him. You know how we told you we'd had a dispute over a girl at college. It was a bit more complicated than that. The girl was Libby.'

'Your ex-fiancée?' When Matt and Charlee met, they'd both been in bad relationships but had thankfully seen sense and called time on them before getting together. I'd never thought Libby was right for Matt but, just like Matt hadn't interfered in my relationship, it hadn't been my place to pass comment on his choices.

'Libby's dad walked out when she was seventeen. He had a new life lined up with another woman who was pregnant with twins and it broke Libby. She went on a spiral of self-destruction which started with self-harming and continued with drinking, sleeping around, drugs...' He winced.

'And this had something to do with Leyton?' I asked.

'He was a bit wild at college – the sort who's naturally bright so puts no effort in and somehow gets good grades. He was always out drinking and Libby started hanging around with him and his gang. Her grades suffered and she only just scraped through her A Levels. Leyton had started dealing. I don't know what, but he was the man to go to if you needed something and Libby always needed something. I'm sorry.'

'Me too,' Charlee said.

I looked from his concerned face to hers then back to Matt. 'Forget it,' I said, giving them both a reassuring smile. 'It's in the past and so is Leyton. I don't think he's still a dealer, but I didn't think he was a gambler either. I guess there are some people you never really know.'

'You're sure you're okay?' Charlee asked.

'He's not in my life anymore. I'm definitely okay.' And I really was. That full moon had worked her magic and all that negativity in my life was long gone.

* * *

'Did you have a good night?' Finley called from the kitchen when I returned to Lighthouse View.

'Really good, thanks. How was your evening of studying?'

He stepped into the hall with a mug of tea. 'Good. Although I got a bit distracted. Do you want to go straight to bed, or do you have a moment for me to show you something?'

I hoped he couldn't see my blushes as my mind wandered. 'I've got some time.'

In the office, he led me over to my drawing board.

'When we were in the church, I said some ideas were brewing for your design problem. I've been mulling them over and I wondered what you think of this? I haven't touched your blueprint. I've used tracing paper.'

I studied the drawing when he stepped aside and my heart leapt. 'Oh, my God! This is perfect!'

He stepped closer and I experienced a heady whiff of his body spray as he moved his arm across to point something out. As he explained the logic behind his adjustments, all I could think about was how close he was and how little movement it would take to kiss him.

'Anyway, I know you have an early start, so I'll say good night and see you in the morning.'

And then he stepped away and that delicious moment was gone.

'Thank you, Finley,' I said, my voice catching in my throat and sounding husky. 'I love it.'

And I love you! I ran my fingers across the drawing, my heart melting at the consideration he'd shown by using the tracing paper. It wasn't tentative feelings I harboured anymore. Somewhere along the way, I'd fallen in love with him. This was bigger than I'd expected. If I told him like I'd planned and he wasn't interested, this really could mess up everything. These past five weeks living at Lighthouse View with Finley had been the best five weeks of my life. We'd talked endlessly, laughed, teased. I felt like I knew him better than I'd known Leyton or Ewan, and I felt like he was the only person in the world who'd ever really got to know me. But wasn't that what a brilliant friendship was all about? How on earth did anyone take the leap from that into something more when the risk of saying or doing something was losing the person you cared about more than anyone in the world?

52

HOLLIE

On the last day of June, I stood behind the brand-new serving counter enjoying a moment's peace and quiet as I surveyed the 'awesomeness' of version three of The Starfish Café. Tori was an exceptionally talented designer who had managed to make the space feel bigger and brighter with her careful use of colour and placement of furniture.

After being hands-off for most of Operation Driftwood, the past week had been a frenzy of activity involving the whole team as we'd cleaned several times, arranged the stock upstairs and prepared the food and decorations for tonight's grand opening at six.

Everyone had gone home an hour ago, but Jake and I had returned early so I could have some alone time in the café to take it all in before the party started.

Jake had disappeared, saying he needed to do something in the kitchen, which I took as code that he was hungry and planning to raid the fridge.

'Happy grand reopening,' he announced, reappearing with a bottle of bubbly in an ice bucket and two champagne flutes.

'I wondered what you were up to in there,' I said as he filled the glasses and we sat in one of the window booths.

'I thought it would be nice to have a private celebration. To new beginnings at The Starfish Café.'

We smiled at each other as we clinked our glasses together.

'What a transformation!' he exclaimed, looking round the room. 'How do you feel about it all now?'

'It's amazing. I love it so much and Mum would have too. I'm a bit embarrassed I had a meltdown about it.'

'I think that was justified. It's hard to let go of something that's so strongly connected to a loved one. It doesn't mean you're letting go of that person. You've still got your memories and a few changes – even major ones – aren't going to erase those.'

'Are you thinking about Lighthouse View too?'

He smiled. 'I suppose I am. I'm going to see if Bart and Tori want to take out a longer lease like six months or even a year.'

'I reckon they'll appreciate the stability. I know they both love living there.'

'What do you think about me saying they can have first refusal if either of them want to buy it down the line?'

'I think that's a great idea. You're sure you're ready?'

'I'm ready.'

There was a knock at the door.

'That'll be Charlee and Jodie with the cake,' I said, standing up.

'I'll get it,' Jake said. 'You enjoy your final moment of peace.'

As he went to let them in, I looked out the window and across the terrace. The weather was appalling for the summer, although typically British. It was mild but dark skies had threatened rain all day with the occasional short cloudburst. Heavy rain was forecast from seven, so we'd erected a huge gazebo across the terrace so guests could get some fresh air without getting drenched.

'Happy reopening!' Jodie called, holding open the inner porch door.

Charlee stepped into the café holding an enormous cake board covered with a box. I'd ordered a starfish cake from Carly's Cupcakes to celebrate the reopening, with icing to match the colours of the mosaic, and Charlee had offered to collect it for me.

'Where do you want this?' she asked.

I slipped out of the booth. 'You can pop it on the counter. I can't wait to see it.'

She lifted off the cover and I gasped. 'Aw, it's fantastic.'

'Where do you want this one?'

I spun round to see Jake holding another large wooden board, also covered in a box, out in front of him. Jodie had closed the door and the three of them were grinning at me.

'What's going on?' I asked.

Jake placed the board beside the starfish cake. 'I asked Charlee and Jodie to create something a little bit special.'

He lifted off the box and I gasped again. They'd made an enormous chocolate driftwood log with stubby branches protruding from it.

'Is this all chocolate?' I asked. 'It's so realistic.'

'We used a mixture of milk and dark chocolate to get the colour right,' Charlee said, 'and the bark effect comes from a silicone texture mould.'

The quote 'With courage, nothing is impossible' had been piped in white chocolate in the middle of the log with the names of all the staff round it.

'You embody that quote,' Jake said, slipping his arm round my waist.

I had a huge lump in my throat already and I felt tears rushing to my eyes when he said that but, when I spotted the names

'Norma' and 'Heather' – Granny and Mum – among the staff
names, a sob escaped.

'Don't cry!' Jodie said. 'You'll set us all off.'

'Sorry! I can't help it. It's incredible. Thank you, all of you.'

I dished out grateful hugs and laughed as Jodie and Charlee
both had to wipe away tears, jokingly muttering about smudged
make-up. While they headed to the toilets to sort themselves out, I
hugged Jake.

'Thank you for everything. You really are the best of the best.'

'Right back at you.' His lips brushed gently against mine.

* * *

A little later, with all the guests arrived, I stood on the second step.
In one hand I held a champagne flute and, in the other, a pair of
scissors ready to cut the shiny turquoise ribbon behind me.

My eyes scanned the crowd, bursting with pride at so many
wonderful people gathered to support the next phase of the venture
my granny had originally started sixty years ago. Some of the guests
had been in my life for a long time like Angie and Martin, Katie and
Trey, and regular customers Betty, Tommy, and Sylvia 'Mrs Sultana',
back from her cruise and looking radiant. Some had only just
entered it, but had rapidly become good friends, like Tori, her
uncle, cousins and their families, Irene, Jim from The Hope Centre,
and Jake's Uncle Adrian and Auntie Maggs. And there were those
who'd been absent from my life for a little while but never gone
from my thoughts like Bex, Kyle, Artie and the RNLI crew.

Plus I had the most amazing members of staff who had been so
helpful and supportive throughout the whole episode. I felt like I
knew them all so much better now that we'd had some time away
from customer demands; an unexpected benefit from what had
happened.

'Thank you, everyone, for joining us for a very special event tonight and particularly for coming out on such a shocking evening.' It was now raining so heavily that I had to shout to be heard.

'When I last had The Starfish Café refurbished, I never expected it would only last for four years, but somebody had other ideas and wanted this place so badly that he tried to destroy it. He destroyed his own life instead and is thankfully now going to spend a long time at Her Majesty's Pleasure.' I paused for a cheer and caught Irene's eye, thinking about the justice she'd finally got for her husband, Derek.

'The Starfish Café will officially open for business tomorrow and I can't wait to share our new menu with you. You'll see all your previous favourites but we've been through old recipe books of Mum's and from Jake's nanna and I know you're all going to be delighted with what we've found, including some exciting new chocolate-based recipes, just for you, Betty.'

She gave me a grin and a thumbs-up.

'I know many of you have noticed it already, but I just wanted to point out the mosaic starfish you can see on the wall over there. Avril and I created this from the broken crockery to show that good can come from bad situations.

'Thank you to my regulars and new customers for your unending support and lovely comments while we were closed. I'd like to thank my amazing designer Tori for her inspired vision and Hugh, Matt, Tim and the amazing team at Richards & Sons for executing it. I'm so grateful to Angie and my fabulous staff for all their support among the chaos and to my partner Jake for always dancing with me in the rain.' I held his gaze for a moment, butter-flies swirling in my stomach.

'Upstairs you'll find Driftwood Dell which is the new home for Hollie's Wood. The range still includes all your favourites, but I hope you'll love the new pieces as much as we do. Also in Drift-wood Dell is Jake's Wood, which contains stunning photos of the local landscape from the amazingly talented Jake MacLeod. And finally we have the Beach, where you'll find a few surprises. Don't forget that a percentage of each sale goes to charity. We still support the RNLI, Macmillan Cancer Support and Paws Rehomed, a dog charity in Whitsborough Bay, but we've now added in The Hope Centre, so dig deep.'

I opened the scissors and poised them over the ribbon. 'I'm delighted to declare Driftwood Dell at The Starfish Café officially open.'

I cut the ribbon to applause and posed for photos with Jake and the staff before our guests made their way upstairs. The oohs and aahs and excitable chatter warmed my heart.

Angie's eighteen-year-old niece, Grace, had just finished her A levels at college and was looking for a summer job so we'd recruited her to work in Driftwood Dell. It was the ideal solution, as we had no idea yet how busy it would be and whether we could justify the salary of someone working up there permanently.

Avril and Kerry had volunteered to work with Grace tonight, wrapping and restocking while she operated the till, so that I could mingle and enjoy my special evening.

Within minutes, they'd sold the first Jake's Wood photo. His face was an absolute picture. He'd had his three days with Philip Heslington earlier this month and Michael had joined them on the final day. Jake hadn't quite been able to believe it when Philip looked through his photos and told him he had serious talent. The pair of them had become firm friends, had exchanged several tips and were already planning their next jaunt out with the cameras.

Philip and his wife Kay, who'd been a good friend and neigh-bour of Jake's nanna, immediately rushed over to congratulate him on his first sale and I could hear them saying, 'We told you so.' I'm not sure Jake would have believed it if he hadn't seen it for himself.

The Beach had been Jake's suggestion. He'd pointed out that the café was frequented by families, yet there wasn't anything in Driftwood Dell that children would love, so I'd sourced soft toys, stationery and gifts with a seaside theme. The main focus was on seals and starfish for obvious reasons, but I'd thrown in a few other sea creatures and some mermaids for a wider appeal.

We were also carrying an exclusive range of seaside-shaped chocolates from Charlee's Chocolates – starfish, seals and shells – which I expected would prove very popular. I'd already sampled a few and they were amazing.

It was wonderful hearing all the positive feedback about Driftwood Dell and the overall refurbishment, but it was the love for Jake's photography that gave me the biggest thrill. The doubts that his vicious sister had driven into him had faded away at last. He finally believed in himself as much as I believed in him and now, with his photos adorning the walls, it felt like he'd become a key part of The Starfish Café, like all the people I loved.

53

TORI

One of my favourite things about working on a café, restaurant or pub is that there is nearly always a grand opening and I'm on the guest list. I can't deny that there's a thrill in being there to see the reactions of the guests and bask in the compliments, but what fills me with joy is observing the owner in their new setting, knowing that I've created the physical appearance of the business that means so much to them.

Tonight at The Starfish Café was no exception. Operation Driftwood had to be my favourite project to date. I loved the building and the setting from my very first visit, but now I also loved the owner and her story. Hollie was such an inspiration with the way she'd overcome her devastating family losses and kept her mother's spirit alive in the business. She'd been on the receiving end of the most heinous attack from Slippy Smythe and she'd picked herself up from that too. We could all learn something from her determination.

The part of the new spectacularly awesome version of the café that I loved the most actually had nothing to do with me. It was the starfish mosaic from the broken crockery. The symbolism of that touched me because it echoed not only Hollie's journey, but also the one I'd been on. The day Hollie came into my life was the day my eyes opened and I began my journey of rediscovery and reconnection. I nearly lost my life that day and it had taken a little while to regain control of it, but now I felt like I'd started properly living. Almost.

Nearly every part of my life was perfect right now. My relationship with my parents was unrecognisable, in that it actually was now a relationship – a proper one with admiration, respect and understanding of each other. A friendship was slowly but steadily building with my sister too and she and Mother were going to meet me here for lunch tomorrow so they could see my design. Mother had suggested attending tonight but I'd registered the fear that crossed Father's face and knew that the thought of Mother in a crowd – even one made up of people Hollie knew – made him anxious. I'd thanked her but said I probably wouldn't get much opportunity to chat and perhaps a lunch date would be better. The relief on Father's face was touching.

Outside of my family life, my business was thriving and I had friends who I was finally letting in. There was just the situation with Finley that wasn't quite there.

I looked over towards where he was talking to Jake. Every day, I swear I fell in love with that man a little bit more and every day I blew hot and cold on telling him how I felt. Finley glanced in my direction, our eyes locked, and he smiled at me, sending my stomach into spin cycle. A hot flush swept through me as I imagined what might have happened between us in *l'eglise des arbres* if those gunshots hadn't ruined the moment.

I needed some air and some space to think. Putting my empty glass on a nearby table, I slid open the door, and slipped outside. The heavy rain this evening had brought a drop in temperature and a delicious freshness to the air after several muggy days.

Standing at the edge of the terrace, I took several deep breaths. As light splashes of rain bounced off the metal railings onto my arms, I focused on the steady patter of rain on the canvas of the gazebo and the sound of the waves below.

I gazed up at the sky. The new moon rose and set with the sun, so she wasn't up there, but I still felt her comfort. New moon, new beginnings. Phipps had suggested I should take advantage of what she represented and tell Finley and he was probably right. I'd wasted too much of my life being with the wrong men, without my family, with a head full of confused and angry thoughts. Now was the time for action and if Finley wasn't interested in anything other than friendship, at least I'd know and I could stop fantasising about us being together. Or try to.

The only thing stopping me was fear. Fear of failing. Fear of the damage my admission could do to our relationship if my feelings were unrequited. I couldn't bear the thought of saying goodbye to Lighthouse View or Finley.

But what if Finley felt the same as me but was also gripped by the fear? In those brief moments where I'd felt something could happen, like in the church, what if he'd felt it too? When we hugged and I longed for it to be more, what if that had been going through his mind too?

I'd been out for drinks with Hollie and spoken to her about it. She was convinced he had feelings for me but I'd dismissed the suggestion because he hadn't said or done anything. But neither had I! What if he'd been waiting for me to give him a sign that I was interested before he opened up and I'd been too focused on not giving him any signs in case I scared him off?

On the chocolate log which Charlee and Jodie had made for Hollie, there was a quote – *with courage, nothing is impossible* – which was perfect for Hollie and Jake's story. Could it be perfect for Finley's and mine?

Taking another deep breath, I made my decision. I'd show courage and tell Finley how I felt tonight and, whatever his reaction, there'd be a new start. The dream scenario was for Finley and me to be together but, if he didn't feel the same and couldn't imagine ever doing so, it would be a fresh start for me in accepting it was unrequited. The fear of losing his friendship was very real, but I was willing to take that risk. Courage didn't mean there was no fear; it simply meant that fear didn't stop you.

The muted sound of music and laughter intensified for a moment, indicating that somebody had opened the door. I turned round to say hello to whoever had joined me, and my heart leapt. Finley was standing in the middle of the terrace, his head dipped to one side, an expression of curiosity on his face. The lanterns strung across the terrace bathed him in warm light.

'Watching the moon?' he asked.

'You know me. Drawn towards it, as always, although it's a new moon tonight so I can't actually see her.'

He took a couple of steps closer. 'Oh, yeah, it's a spring tide again.'

'It is.'

'I've just been talking to Jake about Lighthouse View.'

Another couple of steps closer.

I tried to sound casual. 'Oh, yeah? What about?'

'Whether he'd consider a longer-term rental.'

'Oh! And?'

'He's open to six months or even a year if that's what we want. I love living there. You do too, don't you?' His voice was husky, his gaze intense.

He was only an arm's length away from me now, his eyes locked with mine, and my heart was thudding so rapidly, I felt quite light-headed. This was my moment and I had to take it.

'I do. And not just because it's a great house. It's because of the great company.'

He smiled gently then stepped past me and rested his arms on the railings, looking out to the sea. I kicked myself for my naff turn of phrase.

I mirrored his stance by the railings, leaving a gap – enough for another person – between us.

'It was a spring tide the night we met at Dean and Jodie's wedding,' he said, 'but it was a full moon. You told me that the full moon was time to get rid of the negative energy in our lives. We both had plenty of that back then.'

'Tell me about it. But it's all dealt with now.'

He turned to face me. 'What does the new moon mean?'

'New beginnings, fresh starts, setting goals.' *Tell him!*

He edged a little closer. 'I've been thinking a lot about that blueprint to happiness we spoke about that night – an equal partnership with trust, respect, loyalty, support, shared passions. What I had with Demi was nowhere near that. You didn't have it with Leyton either, did you?'

'No.'

My heart raced as he slid a little further along the railings, narrowing the gap between us. There was an intensity to his gaze that I'd seen on the few occasions I'd felt the chemistry between us.

'It shouldn't be like that, Tori. We both deserve better.'

'We do.'

His eyes searched mine and I held my breath, my heart pounding, anxious to know where he was going with this. Was this a lead-in to saying he wanted to be with me? The silence was agonising. Should I get in there first? *With courage...* But what if this was his way of telling me he'd found someone else? My courage retreated.

'Thing is,' he continued, 'I think I might have found my blueprint when I didn't expect to. At the wedding, I went up onto that roof terrace to escape from my messy life. I thought that being alone that night was what I needed, but it turned out that finding you was what I really needed and I've been so worried about saying something in case you didn't feel the same and it damaged our friendship, but I saw that message on the chocolate log Charlee and Jodie made about courage and—'

His nervous rambling was so endearing and all I could think of was how actions speak louder than words. I edged closer and lightly brushed my lips against his.

'I wanted to be alone that night as well, but it turns out you were exactly what I needed and now I've found my blueprint too.'

I closed my eyes as his soft lips met mine once more in a slow, sensual kiss that was everything I'd dreamed it would be in my many fantasies, and so much more. He ran his hand through my hair and down my back as he pulled me closer.

'I've been wanting to do that for so long,' he whispered.

'Me too. How long has it been for you?'

We leaned against the railings once more, hands clasped and he wrinkled his nose, his eyes twinkling in the light.

'I felt something on the roof terrace at the wedding. It was surprising and unexpected, especially in the circumstances. You know I said I'd avoided the dance floor because it reminded me of family time? That was the truth, but there was something else too. I knew if I danced, I'd want to dance with you, and that meant we'd be really close and...' He shook his head, smiling. 'I didn't trust my feelings. I thought it was a combination of the romance of the day and a free bar getting to me.'

'But you couldn't stay away in the end,' I teased.

'We hadn't finished our conversation and I wanted to see if I could help you like you'd helped me. But, also, I couldn't let you walk out of my life.' He squeezed my hand. 'I was on the verge of asking you out and thought *what the hell am I doing?* You were with someone and so was I. We knew both our relationships were over but, until our partners knew that, it wasn't fair. So I put the thing about The Lobster Pot out there and hoped that you'd take me up on it. After that, friendship kind of took over and I wanted to be there for you. When we talked about renting together, I was very much thinking about two friends helping each other out at a time of need but, once we'd moved in and I got to know you, I knew what I felt for you was so much more than friendship. What about you?'

'There were moments and, like you, it started at the wedding but I didn't realise until after we'd moved in. I didn't know what to do about it. At first, I was worried it was a rebound thing and then I thought I was getting carried away because of reading all those romance novels and, when I was sure it wasn't either of those things, I was scared to say anything and lose your friendship too. The day we stood in *l'eglise des arbres* was my absolute moment of clarity. I thought something was about to happen.'

'Those damn gun shots! I'd been building up the courage to say something all day and that seemed like the perfect moment, but I panicked again and bottled it.'

'But you saw the words on that chocolate log. *With courage, nothing is impossible.*'

He nodded. 'It was now or never.'

'If you hadn't said something tonight, I was going to, and that quote was what convinced me too. New moon, new beginnings. Together.'

Finley lowered his lips to mine and I melted into another heart-racing, spine-tingling kiss. The spring tide at The Starfish Café had brought us our new beginning and, third time lucky, I'd finally found a relationship that was based on a friendship and a true partnership. Not unrequited as I'd feared, but redamancy, just like my parents. When both of our lives seemed to be falling apart at Jodie and Dean's wedding, they were really falling into place. Everything in my life was now finally aligned and I had my constant friend, the moon, to thank for that.

As our kiss deepened, Charlee's words from when I caught the bridal bouquet came to mind: *You next! The flowers have spoken.* It seemed they really had.

54

HOLLIE

'I'd call that a successful opening,' I said, sitting beside Jake on the top stair after the guests had dispersed, with Pickle curled up on my knee.

'You sold loads tonight,' Jake said, his voice full of admiration.

'*We* sold loads. That's five of your photos sold, two reserved and lots of interest. Still think you're not good enough for a gallery?'

'I submit. You called it. I might not be too shabby at this photography lark.'

'I don't think there's anything you're shabby at,' I said, nudging him playfully. 'Come on, you. Let's get this little dog home. He must be shattered after all the excitement and attention he's had tonight.'

Jake helped me to my feet and the three of us headed towards the door.

'You know what else I'm not too shabby at,' Jake said after we'd switched the lights off and stepped into the porch. 'Dancing in the rain.'

I smiled at him. 'And what do you know? It's still raining.'

'Leave your bag here and we'll lock up shortly.'

He took me in his arms and we slow danced across the car park, not caring that the rain was plastering our hair to our heads or soaking through our clothes. Pickle ran round the car park, bouncing in and out of puddles, making me think of the little girl in the pink tutu on the card from my mum, dancing in the rain with her dog.

Jake twirled me, just like he'd done in February when we'd danced in the snow. He stepped back and took a bow and I curtseyed in return. He then took what I thought was going to be another bow, but he dipped down even further onto one bended knee.

'Oh, my God!' I gasped, pressing my fingers to my lips, my heart racing.

'Hollie Gabrielle Brooks, owner of the finest café in the whole of Yorkshire, re-purposer of driftwood, saver of seals and people, and expert with the spindle roughing gouge, you have taken a broken man and helped to fix him. You've brought sunshine and meaning to a life half-lived, and you've believed in me and never given up and now I finally believe in myself. It would be an honour and a privilege to spend the rest of my life making you as happy as you've made me.'

He dipped his fingers into his shirt pocket and held out a ring.

'Will you dance with me in the rain for the rest of my life as my wife?'

'Yes! *Yes!*' I squealed.

He stood up and slipped the ring on my finger, then drew me into a passionate kiss. I'd laughed at the 'romance' of Trey proposing to Katie in the hospital car park but, right now, I couldn't imagine anywhere more romantic or perfect than a proposal in the car park of my family's café in the torrential rain. I'd found my dance partner who made me laugh every day, just like my parents had. Laughter was how our relationship had started and was the reason my parents' marriage had been such a success, just like ours would be.

Mum used to say: *smile, sparkle, you've got this!* In my life before Jake and Pickle, I'd repeated that to myself frequently to help get me through the day. Now it was how I naturally felt all the time. The Starfish Café had been badly damaged but, with courage, trust and belief, it had emerged brighter and better than ever before. So had we. We'd continue to face whatever challenges life threw at us, but we'd do it together. Forever.

ACKNOWLEDGMENTS

Thank you for reading/listening to *Spring Tides at The Starfish Café* – the second book in The Starfish Café series. I hope you loved how Hollie and Jake's story has developed and that you enjoyed meeting Tori and Finley as they took their chance on the new moon signifying new beginnings.

Book 1 – *Snowflakes Over The Starfish Café* – was an emotional story as Hollie and Jake came to terms with their tragic pasts. I went through a few boxes of tissues writing it and I know many readers were reduced to tears too. I've received many gorgeous messages and read such lovely reviews about that story and am so grateful for them all.

I don't deliberately set out to make anyone cry – I simply tell the stories that my characters want to tell – and sometimes those tales happen to be weepies. I'm conscious that *Spring Tides at The Starfish Café* won't have tugged at the emotional heartstrings in the same way and that's because Hollie and Jake have found the courage to move on and dream of a happy future together. That doesn't mean they won't have challenges thrown at them, as you've discovered.

This is my fifteenth book, and it seems like only yesterday that I was writing my first one, wondering if I'd ever make it to the end and create a story and characters that readers would take to their hearts. I still can't believe this is now my full-time job.

If you read book 1 – *Snowflakes Over The Starfish Café* – and the acknowledgements at the back, you'll know I had quite a journey with that book. I started writing it as a Christmas novella many years ago but soon realised that the story was too big for a novella. I returned to it as a full-length book, but I was still thinking too big. The story in *Spring Tides* around Slippy Smythe destroying The Starfish Café was originally in book i, but including it there meant I hadn't done justice to Hollie and Jake's story of finding each other and the courage to stop their pasts controlling their futures. So, with some major re-work, I removed that entire storyline, leaving only essential seeds about Isaac's love for nautical history and the creation of The Smuggler's Key.

I thought it would be easy to write *Spring Tides* because half the book was already written. Silly me! It was actually harder to write because the context in which that part of the story unfolded was completely different. In the end, it took me longer to unravel and knit it back together than it would have taken to write it from scratch. Oops!

My first thanks go to the team at Boldwood Books. I have the most phenomenal editor in Nia Beynon. She's worked on every book I've written and is as passionate about Whitsborough Bay and Hedgehog Hollow as me. I'm eternally grateful for her invaluable editorial guidance. Thank you to Boldwood's fabulous CEO and founder, Amanda Ridout, for continuing to drive an innovative, award-winning, and friendly publisher. Huge thanks to Claire Fenby for the digital marketing, and Megan Townsend and Laura Kingston for the behind-the-scenes support.

I've dedicated this book to an amazing friend and fellow-author, Sharon Booth, who I had the pleasure of meeting before I was published. We've been through our writing journeys together and, as we both live in Yorkshire (albeit a couple of hours apart), we meet up regularly and talk all things writing. She's a sounding board for new ideas and tricky plot points, she provides support and encouragement, and I couldn't imagine not having such a fabulous friend in my life.

Speaking of friends and fellow-authors, a shout out goes to my writing families, the Write Romantics and my TeamBoldwood buddies. You are all absolute superstars.

Another massive thank you goes to Scarborough Lifeboat Station and particularly to Colin Woodhead, who organised a tour and a photo opportunity with the crew to help promote my first book. The RNLI were my chosen charity and I was thrilled to make a donation to them earlier this year for the incredible work they do in saving lives at sea which provided the original inspiration for this series. If you would like to make a donation to the RNLI, you can do so here: https://rnli.org

There are more seals in this book than book 1, although, unlike Samantha in the Hedgehog Hollow series, Hollie doesn't run a rescue centre, so this is not the intended focus of the book. I wanted to find out more about the rescue of seals on the Yorkshire Coast and arranged a private seal experience with Scarborough's Sea Life Sanctuary. It's run by Merlin Entertainments' Sea Life Centre division and Minnie and Teigan were amazing guides who I bombarded with questions to ensure I accurately conveyed Alice's rescue details.

Thank you to my good friend Liz Berry for the brilliant name Sebastian Smythe – perfect for my antagonist. I'd also like to thank Jemima Peacock and the wonderful community in Redland's Readers, my Facebook group, for the suggestions around what medical condition might affect Robyn as a baby. If you love my writing and would like more insights into the worlds of Whitsborough Bay and Hedgehog Hollow, please do search for 'Redland's Readers' on Facebook and you'd be very welcome to join us.

Thanks to Cecily Blench and Sue Lamprell for the brilliant copy-editing and proofreading, Debbie Clement for another amazing cover, Rachel Gilbey for organising the blog tour, and all the bloggers and reviewers who took part. Thank you to Lucy

Brownhill for bringing Hollie to life again with her amazing narration on the audio version of *Spring Tides at The Starfish Café* and Polly Edsell for Tori's chapters. Thanks also to ISIS Audio and Ulverscroft for the production and distribution.

Nearly there with the thanks! My eternal gratitude goes to my husband and daughter, Mark and Ashleigh, and my mum Joyce for being the absolute best, supporting and encouraging me every step of the way. I think my mum checks my reviews and chart rankings more often than me! Mark, I really couldn't do this without you xxx

Finally, thank you to you my reader/listener. Thank you for buying, borrowing, downloading and/or streaming my work. If you love what I do and want me to keep bringing you uplifting stories of love, friendship, family and community, the best thing you can do is spread the word. Tell your friends, colleagues, neighbours and family about books you've loved and hopefully they'll discover them too and pass the message on. Reviews are so helpful too. You don't have to write an essay. A sentence or even a few words is amazing. Or just a rating. All of this helps in kick-starting algorithms and making books more visible.

Thank you once more for choosing *Spring Tides at The Starfish Café*. There are lots more books set in Whitsborough Bay you might like to try if you haven't already done so, and I have another series – Hedgehog Hollow – set on a rescue centre in the beautiful countryside of the Yorkshire Wolds.

It's not the end for The Starfish Café. If you've loved the series so far, you'll be pleased to hear there's one more book planned. Will Hollie and Jake get married or will there be baby news first? What's next for Tori and Finley? And will Angie finally tell Martin she still loves him and wants to try again? All will be revealed in the final part...

Big hugs,
Jessica xx

MORE FROM JESSICA REDLAND

We hope you enjoyed reading *A Wedding at Hedgehog Hollow*. If you did, please leave a review.

If you'd like to gift a copy, this book is also available as an ebook, digital audio download and audiobook CD.

Sign up to Jessica Redland's mailing list for news, competitions and updates on future books.

http://bit.ly/JessicaRedlandNewsletter

ABOUT THE AUTHOR

Jessica Redland writes uplifting stories of love, friendship, family and community set in Yorkshire where she lives. Her Whitsborough Bay books transport readers to the stunning North Yorkshire Coast and her Hedgehog Hollow series takes them into beautiful countryside of the Yorkshire Wolds.

Visit Jessica's website: https://www.jessicaredland.com/

Follow Jessica on social media:

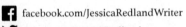 facebook.com/JessicaRedlandWriter

twitter.com/JessicaRedland

 instagram.com/JessicaRedlandWriter

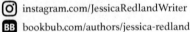 bookbub.com/authors/jessica-redland

ALSO BY JESSICA REDLAND

Welcome to Whitsborough Bay Series

Making Wishes at Bay View

New Beginnings at Seaside Blooms

Finding Hope at Lighthouse Cove

Coming Home to Seashell Cottage

Other Whitsborough Bay Books

All You Need is Love

The Secret to Happiness

Christmas on Castle Street

Christmas Wishes at the Chocolate Shop

Christmas at Carly's Cupcakes

Starry Skies Over The Chocolate Pot Café

The Starfish Café Series

Snowflakes Over The Starfish Café

Spring Tides at The Starfish Café

Hedgehog Hollow Series

Finding Love at Hedgehog Hollow

New Arrivals at Hedgehog Hollow

Family Secrets at Hedgehog Hollow

A Wedding at Hedgehog Hollow

Chasing Dreams at Hedgehog Hollow

ABOUT BOLDWOOD BOOKS

Boldwood Books is a fiction publishing company seeking out the best stories from around the world.

Find out more at www.boldwoodbooks.com

Sign up to the Book and Tonic newsletter for news, offers and competitions from Boldwood Books!

http://www.bit.ly/bookandtonic

We'd love to hear from you, follow us on social media:

facebook.com/BookandTonic

twitter.com/BoldwoodBooks

instagram.com/BookandTonic